THE CHOSEN ONE

Book One of the Savior Project Series

FRITZ FRANKE

2/28/15
Adam,
It's been awesome working + talking with you on tech stuff. Please enjoy it,
All the best,
Fritz

Published by Imagination Pro

IMAGINATION PRO

www.imaginationpro.net

Cover production by Gravitys Edge

www.gravitysedge.com

The Chosen One: A Novel
ISBN: 0985539615
ISBN-13: 978-0-9855396-1-0

This is a work of fiction. Names, characters, places and incidents are products of the author's imagination or are used fictitiously. Any similarity to actual persons, organizations, and/or events is purely coincidental.

Visit Fritz's website - www.FritzFranke.net

Published by Imagination Pro - www.ImaginationPro.net

Cover Design by Gravitys Edge Productions
Gravitys Edge, LLC - www.GravitysEdge.com

DEDICATION

To my Mother, who never stopped believing in me.
I wish I could have put the first copy of this book in her hands. At least there is solace in the fact that she was with me every day, in my heart, helping me finish the book.

VOCABULARY - DEFINITIONS AND PRONUNCIATIONS

Savior: 'save~your' - One that saves from danger or destruction, and/or one who brings salvation.

OTHER WORLDS
Terlokya: 'tur~lo ~key~ya' - Home planet of "Those Who Watch Over Us", the Terlokyans.
Kukno: 'kuck~no' - Terlokyan capital
Donar: 'doe~nar' - Largest moon of Terlokya.
Velox: 'vel~locks' - Enemy planet of the Veloptors.
Kekter: 'keck~tur' - Uninhabited planet in the Hastin solar system. Has Costine.
Cezzeck: 'sez~zeck' - Sparsely inhabited ice planet, used mostly as a layover for ships. Has a black sun.

LIFE FORMS
Terlokyans: 'tur~loke~e~ans' – Human, highly advanced.
Veloptors: 'vel~lop~tors' – Evolved on Velox, highly intelligent. Descended from Velociraptors.

TERLOKYANS (in order of importance and story relevance)
Sohan: 'so~hahn' – Supreme Commander of Terlokya. Father of Zenta.
Zenta: 'zen~tuh' – Captain, in charge of development/training phase. Daughter of Sohan.
Tish: 'tish' – Lieutenant, on Zenta's team. Daughter of Marsitta. Childhood friend of Zenta.
Xander: 'zan~dur' – Captain, on development/training team. Younger brother of Jzet.
Jhall: 'juh~hall' – General, head of Terlokyan moon base GAIA.
Hajeck: 'hi~jeck' – Major, Chief of Staff for Sohan.
Donac: 'don~nack' – Major, second in command of GAIA.
Marsitta: 'mar~seat~ta' – Major, GAIA's communications officer. Mother of Tish.
Prahash: 'pra~hash' – Colonel, Chief Health Officer.
Braaddy: 'bray~dee' – Colonel, head of the Savior Project, all phases.
Gunstot: 'gun~stot' – Lieutenant, on development/training team.
Jzet: 'juh~zet' – Major, head of security and the Anti-Detection Unit. Older brother of Xander.
Dlocto: 'duh~lock~toe' – Captain, second in command of the ADU.
Callun: 'call~lun' – Lieutenant, Jzet's right-hand man on the ADU.

Tuu: 'too' – Specialist, member of the ADU. Assists development/training team.
Bal: 'ball' – Specialist, member of the ADU. Assists development/training team.
Benswear: 'ben~swear' – Colonel, in charge of Flight Ops and Hanger.
Kressa: 'kress~sa' – Major, second in command of Flight Ops and Hanger.
Achted: 'ach~ted' – Master Chief in charge of Maintenance and Facilities Operations.
Tearcut: 'tare~cut' – Specialist, member of Maintenance and backup to the ADU.
Maczee: 'mack~zee' – Captain, pilot, squadron leader on GAIA.
Johono: 'joe~hoe~no' – Lieutenant, pilot on GAIA. Assists development/training team.
Aiko: 'a~ko' – Lieutenant, pilot on GAIA. Assists the development/training team.
Runba: 'run~bah' – Lieutenant, pilot on GAIA.
Kainel: 'kay~nell' – Captain, pilot, squadron leader on GAIA.
Kaioc: 'kay~ock' – Admiral, commands the Battle Cruiser, the TRAZ.
Craymack: 'cray~mac' – Admiral, commands the War Carrier, the CURC.
Dobbie: 'dob~bee' – Colonel, commands the Planet Transport, Mover 1.
Kelta: 'kell~ta' – Lieutenant, Communications Officer on Mover 1.
Qwan: 'kwan' – Major, second in command of Mover 1. Commands Zaw One.
Roial: 'royal' – Lieutenant, copilot on Zaw One.
Klovsew: 'clove~sue' – Head of the Supreme Council.
Dienong: 'die~nong' – Supreme Council member.

TERLOKYAN WORDS

Bonzoon: 'bon~zune' – An alcoholic liquid, clear and slightly syrupy. Needs no mixing. Emits an intoxicating aroma. Can be drank or breathed in.
Contem: 'con~tem' – The state of being despised. Being called a **Conte**, 'con~tea' - is the lowest thing possible.
Farrook: 'far~ruke' – Slang term for crazy or out of your mind.
Flash: 'flash' – To travel at the Speed of Dark. Sometimes used as slang to say "travel as fast as possible"
Glaze: 'glaze' – (noun) A compound that can put someone to sleep and erase memory depending upon the strength of the mix. (verb) To put someone asleep and/or to erase certain parts of their memory.
Sentar: 'cen~tar' – A horse sized mammal with the body style of a tiger and the head of a bear with swept back horns.

Trace: 'trace' – (noun) A communications device worn on the wrist. (verb) To contact someone, usually using a Trace.
Troid: 'troid' – Computer system on GAIA.

TABLE OF CONTENTS

FRITZ FRANKE

THE CHOSEN ONE

FRITZ FRANKE

FRITZ FRANKE

01 – HE RISES

As Chris Gates stood on the pitcher's mound, a familiar uneasy feeling returned. He concentrated on trying to hear that haunting buzzing sound. Little did he know that this sound was an omen, signaling that his life was about to change forever.

In frustration, he pulled at the neck of his soaking wet jersey. His inability to hear the sound, coupled with the summer heat, had him sweating like a pig.

The humidity hung in the air as it always did during July in central Virginia. Perspiration ran down Chris' cheek as he watched for the catcher's sign. He wiped it with his dirty sleeve creating a streak of mud on his face. Cheers came from the bleachers, distracting him. Besides the regulars who came to softball games, most of the player's families were also in attendance. This was the 2012 league championship so the crowd was much larger than usual. For a moment, he forgot about the buzzing when he saw his kids.

Chris' children, Taylor and Michelle, were hanging on the fence. Taylor was a spitting image of Chris with his long wavy, blond locks. He and his middle school friends had climbed higher than the elementary school age kids like Michelle. His little towheads stuck out in a crowd, their voices easy to recognize as they hollered, "Strike him out, Dad!"

"That's high enough, children," Chris heard his wife say. Lisa was sitting in the bleachers with the other player's wives and girlfriends on the first base side of the field. Her blond hair and slender build always turned guy's heads. But once recognized as the wife of the well-known Chris Gates, the gawkers would just say 'Hi. How's Chris?"

Lisa caught Chris' eye and gave a little wave. He smiled back and gulped while feeling extra pressure to look cool and play well. At a youthful looking age of forty-six, he still acted like a teenager trying to impress his girl with his athleticism.

But other things were bothering Chris far more than his softball image. He felt that something unusual was going to happen that night. The soft, high pitched buzzing heard by him and others at a game last April still resonated in his mind. Memories of a softer version of the sound would sometimes bubble to the surface. No one else had ever heard it, as far as he knew. Shutting his eyes, he shook his head trying to refocus on the present. He swatted at the gnats flying around his face as he thought of his next pitch.

Jeff Lambert stood at the plate with his bat cocked ready to swing. The big guy was the only batter to ever hit one of Chris' pitches out of the park. He grinned and playfully winked at Chris.

"C'mon, boy. Gimme a pitch I can carry outta here."

Jeff and Chris were longtime friends, having met through Jim Glendale who played on Chris' team and was Jeff's roommate. Jim was out in right field yelling something about the batter being a sissy.

"You hear that Jeff? Even your own roommate is calling you names."

"What do you expect? He's on your team."

Their softball league had been around for a while. Many of the players had gone to local high schools, some having played baseball with or against each other. It was a fun league so gentle bantering and kidding was expected. Chris' team was known simply as The Boys. Tonight they were playing The Roadies in a tough contest. Down two runs, Chris had no desire to feed that lead. When they were behind, the team always relied on him to provide the spark to get back into the game, just like when they were in high school.

As Chris got ready to pitch, the buzzing started. He looked up and watched seven bugs that looked like horseflies fly about five feet over his head toward the woods outside the left field fence.

They're in a perfect triangle formation flying in a straight line, he thought. *What kinds of bugs do that?* He watched them fly over Cory and Ian. Neither one of them noticed.

Am I the only one seeing this?

He looked straight up and the night sky was clear. He thought he saw a swarm of bugs around the trees near left field but it was too dark to be sure. Chatter broke out from behind the plate breaking his concentration.

"C'mon batter. You're gonna swing and miss. Hey batter batter." Alex Savvas, the catcher, always gave opposing batters an earful of noise when they stepped into the batter's box. Most everyone was used to his insistent chatter, but it usually worked well enough to distract the hitter while the pitch signal was given. Alex called for a short, inside pitch by moving his glove close to the plate and the batter.

After one last glance at the woods, Chris decided he'd better not say anything yet.

If no one saw this, everyone will think I'm nuts. I'll check between innings.

Chris tossed the first pitch high and just inside the back corner of the plate. WHOOSH! Jeff swung and missed. WHAP. The soft sound of the ball going in Alex's glove gave Chris a sense of relief.

"Steeeerrike one!!!" shouted Jerry, the umpire working tonight's game.

Alex laughed as he threw the ball back. Chris and Alex had been a pitcher-catcher combination since they formed the team some fifteen years ago. Chris' older brother, Cory, played shortstop. Ian Johnston played third base, Gene Hudson held down second base, and Jay Greenfield was in center field. The friendship of these six boys went back to pre-school.

From behind the dugout, a light flashed out onto the field. Chris quickly shielded his eyes thinking it was a car's headlights, but then saw it was coming from the spotlight on a video camera. The six o'clock news had reported earlier that a TV crew would be at the park tonight doing a special on the city softball leagues. Someone was interviewing Bernie Gold, the city's athletic director of Parks & Recreation. Bernie played on one of the teams in the league and everyone knew him. Players started hollering wisecracks.

"Hey Bernie! Can ya keep the flashes down a bit?" Chris yelled. "I know you're famous and all, but we're trying to play ball here!" A few more friendly jeers rang out.

Bernie laughed and held his hand up to the news crew as he shouted toward the field, "You just want your mug on the TV screen, Chris. Not all of us are big time celebs like you. I'll put in a couple of good words about you, don't worry." Bernie then turned back to the reporter.

"Come on Chris," Jeff shouted. "You want to pose or pitch? I'm gonna knock the next ball right through that magic glove of yours." Jeff showed that big broad grin of his.

Chris knew he was kidding but Jeff really hit the ball right at the pitcher if the pitch came down the middle. That was an area to avoid.

Chris did seem to have a magic glove though. He had it about ten years now. There were no manufacturer's markings like Wilson, Spalding, or Rawlings anywhere on it. It was just smooth, clean leather that never got dirty and always looked brand new.

Ending up with that glove happened by chance. It just showed up. Players usually got to the field thirty minutes before a game, put their equipment down near the backstop, and took their gloves to go warm up.

One particular evening Chris dropped off his bat bag and grabbed his old glove to go throw. When he returned, this new glove was in his bag. He couldn't find a name or any other identifying marks. He looked around but didn't see anyone who appeared to be searching for a glove. He shouted out, "Anyone lose a glove?" All he got were some blank stares and a few, "Not me's." So he used it that game … and every game since.

"Quit looking at your glove and pitch the ball. Cold beer is waiting for us," David Smith hollered from left field.

Jeff added, "Listen to that will ya. Even your own team wants you to hurry up."

"They know I'm gonna strike you out." Chris saw Alex's signal for a high, inside, deep pitch. He delivered.

WHACK!! All heads followed the ball sailing high along the third base line. It curved slightly and landed in foul territory just past David's glove.

"Almost got ya," Jeff was gloating.

"Almost ain't enough," Chris countered while scraping the dirt off the white rectangular pitching rubber with his cleat. He then placed his left foot in the customary place of the far right of the rubber and had his right foot extended about two feet outward toward third base. This would allow for him to pitch the ball so it would look like it is going inside but would curve to the outside of home plate.

Chris delivered his pitch and immediately knew that he had released the ball too late. The ball was going to drop in the middle of the strike zone right behind the plate. This was called a 'meat pitch'. In other words, Jeff was going to kill this ball.

Chris knew he had screwed up. His mind raced.

Crap. He's gonna smash this. Please oh please swing high, Jeff. Miss it.

It looked like slow motion to Chris as he watched Jeff swing his bat well above the ball, missing it by a mile.

"Steeeerrike three! You're out!" shouted the umpire. "That's three outs!"

After the ball landed in Alex's glove, cheers erupted from the field and the stands almost drowning out Jerry.

"Wow! All right Chris!" Alex hollered as pumped his fist and headed to the dugout.

Jeff lowered his head, then his bat, and slowly walked away.

"Way to strike him out and get us out of that inning," Ian yelled.

"That's the first time he's ever struck out isn't it?" Cory asked David as they trotted off the field.

"I believe so," David replied.

Once in the dugout, Cory sat down near the end of the bench where Chris was and patted him on the knee.

"Nice job, Bro," Cory said excitedly. "How'd you get Jeff to swing at that junk? He never strikes out." Cory started fishing around in his bag for his batting gloves.

"You wouldn't believe me if I told you," Chris said shaking his head. "But I've been meaning to talk to you about this."

"This? What's this?" Cory asked. "Wait. Wait. David is up and we need a hit."

Both of them stood up at the dugout fence and saw David hit a shallow line drive into center field for a base hit.

"Great hit, David!" Cory yelled jumping up and down. "Now we've got the tying run coming up to bat."

The players groaned as their next two batters grounded out.

"Jay!" Alex hollered. "You're up to bat."

"Yeah, right." Jay grabbed a bat and hustled to the batter's box.

"This doesn't look good, man. Jay has been in a slump." Cory bit his lower lip.

"Sit down a sec," Chris said as he grabbed Cory's jersey and pulled him down onto the bench. "I'm trying to tell you something."

"What, dude? We've got Jay out there and we need a hit. There're two outs and the Roadies pitcher is throwing his back-spin curveball."

"So what. Listen up," Chris demanded.

"Can't it wait?" Cory asked standing up. "Jay has got to get on base."

"All right then," Chris said as he got up. "I'll get him on base."

"You'll what?

"Keep your voice down. I don't want the rest of the guys to hear this," Chris said as quietly as he could. They were still at the far end of the dugout, away from the others.

"Hear what?" Cory asked.

"Steeeerrike one!"

Jay had wildly swung at the first pitch and totally missed it.

"You want me to have him hit a home run?"

"Who? Jay? What are you talking about?" Cory was definitely confused.

"Listen this time you twit." Chris' frustration was evident. "I've been trying to tell you that I can affect events. Do you want me to have Jay hit a home run?"

"Are you nuts? He can't even hit the ball past the pitcher's mound," Cory said as he turned away from his brother to watch Jay. "But if you think you can make him do it, then you go right ahead."

"Okay." Chris stood next to Cory and said in a defiant voice, "Watch this."

The pitcher for the Roadies smiled as he eyed Jay. He calmly stepped forward as he released the ball. His expression changed from cool and confident to one of distress as he watched the ball sail lazily down the middle of the plate with no spin on it what-so-ever. Jay's eyes lit up as if this ball was coming in on the proverbial silver platter. He swung the bat as hard as he could. WHACK! All eyes followed the ball as it sailed toward the fence. The Roadies left fielder jumped to snag it but the ball flew a foot over his outstretched glove. Cheers erupted everywhere.

"I did it! I hit my first home run!" Jay yelled as he jumped up and down toward first base.

"Way to go! You tied the score!" Alex yelled as he ran out of the dugout followed by half the team, all of them cheering Jay on as he rounded the bases.

Cory didn't move. He stood next to Chris inside the dugout, disbelief covered his face.

"What did you do?" he said as he slowly turned to Chris.

"I tried to tell you. I can move things. I can affect other people's movements too" Chris had his head bowed down not watching the commotion on the field. He was kicking his cleat softly against the fence making a rattling noise.

"Are you serious? That's so cool. Really? Are you really serious? So when did you find this out?"

"Wow, dude. Calm down." Chris was smiling now. "I'm not really sure what to do about this. I figured it out a couple of weeks ago. Things kept happening that didn't make sense."

Cory reached behind him and grabbed his glove off the bench.

"Here. Make my glove jump onto the bench."

"Nah, man. I'm serious. I need to know what to do and how to handle this."

"Have you moved anything big? Come on, tell me," Cory asked as he grabbed Chris' arm and shook it a bit.

"I picked my car up a couple of days ago." Chris shyly replied.

"No way. Here, make my glove jump. Come on."

Cory held his glove up and it suddenly flew out of his hand and hit against the dugout fence behind the bench. His jaw dropped.

"You really can move things. How did you do it?"

"I dunno. I just willed it to happen. It's hard to explain."

"Cory!" Alex was standing on the field just outside the dugout hollering. "You're up! Get your butt out here!"

"Geez," Cory said as he pulled his batting gloves out of his rear pocket. He punched Chris in the shoulder. "Hey, make me hit a home run too."

"Get out there and do it yourself," Chris said as he pushed his brother along to the dugout opening. "Just get on base."

Cory stood at the plate and swung his bat with everything he had.

"Steeeerrike one!"

He was shocked. He let his bat drop to the ground as he stared in disbelief at the dugout searching for Chris. But his brother was sitting on the bench putting oil on his glove. He hadn't even bothered to watch.

"Yo. Dude!" he yelled trying to get Chris' attention.

"What's your problem?" David asked from the warm-up circle.

"We've got enough breezes going tonight without you adding to it. Hit the ball!"

Chris didn't see Cory hit a weak grounder to the shortstop who calmly threw the ball to first base securing the third out.

Cory glumly passed by his teammates taking the field as he went to retrieve his glove. Chris met him half way in the dugout.

"Here ya go, man," he said as he held out Cory's glove. "Tough break out there. At least we're tied so cheer up,"

"Why'd you let that happen? You didn't even look," Cory said as he threw his bat down. He snatched the glove out of Chris' hand and headed out to the field. Chris grabbed him by the shoulder.

"Look, dude, I never said I was going to get you a hit much less a home run."

Cory stopped.

Chris continued, "I'm sorry you got out but I can't go around changing the way things are supposed to happen. It wouldn't be right."

"You could have this time," Cory said as he kicked his foot in the dirt raising a cloud of dust.

"Then what about next time? And the time after that? When is it supposed to stop? I don't even know why this is happening to me. But I can feel it's all leading up to something big." Chris still had his hand on his brother's shoulder. "Have you been hearing any buzzing sounds tonight?"

"What?"

"Hey!" Alex hollered from behind home plate. The umpire and batter were also staring at them. "Are you two gonna get out here? Everyone's waiting."

"Y'all better hurry up or I'm going to put this batter on first base," Jerry added from the umpire's position behind Alex.

"Come on. Let's take the field," Cory said as he trotted to his position. "You can tell me after this inning."

Chris got on the mound and stared at the batter. Alex started his obnoxious chatter.

"Heyyyy batter-batter. Come on now swing at the ball."

Chris was about to toss his inside-outside pitch when the buzzing sound overhead caused him to look up in time to see hundreds of bugs flying in formation toward David in left field. As he watched, a louder buzzing started up from the woods near left field. Chris stared at the trees and then looked at Alex, who had stopped chattering. He was standing now, his head moving all around as he searched for the source of the buzzing. Chris spun around and saw David and the other outfielders point at the woods, yelling something that he couldn't make out. He turned back to Alex. Their eyes locked with recognition that there was something terribly wrong. This louder buzzing had an eerie, frightening pitch to it. Checking the bleachers, Chris saw that the spectators heard it too. Fear was in Lisa's eyes as she called out to Taylor and Michelle. Other women grabbed their children and pulled them along to the parking lot, some covering their ears to shield them from the terrifying sound. Pandemonium had erupted. Players ran off the field while both dugouts were a frenzy of guys grabbing equipment and bumping into each other as they quickly exited.

Chris just stood on the pitcher's mound watching the chaos around him. He was in disbelief having thought that no one but him would ever hear this. But tonight was different.

Everyone can hear it, he thought. *Why now? What is happening? It sounds so much worse than last time.*

"Ow!" he yelled as he flung his glove to the ground. Something in his glove had stung him.

Suddenly, the sky brightened as if a huge floodlight was illuminated hundreds of feet in the air. Chris froze as he looked up, mesmerized by the bright light above the field. It hypnotized him. He felt dazed and confused.

Ian hollered from behind the dugout, "Wake up Chris! Get your butt over here!" He was the only player left on the field.

Chris snapped out of his daze and bent down to pick up his glove. The buzzing was at a deafening level. The bright light from above had the park lit up like daytime. As Chris stood up, an even brighter cylinder of directed light came down and totally surrounded him making it appear like he was in a cloudy glass tube. A loud humming noise resonated inside the tube. Chris reached out and touched the wall of light that encased him. It felt wet. Trying to push his finger further into the unknown material met with resistance and a stinging sensation. He quickly pulled his finger out and looked up for the source of the beam. He tried to shield his eyes with his hand. With the light making it too bright to see anything, he diverted his eyes toward the bleachers, frantically searching for Lisa. He saw the terrified expression on her face as she shielded the children behind her. Her eyes were locked on his, but he kept losing sight of her through the swirling clouds of white vapor.

He watched as Cory and Ian reached her at the same time.

What's going on? His mind was full of jumbled thoughts. *What is happening to me?*

Memories screamed into his head as he racked his brain for answers. *I've heard a similar sound before, but when was it?* A memory flashed of a black bug staring at him. Then he saw a blurred image of what looked like a girl with bright white hair. She was speaking to him, saying something about coming for him. As he tried in vain to recall more detail, his thoughts were interrupted when the ground shifted under him. Chris watched as something moved below his cleats. Then he felt himself being lifted up.

As everyone in the park watched, the bright light beam retracted slowly up into the night sky leaving a small cloud of dust swirling around the pitcher's mound. Everyone could see Chris at the end of the beam as it continued to rise. He threw his glove down and pushed on the sides of the tube encasing him, pulling his hands back after the pain became too much to bear. Again, images surfaced of a girl with white hair talking to him.

What's she saying? I can't understand her.

Dropping down to his knees, he began to dig in the dirt that had been captured with him. An inch of dirt later, he hit some type of hard clear material.

At that moment, the humming ceased and a familiar melody began. He looked everywhere but couldn't find the source of the sound. Finally realizing it was in his head, he could distinguish a voice similar to his mother's, singing to him, like she did when he was a baby. But he knew this wasn't his mother singing now.

I know that voice, he thought as he stood up.

He looked up to see if he could tell where he was going. He saw only light.

Unexpectedly, a very warm, peaceful feeling washed over him. He calmly looked down at the throngs of people watching as he ascended into the night sky. He spotted Cory.

Take care, my brother. Let them know I'm all right.

He felt like a different person now.

As the light continued to rise with its captured cargo, it suddenly vanished and Chris was gone.

02 – IN THE BEGINNING

It was a hot and humid Virginia night; so much so that a person could step outside for ten minutes and come back in with a wet shirt. Thank goodness for fans which helped folks put up with the heat, and that included the Gates family.

Kelli Gates stood at the side of her baby's crib and leaned on the rail singing softly to Chris. Her sweet voice always calmed her baby boy. She touched his soft, fuzzy blond hair, wondering how long he would remain a towhead. It was the middle of the summer, July 14th, 1966, and Chris was just one month old.

He's so tiny in his crib, thought Kelli.

The polished wooden rails gleamed in the night light. His maple crib was a gift from her mother-in-law; the same crib Pete slept in as an infant. Maple furniture, her favorite, dominated the nursery. The crib, night stand, dresser, and her Grandfather's rocking chair she used when feeding Chris or getting him to sleep, reminded Kelli of her own room when she was a child. Looking at Chris, she noticed just how little space he took up on the mattress.

He's so small, but he sure was a big nine and a half pounds when he came out. Kelli wondered about his future size.

How tall is he going to be?

Everyone was tall in her family and Pete's too. She stood 5 foot 9 inches and Pete was 6 foot 2.

Will Chris be famous?

There weren't any real famous people in either family. Pete was a direct descendent of Frank and Jessie James, if that was any claim to fame. She knew Chris wouldn't turn out to be like Frank and Jessie.

He looks like a little angel. His little blond fuzz was shining like a halo in the soft glow of the night light.

Will he change the world? Not too many Gates have had the opportunity to do that. He can be President or anything he wants to be. Kelli let her thoughts wander as she continued to sing.

Chris was a normal little baby, her second child. Pete was so glad to have another son even though Kelli had hoped for a girl. Chris' older brother, Cory, was 13 months old and a handful. Having a toddler and a baby in the house kept Pete and Kelli on their toes.

Kelli liked to sing Chris to sleep, especially during these hot summer evenings. The sky blue walls in his nursery gave it an open air feeling. In the window, Kelli had an old box fan set on low, the gentle breeze blowing toward the crib making her feel cool in her shorts and tee-shirt. Chris was in a fresh diaper and getting droopy eyed as Kelli rubbed his back and continued to sing. She wondered what Chris was thinking as he lay in his crib on his tummy.

Do babies think thoughts like we do? she wondered.

Babies do think, but not like adults. Chris was still awake, hoping the little one-eyed bug would come and visit him again tonight like it did the night before. When he saw it for the first time last night, it sang beautiful songs to him. He waited in anticipation as he fought drifting off to sleep.

Will it come see me again? he thought, fighting to stay awake.

As Chris' eyelids began to get heavier, Kelli gently lifted her hand from his back. The breeze of the fan kept his little night shirt dry to the touch. Pete came tip-toeing into the room in his stocking feet, his blue jeans making a slight rustling sound.

"Is he asleep?" Pete whispered as he leaned over the rail of the crib looking at his son.

"He dozed off right as I finished singing to him."

"He's beautiful, Kelli. You did well." He slipped his arm around his wife and gave her a hug.

"It took two of us, dear. You did it too."

I am so glad I married this man. He is so wonderful, so perfect. If I hadn't met him at that football game, it's no telling who I would have ended up with.

Kelli gazed up at Pete with dreamy eyes. "I love you sweetheart."

"I love you too"

"Did Cory go down easily?" Kelli had the routine of getting Chris to sleep while Pete read to Cory.

"He's almost asleep. He did ask that you come in and say night-night prayers with him."

"Well let's go do that before he's asleep."

Pete slipped out of the room with Kelli right on his heels. She turned and quietly closed the door leaving it slightly ajar, blew a kiss in, and headed to Cory's room.

A few minutes passed. All was quiet in Chris' room except for the quiet motor of the window fan. From under the crib, a small bug flew out. When it first appeared, it was the same color as the crib, maple brown. But as it flew up to the crib's railing, it changed to black. It looked like some type of fly in the dimly lit room. About the size of a small horsefly and in the shape of a .22 caliber bullet, the bug flew lazily around the room, stopping above the night stand, then over to the dresser as if examining something. It quickly rose up to the ceiling where it hovered near the ceiling light. Absolutely no sound was heard except a faint buzzing of its wings. It flew to the partially open door and hovered there. It appeared to be investigating the hall as if listening for something but making no move to exit the room. After a minute, it flew to the window next to Chris' crib. It stopped, suspended in mid-air with wings beating so fast that they were almost invisible. Slowly, it descended to the right hand corner of the window where the screen had been cut in a perfect circle slightly larger than its body. A small section at the top was still attached to the screen and held the circle in place. The bug then spun around and flew to the crib.

A light turned off in the hallway and the bug dropped to the floor. When it became apparent that there was no further movement, the bug flew up and over the side of the crib rail, floated down to the mattress, extended four little legs from the lower side of its body, and touched down near Chris' head. Its dragonfly-like wings folded tightly against its body concealing them. It was now perfectly symmetrical. The front part of its body was all black and shiny like a big extended eye. The rest of the body had a dull sheen to it. The bug walked closer to Chris and began to sing, but not in a sound that could be heard. This was a telepathic transmission that could only be heard by the recipient.

Chris' bright blue eyes popped open. He sensed that the little one-eyed bug was back. It must be on the other side of his pillow, away from his face. He could now hear it singing inside his head. It sounded female to him, like his mother's voice. Since he was on his stomach, he had to raise his head and turn it to see the other way, showing advanced muscle development and control for a one month old baby. Now Chris saw the bug. This brought a smile to his face, highly unusual for one so young. The song the bug sang was the same his Mother sang - same words, same pitch, and the same melody. Then it began to talk to him.

Chris was still mastering language so he didn't always understand what his family was saying to him. But he understood everything the one-eyed bug was singing and saying … including that its name was Zenta. Chris liked that Zenta looked similar to the little black and yellow bumblebee in his over-the-crib mobile. It reminded him of other bugs he had seen when his mother took him outside in the stroller.

The previous night, when Zenta visited Chris for the first time, she sang to him until he fell asleep. Tonight, after a few minutes of singing his Mother's song, Zenta changed to one that told him about the world she came from. As the minutes ticked by, she purred many more sweet songs into Chris' sleepy little head, with her tiny body hypnotically swaying as Chris tried desperately to keep his eyelids open. Happy thoughts danced in his head as he slowly drifted off. As soon as he was asleep, Zenta stopped swaying and slowly let the singing subside. Then Zenta began flooding Chris' sub-consciousness with a methodical stream of information: history of Earth and Terlokya, languages from both planets, along with mental exercises to train all areas of Chris' brain. Zenta's fast information stream to Chris continued through the night.

Around three o'clock in the morning, hunger began to stir Chris. Zenta recognized this and stopped the information flow. She pulled up her legs and took off. Flying over the crib rail to the bottom of the crib, Zenta attached herself to the springs and waited for Chris' cries to summon Kelli to feed him.

"Waaaaaaaaa!" The hunger cries began.

Just as Zenta predicted, Kelli came into the room calling out to Chris with her gentle voice.

"Chris, my hungry little boy, Mommy is here." She picked him up, carried him to the rocker, and began feeding him. By the time Kelli was done, Chris had fallen asleep in her arms. Gently placing him in his crib, she quietly slipped out of the room and went back to bed. Five minutes later, Zenta flew out from underneath the crib, landed beside Chris' pillow, and restarted the information flow.

As the very first hint of light started to break, Zenta stopped the flow, began to sing a calming song that put Chris into a deep sleep. Then she flew underneath the crib and stayed until the next night. The training sessions from Zenta continued night after night.

Kelli and Pete were lucky that she could stay home with the boys instead of having to work. There was no doubt in Pete's mind that when they started a family, Kelli was going to take a long leave of absence from teaching elementary school and stay at home with the kids. She was in total agreement. Motherhood and its accompanying duties suited her.

One morning, Kelli was cleaning in Chris' room when she noticed how dusty the screen had become in the window next to Chris' crib. The fan she kept there to move air through the room was probably the culprit. She noticed what appeared to be a hole that had been patched. She touched the spot with her finger and the patch opened slightly.

I'll have to get Pete to fix that. It might let bugs into the baby's room.

September nights in central Virginia were still quite muggy. With the windows open and the shades pulled up, the sounds and sights of the night were evident all around. Whippoorwills sang proudly with crickets and tree-frogs accompanying them in song. Lightning bugs lit up the trees like blinking Christmas lights. An occasional Hoot owl joined the night orchestra. Chris lay awake in his crib. The night was young; a little after 9 o'clock. Kelli had put him down a while ago, singing him to sleep. But he woke up from all the outdoor noise. With all the beautiful sounds filling the air, it was no wonder that Chris had a smile on his face with his little arms and legs just a kickin' and a wavin', just to be moving. He was lying on his back and his little eyes were wide with excitement because he knew that Zenta would be visiting him soon. She told him she was going to see him every night, and had so far. He understood everything she said to him and his comprehension of what his family said to him had increased. Zenta was always teaching him something new. The little bug's sweet voice would sing him songs of majestic lands and creatures.

On a particular stormy night, the thunder and lightning kept waking Chris. Zenta's steady stream of information was continuously interrupted. When a bright lightning bolt streaked across the sky, Chris' whole bedroom lit up as if it were daytime. The lightning strike was so close that a loud clap of thunder sounded off immediately sending Chris into a crying frenzy. Zenta took off and flew under the crib just as Kelli came into the room. She quickly closed the window, picked Chris up and cuddled him in her arms, holding him against her chest, gently rocking him back and forth.

"Shhhhhh, sweet baby. Mommy is here for you. Shhhhhh, sweet Chris. I've got you." Kelli began to sing softly to Chris, slowly settling him down.

After a while, Pete came in and opened the window a bit for airflow.

"The storm is dying down. I think that one big lightning strike was the finale. It looks like the storm has moved away."

"Shhhhhh," Kelli whispered in between words of her song.

"Oh yeah, right," whispered Pete in a much lower volume. He noticed that Chris was drifting off to sleep. The commotion had Pete wide awake.

"Cory never woke up," he whispered.

"Thank goodness. I knew we should have closed the windows," Kelli whispered. "Since the storm is gone, we can leave them open so it won't get too hot in here." Kelli gently laid Chris in his crib. "You go on back to bed. I'll stay and make sure he's asleep."

Pete shuffled off to bed while Kelli gently rubbed Chris' back. Satisfied that he was fast asleep, she tip-toed out of the room leaving the door slightly open.

Kelli sat at the kitchen table wide awake as she watched the remaining storm clouds clear. A full moon beamed brightly down on the Earth. A Fresca in hand, she got up, walked to the kitchen counter, and stared out the window into the night sky. The stars were especially bright and the full moon was so big she felt like it was just as close as the dissipating clouds.

"If only I could travel into outer space, I would fly up to the moon and see what was on the other side," she whispered out loud. After watching the glowing moon a while longer, she yawned and then slowly meandered down the hallway to her bedroom.

Meanwhile in Chris' room, Zenta had gone back to work.

03 – THE DARK SIDE OF THE MOON

The other side of the Moon is sometimes referred to as the dark side, but there really isn't a dark side. The name came about because that side of the Moon is never seen from Earth. The same side always faces us due to the effect from the Earth's tidal forces. The Moon's rotation period and the orbital period are the same, so from Earth, you never see the other side. Both halves of the Moon actually get the same amount of sunlight. However, there are a few deep craters near the poles that get no light at all. We never see inside these craters from Earth, even with the most powerful telescopes.

On the night that Kelli was looking into the night sky, the Soviet spacecraft Luna 11 was orbiting the Moon. Luna 11's trajectory was set up for multiple options depending on its orbital entrance. One of the plans was a polar orbit which would have sent the spacecraft directly over the South Pole's Aitken crater, the largest on the Moon.

Had the Luna 11 been equipped with photographic equipment and flown over the South Pole, it would have seen specks of light emanating from a raised circular area. The surface of this circle appeared like any other area of the Moon – strewn with various size rocks; dry, barren, dusty, with small craters that pock marked the landscape as far as the eye could see. What differentiated the circle from its surroundings was that it was actually a raised dome with ramps aimed downward to large bay doors which burrowed below ground level. Had Luna 11 been shooting pictures; it would have transmitted the first images of an inhabited base inside the deepest part of the Aitken crater. If people on Earth had actually been receiving pictures from Luna 11, they would have discovered a very busy and highly advanced outpost occupied by a familiar life form.

The lights on top of the dome were recessed round windows, placed in haphazard fashion as if they were holes blasted into the dome by a large shotgun. From above, the windows gave the appearance of being small craters.

On this night just outside of the base, three wedge shaped rover style machines moved about. These tan and brown thirty foot rovers were propelled on tank treads. A bay door on the base opened, with bright lights shining outwardly from the new opening. As the door rose up, one of the rovers went inside the base.

Off in the distance, right above the horizon, a tiny speck of light was rapidly approaching the base. A small shuttle craft flew low over the Moonscape. It had the same wedge shape and size of the land rovers, but with gull shaped wings and sled-like rails. Red and green lights adorned the upper area of both sides. As the shuttle approached, a rectangular section on top of the base slowly opened, emitting a blue glow. The shuttle slowed to a hover above the dome opening, and then descended. The rectangular door closed, swallowing the blue glow.

A twenty-five by ten foot rectangular section on the upper part of the dome had been lowered down and was now under the surrounding area, revealing a large observation window. Tinted lights glowed from a large room, twenty feet below. Directly beneath the window was a large white platform. Rows of dark gray workstations with monitors faced a large screen on the wall. Above the screen were large, raised, block letters spelling out S.P. LAB.

There was movement at the furthest right workstation in the first row. A female humanoid with long bright white hair was sitting in a high-back, cushioned chair with her head down on the desk. She stirred slightly and then slowly sat up straight while stretching her arms out and leaning her head back revealing dark bronze skin. Except for her hands and face, the rest of her was encompassed in a skin tight light green and black tiger-striped uniform with knee high black boots. Various emblems adorned each shoulder. A momentary turn of her head as she reached for a small object from the adjoining workstation exposed a beautiful young face. She spoke into the object and then looked at her monitor.

She typed on the keyboard, looking intently at the image facing her. The large screen in the front of the room activated and mirrored what she was typing. The words and objects were in a language unknown on Earth. There were a series of rectangular button images on each side of her monitor, with various words across them. The female touched one of the buttons with her finger. At the bottom of the screen, words appeared on a command line with a flashing red icon in front. Translated into English, the words on the command line were, "BEGIN X13 ZENTA-PROBE TO CHRIS GATES DISENGAGEMENT SEQUENCE." She looked one more time at the image in front of her, which was a baby in a crib, then touched the flashing red icon.

04 – THE REAL ZENTA

People from all around the Mid-Atlantic come to the Skyline Drive in the Blue Ridge Mountains to see the leaves changing into the beautiful colors of fall. The mountaintop road through the Shenandoah National Forest was one of the most popular destinations to see this seasonal transformation. In late October, brilliant bright yellows, oranges, and reds, mixed in with various shades of green blanketed the rolling hills like waterfalls of color.

Pete and Kelli usually made the trip every year. Traveling from the Mount Eagle area, they were in the mountains within thirty-five minutes. But this fall was so packed with things to do that it became apparent they were going to miss it. With a baby and a toddler in the house, things were very hectic.

Kelli sat in their spacious living room with Chris in her arms thinking about the annual fall trip. Her glider chair was a favorite place for feeding Chris. It allowed her to gaze out the big bay window which faced west toward the Blue Ridge Mountains. She was in her robe and big fuzzy slippers, feeling cozy and warm. Pete had Cory up at Nick's store getting the Sunday paper as he always did before church. She was positive that Pete was buying some kind of treat for Cory, who was in need of extra attention now that he wasn't the only child anymore. The world wasn't revolving around him and he had begun exhibiting some minor behavioral problems.

The sound of the car in the driveway shook Kelli from her thoughts. She heard the pantry door open and Cory's footsteps closing in.

"Mama, candy!" Cory's hands shot out from his sides and opened, revealing two handfuls of M&Ms, some spilling onto the floor.

"That's great, sweetie. Did your Daddy buy you those?"

"Yaaaa." Cory ran to the corner of the living room where he had left his Matchbox cars earlier that morning, put his M&Ms in a little pile on the carpet, and began to play.

"It was a bribe," Pete said as he came into the living room. "He was bouncing off the walls. I thought Nick was going to ask us to leave."

"Well, that was a great idea buying some candy for him," Kelli said while getting up. "I bet he's really calm now." She winked and headed down the hall to Chris' room. "He's finished with his bottle. I'm going to put him down while we get ready for church."

"Grab a cup of coffee and come sit with me after he's down. We've got a little time before we have to leave for church." Pete sat on the couch, pulled the sports section out of the newspaper, and scanned the headlines.

Kelli laid Chris down on his tummy in his crib. She covered him with one of his light green blankets and gently rubbed his back. She then turned and tip-toed out of the room pulling the door closed behind her. About a minute later, the small bug flew out from under the crib and landed next to Chris' pillow.

"What's in the news?" Kelli asked while plopping down on the couch next to her husband.

"I think we'll see a man on the Moon real soon," Pete stated with an air of certainty. "The paper has a big article on NASA and the new Apollo Space Program that's going to be replacing the Gemini Program. Won't that be great? It says here that Apollo 1 should be launching sometime in January. Once they perfect space travel, I bet our kids will be able to travel to the Moon in their lifetime."

The individuals inhabiting the Moon didn't share Pete's enthusiasm. They would just as soon have Earthlings remain on their planet for the time being. One such individual was hard at work. As she pulled her headset off and set it down on the dark gray desk, the real Zenta wiped the beads of sweat from her forehead, her bronze skin still glistening. Her uniform felt constricting. She bent over and pulled off her boots, taking a moment to rub her feet around in the deep indigo blue carpet. Leaning back in her sleek black chair, she glanced around at the vast rows of workstations that took up the center of the room, barely visible from the dim lighting emitting from where the walls and ceiling met.

Rubbing her eyes, Zenta leaned forward, her arms resting on her desk. She was alone in the darkened lab, mesmerized as she stared at the monitor in front of her. In the center was an image of a human male infant lying on his stomach, his head on its side facing the screen, eyes closed as if asleep. This image was also on the gigantic wall screen at the front of the room.

Zenta was staring at the image when she heard the lab doors swish open. Sohan had entered the lab. Zenta turned and watched him approach, his shadow looming massively against the dull gray walls. His long flowing black robe made a sweeping sound as he moved across the floor. His green eyes enhanced in color by his bronze face, sternly zeroed in on hers, his square jaw rigid. When he was within arm's length of her, his expression softened to one of care and concern.

"Retire the probe. You look like you're about to fall asleep," he said softly as he slid into the chair next to her. He reached over and gently gathered her long pearly white hair and pulled it back behind her shoulders. "I can't have my only daughter make any mistakes. You have been at this a long time tonight and every night since he was born. The future of the whole Savior Project depends on this," he paused, "and on you. You've pulled a double shift so you should finish up this encounter. Xander will be in shortly to replace you. I know we are at the start of the training and you feel you need to do everything, but there are many more sessions to come."

"Yes Father, I'm almost done. I don't want to miss any of these early training opportunities even if they occur during brief nap times."

"I understand, but I can tell you are tired. Get some rest."

All Terlokyans had pure, bright, white, hair, except for Sohan. His hairless bronze dome reflected the sparse lighting in the lab.

As he got up to leave, Zenta turned up the volume as she put her headset on. She touched the 'X13 Disengage' button on the screen and listened to the session's final exchange between the probe and Chris' sub-conscious state. The sessions were at the point where there was some interaction beginning between his sub-conscious and her. On informational feeds, she only listened at the beginning and the end or when 'critical red' lit up on her monitor, but she was always attentive on exchanges. The recordings would have to be reviewed the next day anyway. The image of Chris' face on the monitor had her longing to see him in real life. She had seen pictures of Earth babies before and thought them cute. But this little blond boy was tugging at her heart strings.

Was it because he was the Chosen One who would save all mankind? she wondered.

Zenta realized she was allowing emotion to affect her work.

This baby was just a subject to be trained for a mission, nothing more. To let my feelings enter into the project would be inexcusable. She shook her head as if to shake the thoughts out and focused on her task.

After the probe was retired, she got up and retrieved a report from her workstation. She stretched her legs and went over to the huge white square that was underneath a large ceiling window and stood on it.

"Platform console: rise." She coughed after speaking. Her voice sounded raspy.

I'd better stop relying on those energy fluids to stay awake. They are affecting my throat.

From the floor rose a small console with a series of buttons on it. Zenta pushed a button and handrails rose through small slots in the floor at the edges of the white square. Then she pushed another button and the square began to rise up toward the ceiling. A covering opened on the roof outside revealing a starlit night through an observation window. This window also began to extend outward creating an observation dome. Once inside the dome, the platform stopped. She gazed out at the twinkling lights. The stars were shining especially bright tonight. Short-range transport shuttles were moving the large light ring into a position near the base to launch a Planet-Transport ship. This process was very time consuming. She remembered being on one of the shuttles for a light placement mission, having filled in for the regular onboard communications officer that day. It was really an experience to watch a large Planet Transport ship off to Terlokya or see one come flashing in. The intense flash of light and thundering sound as the transport appeared made even the toughest outpost soldier jump.

Zenta had been so busy since Phase Three started that she hadn't kept up with the travel schedule of who was coming to the Moon or going to Terlokya. She missed home; seeing her mother and the rest of her family. How long had she been on this forsaken space rock working on the Savior Project? It had been seven Earth years. She had arrived during Phase One. That first phase of the project, the Parental Unit - Meeting & Mating, involved the research and selection of parental subjects. Then she immediately became immersed in Phase Two, the Savior Selection which involved evaluation and selection of the offspring. Everyone marveled at the precise execution of the plan.

Sohan had played a major role as the senior officer of the group that planned the entire project. Zenta drew great comfort in that Sohan, the greatest and most brilliant leader Terlokya ever had, chose to be at Base GAIA during the launching of Phase Three of the Savior Project. She knew that failure was not an option under his guidance.

Zenta studied the report she had in her hand. It was last summary of key events from Chris' parents file before he was born. She reviewed the information on the first page.

CHRIS GATES – PARENTAL PROFILE SUMMARY

- Pete Gates and Kelli Barry met at a 1959 University of Virginia football game, introduced by Pete's Delta fraternity brother, Kelli's brother, Joe Barry.
- Pete graduated from the University of Virginia with an undergraduate degree in history in May 1960.
- Kelli graduated from University of Maryland in 1961 with an English degree.
- Pete received his Masters in History from the University of Virginia May 1962.
- Pete is employed by the University of Virginia as an assistant history professor.
- Pete and Kelli married June 8, 1962.
- Kelli was employed as a school teacher before having Cory, older brother of Chris.
- Cory was born on May 12, 1965 in Mount Eagle, Virginia

Zenta stopped reading and leaned on the railing. Getting Pete and Kelli together had been one heck of a chore. As she pushed a button to lower the observation platform, her thoughts raced as she felt the enormous responsibility of this project. The sudden jolt of the observation platform stopping momentarily had Zenta off balance. She kept thinking about when it all began.

Zenta was not part of the Generation Team that was responsible for the selection of parental units that would have offspring to be evaluated. She never fully understood the insistence of the host family having an older male sibling to the Chosen One. "It needs to be there for protection during childhood," her father told her.

What if something happened to the older sibling, or they developed animosity toward their younger sibling? It should never have been a requirement.

Zenta remembered reading the detailed reports on the selection of Pete Gates and Kelli Barry as potential parental units for the Savior Project. They were the top candidates from the group of ten couples.

The amount of work, planning, and manipulation the Generation Team accomplished to have all the selected couples meet and then be so compatible was amazing.

Out of the ten couples monitored during Phase One, only one couple split up. The Selection Team didn't have as tough an assignment but certainly had as much research and work to do. After all, they were selecting The Savior. These offspring of the couples were evaluated, and the selection was carefully made. It took nine years to complete Phase One. It took less than a week to evaluate each child after birth. Pete and Kelli were the seventh couple from the parental pool and Chris had the highest evaluation of the nine offspring. Due to Chris' high score, training for him began immediately after his evaluation even though the offspring from the eighth and ninth couples had yet to be born. The Selection Team believed that those offspring would not score as high as Chris. Probes were sent to evaluate them and the conclusions were confirmed.

Zenta knew that Phase Three, Savior Development, would be the longest phase; about thirty to forty Earth years, depending on the war between the Terlokyans and the Veloptors and the eventual career path of the Savior.

I could possibly be about 60 Earth years old by the time the Extraction Team launches Phase Four, almost in my prime.

Zenta lost herself in her thoughts as she gazed at the blank wall screen where just a few minutes ago, the most beautiful face she had ever seen lightened the lab. She yawned as her mind began to enter that trance like stage one feels when falling asleep while standing. Zenta sat down at her workstation and typed in the commands which restarted the probe to continue Chris' training.

05 – TO CATCH A BUG

Kelli labored in her garden pulling weeds and planting flowers. Out of the five flower beds around the house, the one in the middle of the backyard was her favorite. The tropical hibiscus and petunias were so colorful. She stopped for a second and looked around for a place where her rose trellis could go.

I need to get Pete to build my trellis, Kelli thought as she wiped sweat from her brow.

I really should have started this garden work before ten. The white tee-shirt she was wearing, emblazoned with 'UVA FOREVER' on the back, was already damp.

"EEEEEEEEEEEEEE!!!"

Kelli's head whipped around just in time to see Cory land on two bare feet on the ground outside of the playpen.

Chris emitted another gleeful shriek, "EEEEEEEEEEEE! Mama!" Wearing an ear to ear grin, Chris was standing inside the playpen jumping up and down pointing at Cory. "Cory go!"

Cory turned and headed straight toward Kelli, running with his little arms waving in the air like a windmill.

"Mama!" Cory leapt into Kelli's outstretched arms, causing her to tumble backward.

"You escaped, baby." She gave him a big hug. At age two, Cory had mastered his climbing and escape routine from the playpen. He liked being in there playing with Chris, but once he figured out how to get out, it became a game. Holding Cory on top of her, Kelli rolled her head to look over at Chris. He was still standing in the playpen, holding onto the top rail and bouncing up and down.

"CORREEEEEEEEEE!" Chris was still hollering his brother's name through his little toothy grin. Kelli and Pete, along with their pediatrician, were amazed at Chris' advanced level of speaking at age one. Using Daddy, Mama, calling his older brother by name, and using four to five word sentences, showed an advanced level of development. He started walking at eight months and running at nine. Not unheard of, but talking as well as he did at twelve months was rare.

Kelli felt so blessed holding Cory while eyeing her youngest. Chris didn't care that Cory would climb out of the playpen leaving him behind because Cory would always come back. Chris was still standing but was now looking up into the big Maple tree that Kelli put the crib under whenever she worked in the yard. It provided a wide swath of shade coverage, keeping the kids cool and out of the sun. He was so intently focused on something in the tree that Kelli turned her attention to Cory who was now trying to tickle her.

"Tickle Mommy. Tickle Mommy."

"I don't think so little man. Mommy will tickle Cory now." Kelli had one arm around Cory holding him on top of her and began to gently tickle him under his left arm. He squealed with laughter.

Meanwhile, Chris glanced over at his mother and brother giggling and tickling each other rolling around on the grass. Having heard the familiar buzzing, he turned his attention to the tree and saw his little black bug, Zenta, sitting on a branch looking at him.

"Hi Zenta," Chris said with a big smile.

"Hi Chris." She spoke to him through the probe so that he would hear it in his mind. "Why don't you climb out of the playpen too? I've seen you do it before."

Chris heard Zenta as if the words were spoken out loud. After his initial greeting, he thought of his responses in his head and Zenta heard him.

"I know I can climb out. I like my playpen. All my toys are here." He reached down and picked one up. "See?" He held up his little yellow giraffe toward Zenta. "Come down and see it. Come down and play with me."

"I can see all of your toys in there. But don't you want to go to the flower garden and play with your mother and brother?"

Chris looked toward the garden.

Far away on the Moon, the real Zenta stared at her monitor, her heart melting as she watched this beautiful child. She happened to have been in the Savior Project Lab or SP Lab as it was called, and overheard that Xander was ill and couldn't cover his day shift of observation-training for Chris, so she volunteered. Lack of sleep would become an issue since she normally slept during the day and trained Chris at night. Interacting with him conversationally while he was awake had not been done before. She couldn't help herself.

Zenta guided the probe down from the branch in the direction of the railing across from where Chris was. While steering the probe in a slow deliberate trajectory to the railing, Chris was momentarily out of view. Chris lunged at the probe, snagging it out of the air. His little hand closed tight around his prey as he regained his balance and stood in the middle of his crib.

"I got the bug! I got Zenta!" he hollered.

Zenta's screen went black. Loud scratchy noises coupled with the muffled sound of Chris yelling in the background forced her to pull her headset off. It sounded as if someone was covering up a recording microphone and that is exactly what Chris was doing. The X13 Probe was designed to be a mobile seeing, transmitting, and listening device and Chris had just captured one.

Chris held his little closed fist high in the air, turned toward the garden, and hollered, "Mama! I got the bug! Mine now!"

Kelli was still rolling around in the grass tickling Cory who was squealing so Kelli didn't hear Chris.

Zenta quickly put her headset back on, adjusted the volume, and began to speak into her microphone. The probe transmitted the soundless thought communication to Chris.

While holding the top rail of the playpen with one hand, Chris put his right arm on the rail for support. As he swung his leg up high to hook it on the rail, he heard Zenta's voice in his head. He let his leg drop back down to the floor of the playpen.

"Chris, I'm so glad you are holding me. Now open your hand so you can see me and I can see you." Zenta had already retracted the probe's wings and was ready to deploy its legs the instant Chris opened his hand. She could then easily fly the probe up into the tree, but she didn't plan on doing that. Zenta saw this as an opportunity to gain Chris' trust by showing her trust.

Chris lowered his fist and stared at it. "You are mine now," he said out loud.

"Yes Chris, I am yours. But you might hurt me if you keep me closed in your hand and then I wouldn't be able to see you and talk about different things. Please open your hand so I can see you."

Chris held his fist out; looking intently as he slowly opened his fingers. As they peeled back, he saw the probe in his palm.

"Oooo! You got a picture of a little blue stick bird on your tummy," Chris gleefully said. "It has wings."

"That's the Terlokyan symbol for 'Flying Forcefully'," Zenta explained.

As the probe rolled over, its legs popped out but stayed in Chris' palm.

Zenta again spoke into her microphone.

"Thank you, Chris. That feels much better. I like being able to see you. I'm going to fly to the rail and sit there so you can show me some of your toys, okay?"

"Okay."

Chris watched the probe fly to the playpen rail.

The sound of the SP Lab doors opening and closing with the usual swishing sound broke Zenta's concentration. She had hoped it was Sohan but she heard Xander instead.

"What happened? I received a probe distress signal," Xander said while still sounding ill. His voice was shaking somewhat, but without a harsh tone his older brother Jzet used when speaking to Zenta.

"Everything is under control," she responded as she covered her microphone. "There was a small mishap." She grabbed a stack of papers out of his chair. "I thought you were sick."

"My Trace went off. Tell me what happened," he asked as he tucked his shoulder length white hair behind his ears.

"It really wasn't a big issue," she lied. Zenta observed Xander, envying his more advanced Trace. She had the basic Trace communication device with voice, screen, and camera functions. He also had additions which were needed for being a secondary backup member of the Anti-Detection Unit (ADU). A scanner, longer range communications, and a bigger screen were all things she desired, but she didn't need those functions for her responsibilities.

"It was just a minor incident, no cause for alarm. Everything is normal." Zenta and Xander both studied the images on Zenta's monitor and saw Chris smiling at them holding up a plastic toy truck.

"Well then, would you please tell me why my Trace went off with a probe distress signal?" Xander asked again.

Zenta knew Xander wasn't much into creating controversy. Being one of the original members of the Development Team, the project's success was just as important to him as it was to her.

"I flew the probe down to the rail next to Chris to test his physical abilities."

She snuck a quick glance at Xander. His hard expression softened when their eyes met. A few inches shorter than his older brother, Xander wore his hair down to his shoulders, unlike Jzet's closely cropped cut. His uniform was decorated with only half as many military achievements as Jzet, but then again, his brother was a battlefield warrior. Xander leaned his tall lanky frame over and redirected Zenta's attention to the issue at hand.

"Do you mean to tell me that the probe is in Chris' confinement unit?" he asked while pointing at the monitor.

"Yes. I directed it there to try and encourage Chris to exit the confinement unit which, by the way, is called a playpen. Then my monitor went black for a few moments."

"Why did your monitor go black and why would you expose the probe to the child? And isn't the confinement unit, or the playpen thing, as you call it, supposed to keep the Earth child confined?" Xander nervously tapped his fingers on the top of the monitor.

Zenta saw Chris was waving his small stuffed giraffe at the probe. She and Xander couldn't help but smile.

"Wait a second," Zenta said glancing at the screen. She uncovered the microphone and pressed the talk key.

"I like the giraffe, do you have another animal?" As Chris was leaning down to find another toy, Zenta turned her attention back to Xander.

"I am trying to encourage him to climb out of his playpen to further challenge his dexterity. And don't call him Earth child, you sound like your brother. He is the Chosen One, or call him the Savior, or even Chris."

"Fine. Chris it is. But you still haven't answered my most important question. Why did the monitor go black?"

Zenta slumped forward, unable to make eye contact.

"Chris grabbed the probe out of the air as I was flying it down from the tree," she said quietly.

"He did what?"

"He grabbed the probe out of the air with his hand." Zenta shrugged as she made the statement. They both looked at the monitor and Chris was now holding a little teddy bear waving it at the probe.

"Come and play, now," Chris said while bouncing up and down.

Xander looked at Zenta and exclaimed, "How can a one year old child, or even the Chosen One, grab an X13 Probe out of the air?!"

"I don't know how, but he did." Zenta looked up at Xander and smiled. "And he did it without holding on or falling down. He is extremely advanced." Zenta said smugly. However, Xander's reaction was not what she had expected.

"Remove that smile. You should not be using an X13 Probe to interact with him while he is awake." Xander crossed his arms over his chest and glared at Zenta. "If Sohan heard about this he'd be furious."

"I'll tell him myself." Zenta's head snapped back to her monitor. "I'm in charge of his training and I saw an opportunity to test his physical abilities."

As Xander walked toward the door, he departed with these words, "I want to be there when you tell him."

Zenta heard the doors close.

"You can be there and anyone else you care to bring." Zenta knew Xander wouldn't tell anyone. Anybody could review the day's log, so it wasn't as if she was trying to hide anything. She would deal with this later.

Zenta saw Chris eagerly pointing at Kelli and Cory. They were holding hands and giggling as they walked to the playpen.

"Chris," Zenta spoke into the microphone.

Chris turned his head and smiled.

"I need to go now," Zenta said. "We'll play some more later. I had fun."

"Okay." Chris then looked at Kelli and Cory. "Mama, Mama! Look!" Chris turned back around, but the probe was gone.

Watching from the probe's new position in the tree, Zenta saw Chris' smile fade. Just then, Kelli reached into the playpen and lifted Chris in the air.

"And what's my baby doing?" she said holding him high. "Is a bug bothering you?"

Chris let out a squeal, "EEEEEE!"

Zenta could see that Chris' big toothy grin had returned.

06 – WINTER WALKS

The Gates' 'country mile' driveway meandered to the county road. Their closest neighbor, the Sprouses, lived about a mile away. Country living gave ample time for wonderful outdoor walks. Gravel and little children made for very slow walks unless you were on a well-worn road. The Gates driveway had gravel packed deep in the ground. Trees lined both sides until the first bend where a huge field opened up on the right. A forest full of life surrounded their house and Kelli felt like she lived in the middle of nature's kingdom.

She really enjoyed their four bedroom one story contemporary style brick house with a slate patio next to the carport. They bought it about three years earlier. Since it was built into a small rise, it had a smaller lower level. The best part was the living room with its huge picture window facing toward the mountains. Kelli and Pete had turned that house into a home.

Kelli looked forward to taking Cory and Chris out for walks. The weather was quite mild during the first week of December. The boys only needed light jackets while Kelli, who was a bit cold-natured, wore her long fleece coat. The boys really enjoyed these walks. Lots of sounds and smells filled the air, like crows calling out to one another, leaves rustling as the last few non-hibernating squirrels ran from tree to tree, and the occasional Hoot Owl. On this particular day, Cory was running from the bushes to the trees, chasing squirrels, and squealing at birds. It was just after his nap and he was raring to go.

I hope the walk will wind him down some before Pete gets home. And then again, maybe the Moon will fall out of the sky, Kelli thought.

Chris was keeping up with Cory. She marveled at how coordinated he was at eighteen months. But his advanced development led to certain challenges. She sometimes had Chris running off in one direction and Cory in another.

"Mommy, water please." Kelli looked down at her beaming little one.

"Of course, sweetie. I brought two bottles with us. Here, let me take the top off for you."

"I can do that."

"Okay. Here you go." As she handed the bottle to Chris and watched him unscrew the top, she thought about how Pete would be mortified if he knew she was using his plastic football game flasks to carry water for the boys.

"Thank you. Going to the woods now." And off he went. Kelli was surprised to find the top screwed back on tight.

That boy has some muscle to him.

As Cory ran down the road, Chris inspected the woods, his little eyes wide open, darting here and there. He was talking a bunch of gibberish that Kelli couldn't make out. He was filled with excitement, evident by his little arms waving in the air as he ran.

"You're a little windmill," Kelli said while watching him.

"Daddy coming now?" Chris had stopped waving his arms and turned to Kelli.

She recalled how quickly he was picking up on time related events such as when Pete came home from work.

"He'll be home real soon."

Chris smiled and looked back into the woods. He was studying everything. The contents of the world were still so new. He wanted to touch the leaves, dirt, rocks, tree bark. He wanted to see, feel, and hear the outdoors.

But Chris was also waiting for Zenta. He had seen her before on walks and knew she would be somewhere close. Suddenly, he heard the buzzing and knew that 'his bug', as he called it, was going to be around for today's walk. Whenever he saw it, he reached for it.

From her monitor on Base GAIA, the real Zenta knew it was time to begin visual separation with Chris. His development was progressing rapidly. He was speaking very clearly now and could recognize the probe. She flew the probe out of Chris' view, aimed it at Kelli, and studied her expression. The last thing this project needed was for a probe to be discovered by the Chosen One's mother.

My dear Kelli, thought Zenta. *You have no idea how famous your son will be.*

Kelli noticed that Chris had stopped what he was doing and was watching the road. She was about to say something, but he spoke first.

"Daddy coming now."

"He'll be here soon, sweetie. Did you hear his car?" Kelli listened but didn't hear anything.

"I feel him coming now."

"You feel him? What do you mean, you feel him, sweetheart?" Kelli walked over and bent down next to him, but he didn't take his eyes off the road.

At that moment Cory, who was further up the road, shrieked in delight as he saw Pete's car rounding the bend. Pete tooted the horn a couple of times and slowly rolled to a stop. Kelli quickly forgot about

Chris and his 'feeling' moment and walked to Pete's car. Cory reached the door first with Chris right on his heels.

"Hop in little buddy." The car door opened for Cory to climb in.

Kelli strolled over to the open door. "Got room for one more?" Chris was now climbing into the car to get on his Daddy's lap.

"Always room for my boys and my pretty girl. Want to hop in too? Four is my magic number."

"You go ahead with the boys and I'll walk back." She leaned in and pecked Pete on the lips. "Besides, I could use a few moments of quiet time."

"Sure thing, babe. See ya at the house. You ready boys? Hold it a sec, Chris. Let me get that newspaper out from under you before you get newsprint on your fanny." Pete picked his youngest son up with one arm and slid the newspaper out from underneath him with the other. He set Chris down and tossed the paper on the back seat. Kelli saw the headline in big bold print on the front page.

APOLLO 8 MISSION TO CIRCLE THE MOON.

07 – SAVIOR ADVERSARIES

Major Jzet stood up from his seat and slammed his fist on the oval table. Everything rattled in the Council Communications Room along with a jarring wave that went through the hard, clear plastic-like surface. Marsitta, the communications officer, jumped in her chair at the sound. Even the commander of Moon Base GAIA, General Jhall, with years of battle hardened military experience, appeared startled at this display of anger. Major Jzet glared at everyone around the table and then glared at the Supreme Council members. Only ten minutes into the project update for the council, Jzet was already stirring up trouble. He had wasted little time in jumping up to speak after Sohan finished his opening remarks.

"I really don't think any of this is necessary. We can take on this endeavor without an Earthling's involvement. Everyone knows that I can lead the entire operation. We have plenty of time to prepare: about forty more Earth years. And we could possibly cut that time in half."

The room fell silent as Sohan listened intently, his brow slightly raised. His seventy-five years of leadership and military experience had exposed him to many such outbursts. He scanned the faces of everyone in the room judging their reactions. Zenta's expression did not change one bit, with contempt written across her face. Her green eyes appeared like they would burn right through Jzet. A furrowed brow along with tight lips caused wrinkles in her normally smooth, youthful skin. White replaced bronze in her knuckles as she pressed tightened fists into the table surface. Sohan knew she despised the fact that the Major was constantly meddling in her phase of the project while conniving to impress her with his other actions, deeds, and words.

That look on her face, thought Sohan, *is the same look everyone wears when confronting Jzet's angry eruptions.*

The senior officer in charge of the Savior Project, Colonel Braaddy, sat expressionless next to Jhall. This grizzled war veteran had long ago tired of Jzet. Sohan hoped there would not be another confrontation between them. Braaddy never hesitated to use his rank and years of military experience to put Jzet in his place.

Sohan glanced at the council members, their images displayed on the gigantic communications screen. Their flowing robes gathered about them as they sat behind the elegant and stately six foot high Supreme Council Bench. The bench, made entirely from glass, gave the illusion that the council members were floating. Their life size images on the screen made them appear as if they were in the room. None of them had reacted or showed any emotion to Jzet's outburst.

"Can anyone justify to me why it is necessary to spend our resources training an Earthling fresh from the womb? We have fully trained Terlokyans capable of leading these people," exclaimed Jzet.

Sohan thought he heard a growl come from Zenta at that last statement. Jzet was strong willed and tried to project his will on others, but it never worked with Zenta. He was an imposing figure, tall for a Terlokyan at six and half feet, strapping, solid muscle, and only fifty years younger than Sohan. His closely cropped white hair framed a rugged, sharp featured face adorned with a few scars. He was a soldier warrior who had risen rapidly through the military ranks. His tough colonial background, and his upbringing on the cold, war weary planet of Cezzeck, created a certain aura about him. The wars he had fought in, coupled with his daring leadership on the battlefield, had made him a hero to the population, as his impeccable uniform showed with its ribbons, metals, and rank insignia. He appeared invincible at times and was very convincing in his arguments.

"To go through all the trouble of training an Earthling to undertake this important mission is a huge waste of time, energy, and effort. We should be readying a Terlokyan to do this. That way we know the mission will be done correctly and successfully."

Jzet's glaring eyes moved quickly from face to face searching for acceptance. "We always have to save Earthlings from themselves. This time it should be different. Now they will need to be saved from someone else." Jzet continued to stare at everyone as he slowly sat down. He was a warrior and argued like one, using words as weapons to win. Defeat was not a word he used, except when speaking of his enemies.

Sohan thought carefully about how he would respond. He rose from his seat at the head of the table and slowly walked around the outer edges of the room. The soft overhead lights gave a shine to his hairless head; his footsteps were silent as he stepped upon the lush, soft carpet. He walked behind Zenta's chair, not making eye contact with his daughter as she watched him. He passed by Major Marsitta, who sat quietly at the communications workstation with its multitude of lights, gauges, and small screens emitting a colorful glow. She had been the communications officer for Sohan for almost forty years. Before that, she had risen through the military ranks with him after they had joined the Terlokyan Colonials together and fought in the colonial wars. She was a tall, well chiseled woman who had seen her share of combat. As Sohan advanced in rank, Marsitta was at his side. He always believed that communications was one of the most important positions in a military organization and he relied heavily on Marsitta.

Rounding the side of the table, Sohan caught Lieutenant Callun's eye. Callun quickly broke eye contact and glanced at Jzet. The short, rotund Terlokyan had been Jzet's aide and apprentice for quite a while. He would side with his superior no matter what the stakes.

Sohan stopped near the communications screen and began to speak.

"We must continue on the path that we started. Things are different and we are living in troubled times. Keep in mind that we are in our own crisis." He paused and resumed his walk around the table. Stopping in front of the council members, he continued.

"We all knew the time would come for us to pass on our knowledge to Earth and separate ourselves from them. Time used to be a luxury which allowed us to dictate the separation pace. However, considering the current hostilities with planet Velox, we've had to make drastic changes in our overall plans."

Sohan closed his eyes for an instant. He felt he had to convince the council once again that this plan was the only option. He continued, "With a carefully planned and executed separation, we will then have more time and resources to concentrate our efforts on our own defense. We have all reached the conclusion that Earthlings will be more likely to unite behind one of their own and follow that leader into battle versus someone from a distant solar system. This will free us for what lies ahead: for if we do not bring the Earthlings up to our level of technology and concentrate our strongest efforts on the threat before us, then it is possible that we shall not survive as a species."

Sohan walked back to his seat, sat down, then stared right at Jzet, awaiting the response he knew would come.

"But they don't have the knowledge or the resources to defend themselves against this upcoming onslaught," Jzet said as a few of the members of the council nodded in agreement. "They are weak and disunited. They have wreaked havoc on their own planet and are at war constantly among themselves. They kill fellow humans as if they were killing a lower life form or an external enemy. With all due respect, Supreme Commander, not one of them is fit to lead anything."

Sohan pondered the situation in front of him. He glanced at the images of the council members looking past them at the large paned window behind the council bench. The resolution and size of the screen made it seem as if he was on Terlokya, looking out that very same window. It was evening, both suns having set hours ago. The skyline of the Terlokyan capital Kukno gleamed in the night.

The room fell silent as Sohan rose from his seat. Standing tall, he pointed his outstretched arms toward the center of the room; his hands clenched in fists, turned downward, eyes shut tight. His concentration was apparent. Everyone wondered if he was communicating with the Source.

A minute passed. As he opened his eyes, he slowly spread out his arms. With the oversized sleeves of his gray and black robe draped downward, it gave the appearance of a Terlokyan War Bird, with wings of feathers spread wide ready to take flight. Unclenching his fists and turning his open palms up, he began to speak in a soothing, but firm, clear voice, the same voice that had continually convinced his people that his wisdom was always the best choice.

"The time is approaching for us to end our caretaker role and prepare Earth to defend itself." He lowered his arms and continued. "This separation was going to happen eventually. The Veloptor's progress in the development of their space travel technology has allowed them to engage our forces in more locations. Our recon units have spotted their sensor units on the far reaches of this galaxy. Our outposts on the planet Mars and the Jupiter Moon, Europa, are on constant alert."

Sohan began another slow walk around the table.

"Their persistent espionage and constant attacks have emphasized the need to continue with the plan we developed for the Savior Project. The Veloptors are a formidable enemy. With their increasing ability to thoroughly search solar systems, and their willingness to travel long distances, they have shown a determination to hunt down humanoids and will spare no resources to find Earth."

Sohan paused to give everyone a moment to digest his words. He stopped his slow stroll at the entrance doors and turned to face the conference table and the communications screen. He held his hands out in front of him and noticed not a trace of movement. Raising his head, his green eyes were keenly focused, his brow slightly furrowed, and a stern and confident expression radiated throughout the room. He continued.

"We will never be forgiven by the Veloptors for what happened on Earth before humans evolved. Even though it was not our fault their species died out on that planet, they will always blame us. They know we will defend our own species throughout this galaxy and that includes Earth. Terlokyans have never backed down in the face of an adversary. Our two civilizations are on an inevitable collision course that is only going to lead to all-out war."

After a dramatic pause, he finished with, "The inhabitants of Earth will subject themselves to the leadership of a fellow human who possesses superior super-natural abilities. With the resources we will provide to the Savior during the Return Phase, he will unite the various tribes of Earth. As seen in the reports before you, we are well ahead of schedule in the training phase of the Savior Project. Our selected Earthling has exhibited far more superiority than we could have hoped for."

"These issues have been thoroughly researched and discussed. We can, and we must continue with the Savior Project as it is laid out. It is the best way to control the Velox threat and preserve humanoid life."

Zenta and Braaddy both jumped to their feet and began clapping. Seeing this, Marsitta and Jhall followed suit. Then the council members slowly began to acknowledge Sohan and his unifying speech with much head nodding and polite, quiet clapping: the usual dignified response of a council member. This left Jzet alone with his views. To appear loyal, he too began clapping, although without the same enthusiasm the others showed. Callun clasped his hands together on the table, his eyes cast downward with his mouth slightly ajar. He wore the look of defeat but finally managed to move his hands in a clapping motion.

Sohan raised a hand, quieting the room.

"This is not a time for rejoicing." He paused for everyone to grasp that. "These were merely words that must be followed with action. We have a difficult road ahead. The only way we will achieve success is to continue to support these efforts with a united front." His eyes fell on Jzet as he finished his words. The look he saw in Jzet was not one of cooperation. Sohan knew there would be more confrontations and they would become more intense and complex as the time drew nearer to extract the Savior. He would have to develop a plan to occupy Jzet. Sohan decided to table those thoughts for now. He had the very pressing matter of the upcoming Apollo 8 mission. The space programs from Earth had never sent a human to the moon before. He needed information on the status of that mission and he needed it right away.

He closed the meeting, bidding the council members farewell till the next scheduled time. The council had appeared pleased with the final outcome of the meeting. With that, Sohan nodded toward the smiling faces of Zenta, Marsitta, and a few others in the room. Sohan shot Jzet a glance, no more than just an acknowledgment of his presence, then turned and walked to the door.

"Supreme Commander. Wait," Marsitta said with an alarmed tone. "General Jhall. I need you to stay too."

Both Sohan and Jhall stopped and walked back to the communications workstation.

"What is it, Marsitta?" asked Sohan.

Everybody in the room turned their attention to Sohan.

"Sir," Marsitta began. "I'm getting a trace from the Command Center. We are receiving communications from our outpost on Europa. Apparently they have detected a Veloptor presence on the other side of the solar system near the planet Neptune."

"Put the communications on speaker," Jhall ordered.

"General Jhall" Everyone recognized the voice coming through the speaker was that of Major Donac, GAIA's second in command.

"Please report to the Command Center as soon as possible. We've had to scramble fighters from the Europa and Mars outposts. I've ordered the launch of GAIA's Kahn Fighters. Majors Hajeck and Kressa will also deploy with the GAIA squadron."

Jhall quickly exited the room.

"He's on his way," Marsitta notified Donac.

"Supreme Commander."

Everyone immediately became aware that the Supreme Council had not yet signed off after the meeting. The image on the screen showed Councilor Klovsew, the head of the Supreme Council. He was now standing while the rest remained seated.

Klovsew continued, "Would you please enlighten the Council as to the current threat occurring near one of the outposts?"

"Not having the benefit of hearing the ongoing communications in the Command Center, I can only give you my impression and assessment based on the information I've heard and my experience in dealing with similar events."

"That will suffice." Klovsew sat down.

"It appears that Veloptor raiders have entered this solar system near Neptune, the seventh closest planet to this system's sun." Sohan took a step closer to the screen. "For the last five Earth years, the Veloptors have been probing various solar systems scanning for a human presence. As you are aware, their aim is to find early human civilizations such as the one on Earth and exterminate the inhabitants as revenge against a perceived wrongdoing by Terlokya many millenniums ago. They have recently decoded the magnetic fields in this part of this galaxy."

"Then have they perfected their split-magnetic-field travel?" one of the other council members inquired.

"Not quite," Sohan responded. "The Veloptors call it magnetic plate splitting. That is why you will hear their high speed travel referred to as 'plating'. It is still a highly inaccurate way of high speed space travel. The final destination point can never be accurately predicted due to the varying shapes and sizes of these magnetic fields and how they constantly change. Their entry into this solar system could be attributed more to luck than anything else."

"I see," Klovsew replied creasing his brow. "How many of these sensor units or raiding parties have there been since the Savior Project began?"

"I am going to let Colonel Braaddy answer this since he has been here for the entire duration of the project."

"Thank you Supreme Commander," Braaddy began. "Councilors,

this is the second and closest Veloptor expedition into this system. The first occurrence was right after we constructed the base. Those particular Veloptorian ships from their home planet of Velox were very primitive and only appeared at the far boundaries of this system. From what I've heard, they now have new raiders of a different type."

"Do you believe they are searching for Earth and do you think they have knowledge of the Savior Project?" Klovsew asked.

"I'm sure they have no knowledge of the Savior Project. They have been hunting for Earth for some time now. It could also have been a food expedition. They are strictly carnivores and are constantly hunting for planets with new food sources."

"Is there any cause for alarm?" another council member asked.

"Absolutely not. The Velox sensors are strictly short range so I am positive they have not detected our presence. We will eliminate them before they can detect us."

"Colonel, I trust that this manner will be handled quickly and efficiently. The Council will let you attend to this matter. Please send a communiqué of the final results when completed."

"Thank you, Councilors," Colonel Braaddy answered. "You will be updated as soon as this has been taken care of."

As the communications screen went dark, Sohan and Braaddy were already heading out the door.

While others were leaving the room, Zenta went over to Marsitta's desk and asked, "Heard anything else?"

"They've launched Reep fighters from Europa and Mars." Marsitta paused, focusing on what was coming through her headset. "Now they are preparing our big Kahn fighters in the hanger. It appears there are quite a few raiders that have appeared near Neptune."

"How many?"

"Over fifty."

Zenta turned and ran out of the room without saying a word while Marsitta secured the communications workstation and also left for the Command Center.

The first sounds that greeted Zenta upon entering the center were communication bursts from launched fighters to Command.

"Base Control, this is Kahn Fighter Kappa 252 Captain Maczee, GAIA squadron. We are forming to flash to the rendezvous point near Saturn."

"Affirmative, Captain Maczee. I am now transferring communications control to the Command Center. Base Control out."

Tuu was operating the Command Center communications

workstation until Marsitta arrived.

"Have Majors Hajeck and Kressa joined up with the GAIA squadron yet?" The general asked as he walked up behind Tuu.

"Sir," Tuu quickly replied, "they are not in probe view yet. I will make sure Captain Maczee is aware of the additions."

Tuu keyed his mic. "Command Center to Captain Maczee."

"Go ahead Command."

"Major's Hajeck and Kressa in Kahn Fighters Kappa 671 and Kappa 349 will be joining up with GAIA squadron under your command."

"Affirmative, I have them in sight."

Zenta had taken a seat next to Sohan, transfixed by what was happening.

"You know the rules, Zenta," Sohan whispered while leaning over to his daughter. "Only essential personnel are allowed in the Command Center during emergencies."

"I know, Father," she whispered back. "I just had to see what was going on. I'll leave once they flash to Saturn."

"That'll be fine. Marsitta has taken over from Tuu. I'll make sure the transmission feeds from the Command Center are available to the Lab."

"Thank you."

Zenta was taking in all the action. On the raised area behind the workstations was the communications console where Marsitta was now positioned. Standing beside her was General Jhall, nervously rocking back and forth on his heels. The rows of workstations in the middle of the room were occupied by various Terlokyans monitoring different parts of the mission. Jzet, Dlocto, and Callun, all members of the Anti-Detection Unit, were sitting in the front row along with Major Donac. They were focused on the data feeds that were being transmitted by the larger X5 Probes monitoring the raiders near Neptune. Noticing that Tuu was now sitting next to Callun, she traced Xander.

"Xander," she whispered. "There are four members of the ADU in the Command Center. Who is deployed on the Intervention Mission to Earth with Bal?"

"That would be Tearcut. He was scheduled for it. Anything wrong?"

"No. I just didn't remember and saw everyone but Bal here. Thanks."

"Captain Maczee." Hajeck's voice roared over the speaker catching Zenta's attention. "Majors Hajeck and Kressa request permission to join GAIA squadron under your command."

"Permission granted, Major," Maczee answered, no obvious change in her voice due to having senior officers under her command.

"Please form on my right flank. Lieutenants Johono and Aiko are on my left."

"Affirmative, Captain."

The visual on the Command Center screen in the front of the room was from an X5 Probe. Everyone watched as the five Kahn fighters lined themselves up in a V with Captain Maczee's Kahn on point. These sleek white fighters looked so graceful as they hovered together. The Kahn was the second largest fighter in the Terlokyan arsenal. With its advanced and larger weaponry and superior maneuverability, its size also gave it the capability for being used on small military transport missions. Behind them were ten Reep fighters.

Jhall tapped Marsitta on the shoulder indicating he wanted to communicate with the pilots. She handed him the extra headset with an attached mic.

"GAIA, Mars, and Europa squadrons, listen carefully. This is an extremely important mission. We must be sure that the Veloptors do not discover our presence here or the presence of any life in this solar system. They are possibly searching for Earth and we can't let them find it. Captain Maczee will coordinate and lead the attack. Good luck and fly forcefully. Captain, it's all yours."

"Thank you, General. All right you Terks, let's cut the chatter and get straight to the plan." Maczee's voice now filled the room. "We will be using the Laser Fire Flash attack. Captain Jespa, you will take the Mars Reep Fighters and flash in just under the raiders. Captain Havok, you will take the Europa Reep Fighters and flash in on top them. Both squadrons need to come in at 45 degree angles. I'll bring the GAIA fighters in for a full frontal assault. Check your computer screens now for the attack diagrams."

"Why do they have to flash in at such a high speed," Zenta asked Sohan quietly. "Would it be just as effective to come in on Speed of Light or even conventional power where high speeds are more controllable?"

"Let us not question the mastery of our military experts," Sohan replied. "The Savior Project has the best of the best protecting it."

"Order the squadrons to deploy their X5 Probes," Jhall ordered.

"Deploy probes to the front of the squadrons now," Marsitta repeated. "Sir, probes are deployed. Split the screen now?"

"Affirmative," was Jhall's gruff reply.

With Marsitta splitting the screen, there were now four views. Three of the screens showed the Terlokyan fighter squadrons lining up in attack formations with the fourth screen showing a transmission feed near Neptune of the Veloptor raiding party. Screen two showed twenty Reep fighters from the Mars squadron commanded by Captain Jespa. The

Europa squadron, commanded by Captain Havok, was on screen three. These smaller Y shaped fighters, bristling with weaponry, were sleek and fast.

"General, sir," Jzet said as he stood up and looked to the back of the room to get Jhall's attention.

"Yes, Major."

"We are detecting a split in two magnetic fields next to the raiders. There have been two small nuclear detonations on each side of this particular field border. It appears that the raiders are about to leave."

Jhall quickly spoke into his mic.

"Squadrons, abort the attack. I repeat, abort the attack. Do not flash. All squadrons confirm this order."

The room was tensely quiet.

"GAIA squadron, order confirmed," Maczee's voice crackled over the speakers.

"Mars squadron confirmed," Captain Jespa followed.

"Europa also confirmed," Captain Havok being the final response.

"Squadrons standby," Jhall was relieved. "Major Marsitta is going to patch you into the X5 probe visual of the raiders."

"Done," Marsitta responded.

Three of the front screens showed the Terlokyan fighter squadrons holding formation. The fourth screen showed movement of the Veloptorian raiders into a formation.

"Major Jzet, do you have updated information on the Veloptorian magnetic field split?" Jhall asked.

Jzet, without getting up this time, loudly gave his response.

"Sir! I have detected that six raiders have entered the field split with more following!"

Zenta noticed that Callun had jumped when Jzet's voice blasted the room.

"Father, how many X5 Probes do we have out there?"

"There are thousands around the solar system," Sohan answered.

"I wish we could use a few of those on Earth. Think of what we could do."

"They are ten times the size of an X13. They're only used in space."

"Major Jzet," Jhall continued. "Please try and get us a better visual."

"Sir, yes sir."

As everyone watched, the angle of the X5 Probe transmitting the image began to shift so that a clearer view of the raiders, lined up in pairs and rapidly entering the split between two magnetic fields, filled the screen.

"Major Marsitta," Jhall began.

"Sir, I am already feeding the image to the squadrons."

Jhall smiled and patted the major on the shoulder.

"Always one step ahead. I see why the Supreme Commander values you so much."

As the last pair of Veloptorian raiders entered the split and disappeared, the room erupted in cheers. Zenta jumped up from her seat and slapped her father on the arm eliciting a stern look.

"Well, everybody," Jhall announced to the Command Center and into the microphone. "It appears that we have avoided a confrontation. "Squadrons," Jhall continued. "Stand down and return to your base of operations. The Veloptorian raiders have left the system." As he listened to the cheers, Jhall went over to Sohan who was discussing the incident with Zenta and Donac.

"Supreme Commander."

"Yes, General," Sohan responded with a smile and a firm handshake to Jhall's out stretched hand.

"It looks like we dodged a bullet, as the Earthlings say."

"You are correct my old friend." Sohan's tone then turned serious. "But we must always remain vigilant. Even though we've only seen two raiding parties since we started the Savior Project, we both know there will be more."

"I am going to put a robotic outpost on Saturn's moon, Titan. This way we can launch and service X5 Probes. We need to expand our coverage."

"By all means, General. You don't need my permission for this."

"I just want us to be ready, sir. Terlokyans are always ready."

08 – MAKING A SAVIOR

"Why won't I see you for a while? Where are you going?" Chris asked Zenta while sitting in the middle of the floor of his room. Little toy Matchbox cars were spread out all around him. He looked up at the sunny windowsill where the X13 Probe was perched on the ledge. His eyes were watering while his lower lip began to quiver. The sadness carried through the probe directly into Zenta's heart.

"You said you would always be with me and teach me everything." Chris turned away from the probe and stared at a toy fire truck next to him. He rubbed his bare feet back and forth in the lush fibers of the rug in the middle of the hardwood floor.

"Chris, I told you I will always be with you and I meant it. The only difference now is that you won't see me in the daytime anymore. I'm going to be with you every night while you sleep, just like we've always done." Zenta hoped this explanation would satisfy Chris.

The room was quiet, without a sound having been made. Zenta and Chris had been communicating as they normally did, via telepathy.

Chris' image filled Zenta's monitor with his sad, dour expression. She would have to hurry. Chris' mother could come in at any time.

A tap on her shoulder prompted her to turn and see Xander's hand swirling in a churning motion, indicating his desire for her to speed up the process. He was sitting at the adjoining workstation.

Careful to sound upbeat, Zenta coaxed Chris on. "I need you to do something for me, Chris. I need you to lie on the floor and close your eyes. I want you to think about the world of Terlokya and the wonderful images I've helped you see at night."

"Okay."

"Are you comfy now? Can you see Terlokya?"

"Yes." Chris was now lying on his floor, eyes shut. He wiggled his feet as images of life in the Terlokyan capital of Kukno danced in his head.

At that moment, Zenta and Xander instantly turned to the swishing sound of the lab door opening with Tish striding through the doorway.

"Hello there Zen..." Tish stopped her greeting after seeing Xander jump up from his seat while giving the 'slash across the neck' kill sign. She now noticed that Zenta had a live microphone on so she quietly slid into an adjoining workstation seat next to Zenta. She nervously pulled at her uniform collar while her eyes darted from face to face, checking to see if her actions had caused problems.

With the room settled again, Zenta continued. "Now Chris, you keep watching those images, and I will give you some new ones tonight."

"Okay."

"Glaze him now," Xander whispered as he intently watched Zenta lift the probe off of the windowsill.

Zenta growled quietly while carefully guiding the probe over Chris' face. She typed in a command and the probe released a mist. Everyone in the lab watched the mist enter Chris' nostrils as he breathed in. His eyes opened momentarily, then slowly closed. With the probe hovering above his head, Zenta checked his vital signs.

"Everything is normal." Zenta flew the probe to a vantage point on the floor just under the front overhang of the dresser. "Those memories are now erased."

From there, she still had a good view of Chris, who was now sound asleep. She sighed, turned off her microphone, and stretched her arms above her head.

"And I would appreciate it if you would refrain from even whispering orders to me." Zenta glared at Xander. "You are not my commanding officer, nor the head of this project. As a matter of fact, I am running Phase Three and don't you forget it."

Tish squirmed uncomfortably in her seat. She glanced at Zenta who returned the look with a wink.

Not seeing this exchange, Xander gathered a folder of papers from his workstation and stood up. He looked down at his monitor, then at Zenta.

"I'm sorry. I really am. After that incident in the Earthling's confinement unit ..."

"Playpen."

"What?" Xander's upper lip turned up slightly as he quizzically stared at Zenta.

Zenta stood up, took Xander's arm, and guided him around the chairs to the lab doors.

"It's a playpen. Not a confinement unit. I've told you this before. Since you are part of this project I would strongly suggest that you learn what these objects are unless you are doing this just to aggravate me."

"I ... I will make an effort."

Now standing near the exit, Zenta gently pushed Xander to the door.

"I know you will do better than just try. Now I must brief Tish on the project status since she just got here. There is a lot for her to assimilate."

With that, Xander exited.

Zenta turned in time to see Tish jump up from her seat and run to her. Zenta barely ran two steps before both of them met for a big hug.

"It's about time you got here!" Zenta exclaimed. "What's it been? It's at least three years since we've seen each other."

"More like four, I think," Tish said as they both walked back to their seats. "I thought you were going to meet me in the hanger."

"I was going to but I had a separation protocol to take care of." She slid into her seat. "Give me a few minutes to finish this and we'll catch up."

"All right."

Zenta saw on her monitor that Kelli had just come into Chris' room. She turned up the volume.

"So my little one has tuckered out," Kelli whispered as she bent down and tenderly picked up Chris.

Zenta adjusted the probe to keep Kelli in view. She and Tish watched as Kelli carried Chris to the crib and laid him down, covering him with his blanket. She then tip-toed out of the room.

"I am so glad you finally got here," Zenta said as she turned away from her monitor. "We've been down one team member for almost a year now." She finished securing her workstation and then faced Tish.

"You mean you're only glad I'm here so that I can help out on the project?" Tish pouted and lowered her head. She fiddled with a valor ribbon attached to the shoulder of her new uniform. It was adorned with a few ribbons and metals. Like Zenta, she had also two combat valor patches from the Seth colonial wars against the Hesters. They both had earned these patches together. But where Zenta wore the rank of captain with a designation patch showing she was a Project Phase Chief, Tish's rank insignia was that of a lieutenant. Even though she was assigned to the Savior Project, specifically the Savior Development Phase, her designation patch had yet to be given to her.

Zenta reached out and put her arm around her friend.

"Are you crazy?" she said cheerfully. "I'm glad to finally have my best friend here."

Tish looked relieved.

"You had me worried. I was wondering if your time on this rock had changed you into a Jzet."

"A Jzet? Is that what they are calling a 'conte' now? That is the lowest thing you can call someone." They laughed. "Look, we will have to catch up while I make a run down to the hanger." Zenta turned on the auto-monitoring system and then stood up. "I accidentally left my Pulsar in a shuttle I was copiloting last night."

"You can't leave a Pulsar lying around," Tish said as she stood up to go. "Normal punishment for that is…"

"There's no problem here," Zenta interrupted. "Hajeck was the shuttle pilot with me. I traced him right after I got on an Itran to go to my quarters. Let's go. We'll talk more on the way."

Outside the lab, Zenta pointed to the right and headed down the long wide hallway with Tish by her side. The bright white walls also served as the light source for the maze of hallways that snaked in all directions throughout the base. If Tish's hair was longer than her current shoulder length cut, it would be difficult to tell her from Zenta. They were born within months of each other and could easily be taken for sisters.

"An Itran station is just down here." Leisurely strolling along, Zenta continued their conversation.

"I'm not sure how much time you've had to look at the project data of how many briefings you've had, but I'll give you a quick, abbreviated version of some necessary information. You are part of the Savior Development Team. This is Phase 3 of the project."

Zenta and Tish stopped in front of the Itran doors. The illuminated sign above the doors read 'DECK 99 – MAIN HALL B'. Zenta pressed the call button and said, "Hanger."

"Unfortunately, I haven't been briefed yet. I didn't think I was deploying for another two weeks so things have been in a rush. Refresh my memory on Phase 2," Tish asked as she looked at the lighted display showing the time until an Itran arrived. Glancing at the small print on the deck location sign above the Itran door, Tish read the sign to herself. ANOTHER INNER TRANSPORTATION SYSTEM BY SOKO. She re-read the sign then asked, "What is SOKO?"

"I'll tell you about SOKO in a minute. Many forget that Phase 2 was the child selection phase. There were ten potentials to choose from, so it took us a while to research and analyze the data during that first month after the birth of each one. We tried to have them all born around the same time, but we could only be so involved. The lab was overflowing during that time."

The Itran doors opened and they stepped into a large empty space. The walls and ceiling were an extreme light blue with the floor being a very dark blue. The walls provided the light the same as the hallways, with light shining evenly from every square inch outward into the compartment.

"Isn't this unusual to find an empty Itran?" Tish asked.

"Sometimes, but we are on the top deck. We'll pick up riders before we get to the hanger."

The Itran started to move.

"What deck is your father's quarters on?"

"Deck sixty. Did you want to see him?"

"If that's possible. It has been a while. After all, he is like a father to me."

Zenta gave new commands to the Itran. "Re-route. Deck sixty, Main Hall C."

"Entered," the computer generated voice replied through the internal speaker.

Zenta spoke into her Trace. "Locate Sohan."

Sohan's deep voice immediately came thru her Trace filling the Itran. "Yes, Zenta?"

"I was wondering if you were in your quarters."

"Affirmative."

"May I come by? I have something to show you."

"By all means."

Zenta glanced up at Tish and smiled. "He'll be happy to see you. Have you seen your mother yet?"

Tish frowned and looked away.

"No, I haven't seen Marsitta yet," she said quietly. "I suppose I'll run into her somewhere."

"I still don't understand why you don't call her 'Mother' like you used to."

"You know the answer to that," Tish replied. "Mothers are there for you when you're growing up. I'm closer to your mother. She practically raised me."

"You can't really blame Marsitta for constantly being deployed with …"

Tish raised her hand.

"That's enough. I'm not interested in talking about her. Don't spoil a good mood. Please."

Zenta saw the hurt in Tish's eyes.

"All right then," Zenta said as she put her hand on Tish's shoulder. "Now where was I?"

Tish brushed a couple of strands of her short white hair off her forehead. "You were explaining Phase 2." She then habitually placed her hand on her Pulsar strapped to her thigh.

Zenta continued. "You will be doing night education and training. I've been handling the bulk of that so it will be nice to get some help." She glanced up at the location screen above the door which read 'DECK 78 – MAIN HALL B'.

"This is done every night?" Tish inquired.

"Yes. You will also be part of a Secondary Backup Intervention Unit. This is new for me too so we both have a lot to learn. We help backup the Intervention Units, which are the groups that intercedes to protect the Savior in times of need. It's run by Jzet and his Anti-Detection Unit although Colonel Braaddy really makes the critical decisions. The primary unit consists of Hajeck, Donac, Maczee, Johono, and Aiko. The Savior Project Development Team, you, Xander, and I are in the secondary unit."

"Isn't Hajeck Sohan's apprentice?"

"Yes. And Callun is Jzet's stooge. Be wary of him."

"Why are we just secondary?"

"Our main responsibility is to develop the Savior. The primary unit does regular rotations with the main unit. Secondary backups only go if there is a need."

"Well, I want to be able to go on one of those missions."

"So do I. Good luck with that quest."

The Itran's computer announced their arrival. "Deck 60, Main Hall C.'

"Here we are. Father's quarters are not too far from here."

They stepped out into the hallway right as a two-seater Otran passed by. Tish read the words on the side of the unit as it passed, "OUTER TRANSPORTATION POWERED BY SOKO."

"There it is again. What is SOKO?" inquired Tish.

"It's the development company founded by the boy genius, Ttocs; the one who re-engineered space travel. He designed the transportation systems and the Troid computer system for the GAIA Moon Base. You will get to know Troid quite well." Zenta picked up the pace. She really wanted to get to the hanger to retrieve her Pulsar. But she knew Sohan would be glad to see Tish so she must be patient.

"Keep in mind that on this rock, you can be pulled from any duty at any time and be assigned temporarily elsewhere. Your main assignment is to the Savior Development Team, but there are a lot of base operational efforts going on here too. The most important thing to remember is that the Savior comes first." Zenta glanced at Tish to see if she understood the severity of the statement. "We drop anything around here, short of discovery by others, to protect and develop the Savior. He is of the highest intelligence imaginable. He would top the charts if he were Terlokyan. His development must go according to plan. Clear?"

"Got it. What are the other phases?"

"Well, Phase 1 was the task of selecting suitable parental units according to the Mate Guidance Plan that was put together. Jzet referred to it as the breeding stage. Thirty individuals were selected, fifteen male and fifteen female, which we hoped to get ten couples with the desired goal of producing children. It worked. Phase 2 involved the evaluation and selection of the best child to be the Chosen One. I already told you about that phase right after we left the lab."

"The Savior Project lab?"

"I'm sorry. Yes, when anyone refers to the lab, they mean the Savior Project lab. Phase 3 is the development and training of the child. That is what we are currently working on and what your training and briefings will be about for the next few days."

Zenta noticed that Sohan's quarters were right around the next corner. She reached out and touched Tish's arm to stop her.

"Real quick before we get there; Phase 4 is the extraction of the Savior, Phase 5 is the training and Phase 6 is his return to Earth. There is a lot more to those phases than what I've told you. Phases 3 and 5 seem to be the most controversial ones since a definite time frame cannot be established."

"Why not?"

"It is hard to define how long it will take to establish Chris Gates as a well-known and well thought of citizen of Earth. So much of that will be decided based upon circumstances beyond our control."

"So you mean that much of his life will be influenced by Earthly factors."

"Yes. Just the fact that he has to live on Earth and grow up in that setting will partially determine what kind of person he will become and how well known. We can only do so much." Zenta started walking again.

"I'll bet that this is the reason Jzet is against having an Earthling in this role," Tish said quickly recognizing a major problem.

"You are a quick-study. Here we are." They stood in front of a door with a sign above that read '60-C-147'. Before Zenta could raise her Trace up to announce their arrival, the door opened and Sohan's beaming smile greeted them.

"Greetings and salutations. Come in my children." Sohan appeared to float as he ushered them into his quarters. He had known Tish would be with Zenta. The Supreme Commander had a way of sensing things.

They sat in his outer living area and chatted about the current project. Tish caught them up on some family news and other minor events on Terlokya. Zenta finally reminded Tish that they had an appointment to keep down in the hanger. Sohan didn't inquire as to the nature of the appointment and bid them farewell.

Back in the hallway and heading for an Itran, Tish said, "That was great to see him again. I really wish I could work with him on what he is researching."

"Here's an Itran station," Zenta said as she pushed the call button. "Hanger." She turned to face Tish. "What research? What do you mean?"

"Didn't you see the reports on his desk and the images on his screen?"

"I guess I missed that. I'm really focused on getting to the hanger and getting my Pulsar. Does it have to do with the Savior?"

The Itran arrived and they got in.

Tish looked at Zenta and said, "There was a lot of information on past Earth space satellite missions to the moon. He also had a lot of printed images of Earth spacecraft on his desk with a number of Apollo craft pictures. From the bold print I could read, there was a lot of information on the upcoming Apollo 8 spacecraft which is scheduled to orbit the moon very soon."

Zenta gathered her thoughts as the Itran hummed along.

"That Apollo mission has a lot of us worried. One of its planned trajectories is directly over Base GAIA."

Suddenly, Zenta's Trace went off.

"Zenta." She recognized her father's voice.

"Yes?"

"Sorry to trouble you, but I need you to return to my quarters as soon as possible."

"On my way," Zenta answered. "It appears that my Pulsar will have to wait." Zenta faced the Itran communications speaker. "Re-route. Deck sixty, Main Hall C."

Tish smiled. "It appears so. I'll bet it's about the Apollo mission."

"You're probably right. Either way, I have to go back. I'll trace you when I leave." The Itran had arrived and the doors opened. "If it's not too late," Zenta said upon exiting the Itran heading to her father's quarters.

09 – THE SEARCH FOR TRUTH

While waiting for Zenta to return, Sohan sat at his desk and reread the document that he had discovered folded and taped to the door of his quarters earlier in the day.

> *The space race between the United States and the Soviet Union started on October 4, 1957 with the launching of the first artificial satellite from Earth: Sputnik I. Sputnik was small and weighed just over 180 pounds. Both programs wanted to be the first to put a man on the moon.*
>
> *In early 1967, the National Aeronautical Space Administration of the United States was finalizing a new type of space vehicle, Apollo that would replace the Gemini program. Apollo was aimed at longer space travel, specifically, the Moon. The first in a series of missions was Apollo 1 and was to test the spacecraft in Earth's orbit.*
>
> *On January 27, 1967, a launch 'test run' was in progress with Astronauts Gus Grissom, Edward White and Roger Chaffee in the command module strapped in to their seats. At 6:30 P.M. a flash fire caused the Apollo Command Module to burn up killing the three astronauts by smoke and fume inhalation during this preflight test. An electrical arc in an equipment area caused the fire.*

Sohan stopped reading and laid the paper down. He stared at the scribbled handwritten note at the bottom of the page, 'check satellite interventions' in a handwriting he didn't recognize.

"Father, I'm outside your quarters." Zenta's voice came through his Trace.

"Enter."

The door to his quarters opened and Zenta came in. She quickly took a seat on one of the long, elegant red couches that were against the walls of Sohan's outer living area. She glanced over at the food preparation counter.

Sohan noticed his daughter's look toward the kitchen and said, "Thank you for coming. Do you want something to drink?"

"Yes, I think that would be nice."

Sohan started to get up from his chair, but Zenta popped up from the couch first. She smiled at her father. "Please, don't trouble yourself. I know my way around here."

"Of course you do." Sohan relaxed into his high-back chair and put his feet up on his desk. The Earth Space Program summary lay in his lap.

"So, what did you need me for?" Zenta called out while fixing herself a glass of water. "Can I get you anything while I'm here?"

"No thank you, my child. I'm in a bit of a quandary right now. I need a set of trusted eyes to go over something with me."

Zenta's interest was heightened now.

"This must really be something out-of-the-ordinary for you to not invite Tish. After all, she is like a daughter to you and a sister to me." She sat down on the couch, putting her drink on the stone table in front of the couch waiting for her father to begin. He was flipping through some of the documents on his desk. After a couple of minutes, Zenta said, "I would like to have seen the Moon rock your table was cut from. This top has the most beautiful swirling colors in it." When Sohan didn't respond and continued staring at a document in his hand, Zenta tried a different approach. "I think I'll pick this table up and put it on your desk."

"That's fine," Sohan responded without taking his eyes off the paper.

"You haven't heard anything I've said, have you?"

"What was that? I'm sorry." Sohan looked up. "You said something about Tish?"

"That was a while ago. Tell me why you need my trusting eyes?"

"Pull up that chair that's next to the bookcase and sit with me. I've got some documents to show you and we've got a bit of research for Troid to do."

Zenta picked up the gray molded plastic chair. It weighed very little with arms that swept up to a tall back, its cushions were attached to the seat and back and had a soft and fluffy feel to them. She carried it easily with one hand and moved it next to the desk. After settling into its confines, she asked, "Does the piece of paper you are holding have anything to do with what we are going to discuss?"

"Why yes it does. Here," he said while handing her the paper. "You read this while I pull up some data on the computer."

"On." Sohan gave a voice command to turn on his computer which connected him to Troid, the GAIA moon base computer. "Deliver all Anti-Detection Unit satellite intervention report summaries since the beginning of Earth's space programs."

"Voice recognition confirmed," Troid replied. "Reports delivered."

On his monitor was a list of the various reports generated by Jzet's Anti Detection Unit. Opening the report summaries, Sohan began to review the information.

"So who wrote this note at the bottom of the page?" Zenta asked while holding up the paper and pointing to the scribbled message.

"I don't know. It is not a handwriting that I immediately recognize. Have you seen it before?"

"No, I have not," she replied while studying the handwriting.

Sohan turned away from the monitor to look at Zenta. "Tell me what you know about Earth's satellite programs."

Zenta put the paper on Sohan's desk. "Well, the Soviet Union started space exploration when they launched Sputnik 1 in 1957. Then there were a succession of missions by both the Soviet Luna series and the American Surveyor series. Their orbital prep missions led to moon missions that we had to monitor closely." She paused to gather her thoughts further. "I remember that the Anti-Detection Unit was very busy during that time with all of those satellites coming to the moon."

Sohan raised both hands and with a smile said, "I should have known better than to ask someone with such a precise memory. Let me get straight to the point."

"Please do because I'm not sure where you are going with this." Zenta took a drink from her glass.

Sohan sighed, and then said, "It is no big secret that Jzet always feels that his decision making skills are unparalleled."

"That is an understatement."

Zenta's quick response brought a chuckle.

"I have suspected that he may have gone too far in his zest to keep this base from being photographed by the Earth's satellites." Sohan paused. "Everyone was on alert during satellite missions that were deemed critical by detection standards. Do any of the Anti-Detection Unit interventions stand out in your mind?"

"I remember the intervention by Jzet's group on the Luna 3 mission. X-5 Probes were sent to guide the satellite in a loose equatorial orbit so that no photographic images of the Polar Regions were possible. Since the satellite lacked a propulsion system, the probes were successful in altering its course." Zenta stretched her legs out then yawned.

"Are you getting tired my dear? We shouldn't be that much longer."

"No, I'm fine. I'm actually interested in where this is leading."

"Please understand that I already have an idea of what has transpired here with these events. But I need to run all of this by someone before I take action. And as I stated before, it has to be someone I completely trust."

"I understand. So which intervention by the Anti-Detection Unit has led you to your conclusion?" Zenta's fatigue evaporated now that she could put the pieces together.

"Have you ever read the complete Counter Technology Options Plan?"

"Not in detail."

"Well, the Counter Technology Options Plan, or CTOP as it is commonly known, outlined various options to thwart discovery of Base GAIA by Earth's space programs. The developers of the CTOP plans were Jhall, Marsitta, Dlocto, second in command of the Anti-Detection Unit, and Hajeck, my Chief of Staff. Jzet's Anti Detection Unit is charged with carrying out CTOP recommendations for different scenarios. Besides developing anti-detection plans, the CTOP outlined various options to slow down both of the Earth's space programs. When an option is chosen, it is Jzet's unit that carries out the mission, either using X5 Probes, or in dire cases, use of direct Terlokyan intervention." Sohan waited for a response.

"I understand. This is for our security and protection of the entire project."

"Correct. You also have to keep in mind that the Anti-Detection Unit has strict guidelines that it has to abide by. Lean over here and read this Satellite intervention report on my monitor."

Zenta scooted her chair closer to the desk and leaned forward to get a good view of the report.

USA Surveyor 2 - Sep 20, 1966 - Attempted Lander

The Surveyor 2 spacecraft mission was to achieve a lunar soft landing and to transmit photographic data to Earth. The target area proposed was within Sinus Medii.

POSSIBLE THREAT - Detection Concern and Observation Concern (OC)

ANTI DETECTION UNIT INTERVENTION – Yes

REASON - Satellite mission was to photograph the surface, achieve landing on the moon, and commence with further photographic efforts. Projected early satellite trajectory was over the Terlokyan Moon Base: GAIA.

OC Mission summary: The Unit sent a rogue computer command to the satellite's onboard computers causing one Vernier engine to fail ignition, resulting in an unbalanced thrust that caused the spacecraft to tumble. This caused the satellite to crash on the Moon's far side resulting in satellite mission failure. The Unit investigated the landing site.

Zenta finished reading and leaned forward in her chair.

"Nothing seems out of the ordinary here except for the site visit."

"Correct. Now let's review the facts. The Surveyor satellite program had a primary objective of photographing areas to support eventual crewed Apollo landings. The Surveyor 1 craft was successful in its mission but landed far away from Base GAIA so it was no threat. It never flew across the South Pole. The Surveyor 2 craft had a planned satellite trajectory over the Moon's South Pole where the Aitken crater is located. This, of course, is our location."

"That seems to justify the heightened threat that this satellite posed. Right?"

"Yes, one would assume that. But why the site visit? If the CTOP recommendations were followed, and a computer command forced the satellite to crash, then why was the visit necessary?"

Zenta sat up straight. "There must have been something that Jzet needed to get from the site."

"That's what I think. Since he did visit the site, he has already retrieved whatever it is. So we must determine what he needed to get."

"We need to go to the site." Zenta made the statement so matter-of-factly.

"That would certainly raise suspicions." Sohan stood up and walked over to the couch, robes billowing as he walked, and sat down.

"It absolutely would raise suspicions. But only with Jzet." Zenta had moved her chair to face her father and was leaning forward, elbows on her knees, her face tight with intensity. "Maybe it would shake him up enough to give up the information."

"Well, talking with you has now raised another issue. I was also going to discuss with you my suspicions about the Apollo 1 disaster. That craft was destroyed on the launch pad by an electrical arc, of all things. He could have easily set that up to happen."

"I see what you mean. Do you really think Jzet would go that far?"

"I have my doubts as to how closely he obeys orders when he feels his situational evaluation is far superior to that of his commanding officers. Don't get me wrong about one thing. I would never doubt Jzet's loyalty to this project and to Terlokya. But I do think that he believes that his way is the best course of action to take regardless of orders."

Zenta glanced down and asked, "What are you going to do?"

"I'm going to take your advice and make a site visit tomorrow. And I'm going to take Callun along. That should get Jzet worried."

Zenta smiled at this. "You know he's going to demand to come."

"I'm sure he will. But he has to report to the CTOP developers tomorrow with a contingency plan for the upcoming Apollo 8 mission. He wouldn't be able to go because of that." Sohan stood up looking determined. "I knew you were the best choice to analyze this with me."

"What other choice did you have?" she said as she got up. "I think my work is done since you now have a plan. I have a feeling tomorrow is going to be a big day."

"It appears that way. It will be very reveling, so to speak. Thank you for returning. Please give my apologies to Tish, and I will keep you updated."

"Please do." Zenta walked to the door. "Thank you."

"For what, dear? I should be thanking you."

"For always trusting me. It means a lot."

"One last thing." Sohan looked into his daughter's eyes. "I will be returning to Terlokya after the Apollo 8 mission."

Zenta sighed. "I knew this was coming. You have been here since we chose the Savior. So it really is time for you to go home. Terlokya needs you more than we do."

"You never cease to amaze me. You are, by far, much more mature than your age would tell." Sohan placed his hands on Zenta's shoulders and was smiling now.

"I am pretty lucky. I have the best teacher." Zenta kissed him on the cheek. "Good night, Father."

"Good night, Zenta."

After she had left, Sohan sat at his desk.

"Troid. Take down this information and send it to the following personnel via Trace."

10 – CORNERED

It was getting hot in Jzet's quarters. The pronounced scuff marks on the carpet were due to his constant pacing. Ever since Callun had traced him about the time change for the Surveyor 2 crash site inspection, Jzet couldn't sit still. The departure time had been moved up. Jzet had been trying to contact Callun, but couldn't raise him. He finally sat down at his desk.

He had been poring over various reports laid out across his desk. His presentation to the CTOP developers on the Apollo 8 contingency plan was due later in the morning and he had been working on it since last night. Suddenly his Trace went off.

"Jzet, Callun here. Sorry I couldn't answer you before, but I'm with Hajeck and we are readying the Dagar for a site inspection. How's the report coming?"

"It's driving me crazy. They want an entire Apollo program analysis and it is such dry information. The Apollo 1 mission failed. Apollo 4, 5, 6, and 7 were all test missions to ready this new type of spacecraft for a trip to the Moon. Everyone has this information already but they want more details. The most important issue right now is that Apollo 8's projected orbital paths will take the spacecraft directly over the Moon's South Pole and that means it will fly over Base GAIA." Jzet stood up and started pacing again. "Everyone knows this, so why do I have to compile a report about past missions?

"The CTOP developers are requesting it. We have a good plan to avoid detection from Earth satellites. What have you come up with so far to avoid detection from a manned mission?"

"I've got it partially completed. Whatever contingency I develop, it will be the Anti-Detection Unit's responsibility to ensure that the Apollo 8 mission will not have any impact on the Savior Project. I feel we should use one of the satellite plans."

"I don't think you should do that. This is a manned mission so developing a similar plan doesn't appear to be complicated. We turn off the lights, remain quiet, and let them fly over."

"I wish it were that simple." Jzet's pacing was beginning to make him sound breathless. "The Apollo 8 crew is also tasked with photographing potential landing sites for upcoming missions. They are going to be taking pictures of everything and if they get these back to Earth for analysis, someone may detect our presence."

"Are you all right?" Callun was concerned.

"I've got to finish this report, but I need to go on this Surveyor 2 site inspection." Jzet stopped dead in his tracks. "I've got it. You need to delay the mission."

"I can't do that. Sohan is in charge of this and I'm not going to be responsible for any delays," Callun responded curtly.

"You've got to do something. You know what they'll find out there." Jzet wiped the perspiration from his forehead with his sleeve.

"I'm not about to make matters worse."

"You must do this," Jzet barked into his Trace. "Your loyalty is to me. I am the one who advanced your career. You owe me."

"I...," Callun paused. "Hajeck is tracing me. I've got to go. He is waiting on these air tanks. Callun out."

"Wait, Callun." Jzet saw on his Trace that Callun had terminated the communication.

"I need to be on that Surveyor 2 inspection trip," Jzet said out loud. He pushed the reports on his desk in a pile and strapped on his Pulsar, his hands shaking.

I am going to be the one to save Earth and there is nothing that will get in the way of my plans. This report can wait.

With his mind made up, he quickly exited his quarters and headed for the nearest Itran.

The vast hanger of Base GAIA was a hub of activity. Crews were working in the Ground Transportation Wing and the Dagar Shuttle Wing, located on opposite sides of the large bay doors that led to the floor level decompression chamber. Ground Rovers, wedge shaped vehicles used outside of the base, were the same shape and size as the Dagars. The obvious differences were the gull type wings and sled rails on the Dagars with Rovers having tank treads. The Dagars were the workhorses of the base fleet, carrying supplies, personnel transportation, loading and unloading transports, special missions, and inspections.

Hajeck and Callun were loading one of the Dagars for the Surveyor 2 site inspection. Orders had been traced to both of them to ready a shuttle as soon as possible.

"This mission came up fast," Hajeck said as he loaded a rack of five moon suits. "Who else is coming?"

Callun stopped at the ship's ramp and set down a crate of portable air tanks. He faced Hajeck, his shoulders drooped as he breathed heavily, sweat was dripping from his chin.

"As long as we've been on this moon working together, you should know by now that our superiors only tell us what they think we need to know. That way there is always a surprise for us. But judging from the fact that the orders were to load five moon suits and support equipment for five Terlokyans, my guess is that there will be five of us making the trip. As for whom they are, I only know of Sohan, you, and me." Callun grunted as he picked up the crate and carried it up the ramp.

"That wasn't much help." Hajeck rolled the suit rack up the ramp and into the Dagar.

"Hajeck!"

At the sound of his name, Hajeck spun around to see Tish walking toward him. He secured the rack in the ship and came down the ramp followed by Callun.

Hajeck was at a loss for words. "I know her, but I can't remember her name," he whispered to Callun. "She is beautiful."

Callun also stared. "She makes that green and black uniform look good. She and Zenta are hard to tell apart except for the short hair. Don't you think so?"

"They do have similar features," Hajeck replied as he picked up his clipboard.

"They sure do. You've heard the rumors, haven't you?"

"Shut up, Callun. How dare you speak of the Supreme Commander in that manner?"

"So you have heard them?"

"I said shut up, or I'll have to speak to the Supreme Commander about your loose tongue. Now try and look sharp. She's almost here."

Tish walked right up to Hajeck and saluted.

"Lieutenant Tish reporting for duty, sir."

Returning the salute, Hajeck stammered, "Uh... fine, uh ... how are... I mean ... at ease."

"What?" Tish smiled at his confused expression and dropped her bag. "You don't remember me, do you?"

"Of course I do. You're Tish."

"Yeah. I just said that. You look taller than the last time I saw you. Your uniform is as impeccable as ever with more insignia on it than I have seen on anyone else since I've arrived." Tish crossed her arms and cocked her head to the side. "I was there on Donar when Sohan made you his Chief of Staff. You probably don't remember. It was a few years ago."

"Hi, Tish."

Her train of thought was interrupted as Callun finally spoke.

Callun stepped forward and gave her a hug. Hajeck stood there dumbfounded, looking a bit surprised as was Tish. She and Callun barely knew each other.

"Well, hello Callun," she said as she carefully broke out of the hug but not so quick as to make the moment seem awkward. "How have you been? You haven't changed a bit."

Callun did not wear the uniform well. He was short, slightly overweight, and quite pale for a Terlokyan; but he had a pleasant disposition and was known for his intelligence and allegiance to Jzet.

"I am doing fine, thank you. I hear you recently arrived at GAIA. Has anyone shown you around?"

Tish quickly seized the initiative, "Actually, no. Hajeck was just about to show me the hanger area and brief me on the mission."

Before either could utter a word, Tish put her arm under Hajeck's arm and led him off toward the Fighter Wing. Tish then glanced back at Callun and shouted over her shoulder, "And I was told to tell you to put two Riser Packs on the Dagar."

"Who told you that?" Callun tried to get an answer, but they were moving further away and the noise of the hanger drowned his voice out. He tried one more time, "Are you coming on this mission?"

Tish and Hajeck moved quickly into the Fighter Wing area so as to avoid having to respond to Callun's inquiry. She let go of Hajeck's arm, walked straight up to a Gust Fighter and turned to face Hajeck.

"So why do we need Gust Fighters on the Moon if we are not going to engage any enemies here?" She put her hand on the ship while awaiting Hajeck's answer.

Hajeck stood next to the fighter, crossed his arms, and stared at Tish. She smiled then looked up at the Gust. "Well, are you going to answer me?"

"I have my own questions. First of all, are you going on the mission? Second, who told you to load Riser Packs? Third, why did you lead me away from the Dagar?"

Tish frowned. "Why won't you answer me? It was a sincere question, and I asked mine first."

Hajeck looked down for a moment, then into Tish's questioning green eyes.

"I'm sorry," he said. "You're correct. I should have been more polite. It is standard operating procedure to carry all types of fighters on missions that will either last more than a year or are over three flashes in distance from home. The Gust is used mainly for ground base defenses. Its star shaped design makes it extremely maneuverable for combating ground threats." Appearing pleased with his answer, he said, "Your turn."

"Thank you. That was a great tour guide description." She crossed her arms and took two steps toward him. "First, I was ordered on this mission as the Dagar pilot. Second, the Supreme Commander traced me about the Riser Packs. And third, I wanted to talk to you away from Callun, but I am equally interested to know about the fighter deployment."

"You fly Dagars?"

"Don't look so surprised. Females can fly too you know." Tish moved away from Hajeck and slowly strolled to another section of the fighter wing.

As Hajeck followed her, he continued, "I knew that. I just didn't think ..."

"You didn't think that I could be a pilot. I know that you fly. My main assignment is to the Savior Development Team with Zenta, but flying has always been my first love. You're a Gust pilot, right?"

"Wrong."

Now in the Reep Fighter Section, Hajeck had taken the lead in their walking tour and headed straight for the fighter with RF-R155 on its tail fins. It was the first one of the arranged rows of fighters.

"Reeps are my style," Hajeck said with a gleam in his eye.

Tish stood behind Hajeck as he walked along side of the Reep. He had both hands touching the fuselage, maintaining contact, rubbing his hands on the ship as he slowly walked along its length. It was a graceful ship but also fierce in its size and shape. Slightly bigger than the Gust and shaped like a Y, the Reep was primarily used for space combat. She could tell he was one of those pilots that became one with his ship when he flew. He never took his eyes off of it as he walked the full length.

"From the way you are touching that Reep, I'd guess it's yours," Tish said to Hajeck as he turned to face her.

"You guessed correctly," he dropped his hands to his side. "I also fly the Kahn, but primarily the Reep. This bird and I have seen some combat together. But before we continue the tour, tell me why you wanted to talk to me away from Callun."

Tish started fiddling with her Pulsar, obviously displaying uneasiness to the question.

"I can only tolerate Callun in small doses. But I also wanted to know if you had any idea why we are going to the Surveyor 2 crash site."

Hajeck motioned toward the Kahn Fighter section and headed that way with Tish beside him.

"You might not have heard yet since you've just arrived, but Jzet has been giving Sohan trouble with the Savior Project."

"I've heard some things."

Hajeck stopped walking.

"He is trying to undermine the project so that he can be the one who unites Earth to prepare for the coming of the Veloptors. He has gone so far as to voice his opposition to the plan during a project briefing to the Supreme Council."

Tish's jaw dropped. "How can Jzet get away with opposing the Supreme Commander? And in front of the council?"

Hajeck started walking again. “Well, let’s just say that Sohan never allows anyone to gain the upper hand on him. I figure that Sohan discovered something unusual about the Surveyor 2 site and is going to confirm it.”

Tish looked puzzled.

Standing in front of a huge Kahn Fighter, Hajeck added, “Jzet personally handled the Anti-Detection Unit’s response to the Surveyor 2 threat. He must have slipped up somehow and that’s why Sohan wants to investigate. We’ll have to see how this plays out. One thing’s for sure, anyone on that Dagar will be the first to know.”

“When I was in his quarters yesterday, I noticed some satellite reports on his desk so he has definitely been researching this.” Tish saw that Hajeck was lost in thought, so she changed the subject.

“Have you ever flown one of these birds?”

Looking up at the huge spacecraft, Hajeck told Tish about the Kahn Fighter and his experiences with it.

“It is designed to handle ship to ship along with ship to ground combat. Its size reduces its maneuverability, but it can still pull a tight 11G turn. Plus it can carry a heavy payload of weapons and personnel.” Hajeck looked at his Trace.

Tish’s Trace was also receiving a message.

“Did you just get a message from Sohan?”

“Yes. He’s on his way down. We’d better get back.”

“One more thing,” Tish asked as they were walking. “How come we only have eight Kahns here? There’s enough space in their section of the hanger for at least ten more.”

“That section will fill up with more when the Savior returns to Earth. But that will be some time from now. And it will also depend on any increase in Veloptorian probing missions.”

Within sight of the Dagar, Tish saw Major Donac, second in command of Base GAIA, going up the ramp. She reached out and grabbed Hajeck’s arm and stopped him.

“Did you know Donac was going on this mission?” Tish sounded irate.

“Yes. I’m sure he’s here on General Jhall’s request. Why? Is there something wrong with that?”

“He and I have had some problems. I hope that he can …”

“Hajeck! Tish! Wait.”

They spun around at the sound of their names being called out.

Sohan hurriedly walked up to them, “Glad I caught up. You were covering ground fast. I was hoping to have a word with both of you out of earshot of the rest of the mission crew.”

Tish noticed that Sohan was wearing his military battle gear meaning he wore his Life Suit under it. She quickly glanced at Hajeck to see if he noticed.

"Sir, why are you wearing battle gear?" Tish asked.

Sohan instinctively glanced down at his attire. "I will be donning a Riser Pack and since I have not been issued the new style flight suit, this is the only allowable alternative."

"Sir, would you please let me get a flight suit for you?" Hajeck inquired. "I can have one delivered to the Dagar in a matter of minutes."

"That won't be necessary. But I would like to take a brief moment to update you on this mission. It is being conducted to verify that procedures were followed by the Anti-Detection Unit on their mission to the Surveyor 2 crash site. It has come to my attention …"

Sohan was cut off in mid-sentence as two Rovers rumbled by on their way to the decompression chamber, their tank treads clanking against the solid rock floor. Sohan and Hajeck watched the vehicles pass. An officer atop one of the Rovers saluted smartly to Sohan who returned the salute.

Tish, uninterested in the Rovers, looked up at the massive clear inner roof with the huge sliding doors that led to the upper decompression chamber. Ships passed through these clear doors to the upper chamber then through another set of doors out into space. She would soon be taking the Dagar out that way.

Sohan continued after the noise faded, "I'll make this short. I believe there were unauthorized actions taken by Jzet's group in dealing with Surveyor 2. I want you to search for anything that might be out of line with our standard protocol for site visits. Do not say anything during the mission but report to my quarters after we return. Are we clear?"

Both Hajeck and Tish responded, "Clear, sir."

"I might add that I did not find approval for the Anti-Detection Unit's visit to the Surveyor 2 crash site." Sohan expected more of a reaction but only got raised eyebrows. "I have a feeling that Surveyor 2 has one more piece of data to share."

"I would like to see that data, sir," responded Tish.

"Then let's get on with it." Sohan gestured toward the Dagar and they headed that way.

"Supreme Commander present!" Upon seeing the approach of Sohan, Donac had given the order for attention from the top of the ramp. Callun, who was at the bottom of the ramp also snapped to attention.

"As you were. Are we ready to go, Major Donac?" Sohan asked.

"Sir, the ship is loaded and ready. Who will be flying us out, sir?"

"Lieutenant Tish will be at the controls."

Donac and Callun exchanged looks. Tish caught Donac's expression and allowed a slight smile to show.

"Sir, I would like to point out that the Lieutenant," Donac nodded in Tish's direction, "has not yet traversed the moonscape and it would be …"

"And Hajeck will be her co-pilot," Sohan had cut him off. Facing Donac, he continued, "Let's get moving, Major. You stated we were ready so let's not waste time." Sohan stretched out both arms as if to herd everyone aboard the Dagar.

"Supreme Commander, wait!" Jzet yelled as he hurried across the tarmac.

Sohan's head snapped around at the sound of Jzet's voice. He squinted as the corners of his mouth slowly turned up. The rest of the mission crew watched Jzet who was wearing his fight suit and carrying a Riser Pack, run toward the Dagar's ramp.

Sohan, looking very imposing in his military battle gear, met Jzet at the bottom of the ramp.

"Sir, I respectfully request permission to accompany you on this mission." Jzet stood ramrod straight in front of Sohan. "I believe I can be of great assistance since I was on the original site inspection." An air of desperation surrounded him.

"By all means Major, please join us. By your being here, I would assume that you have completed your task for the CTOP developers and delivered your report to them. They are very interested in analyzing the data that you have compiled. I was just with them in the Command Center before coming down here. General Jhall mentioned before I left that you had not yet delivered your report. I assume he has it now."

With all eyes focused on him, Jzet stumbled for words, "It is not quite complete. I just wanted to be of assistance to you on this mission and upon my return, I could complete…"

Sohan raised his hand to silence Jzet.

"While I appreciate you wanting to help with this task," Sohan paused and took the tone of teacher and lecturer, "your report to the CTOP developers takes priority. Rest assured that we will do our best to succeed in this endeavor, although we realize your knowledge would have made things much easier. I will brief you when we return. I am also looking forward to reviewing your report."

With a satisfied expression, Sohan headed up the ramp. The sound of his boots hitting the ramp on his way up gave a feeling of finality as if a Pulsar's energy blasts were knocking a hole through a steel wall.

"But …" Jzet was losing his composure.

"We can handle this, Major. If I were you, I would hurry and complete that report. General Jhall appeared impatient when I last saw him." Sohan stepped inside the Dagar. "Lieutenant Callun, raise the ramp so we can get underway."

"Yes, sir," Callun looked down the ramp at his immediate superior who looked defeated. The door slammed shut in Jzet's face.

Jzet stood motionless for a minute as he heard the Dagar's Magnetic Field Realignment unit start up. With his head hung low, he shuffled his boots along the tarmac away from the Dagar and seemingly dragged himself over to one of the hanger's side viewports. He looked up through the window and was struck with a beautiful view of space.

Earth is supposed to be my planet. That Savior child better not screw this up.

11 – HILTON MILLS

Chris' little hands gripped the windowsill as he quietly stared at the bright, full Moon through the dining room window. Eerie shadows appeared to dance across the yard on this cloudless, breezy night.

"Come back over here and play tanks with me," Cory said while watching his little brother.

"Not yet."

"Why?

"I feel someone looking at me."

"Who? Where are they?"

"The Moon."

"Why would someone want to watch you? You're a little kid. No one's on the Moon anyway. Come play."

"Okay." Chris went and sat next to his brother. He pushed a toy tank around, then suddenly stopped.

"Someone's on the Moon. But don't tell anyone. You'll see."

Cory glanced at Chris and then continued playing.

Pete sat at the kitchen table while Kelli stared at the realtor's brochure lying on the counter like it was a death warrant. She dried her hands with a towel and picked up the paper but handled it as if it had a disease.

"I can't grasp the concept of us ever moving out of this house." The brochure fell from her hand as she leaned against the counter, arms crossed. "I mean, look in the dining room."

Pete got up and peered through the doorway.

"Vrooommmmm!" Cory was lying on his stomach next to the dining room table pushing a little toy tank along the floor. "Boom! Boom! It shot that other tank."

"Bam! Got 'em." Sitting across from Cory, Chris leaned over and flipped the tank onto its side. Both pant legs on his little blue jean coveralls were pushed up just below his knees. He had at least two little army men in each hand. The white socks on both boys showed signs of having been worn outside without the benefit of shoes.

Kelli was next to Pete, watching their sons, her head resting against his shoulder. The boys acted unaware that they were being observed. Just as they turned away, Chris looked up.

"And you want to leave this?" Kelli asked with her hands out, pleading.

"Sweetheart." Pete led her to a seat at the kitchen table. "This is our first house and that makes it special." He gazed tenderly at his wife and continued. "But what the boys are doing in there is creating memories and those are what make up a home. We can do that wherever we live."

Kelli stared at the brochure's picture of the two story brick contemporary house. A tree lined, meandering, paved driveway led up to a two car garage.

"This is a neighborhood and we're used to being in the country."

"Honey, this house is surrounded by plenty of trees, sits on five acres, and is set back from the road. All the houses have four acres or better. See how the driveway kind of bends around to the house?" he asked, pointing at one of the brochure pictures. "The house is even at an angle so it doesn't directly face the road."

Kelli put the brochure down, leaned on the counter, and massaged her temples.

"Pete, you know I was born and raised in the country. Down near Spartanburg, if we could see a neighbor's house, we were too close. Besides, we don't know anybody in Hilton Mills and I hate being a newcomer."

"That's not entirely true. The Savvas' live there."

Kelli cocked her head and raised an eyebrow.

"You know who I'm talking about. George owns the steak house on the other side of town. They've got two kids about the same age as Cory and Chris. And the Hudsons live there too. They go to our church. The boys always play with their youngest son, uh, what's his name?"

"Gene."

"Yeah that's it. They play together after Sunday School."

All was quiet except for the boys. Pete watched as Kelli came over and sat at the table. She straightened the napkins on the Lazy Susan then lined up the salt and pepper shaker in front of the napkin holder.

"Kelli," Pete said as he gently put his hands on hers, stopping her tidying. "If you don't want to move, then we won't. You know I'd never make you do something that you didn't want to do. Let's just take a look at the house and see if you like it. If you don't, then you won't hear another word from me. Deal?"

"Okay. I guess it wouldn't hurt to go see it. I always wondered what it would be like to have kids running around in a neighborhood." Kelli turned her hands up under Pete's and gave them a squeeze. "You call the real estate agent and set something up for Saturday." Her eyes widened. "Wow. That's tomorrow. Do we take the boys?"

"I think we should. This might be a good way to break them into the idea of moving. That is if you like the house," Pete said, smiling.

A few minutes past eleven on Saturday morning, the Gates were at 1706 Hilton Circle in Hilton Mills.

As Pete parked their 1968 Chevy Impala station wagon next to a white Mercedes, a tall man in a dark grey suit got out of the car. He was wearing an expensive London Fog overcoat and gestured with open hands as he said, "Welcome to the finest house you will see today." Steve had a broad, good looking face, which had so many freckles that he looked tanned.

"That's Steve White, the real estate agent," Pete said to Kelli as he unbuckled his seatbelt.

Chris had his seatbelt off, his door open, and was out of the car before anyone could say a word. He blew past Steve like a blur with Cory right behind him.

Kelli jumped out of the car.

"Chris, where do you think you are going?" She stood in the driveway looking at her boys bound up the front steps.

"I wanna see my new room," Chris quickly replied as he and Cory pushed the door open and disappeared into the house.

Steve walked up to Pete with his hand extended. "Those are fast boys you've got there. Good to see you, Mr. Gates."

"Howdy, Steve. Yeah, they're speedsters for sure." Pete gestured toward Kelli. "Steve, this is my wife Kel ..."

"Pete!" Kelli cut him off in mid-sentence. "What do we do about the boys?" Kelli was still standing next to the car, hands on hips. "Shouldn't you be going after them?" She then eyed Steve. "Sorry. Hi. I'm Kelli, pleased to meet you." After a quick handshake, her hands went back to the hips with her head cocked to one side. "Pete?"

"Yes, dear?"

"Remember? Our sons just ran into the house?"

Pete walked around the car and placed his hand under Kelli's right arm to escort her to the house. "The boys are fine. Chris said he was going to his room. That's okay isn't it, Steve?"

"Sure." Steve said, with widened eyes. "How does he know which room is his?"

"I don't know. I'm assuming that the boys have worked it out already." Pete broke his stare away from the house and turned to Steve. "They've always been like that."

"Well, good. Maybe they can give me some tips on how my kids could get along better." All three of them chuckled.

"So, Kelli, how old are your youngins?" Steve asked while holding the front door open.

"Well, Cory is a little over three and a half and Chris is two and a half."

"They seem to get along great." Steve closed the front door.

"Yes they do," she replied while taking off her coat. "But Chris behaves like a three year old. The boys they act like twins."

"That's a good thing. At least Chris is avoiding the terrible twos."

Down the hall in the far back bedroom that faced the road, Chris was sitting in the middle of the floor. Cory was in the bedroom across the hall and shouted, "Come here, Chris."

Chris walked into the other bedroom dragging his big fluffy winter coat behind him.

"What?"

"You like your room?"

"Yeah." Chris sat down cross-legged.

"Why did you pick that room?"

"It's easier to see the Moon at night."

"How do ya know? We've never been here at night."

"I just know."

Cory learned long ago not to question Chris' intuitions.

"Let's go outside and explore," Cory said.

"Okay."

The boys donned their coats and headed for the front door. They almost plowed over the adults as they raced through the front foyer.

"Boys, slow down." Pete caught his sons as they tried to wiggle past him and out the door. "What's the hurry? Did you pick your rooms?"

"That's a little presumptuous, dear. Don't you think?" Kelli was standing just ahead of Steve in the front hallway, her brow slightly furrowed.

Steve quickly jumped in. "It appears the boys only explored the three bedrooms on this floor." Steve motioned toward the stairs. "Would you like to see the downstairs master suite or start in the kitchen?"

Pete was looking sheepishly at his wife. "What do you want to see first, Kelli?" Pete was still holding onto the two boys who were now watching their parents. Chris spoke up first.

"Kitchens have food. Go there."

That broke the tension. Kelli walked over and put her hand on Chris' shoulder, then brushed his hair off his forehead. "You're not hungry, are you sweetie?"

"No, Mommy. We wanna go outside and play."

"Well, all right. You boys stick close by. Your Daddy and I are going to take a tour of the house with Mr. White." Kelli held the front storm door open so the boys could go out.

"Yes, ma'am."

"And keep your coats on. It's cold out there." She let the door close and turned her attention to the living room where Steve was talking with Pete.

Cory and Chris, wearing their winter snow pants and their puffy down jackets, jumped down the two steps from the front porch and ran down the driveway.

"Why did you want to come down here?" Cory asked.

Chris pointed across the street.

Standing in front of the house across the street were two bundled up little boys, Alex Savvas and Gene Hudson.

Chris looked at Cory and whispered, "They're going to be our friends."

"How do you know?" Cory said without taking his eyes off Alex and Gene as he sized them up.

"I just know. They're gonna be our best friends."

"We don't know them." Cory was now facing Chris.

"We know Gene from church. I think the other kid's name is Alex. Here they come."

Across the street, the front door of the Savvas' two story brick house opened. Stepping into the chilly sunlight, Alex's mother, Lydia, held the door for John and Marsha Hudson, Gene's parents. They pointed across the street at the Gates boys. The mothers gathered up their boys, crossed the street, and walked up the driveway with Cory and Chris in tow introducing them on the way.

Back inside the house, Steve had finished showing the inside and everyone was standing in the dining room.

"Mr. Gates, the boys certainly like the house." Steve was casually leaning against the door jamb leading into the kitchen. He appeared at ease around Pete and Kelli. His laid-back manner and hair over the collar were in sharp contrast to his impeccable blue pin-striped suit. It appeared the real estate market had been very favorable to him.

"Please, Steve, call me Pete. And yes, they really took to this house. Especially Chris."

"I heard him ask Mrs. Gates if y'all could move tomorrow."

"Steve, you can call me Kelli."

"Well then, Kelli, what other questions can I answer about the house? You mentioned you liked the layout of the kitchen with the center island. And you really took to that big bay window in the living room. Please don't forget that under the living room carpet is oak hardwood, the same as the windowsill. If you decide to pull up the carpet, I would suggest having the wood refinished."

Kelli had her arms crossed. "I would like to have the natural wood floors showing." She stepped out into the hallway by the front door and eyed the living room.

Pete glanced out one of the dining room windows and caught sight of their friends walking up the driveway with Cory and Chris. He waved.

"Kelli, we have visitors."

They got their coats and stepped out into the chilly air.

"Hi y'all. Come on up," Pete cheerfully called out.

Kelli smiled as they all greeted each other and did introductions with Steve. While the adults chatted, Alex and Gene stood right in front of Cory and Chris with their hands in their pockets.

"We play at church," Gene said. "This is Alex. He lives there." Gene turned and gestured with his gloved hand toward the Alex's house. "He's almost four, like me."

"Hi. I'm Alex. Are you moving here?" Alex was pointing at the house behind the brothers.

"I hope so," Cory said quietly. "It would be great to have friends to play with."

"We like the rooms," Chris added. "Lots of places to hide."

"You wanna play? There are some good trees out back to climb and swing from. Come on." Gene started leading the rest of the boys around the house. They walked together like they had known each other for years.

"Not too far, boys," Kelli watched as the new little tribe headed to the backyard.

"Don't worry, Kelli," Marsha reassured her. She put her hand on Kelli's shoulder. "Gene and Alex know to stay in the yard. And they know this house pretty well."

"The family that used to live here also had a little boy," Lydia said while pulling her coat tighter around her to ward off the chilly breeze. "They all used to play together all the time," "It would be such a blessing to have another family in this house with children the same age as ours."

"That's right, Pete," John chimed in. "Mr. White, you need to do a real good sales job on these folks. We want them to take this house."

"Call me Steve. I can only show them what a great house and neighborhood this is. The final decision rests with them. Is there anything else about the house I can show you or tell you?" Steve opened both arms in a gesture of servitude; his shiny gold Rolex watch reflecting the sun.

"Well, I think Kelli and I will need to head home and talk about this," Pete put his arm around his wife. "It's a big decision."

"I understand," Steve continued. "You have my contact info so feel free to call me anytime."

"They'll be calling you for sure," Marsha added firmly. "We'll work on them from this end."

"No pressure here at all," Kelli said with a smile and glanced at Pete. "We'd better get the boys and go talk about this." Turning, she almost stepped on Chris who had been standing right behind her. No one had noticed him come around the house.

"Chris, sweetheart. I almost stepped on you."

"I know. You missed."

Everyone laughed at that.

She knelt down and put her hand on his face. "Are you all right?"

"Yes, ma'am."

"Where are the other boys?"

"Out back."

"Why did you leave them?" Kelli gently pulled Chris closer to her.

"We should buy this house." Chris' hands were shoved deep into his pockets; determination etched on his face.

Everyone directed their attention to Chris. Even the talkative Lydia went silent.

"And why is that sweetie? Do you like this house?"

"Yes I do. And we like Gene and Alex. They're our new friends. We want to live here."

"Well, Daddy and I are going to talk about it tonight. Is that okay with you?"

"It's okay. Let's go talk."

With that, Kelli pulled Chris into her arms and gave him a hug. "All right sweetie. We'll go now and talk." Kelli winked at Pete.

The image of Chris in his mother's arms warmed Zenta's heart. She stretched her arms above her head. Turning off her monitor, she looked at Xander at the adjoining workstation and said, "You're on duty now. Make sure you get all the details when Pete and Kelli discuss this."

"What are you worried about?" Xander adjusted his headset. "With everything you've set in motion, it is very likely they will buy the house."

"I know. I just want to see how much Chris influences the decision."

"From what I've seen, it looks like he has already made the decision for them."

"Possibly. But I want to study how he gets them to do this. He is going to have to persuade a lot of people to do many things in the future. And those won't be anywhere as easy as buying a house."

12 – LAST DATA FROM SURVEYOR 2

"Hanger control channel open," Tish said looking at Hajeck for acknowledgment.

"Check," Hajeck responded as he read the next task on his pre-flight check list. His clipboard was in his lap as he pulled down on one of his seat harness shoulder straps.

"Magnetic Field Realignment unit on," Tish continued.

"Check MFR."

From the back, Donac, strapped into his seat, leaned over to Callun and asked, "Didn't the new MFR model get installed on all the Dagars last week?"

"Yes. Why do you ask?"

"I was just wondering if the lieutenant had been trained in operating the new unit."

Sohan spoke while securing his front belt harness, "The new MFR operates no differently from the old model. It's just new technology. Major, do you have a problem with our pilot?"

"No sir. I was just ..."

"By the sounds of it, you seem to be questioning my selection of personnel for this mission. Perhaps I erred in selecting you." Sohan looked at Donac with a suspicious eye.

"Sorry, sir." Donac retreated quickly. "I would never question your wisdom."

"Wise choice. Now let's enjoy the ride."

"Supreme Commander, didn't the new MFR technology improve upon the ability to hover?" Callun asked trying to help Donac.

"Yes it did. The principle technology of having the magnetic disks move in patterns between the inner and outer vehicle hull is the same. The improvements come from using smaller, flatter disks that are magnetically more powerful. Now when operated to lock in on natural magnetic fields, they don't have to move as far or as fast. This reduces friction, heat, and saves conventional startup fuel reserves."

Donac jumped into the conversation with a question. "Were any changes necessary to any vehicle bodies?"

"That's the great part of this technological improvement," Sohan continued. "Engineers only had to remove the old disks and insert the new ones. It was first tested on the duel pilot Zyker fighter. Finding no problems, it was installed on the Falk War Carrier from the new Warship Class. It improved performance and conventional speed dramatically. No changes were necessary to the bodies of either ship so it was installed in every ship of the fleet."

Meanwhile, up front, the flight crew had finished their pre-flight.

"The craft checks out. Let's get moving." Tish stashed her clipboard next to her seat. "Control, this is Dagar Transport, Delta, four, one, three, requesting permission to exit the base on a research mission. We have The Supreme Commander on board. Request priority pattern."

"Permission to exit granted," the front cockpit speaker crackled. "Priority request granted. Proceed at forty-five degrees from present location to the decompression chamber entrance."

Tish eased the throttle, height, and forward controls into prime positions to take the Dagar on course to the chamber entrance. She noticed two other shuttles slow to a hovering state to allow her to proceed ahead of them.

Hajeck gazed out of his side window at the activity on the tarmac. The rows of fighters and transports were quickly becoming smaller. "I'm always so fascinated by how big the hanger is. You can't really get a grasp of it until you go up in a ship."

Tish saw the chamber doors to the overhead canopy slowly open.

"Delta, four, one, three, this is Control. Proceed through to the chamber and wait for the outer doors to open."

Tish moved the ship into the chamber and the lower doors began closing immediately.

With the lower chamber doors closed, the outer doors opened. Tish took the ship up and out of the base. She slowly banked to the right for a course to the Surveyor 2 site.

"It is hard to believe that base GAIA is 80 stories high. It looks so low to the ground from up here. It's beautiful," Tish exclaimed; her eyes were glued to the window.

"I know." Hajeck was mesmerized by the sight. "From up here, you forget that there are also nineteen stories underground. This base covers five hundred acres plus. It's like it is a big round hill inside this crater."

Donac, trying to impress Sohan, piped in from the back, "As you can see, the outside of the structure is covered with different size rocks and dirt and colored like the moonscape itself with various shades of brown, grey, and yellow to create a good camouflage."

There was no response from Sohan. He continued gazing out the window.

"It blends in, doesn't it?" Hajeck spoke without taking his eyes off the moonscape.

Tish slowed the Dagar to prolong their viewing.

"It sure does. Have you ever touched it? What's the surface like?" she asked.

"I have touched it. I accompanied a repair crew one time when they fixed an observation window covering. We walked up the side of the base with ease. Beneath the debris, the surface is smooth to the touch but is dull in appearance, like concrete. You have to brush off all the dust and dirt to get to it. I've felt some of the replacement panels they keep in storage. The covering has the feel of a flexible metal and plastic combination. I'm not sure what material it is. It's a new composite. Without any lights on, the base looks like part of the moonscape. It blends well."

"Tish and Hajeck," Sohan's voice boomed up to the front. "If you tourists are done sightseeing, we should proceed to our destination."

"Yes, sir. Right away, sir," Tish responded, her cheeks burning with heat. She hit the throttle pressing everyone into their seats.

"Wow," Tish said, forgetting her embarrassment. "This new MFR accelerates much faster than the old one."

"I felt that acceleration," Hajeck said. "Let me take the controls for a minute."

Tish saw a boyish twinkle in Hajeck's eyes. "Okay. They are all yours." She took her hands off the pilot side controls as Hajeck grabbed the co-pilot controls.

"This is a big change. It's definitely quicker."

"Don't get too carried away. This is my flight."

"All right. It's all yours again."

Tish covered the distance with the Dagar in a matter of minutes. She brought the ship in over top of the Surveyor 2 site, slowly circling the wreckage at a height of 50 feet. Pieces of the satellite were spread over a 30 yard radius.

"Looks like a big pile of twisted metal, sir," Hajeck informed Sohan as Tish brought the Dagar to a hover facing the site.

"Let's see what we have here." Sohan released his harness and stood behind Tish's seat inspecting the crumbled Surveyor satellite.

"Move in closer using this side of the Dagar." Sohan returned to the middle of the ship and was peering out the right side window with Callun and Donac. "Stop," he said pointing at an area in front of the largest piece of wreckage. "Right there, next to the communication dish in front of those broken antennas. Those are footprints I'm seeing. I'm sure of it. Do any of you concur?"

"Sir, I concur. There are prints in the dust there." Donac had confirmed the visual.

They all looked in total disbelief.

Hajeck leaned toward Tish and whispered, "What was Jzet

thinking? How could he possibly not clean up the site? Did he think the wind would blow the footprints away?"

Tish stifled a laugh which brought an immediate reaction from Sohan.

"I find nothing humorous about this situation."

"Callun, you're part of the Anti-Detection Unit, correct?" Donac asked.

Callun had taken a seat upon the detection of the footprints.

"I didn't go on this mission. This was Jzet's doing. I wouldn't have …"

"That's enough. This will all get sorted out and the truth will rise to the surface. Donac, you, Hajeck, and I will don Riser Packs, photograph the site, and clean up this mess. If an Apollo mission were to ever return here and see footprints," Sohan paused as if searching for the right words, "I can't imagine the fallout."

"Sir." Hajeck had spun his seat around during the verbal exchange to face the back. "I believe we can maneuver the Dagar over the site and use the bottom exhaust vent to blow those prints away. We have full tanks with more than enough oxygen to do this."

"Well, make it happen. Use the Dagars cameras to shoot pictures of the entire area before and after the cleanup procedure. Someone obviously came here in a hurry to do something at this site and it wasn't an Earthling. I want to know why they came here and why they were stupid enough to not clean up after themselves." Sohan slammed the palm of his hand against the bulkhead.

"Sir." Hajeck was pointing to a crumpled outer piece of the satellite. "It appears as if the metal siding got hit with a blast of rocks or something. There are small holes in that one section."

Everyone crowded around observation windows.

"Move us closer, Tish," Sohan ordered.

Tish eased the Dagar like a crab moving sideways. She had the right side observation window within ten feet of the suspect metal siding.

"Those holes appear to match holes made by blast pellets from an X5 Probe," Sohan said. His jaws clenched in a determined effort to not say more.

"The majority of the footprints are around that section of the satellite," Donac added. "My theory is that blast pellets were used to disable this ship and someone came here to retrieve the pellets."

"I agree with that, Major." Sohan's voice shook with anger. His lips had disappeared as his mouth formed a straight line across his face, brow creased. "Are we filming this, Lieutenant?"

"The cameras have been on the whole time, sir."

"Film it all then clean up those footprints. This place is a disaster."

Sohan went back to one of the seats and sat down next to Callun.

Arms crossed on top of his rotund belly, as he slouched in his seat, Callun barely acknowledged Sohan.

Picking up on this discontent, Sohan leaned over and quietly said, "Lieutenant Callun, if I were you, I would get rid of that dour expression and offer assistance in whatever is needed to rectify this situation. No one is blaming you for anything but your superior is responsible for this and is now under the spotlight. Your actions, or lack thereof, are now putting you in under that same light."

Callun quickly jumped up and said, "Sir, yes sir." He then made a beeline straight for Hajeck.

"Major, is there anything I can do to assist in this mission?"

Slightly startled by Callun's abrupt request, Hajeck looked up from the camera and said, "Lieutenant, you can stow away the Riser Packs that Major Donac had gotten out. I don't think we'll need them." Hajeck then turned to Sohan.

"Supreme Commander, I've run a scan and there are no traces of blast pellets."

"Very good, Major. I've seen all I need to see." Sohan shifted slightly in his seat. He bit his tongue and stared out the window.

After the filming was completed, Tish hovered over the site while Hajeck released small blasts of oxygen from the bottom vent onto the various affected areas. Plumes of dust rose from the ground as Tish pulled the Dagar up to avoid the billows.

After the dust settled, Tish hovered the Dagar next to the crash site for a final inspection.

"Supreme Commander, everything is clear now. All sensors show no evidence of blast pellets or marks in the ground. Do you wish to return to GAIA now?"

"Yes, Lieutenant. After we land, I want to see all of you in my quarters. Do not speak about this mission to anyone. Is that understood?"

All acknowledged the order.

Sohan stared out the window. He knew that this incident would give him a certain amount of leverage with Jzet. But what worried him more was the possibility that Jzet and his Anti-Detection Unit had intervened with Apollo 1 causing the deaths of the three astronauts. The death of an Earthling purposely caused by a Terlokyan for any reason other than the protection of the Savior Project was punishable by banishment to one of the barren moons of Qanzazini, the first planet the Terlokyans colonized in the Eck solar system. The life expectancy on one of those moons was very short, even for someone of Jzet's perfect condition.

The return trip was quiet. As Tish entered the hanger area from the decompression chamber, she glanced back at Sohan to see if he also noticed Jzet standing in the Dagar landing area. The scowl on his face, confirmed it.

After landing and powering down the ship, Tish opened the Dagar's door and lowered the ramp. Sohan was standing at the ship's door when he saw Jzet at the bottom of the ramp.

"Greetings Supreme Commander. I have finished my CTOP report and ..."

"Major Jzet. Get onboard and take a seat." Sohan then spoke to the rest of the mission crew. "Lieutenant Tish, would you please upload all of the mission files to Troid and then escort the rest of the crew to my quarters. I will be there momentarily."

"Yes, sir." Tish motioned for the others to move toward the door then she uploaded the files.

"Sir." Hajeck snapped to attention and faced Sohan. "I will return and finish securing the Dagar when we are done."

"Not to worry, Major. I will have that taken care of."

With Jzet sitting in the Dagar now and the crew departed, Sohan closed the ship's door.

"Major, I will give you one and only one opportunity to explain everything."

Jzet shifted nervously in his seat.

"I'm not sure what you are referring ..."

"Stop!" Sohan had his hand up. "I am ready to order your transfer to Qanzazini. Let's try again." Sohan, still standing, crossed his arms and glared at Jzet. "Explain the Surveyor 2 mission and what happened at that site."

Jzet then explained his reasoning for using probes to bring down the Surveyor 2 satellite. The data showed that the satellite's orbital path was going to be directly over base GAIA. His justification was that surveillance data from the Anti-Detection Unit also showed a new more powerful camera system was onboard Surveyor 2. He sounded confident with that explanation.

"As stated in my report, the computer commands sent to Surveyor 2 did not cause the ship to wobble and leave orbit. With the improved camera and our ineffective rogue computer commands, I was left with no choice but to forcefully bring the satellite down using probes." Now Jzet looked uncertain as Sohan's glare remained.

"Major, where in our regulations does it say that the intervention you described, is permitted without the approval of your superiors?"

"Well, sir ..."

Sohan put his hand up and continued, "Some of the actions you've described might have been permitted. The lack of securing proper authorization due to the possible, and I repeat the possible chance of detection might have been met with a minor reprimand. But I also have a real concern in what you DID NOT do. Would you please enlighten me about that?"

Jzet stared blankly at Sohan, obviously clueless as to what he didn't do.

"You have no idea what I'm referring to, do you, Major?"

"No, sir."

Sohan went to the front of the Dagar and turned on the recent recording of the Surveyor 2 sending the video feed to the overhead screen in the back of the ship.

Jzet sat in stunned silence as he saw the images of footprints around the crashed satellite and heard the voices of the Dagar crew discussing the situation. No one but his Anti-Detection Unit could have left that evidence. He knew those large boot prints next to the crumpled shell of the satellite were his.

"Sir?"

"Yes, Major."

"I recall the accelerated pace we were operating under and the ..."

"No excuse." Sohan, unmoved by the explanation, kept his eyes still glued to the screen.

"I know you are well aware of protocol in situations such as this," Sohan continued. "No traces of our presence are permissible under any circumstance; even at the risk of our own lives."

"Yes, sir," Jzet responded with barely a whisper. He was staring blankly at the floor. "What are your orders, sir?"

"You will take an intervention team to the site and alter the holes in the satellite made by the blast pellets so there is no size uniformity. Film before and after."

"When would you ..."

"Now, Major. Right now. Have this Dagar refueled. It is already equipped for the mission."

"Yes, sir." Jzet opened the Dagar's door.

Sohan took hold of Jzet's arm as he headed down the ramp.

"Jzet. At this moment, I can't say whether or not you will be reassigned to another post. It is safe to say that until a decision is made, I will be monitoring your every move. Only the crew from this mission has knowledge of this. If you want to keep it that way, substantial changes are necessary in your conduct."

Jzet kept his eyes diverted from Sohan's.

"Sir, I will ..."
"You are dismissed, Major."
Sohan released Jzet's arm and headed down the ramp.

13 – MAN AROUND THE MOON

The speakers crackled with the sounds from Apollo 8 and Houston Control.

Apollo 8, “Lift off. The clock is running.”

Houston, “Roger. Clock.”

Apollo 8, “Roll and pitch program.”

Houston, “Roger.”

Apollo 8, “How do you hear me, Houston?”

Houston, “Loud and clear.”

The first manned spacecraft with the mission to leave Earth's gravity and reach the Moon had just been launched from Cape Canaveral in Florida. The National Aeronautics and Space Administration’s Mission Control in Houston, Texas was receiving the transmissions from Apollo 8. Monitors there showed the command module aboard the Saturn rocket streaking through the sky. Unbeknownst to anyone on Earth, this mission was also being observed from the Moon. The Command Center at Base GAIA was monitoring Apollo 8 communications as well.

“Check that. Set a time mark for launch.” Donac was hunched over his monitor and didn’t look up to see if Hajeck had acknowledged his command.

“Mark set. December 21st, 1968 at 07:51:00 a.m. Earth Eastern Standard Time.” Hajeck entered the time for Apollo 8 launch.

“Check that. Set an estimated time mark for Moon orbit.”

“Estimated mark set at December 24th, 1968 at 04:59:20 a.m. Earth Eastern Standard Time.” Hajeck keyed in the estimated time when Apollo 8 would enter the Moon’s orbit.

“This is our first real test to see if we can go undetected,” Sohan said to Jhall while sitting in the back of the Command Center. He spoke without taking his eyes off the large screen at the front of the room.

“You are aware that the base has passed all Terlokyan detection tests. The Earthlings have equipment equal to toys our children play with.” Jhall chuckled. Sitting in one of the high-back swivel seats next to Sohan, he stretched out his legs. His boots glistened from the overhead lighting. “The only way we will be detected by these so called astronauts is if we shine a spotlight on their ship and turn on our lights.”

Sohan laughed at that. “When is the projected date for Apollo 8 to return to Earth?”

“December 27th.”

Sohan wondered if Earthlings would remember that their ship orbited the Moon on the anniversary of the eve of their original Savior’s birth.

It will be interesting to see if they celebrate the arrival of this new Savior with a marked day.

"How long will they orbit?" Sohan posed the question as he saw the doors to the Command Center open.

"They will be in orbit for ten revolutions."

Jhall and Sohan watched as Jzet entered the room and stood just inside the doors. He stared at the screen on the front wall, watching the live feed of the Saturn rocket which was barely visible now.

"What is he doing here?" Jhall asked. "I thought he was ill."

"I did too. He must be doing better." Sohan stood up. "I'll go check on him." He walked up to Jzet.

Out of the corner of his eye, Jzet saw Sohan approaching. He turned to face him, snapped to attention, and saluted.

"Sir, permission to participate in the Apollo 8 monitoring program." Jzet lowered his salute.

Sohan stood right in front of Jzet. Not many Terlokyans were of the same height, six foot six inches, as Jzet. But Sohan looked him right in the eye and said, "I thought you were ill; too ill to work I might add."

Jzet was now staring at Callun who was occupying the workstation where he would have been sitting.

"Jzet!" Sohan's stern voice got his attention.

"Sir, may I have a moment in private with you?" Jzet was being unusually courteous.

"Step out into the hallway."

Before the doors closed, Sohan was in Jzet's face.

"We had an agreement. You are to be sick, and I will keep your Surveyor fiasco quiet for now. If the Supreme Council were to find out about your mistake, you would be shipped off this rock to some remote military outpost faster than you could blink. I haven't been able to find anything linking you to Apollo 1 incident but I'm not done researching it. You have zero latitude to be doing anything except for what you are ordered to do. Is this becoming clear to you?"

"Yes sir. But I feel …"

Sohan cut him off. "If you want any chance of remaining with this project, you will do as I say." Then he softened his tone. "Look, Jzet." Sohan started to walk slowly down the hall, Jzet at his side. "I know you are doing what you feel is best for Terlokya. I would never question your loyalty to our people. At one time, you followed my guidance in advancing your career. Why I remember the days when you used to ask me for advice. Somewhere along the way you started to think of yourself as being smarter than everyone else. Are you doing well with that mindset?"

Jzet continued the slow stroll down the hall, head bowed, and at a loss for words.

"No, sir. Perhaps I need to listen now instead of taking action."

Stopping in the hallway just a short distance from the Command Center, Sohan turned and put his hand on Jzet's shoulder.

"I think that's a good plan right now."

Jzet raised his head and looked at Sohan. "Thank you, sir."

"You are a patriot, Jzet. I have no doubt about that. And you appear to be feeling better. Why don't you join me in the back of the Command Center with General Jhall? We'll observe the assembled tracking team and lend assistance if it is requested."

"Thank you, sir."

They walked back down the hall, entered the Command Center, and took their seats. The Command Center continued monitoring the launch. Once Apollo 8 left Earth's orbit, Jhall dismissed most of the staff to rest and get ready for the ship's arrival to the Moon.

On December 24th, the Command Center was again humming with activity. Things had been slow while the spacecraft traveled from Earth to the Moon but on this day, most all of the workstations were occupied with personnel busily going about their duties.

"Let's be ready everyone. They should be entering orbit within the hour," Jhall announced from where he was standing at the front console.

"On my mark, Lieutenant Callun, launch orbital probes." Jhall paused. "Launch."

"Yes, sir." Callun keyed the command. "Done."

"Major Donac, you have the probe controls."

"I will position them in a slow, lower orbit and wait for the Apollo 8 spacecraft." Donac assumed his familiar hunched over position in front of his monitor.

Down the hall in the Savior Project lab, Sohan had wandered in on his way to the Command Center. He stood behind Zenta's workstation, observing her and Tish monitoring the actions of the Gates family. Empty energy fluid containers littered the lab.

"Don't say anything." Zenta raised her hand before Sohan could speak. "I know we need rest, but with the Apollo 8 mission taking Xander, Bal, and Tuu away from us, I needed to be here for this. Look at how the adults are crowded around their television set with their friends watching the Apollo 8 launch."

Tish was looking at Zenta's monitor since she had a different view on hers. Sohan observed from behind them.

"They haven't spoken much," Tish said. "They're mesmerized by this. Space technology that we've taken for granted for generations is just beginning on Earth."

"You have placed the monitoring probe in an ideal position," Sohan said. With his hands on the back of Zenta's chair, he glanced at Tish's monitor and saw children sitting in a circle in a different room from the adults. "What exactly are you two monitoring?"

"Shhh. Listen." Zenta pointed at her monitor and turned up the volume on the speakers.

"This is a great day for us," Pete Gates said without taking his eyes off the television.

"It is a great day for all mankind," John Hudson added. He was standing next to the dining room table munching on a freshly baked chocolate-chip cookie.

"Not so great for those damn Russkies I might add," George Savvas said while shifting in his seat on the couch.

"Don't start something now." Lydia Savvas put a hand on her husband's knee and smiled.

"No, he's right," Pete added. "The Soviets aren't going to just sit back and do nothing. They're going to speed up their program."

"I know this is an important time in history, but Pete and I did want to talk to you all about the house," Kelli announced after standing up. She smoothed the apron she was wearing, bits of cookie dough stained the white material. "I mean we really can't see anything from Apollo 8 yet. They haven't started filming the Moon, have they?"

"Not yet. What's to talk about anyway?" Marsha Hudson stood up and went over to Kelli. "If it's about the house, John and I would love for you and the boys to move to Hilton Mills. That place is just perfect for your family. And the yard; the way it slopes through the woods down to the lake, makes it a wonderful picnic area." Marsha walked to the dining room table, picked up one of the cookies and placed it on a napkin. She continued, "If we weren't so content in our house, I'd seriously be bugging John to buy it."

"I like that house too," Lydia chimed in. "And Alex told me yesterday that he really wants Cory and Chris to be our neighbors. The boys play so well together." She looked at her husband hoping for a confirming nod, but he was focused on the television and obviously hadn't been listening. "Speaking of the boys, where are they?"

"I'm not sure," Kelli said as she looked down the hallway where the boy's bedrooms were. "They're awfully quiet." They went to check on the boys. Peeking into Cory's room, she saw them sitting in a circle on the floor talking.

Sohan, Tish, and Zenta were also watching the boys.

"How many probes are you using in that house?" Sohan inquired.

Without taking her eyes off the monitor, Zenta answered, "We like to keep at least six spread throughout the house." She reached for the volume control. "They are talking so softly. I'm having trouble hearing them."

"I can barely hear anything," Tish added.

"I'll turn it up some more."

"Talk to your momma. She'll listen to you." Gene was sitting with his legs straight out in front of him, tapping his shoes together as he talked. "We can have so much fun."

"Yeah. Your dad wants to move." Alex was also sitting like Gene, legs straight out tapping his shoes together.

The boys were all wearing jeans, tennis shoes, and various colored shirts, some clean and some a bit disheveled. Ian Johnston was also there. He came with the Hudsons since his mother, Helen, was in town visiting his grandmother.

The boys were quiet again so Kelli and Lydia walked back to the living room.

"They all look adorable," Zenta said, mesmerized by what she was watching.

"But they are so pale," Tish said as she scrunched up her face.

"Spoken like a true Terlokyan." Sohan let go of Zenta's chair and walked to the doors. "Your plan is working." Glancing back, he asked, "Did you influence those other families to move to that neighborhood?"

"The Savvas' were already there and Helen Johnston was living a few houses down the street. I did have something to do with getting the Hudson's in there a few years ago," Zenta said smugly.

"And don't forget Tom and Barbara Greenfield and their son Jay. You got them to move in there. Where are the Greenfields anyway?" Tish asked.

"Not sure." Zenta looked up at her father. "It appears you are leaving."

"Yes, I must get to the Command Center. In case you hadn't heard, Apollo 8 will be entering the Moon's orbit soon."

"We heard," Tish replied. "Take Xander's place and send him back here."

"I wish I could." Sohan moved through the open doors into the hallway. "But he's on flight ready status sitting in a Dagar. He'll be returning as soon as Apollo 8 leaves orbit." The doors closed.

"Tish, listen to this." Zenta was so focused on her monitor that she hadn't said goodbye to her father.

Chris glanced at the door to the bedroom. Seeing that his mother and Ms. Savvas had left, he started talking again.

"Momma and Daddy are gonna buy that house," he said as if it were factual.

"How do you know?" Ian asked as he rubbed his head messing up his thick red hair.

Chris looked at Ian. "They are going to tell us today."

"But ..." Ian was cut off by Cory.

"If Chris says it'll happen, it will," Cory said backing up his little brother.

"Yeah, Ian." Gene jumped in. "I've seen him do that a lot."

"What?" Ian looked puzzled.

"When he says something is going to happen, it usually happens." Gene got up on his knees. "I've seen him do it when we want to get some candy from his mom. He knows if we can have it or not."

"Yeah. He always knows if it's yes or no before we ask," Cory added while nodding his head for emphasis. "So if Chris says we are gonna buy the house, then we will," he said with an air of finality.

Inside the lab, Tish turned to Zenta and said, "Well, let's see if this is going to hold up."

Zenta pulled off her headset and wiped her brow with her sleeve.

"Chris has done this many times," she said. "He is really quite adept at predicting others' decisions. And it's usually decisions that he has influenced."

"Look," Tish said pointing at Zenta's monitor.

Kelli and Lydia were standing at the end of the hallway now. Kelli gestured with her hand, waving it in slow, sweeping arc.

"All of this seemed so important just two weeks ago. But I've realized that this is just a house. Granted, it is a special house, being our first," Kelli paused and looked down the hall to the boy's room. "Seeing those boys all sitting together and talking, well, it made me think about how special it would be to see them grow up together."

Lydia was nodding in agreement. "In the Greek community, children who forge friendships at a very early age tend to nourish and keep those friendships for a lifetime."

"I agree." Marsha had joined them at the hallway entrance. "Ian's mother, you know Helen, well, she and I have known each other since elementary school."

"Really? I didn't know that." Kelli sounded surprised.

"Sure. We also went to high school with Barbara Greenfield."

"Wow. You really are locals," Kelli said. "Well, I guess this just adds to my feeling that moving to Hilton Mills will be good for the children. I know that Pete wants to move there, so I guess we're going to do it."

Marsha shrieked in happiness and gave Kelli a quick hug. Their celebration was interrupted by those sitting around the television.

"Ladies, come quickly. We've got Americans orbiting the Moon," John said excitedly.

While the Gates household and their friends were captivated by the images on their television, Terlokyans were captivated by different images on their monitors.

The Command Center was a bundle of energy. Everyone working the Apollo 8 tracking operation was in full uniform and at their duty stations. All other base personnel were in a ready status. Two Dagars were fueled and ready to launch with pilots and crews aboard. A fully crewed Rover sat ready to enter the decompression chamber. Twenty X5 probes were perched on top of the base, and a fleet of five X5 probes were flying in various positions around the Apollo 8 capsule out of sight of the spacecraft's portals.

"Major Donac, have all stations cut exterior area lights?" General Jhall asked. He was at the front of the room manning the stand-up workstation located next to the large video screen.

"Sir, all externally exposed lights are off," the major quickly replied.

Jhall appeared satisfied. "I see that all non-essential radio communications have ceased. We're looking good, everyone. Major Jzet, let's get that X5 video feed up front please."

"Yes, sir." Jzet keyed in the commands and a rolling view of the Apollo 8 spacecraft filled the screen.

"Quite impressive." Sohan was sitting in his customary seat in the back of the Command Center. Right next to him was Colonel Braaddy, head of the Savior Project.

"We should have taken that ship out on its way from Earth," Braaddy said gruffly. He was known for being over-protective of the project.

"Now Braaddy, you know we can't do that. Those astronauts on board would be killed." Sohan knew that the good colonel would never really agree to such an action.

Braaddy crossed his arms over his chest. "I know that, sir. But I prefer to err on the side of caution. I don't want anything to jeopardize this project."

"I know Braaddy. You and your staff have been doing an excellent job considering the circumstances we operate under." Sohan trusted Braaddy completely. He had distinguished himself on many military and civilian projects. Of medium height but stocky with great strength, he had gained the reputation of shooting first and asking questions later.

The conversation halted at the sound of Jhall's booming voice.

"Major Marsitta, please trace all personnel to standby and be ready. Apollo 8 is about to make its first pass over Base GAIA."

"Here's the real test; having someone else fly over us." Braaddy sat up straight, watching the images on the front screen. "If I were in charge of this base, I would fly one of the probes right into the camera lens on that craft."

"General Jhall," Jzet was sitting ramrod straight at his workstation while giving his report. "I've received data from one of the X5 probes that the cameras on board Apollo 8 are activated and filming."

Jhall barked out more orders, "Major Jzet, is the feed capture probe in place?"

"Yes, sir."

Jhall was quick with his orders. "Then let's get a four way split on that screen." He gestured to the front of the room. "Get the craft and ground views up there."

"Yes, sir."

The screen up front was now split into four views coming from X5 probes: the view from probe 1 was showing the Apollo 8 capsule flying. Probe 2 showed a straight ahead view of capsule's orbital path. The ground view of what the Apollo 8 craft was filming was being duplicated by probe 3. Probe 4 was capturing the signal from the Apollo 8 camera and was showing exactly what they were filming.

Braaddy leaned toward Sohan and whispered, "Look at the difference in quality of our probe's view compared to what their camera can pick up."

Sohan looked at the grainy images from the Apollo 8 camera. "I don't think we have any worries about discovery. I'm not sure anyone could tell what planet is being filmed much less see a hidden base. We are safe for now."

14 – FRIENDS FOR LIFE

"Make a wish and blow out the candles," Kelli said to Chris as all the kids bounced up and down in their seats around the picnic table.

"Come on, Chris. We want cake," Gene whined.

"Yeah. Hurry up. You sure are slow for an eight year old," Ian added.

"It's hot, Chris. Blow out the candles," said the usually quiet Jay. He looked down at his dirty bare feet. None of the boys had shoes on that particular Saturday afternoon, June 14th, 1974.

Cory, sitting to Chris' right, leaned over and whispered in his brother's ear, "Gotta hurry up if we're gonna form the club."

Chris looked at his friends. Next to Cory sat Gene, staring at the cake, his curly, dirty blond hair matted down with sweat from playing on the rope swing. Ian was on the end leaning on Gene and crowding him while trying to be closer to the action. Gene didn't seem to notice or care.

Alex was to Chris' left with Jay beside him. Next to Jay were the remaining birthday party guests: Alex's little sister Eve and Jay's little sister Tracy. Both of those five year olds were barefoot and wearing the standard country summer wear, shorts and tee-shirts. The non-brothers treated those girls as if they were their own little sisters.

"Okay." Chris leaned forward. "I'm ready." All eight candles were extinguished.

"Yaaaayyy!!" was the collective cheer.

"Bring on the cake!" shouted Alex.

"Oh no," Kelli said from behind Chris. "I forgot the forks, children."

"Awww Mom," Chris and Cory said in unison.

"Just hold your horses," she replied. "I'll be right back." She passed Pete who was taking pictures from the step leading to the porch. As she went by she whispered, "Do a little song and dance for them while I'm gone. They're getting restless."

"I'm on it, honey," Pete replied. He hopped off the step and raised both hands in the air.

"Kids! Kids! I've got an emergency. Ya gotta help me."

All the children stopped their squealing and looked at Pete as he stood waving his arms over his head.

"What's up, Dad?" Chris asked. "What's the big emergency? We are in the middle of our own sugar emergency."

"I need a picture of all you guys so I can send it off to all the grandparents. Okay?"

The kids all started squirming and talking again while totally ignoring the amateur photographer. Pete shot some pictures anyway seeing that his declared emergency idea didn't work. Kelli came out with the forks and the sweet tooth emergency was averted.

With massive quantities of cake and ice cream finally consumed, Cory got things moving.

"Come on gang. Let's head down to the creek. We've got a mission."

Alex, Gene, and Jay bolted for the backyard path that led down a hill to the lake's feeder creek at the rear of the property.

Tish watched some of the kids run off down the path. Zenta's monitor showed the rest of the birthday party still milling around the picnic table. Leaning back in her chair, she yawned. After rubbing her eyes, Tish checked the time display panel on the front wall.

I've still got two hours left in my shift. I am so tired. Someone needs to come in and relieve this boredom.

Getting up, she took one last look at the monitors, and then walked over to the observation platform. She stepped onto the huge white square that was underneath the observation window.

"Platform console: rise," she commanded and the small stand with a panel attached to it rose out of the trap door in the white square. Handrails came up on all sides. She pushed a button and the square started rising.

Sssswishhhh.

The sound of the lab doors opening turned her head. Xander walked in.

"Where are you going?" he asked while standing below the platform, both hands on his hips. He was wearing his life suit.

"Not very far on this thing, but am I ever glad to see you," she said as she hit a button that reversed the platform, sending it in a slow and easy decent to the floor. "I was about to go crazy from boredom." She stepped off the platform and stood in front of Xander. "I was going to gaze at the stars to wake up. This has been a boring shift."

With Tish standing so close, Xander froze, captivated by her enchanting green eyes.

"Xander?" Tish cocked her head. "Are you all right?"

That snapped him out of his trance.

"Uh, yeah," he said diverting his eyes. "I was passing by on my way from the hanger and thought I'd check on you."

"What were you doing?" she asked in such a sweet and innocent way as to force him to look at that beautiful face.

"I was, uh, doing …"

"Are you sure you're all right?"

Xander shook his head, bent down and adjusted the thigh strap of his pulsar holster.

"I'm fine," he said as he stood up straight. "I've been on a base surface repair mission and it wore me out."

"That's still more exciting than what I've been doing," she said as she grabbed his arm and steered him over to their workstations. "This feels like the hundredth birthday party I've had to monitor since I arrived on base. Chris was almost two years old then and now he's turning eight. With his and all his friend's birthdays, it feels like that's all I do."

"What?" Xander replied staring at her.

"Monitor birthday parties," Tish answered. "Are you sure nothing is wrong? You're acting strange."

"I'm fine," Xander said as he sat down at his workstation. "You mostly monitor Chris during the day so you're going to get the daytime activities. Zenta and I don't get to see half the exciting stuff you see."

"Well, I don't know about that last part."

"From what has been happening with those boys forming a tight friendship, I would say that these are exciting times. Zenta's plan is working."

As Xander finished his sentence, Zenta walked into the lab.

"Hello, everyone." Zenta cheerfully greeted them as she took a seat next to Tish. "I thought I'd see how the birthday party is going."

"Boring," was Tish's reply.

"She's sooooo tired," Xander said mockingly.

"I am tired," Tish exclaimed as she slapped her knees. "Why don't you start your shift early and I'll go catch up on some sleep?"

"I can't do that right now," Xander said with an air of exasperation. "This life suit has got to come off."

Zenta stood up, grabbed Tish's hands, and pulled her up to a standing position.

"I have a good idea. Since I want to observe how these friendships progress, why don't you both go and do what you have to do." She looked at Xander. "You go change and come back for your shift. But please come in a few minutes early for your shift to relieve me." She turned to Tish. "And you go to your quarters and get some sleep. Is everybody agreeable to this?"

Tish and Xander looked at each other and nodded.

"I'm in agreement," Xander said.

"Yes. I am really tired," Tish added.

"Good." Zenta clapped her hands together and sat down at her workstation. "You all get out of here so I can get to work."

Tish and Xander left while Zenta watched the remaining children still gathered around the table.

Ian was still finishing his second piece of cake as Eve and Tracy climbed down from their seats. They started running for the path. Cory and Chris caught up to them.

"Girls. Hey. Wait a minute," Cory said getting their attention. The girls stopped and faced the brothers. Cory bent down on a knee to talk to Tracy while Chris did the same with Eve. Unbeknownst to each other, they delivered the same message to each girl.

"Listen, Eve," Chris began as he gently held Eve's elbow. "The boys have something really special to do, but we need to make sure no one comes down the path and interrupts us. Can you and Tracy guard it for us? Maybe you can help my mom take some stuff in from the picnic table."

"Whatcha gonna do? We want to go too."

"Hey," Ian said as he came up on the others. "Everything all right?"

"Yeah, it's all cool," Chris replied. "You go ahead on down and we'll be there in a minute."

"All right." Ian headed down the path.

Chris focused his attention back on Eve.

"Will you keep a secret?"

"Can I tell Tracy?"

"Of course you can. But I think Cory is telling her the same thing."

"Okay."

"Well, we're gonna form a club. And we need to..."

"That's not fair. You're gonna just have boys."

"No. Let me finish. We are going to add you and Tracey in the club as special members called 'little sisters', but we need to form it first. And that's what we're doing today. You two are going to be in the club. It's not just for us boys; it's for all of us who are going to grow up together. So can you be a guard for me to let us get this thing going?"

"Promise?" Eve offered a timid request with her eyes locked on Chris as she shuffled one foot back and forth in the dirt path. She had developed a little girl crush on Chris last summer which had not diminished.

"Sure. Let's do a pinkie swear to seal the deal."

"Do what?"

"A pinkie swear is like a big promise."

"Okay."

With the deal done and the girls meandering along to the house, whispering to each other and sneaking peeks at the brothers, Cory and Chris walked down the path.

"So," Cory began, "what'd you say to Eve?"

"Same thing you said to Tracy. We gotta form the club then we'll get them in."

"How do we do that all the time?" Cory said as he kicked a branch off the path while they wound their way toward the creek.

"What?" Chris reached down and picked up a long stick.

"You know. Always thinking and saying the same things." Cory also reached down and grabbed a stick.

"I dunno," Chris responded as he broke off the small branches from his stick. "We're just in tune with each other's minds. Know what I mean?"

"I guess." Cory glanced up and saw the other boys down by the dam they had been building in the creek. "Ya think it's weird?"

"Nah. I think it's awesome. We shoulda been twins. We've got that mental connection twins have so there's nothing weird about it. It'll help us in the future for sure."

"Cool. We'd better think about the club thing now. You want to do the talking or me?"

"You do it. I'll get 'em into the fort."

They got to the edge of the creek and saw that the others had piled more rocks and branches on the dam they started last month.

"This is great, guys," Chris said. "Hey, let's go to the fort for a meeting. Cory and I have a great idea."

Gene looked up. "Help us finish this one part here. It's almost done. So then we can seal it off and make our pond."

"Okay," Chris said as he waded in to help out. Cory followed.

"See if you and Cory can move that big rock," Gene said while pointing to the middle of the creek. "We need it in the middle of the dam right here," he said as he slapped at the water running through the big open space. "You'd better get Ian to help. Alex and I tried to move it earlier but we could barely budge it."

"Yeah," Alex jumped in. "It's gotta be at least a hundred pounds."

"Okay," Chris said as he waded over to it, bent down, and picked it up. It was about as big as his torso. "Move so I can put it there."

"Whoa, Trigger," Alex exclaimed wide-eyed as he watched Chris set the rock down right where Gene wanted it. "Where did that come from?"

All of the boys had stopped what they were doing and were dead silent as they watched Chris.

"It came from right there," Chris said nonchalantly as he pointed to the rock's previous spot.

"I mean …" Alex began, but stopped. "Where …" he stopped again and just shook his head.

"How did you do that?" Jay asked.

"What do ya mean? I just picked it up," Chris said, shrugging his shoulders.

Cory slapped him on the back as he waded by him and said, "Stop standing around, guys. We've seen him do stuff like that before. Nothing new here. Let's finish this up so we can go to the fort."

"Really," Xander exclaimed standing behind Zenta. He had returned after shedding his life suit. "Where did that come from? We can't let Chris go around and do extraordinary things like that."

"You're right," Zenta answered. She chewed on her pen with her eyes darting back and forth between her monitor and the notes she had been scribbling.

"You'd better turn something off in his sub-consciousness tonight or we're going to end up with an incident to clean up."

"I'll take care of it tonight."

Down at the creek, Alex bellowed, "Good work, boys. We got a lot done today."

"I think we'll be through with this thing soon," Ian added. "So what did you want to do, Chris?"

"Let's go to the fort so Cory and I can tell you about an idea we have."

"Okay guys," Gene said with an air of authority. "Let's do it."

The boys headed down another path that led toward the lake. Nestled in the woods slightly up hill from the path was the fort.

Ian caught up with Gene and Chris before they went in the fort.

"Hey guys. We should really use those leftover boards from Jay's house to make a roof. I mean the walls of branches really keep the fort hidden but we have to pile leaves on it all the time. If we had a roof, we could hang tarps on the sides and skip the leaves."

"You know, Ian has a great idea," Chris said while crossing his arms and wearing the expression of a concerned architect. "If we nail boards to each of the four corner trees, we can nail more boards on top of those and use the new roof as a floor for the tree-house part we planned."

"You're right. I mean, he's right. Oh heck. Whatever." Gene threw his hands up. "Let's go in the fort and talk. Then we can come out afterwards and plan for the roof."

"Good idea."

With everyone inside, Chris headed to the far corner and plunked down on the oak stump right next to Alex who sat on a rusted metal folding chair. In another corner were Gene and Jay, planted on a log. Ian stretched out on an old pallet in the middle of the fort. Cory stood in front of everyone near the fort's entrance.

"Hey guys, listen up." Cory waited while the boys stopped jabbering. "Chris and I had an idea. We've all been friends for six years now. We're all in the same school, we play on the same baseball team, and we're with each other practically every weekend. We need to make a club or something like that."

All the boys started talking at once. Alex's loud voice finally prevailed. Standing now, he gave his opinion on the idea.

"Boys, Cory has a good idea. We need to come up with some kinda club. You know, like make it official. I mean I don't think any of us are going to be moving for a long time. We are gonna end up in high school together."

"I agree," Gene added as he stood up. "We're a really tight bunch, and I know we're always gonna be there for each other."

"Let's call ourselves the Hilton Mills gang," Ian announced.

"We could get some cool jackets or something," Jay added. "We can even have a secret handshake."

"Let's not get goofy, but the handshake idea is a good one," Cory said quickly. "Let's call ourselves something easy like 'The Boys'. Whatcha think?"

"And how is that going to sound when we're all in college?" Gene questioned.

Chris stood up.

"We all think of each other as brothers, right?" Chris canvassed their faces gauging the reactions. Everyone was nodding and mumbling their agreements. Chris continued. "Why not call ourselves 'The Bros', short for brothers."

Again they seemed to agree. Alex spoke first.

"I like it."

"Me too," Cory and Gene said in unison.

"Yeah, let's do it," Ian agreed.

"Does that mean we can't get cool jackets?" Jay asked. Everyone laughed.

"Jay, we'll get jackets," Cory assured him. "Wait, that ain't a bad idea. We should all get blue jean jackets."

"Hey, that sounds good," Gene agreed. "But how do we make the Bros official?"

"Blood," said Chris.

"What? Are you nuts?" Jay asked.

"I mean like the Indians did; blood brothers." Chris saw the puzzled expressions and explained, "We each prick one of our fingers and then we mash them together so that our blood all mixes. That's how you become blood brothers."

"All right," Alex said as he strode up to where Cory was standing. "Let's do it. Ian, you got your knife?"

"Sure." Ian reached into his cutoffs and produced a small pocket knife. "We should clean it with fire like they taught us in Cub Scouts." He reached up from the pallet and handed the knife to Tim.

Tim opened the knife and felt the tip.

Ian watched him and said, "Don't worry. I sharpened it yesterday."

"Not bad," Alex said as he closed one eye and held the knife up while he ran his index finger along the tip. "This thing is already clean. We don't need to burn it. I'll go first. Y'all get up here so we can each do this fast and get our blood mixed."

"What do you mean we're going to mix blood?" Jay asked as he lingered behind the other boys, his face slightly ashen.

Chris walked over to Jay, put his arm around his shoulders, and told him, "You're going to gently poke yourself in the finger so a little blood comes out. Then we all touch fingers together and we'll be blood brothers, just like the Indians."

"Neat. Can I go next?"

"Hey Alex. Jay wants to go next."

"Well, get him up here cause I'm ready to go. Y'all use your left index finger since you're right handed."

"Chris can use either finger since he's amadex, amadexter, ... uhhh," Gene stumbled on the word.

"It's ambidextrous," Chris corrected.

"What's that?" asked Ian as he poked at his finger with a twig.

"I can use either hand to do stuff." Chris gave Jay a push toward Alex. "Get on up there, Jay."

They were all anxious as Alex held the knife on his left index finger.

"Y'all get ready. Here it goes."

Alex poked his finger with the knife and a few drops of blood came out. He passed the knife to Jay but he didn't take it. So he handed it to Cory.

"Did it hurt?" Gene asked.

"Nah. Hurry up before this thing closes up."

Cory poked his finger and it started oozing blood.

"Cool." He handed the knife to Gene.

Gene poked his finger and got the same results. Then Ian and Jay went. Chris was last.

"All right, boys," Chris prodded the guys together in a tight circle. "Everyone put their finger in the middle and let's rub 'em around."

The boys all meshed their fingers together, blood dripping everywhere.

"Now let's raise them up in the air together and point at the sky."

Everyone slowly raised their hands, fingers extended and still touching, at the sky.

"Repeat after me," Chris commanded. "To the Bros!"

"TO THE BROS!"

"We're all in this together and will be forever!"

"WE'RE ALL IN THIS TOGETHER AND WILL BE FOREVER!"

"Ow!!!" All of the boys pulled their hands back. Jay, Ian, and Gene immediately stuck their fingers in their mouths, pained expressions covered their faces.

"This thing hurts," Alex hollered as he and Cory were shaking their hands vigorously.

Only Chris held his finger up and stared at it. Jay saw this and pulled his finger out of his mouth and looked at it.

"Hey guys. It's not bleeding anymore," Jay said while turning it this way and that.

"Mine isn't either," Cory added as he and the rest of the boys ceased their antics. "It's already healed up."

"Yeah," Alex said, his eyes narrowing. "But I have a scar now."

"So do I," Gene added.

"I bet we all do," Chris said. "And I bet they're all the same."

"What's yours like?" Cory asked straining his neck to try and catch a glimpse of Alex's scar. "Hey. It's just like mine."

"Lemme see. What's yours like?" asked Ian.

"It looks like two connected upside down 'Vs' with an extra piece coming off of one."

"Point your finger down and it looks a W," Gene said as he turned his finger over. "But it does have that extra piece. This thing messed up my finger print."

"Mine too," Jay added.

"They're all alike," Alex said. "How'd you know that, Chris?"

"Just a feeling. What we just did was something really cool; making our club. I don't know how that scar happened, but that really makes us blood brothers now. We all have the same mark."

"Do you know what it means?" Gene asked.

"I've seen it before, but I can't remember where." Chris scratched his head. "It'll come to me eventually."

"It looks like a bird," Ian said.

"It's so little and perfect, like someone drew it." Alex had his finger right up to his eye.

"Well, I think it's pretty cool," Cory added with an excited tone. "We're pretty lucky to have this happen. Just like Chris said, we've all got the same mark now. So let's use that cool handshake we do all the time and make it our official handshake." Cory stuck his hand out to Chris who proceeded to shake it. "Remember, you grip the other person's thumb, not his palm."

"We know," was Alex's reply as all the boys were shaking each other's hands now.

And the Bros were formed.

"So how did you pull that off?" Xander inquired. He had remained in the lab, transfixed by the events.

"Do you mean the scar looking like the mark?" Zenta replied.

"Yes, of course. The probe was up on a branch and I didn't see any kind of energy flow coming from it. So how did you do it?"

"I don't know. I didn't do it."

Xander looked puzzled.

"When you zoomed in on their fingers, we could clearly see that the mark was obviously the 'Flying Forcefully' symbol. That can't happen by chance," Xander said as he stood up from his workstation and started pacing behind their chairs.

Zenta was still staring at her monitor as she watched the boys work on their fort. She didn't respond.

"Well? We've got to explain this somehow." Xander had his hands up and shoulders shrugged in exasperation. He had walked around their workstations and was standing behind Zenta's monitor facing her. "Should we just say it was higher intervention?"

"I guess we could say it was the Source."

"Don't say that." Xander was shaking his head. "I wasn't really being serious."

"Then you come up with an explanation," Zenta almost yelled as she pulled off her headset and threw it on her desk. "I don't know how to explain it. This is a major incident and I have no idea how it happened."

"All right then," Zander said as he tried to calm her down. "Let's just settle down and think about this logically." He walked around and sat at his workstation next to hers, turning his chair to face her. "It was clearly the Flying Forc …"

"Look, Xander," Zenta cut him off as she spun her chair around to face him. "We both know there is no explanation for this. It is the mark. And it hasn't been seen on anyone since Koss broke the speed of light barrier."

"That's right. I remember studying about him." Xander uttered under his breath as he got lost in thought. "He reported that he was touched by something when he broke it."

Zenta didn't respond. She was watching the boys again.

"Didn't he die recently?"

"Who?"

"Koss. That's who we've been talking about." Xander slapped both hands on the top of his workstation and stared at his monitor.

"That's what you've been talking about. I'm trying to figure out how to report this." Zenta put her headset back on. "And no, he didn't die."

The room was silent.

"It's simple. Just report exactly what you observed and see if anyone questions you about it," Xander declared as if that was the perfect answer. "That way someone else can determine how it happened."

Zenta looked flabbergasted. When he didn't say anything and continued staring at his monitor, she reached over and smacked him on the shoulder.

"What was that for?" he exclaimed.

"This is an extremely important event that might shed light on us understanding all of the 'whys' of the universe." Zenta's frustration was evident.

"Well," Xander said as he rubbed his shoulder. "I appreciate the professionalism used to bring it to my attention."

"Sorry."

Zenta got up and walked to the lab doors.

"And where are you going?" Xander asked.

"I can't think right now in here. Like this," she said stopping in front of the doors. "It's the pressure. I've got to leave and think about this. I'm going to talk to Father about it too. I am so glad he got back last week."

"I can't believe he was gone for almost six years. It's good to have his guidance and calm demeanor around here again."

"I agree. So you can write this up any way you want for right now. I'll return for the start of my shift. If I come up with an idea, we'll discuss and amend." The lab doors opened and she was gone.

Xander rolled his chair up to his workstation and started typing.

15 – EXTRA ORDINARY

Sitting in the lab, Colonel Braaddy was at Tish's workstation next to Zenta and was reviewing her latest update on Chris' training.

"You've done a tremendous job here, Zenta. I'm very proud of this work." Braaddy glanced up from the monitor, smiling.

"Thank you, sir." If Terlokyans could blush, she would have. "I feel we're at a highly developed level with the Savior."

Braaddy looked back at the monitor. "I agree. He is just a few months past his eighth birthday, correct?"

"Yes, sir."

"From what I've read in past reports, by age three, Chris had advanced to a level of training that previous estimates said would take five years to complete. I especially like the program that uses songs to suppress Chris' conscious recognition of X13 Probes. It was the ones that had the subliminal training imbedded in them. That was tremendous foresight on your part to avoid any possible probe detection. Did you program those songs?"

"Xander and I did them together."

"That's another characteristic about you that I respect. You share credit even though I know you created them." Braaddy leaned back in his chair, put his boots up on the workstation, and clasped his hands behind his head. "Tell me some of the things that your intuition is revealing."

Zenta was excited that her superior was pleased with her work.

"Chris' personality and will are stronger than any of us had anticipated. We ceased all visual contact with probes at a little past age three. But even now I feel he can sense when probes are nearby."

"Go on." Appearing very relaxed, the normal creases in Braaddy's brow were less pronounced.

"Now at the age of eight, Chris' measured mental usage capacity is up to forty-five percent compared to the normal ten percent of a human adult. His command of Earth's mainstream languages is nearing fluency. His historical knowledge foundation of both Terlokyan and Earth civilizations is almost complete. His ability to communicate in a subconscious state in Terlokyan is astounding. When the time comes to open these knowledge bases to his conscious state, releases will occur in stages or when necessity dictates."

Braaddy put his boots down and leaned forward.

"Zenta, I must say that everything for this phase of the project is in perfect order. I am so pleased that you are heading up phase three." He got up from his chair, arched his back to get a good stretch, and then clapped his hands together. A determined smile showed his satisfaction.

"Well sir, I wouldn't have this project where it is today if I didn't have Xander, Tish, Bal, Tuu and sometimes Hajeck on my team." Zenta stood up to escort her superior to the door.

As Braaddy turned to say goodbye, Zenta saluted smartly.

"While that is proper, I would rather shake the hand of a brilliant analyst, manager, and soldier. That is, if you don't mind, Captain," the colonel said, his hand extended.

"Thank you, sir. I am thrilled to be on this project."

"You've earned this praise. Carry on." With that, he left.

Zenta stood there staring at the doors for a moment. She glanced down and sighed, then went back to her workstation.

"When are you supposed to go?" Gene asked Chris, who was standing on the picnic table with Cory.

Chris took the rope from Cory. He opened and then closed his hands to tighten his grip. Then he carefully wrapped his legs around the rope, his toes barely on the box. "I guess we're going after dinner. That's when most parent-teacher conferences happen."

With a nod to Cory, Chris said, "Okay now. Knock the box out from under me."

Cory kicked the box out from under Chris' feet and he went swinging off the picnic table.

"Yeeeeeah! This is so cool!" Chris yelled as he swung back and forth, his blond curly hair blowing every which way.

Alex and Ian were standing under the big maple tree in the middle of the Gates' backyard. They watched Chris and then peered up into the tree.

Ian shook his head. "I still can't figure out how he got that rope up there."

"I can see how he did it, "Alex said as he watched Chris swing. "I'm just surprised that he was able to do it. It had to be a million to one that he could snag a loop over the thick part of that huge branch."

Gene was now standing on the picnic table beside Cory. He leaned toward the swinging Chris and hollered, "Let me have a turn when you're done."

"Sure." Chris jumped off the rope at the high arc of the swing away from the table and landed squarely on his feet. He pulled off his long sleeve Green Bay Packers football jersey.

"Man, it's hot out here." Sweat was dripping off his chin. Down to his undershirt, he also kicked off his shoes.

"It's September. And it's been chilly the last few days," Ian taunted. "Your momma is gonna get mad if she sees you like that."

"No she won't, Ian," Chris said staring at him. "You gotta admit it's hot out here."

Ian diverted his gaze.

"Yeah," he said as he sat down and leaned against the tree. "I guess you're right. It is hot." He kicked off his shoes.

The sound of the door on the upper deck had all eyes looking up at Mrs. Gates.

Kelli leaned on the deck railing.

"Are you boys having fun?"

"Yes ma'am," came the collective reply.

"I hate to break up the great time, but Cory and Chris need to get cleaned up for dinner. We have a parent-teacher conference tonight." Kelli smiled. "Y'all can play tomorrow. Okay?"

"Okay Mrs. Gates. We'll see ya tomorrow," Alex replied. "Come on guys. I'm sure dinner's almost ready for us."

The boys said their goodbyes and the brothers went inside.

From underneath the railing of the deck, a small black bug flew out and lazily drifted toward the light blue American Motors Rambler station wagon parked in the driveway. It flew through the open window and tucked itself into a side pocket of Kelli's purse on the front seat.

"Mr. and Mrs. Gates, there's really nothing to worry about. We were just," Mr. Clark paused and shifted in his chair, "curious as to where Chris would get such visions. His drawings of spaceships and other worldly creatures are of things I've never run across in all my years in education."

Mr. Hartwell Clark appeared like he should be teaching at a prestigious university instead of serving as the Headmaster at one of the finest private academies in Virginia. His salt and pepper beard, coupled with his slightly receding hairline, gave him the appearance of an economics professor rather than that of an administrator. However, Mr. Clark was well known for his expertise in preparing high school students to succeed in college. The educational programs he designed for the school practically guaranteed that Jefferson Academy graduates would go on to higher education. College acceptance of Jefferson graduates was at 100%. With that reputation, there was a long waiting list to get in.

"Please don't get the wrong impression," said Mrs. Mullins, Jefferson Academy's art instructor, as she looked down and smoothed her skirt. "We feel that Chris is extremely talented. As a matter of practice, I've always encouraged imagination in my student's artwork." Mrs. Mullins looked up and held her hands out. "Mr. Clark pretty much summed up our thoughts. We would like to know how an eight year old could draw and paint with such flair and imagination. Has he had lessons outside of school?"

Unbeknownst to the roomful of adults, Chris' pictures also showed aspects of Terlokyan culture and language, mixed in with his own earthly experiences and awareness. His skill level at drawing is comparable to that of an artistically gifted college student.

Kelli carefully framed her response. She had been studying Mr. Clark's office during the introductions. The large bookcases behind the huge desk had caught her attention. Loaded with classic literature, science textbooks, and elegant hard bound covered books that were obviously very old, they would have to wait.

Kelli set her maroon suede purse on the floor next to her chair.

"We've known for some time that Chris has artistic talent. Many of his pictures are hung around our house. A number of friends and relatives have commented on his talent. However, Chris hasn't had any other art classes outside of school. He just likes to draw and has a vivid imagination. But I am pleased that you are noticing his talent."

Pete still appeared a bit uptight. He was leaning forward in his chair, elbows on his knees, hands extended with palms up as he began to speak. "I don't see anything unusual with a young boy drawing spaceships and rockets flying to different planets in outer space. There are television shows that have these themes." He leaned back and placed his orange and blue tie in the middle of his starched blue dress shirt. His khaki pants were slightly wrinkled from the day's work. He barely had time to eat and get ready for this meeting.

"Please Mr. Gates," Mr. Clark said and quickly turned to Mrs. Gates, "and Mrs. Gates ..." Popping up from his desk chair, he came around the side of his huge mahogany desk and sat in one of the leather wingback chairs next to Mrs. Mullins. "We are not singling Chris out." Mr. Clark leaned back and put his left leg up on his right knee; his impeccable tailored gray suit looked as if it had just been put on. "As the Headmaster of the Jefferson Academy, I have never seen as talented a child as your son, Chris."

"And it isn't just with art," Mrs. Mullins added. "Chris' test scores place him in the hundredth percentile for his age group."

"Actually," Mr. Clark creased his brow and continued, "Chris tests out at Cory's grade level, the fourth grade."

Pete and Kelli looked at each other. Her face flushed a bit.

"To be honest with you, Mr. and Mrs. Gates," Mrs. Mullins said softly, "we are having a hard time placing Chris' grade level."

The parents wore puzzled expressions.

"In other words," Mrs. Mullins caught the non-verbal cues and clarified her statement, "we can't exactly tell how smart Chris is."

"That's true." Mr. Clark was smiling now. "We have discussed Chris' special talents with all of his teachers and we felt that you both need to be involved before we make any decisions."

Mrs. Mullins and Mr. Clark were now in a one-up-man-ship with praise. It was Mrs. Mullins turn.

"Yes. Did either of you know that Chris has an understanding of algebraic principles even though he has never taken an algebra class?"

"Did you say algebra?" Kelli asked. "He's only in the third grade."

"We were just as surprised as you," Mr. Clark added. "Your son obviously needs to be challenged more."

"We've always known that Chris is extremely smart," Kelli replied. "As parents though, it's hard for us to measure it. We can only measure against his older brother and that makes me feel uncomfortable. Cory is also very bright, but the only explanation that Pete and I can come up with is that Chris is just very unique."

"We can see that too," Mr. Clark was quick to add.

"So what are you suggesting?" Pete asked while pulling gently on his collar.

"Well." Mr. Clark clasped his hands together. "Whenever we have a child that we recommend for advancement to a higher grade, and that child has an older sibling in the same grade, we consult with the parents to avoid any negative effects on the older child."

Kelli loudly cleared her throat, silencing the room. "Cory is very intelligent. We've seen his grades and he continually brings home A plus report cards."

Mrs. Mullins made a motion to say something but Kelli put her hand up.

"Please, let me finish." Kelli lowered her gaze while she gathered her thoughts. "I agree that we need to see how this could affect Cory. However, our sons are very close. They are not your typical brothers who compete with each other and get into childish arguments. They actually care for one another and encourage each other in whatever they are doing. They are inseparable."

Mrs. Mullins waited to be sure Kelli had finished.

"We realize that and we've observed them interact with each other between classes and at lunch," Mrs. Mullins began. "We've been evaluating this opportunity for Chris. His teachers are all in agreement that we must accelerate Chris' education and challenge him more or we risk losing him to boredom. It is very early in the school year so any change should be done now. To summarize, we would like to move Chris up a grade level."

The room was quiet. Pete broke the silence.

"I don't want to make a big deal about this. Chris is just an ordinary little boy, just very talented. If we present this to the boys as an opportunity to be in the same class together and be able to study together, I bet they will be more receptive to it."

"That's my thought exactly," Mr. Clark exclaimed. "However, Chris is far from ordinary. He excels at everything he does. But we do feel that both boys would greatly benefit from being in the same class together."

"Both of your sons seem to do things so effortlessly," Mrs. Mullins added.

The room was quiet again, but everyone was looking at each other as if they all wanted to speak simultaneously.

"There is one thing I would like to address with you both," Mrs. Mullins said. All attention was on her now.

"Mr. and Mrs. Gates, have you ever noticed Cory and Chris playing, hmm, how do I put this …," she paused again. "Have you seen them play harmless pranks?"

"Mrs. Mullins," Mr. Clark spoke with a hint of humor in his voice. "I don't think this is really …"

"It's fine, Mr. Clark," Pete spoke up. "We'd like to hear what Mrs. Mullins has to say."

"As you wish." Mr. Clark made a sweeping gesture with his arm and then folded his hands into his lap.

"Well, I believe your boys are jokesters in a way," Mrs. Mullins continued.

"In what way?" Pete leaned forward.

"On our stone pillars at the front of the drive to the school are the words 'The Thomas Jefferson Academy' which are chiseled into the stone."

"We've seen that," Pete said as he glanced at Kelli who was smiling. "Please continue."

"On the second or third day of this school year, someone used clay and molded the chiseled letters to read something else."

"What was it?" Kelli asked and appeared to be stifling a laugh.

"The boys, I mean, someone had used stone colored clay and altered the letters to say 'The Tom and Jerry Academy'."

Kelli snickered and covered her mouth.

"Excuse me. Sorry. Did you say 'The Tom and Jerry Academy'?" Kelli asked the question while again having to cover her mouth, this time with the back of her hand.

Mr. Clark coughed loudly sounding as if he was trying to mask a laugh.

"I dare say I see nothing humorous about this." Mrs. Mullins was staring at Mr. Clark who was trying to look serious but without much success.

Upon seeing the Headmaster's difficulty in suppressing a smile, Kelli struggled even more to hide her own.

Pete appeared totally lost in this conversation as he looked from Mrs. Mullins' serious face to the expressions worn by his wife and Mr. Clark.

"Mrs. Mullins." Mr. Clark had regained his composure. "I don't think that this harmless incident is anything to concern the Gates family with."

"Are you saying my sons did this?" Pete asked.

"No, we are not," Mr. Clark quickly replied.

"Well," Mrs. Mullins huffed. "This one prank may seem harmless, but I still am trying to get to the bottom of who put the dissected frog in the second floor water fountain near the lockers." Her nose rose a few inches.

"I believe," Mr. Clark paused while trying to regain a serious composure. "I really believe that these incidents have no relevance on what we are here to discuss tonight."

"I know, sir. I was just trying to get to the…," Mrs. Mullins stopped when she saw the stern expression on Mr. Clark's face. "Well, I guess we'll find out someday. It's not important now." Again she had her sweet look and folded her hands in her lap.

"Well, then, where were we?" The Headmaster was trying to steer the conversation back to Chris' advancement.

Kelli spoke first. "I think that my husband and I should be the ones to tell the boys about this grade change. I feel we can present it in a positive light."

"We agree," Mr. Clark was beaming, "and the Jefferson Academy will do anything to help you with this transition. Both of your boys are model students as far as I am concerned. Just let us know what you need and I will personally see that it happens."

After agreeing that Kelli would inform Mrs. Mullins Monday morning of the outcome of their conversation with the boys, Pete and Kelli left the office. They headed down to Cory's classroom where they spent the next half hour hearing what an outstanding student Cory was. Afterwards, they found Cory and Chris in the gym with the other children of parents who were in conferences.

"Cory. Chris. Let's go," said Pete. "I know we ate a fast dinner so let's head home and have some of Momma's delicious apple pie."

"All right," the boys said in unison as they ran out the door.

16 – TRAINING HERE AND THERE

The ride home from the parent-teacher conference was quiet.

"So, Mom and Dad," Chris said, breaking the silence. "Are you gonna tell us how your teacher meetings went?"

"Well …" Kelli started to respond but stopped. She turned slightly in her seat so she was facing more toward Pete and could also see the boys. She continued, "Well, first we met with your headmaster, Mr. Clark, and your art teacher, Mrs. Mullins, Chris. The first thing they wanted to know was where you got all of your artistic talent."

Pete jumped in quickly, "That's right. They think you are a very talented budding artist, Chris."

"They really like your space drawings and paintings," Kelli said excitedly.

Chris was grinning now. "They're fun to do."

"We get to use our imagination a lot," Cory stated. "I like drawing, too, but I also like looking at Chris' stuff."

"Well, I like looking at your drawings," Chris said.

"We also met with your teachers, Cory," Pete continued.

"Yes we did," Kelli added. "And we are so pleased to hear what an outstanding student you are."

"Yeah." Cory was smiling. "I know I'm great."

Chris leaned over and playfully punched him in the shoulder."

"Well …," Kelli started slowly, glancing at Pete for approval. Seeing him give a slight nod, she smoothed her skirt and shifted her purse on the seat, obviously buying time to find the right words.

"Your father and I talked at length with the Headmaster, Mr. Clark, and the art teacher, Mrs. Mullins. While they said that both of you boys are very good students and really smart, all of the teachers involved with each of you feel that you two should be in the same class."

"Do you mean that Chris will be in my class?" Cory asked.

Kelli looked worried for a second. "Yes, dear. That's a possibility."

"I knew it!" exclaimed Cory. "This is so neat. Right, Chris?"

"It sure is." Chris started bouncing in his seat. "Momma, is this for real? Can we be in the same class?"

Kelli was taken aback by this. She fully expected Cory to be somewhat upset. "Why of course it's for real." She was again staring at Pete in amazement.

Pete took the lead.

"Boys, the teachers feel that Chris' artwork and math skills are good enough for him to be in the fourth grade."

Chris and Cory were both bouncing up and down in their seats now, squealing like the little kids they were. Pete kept peering into his rear view mirror watching his sons, astonished at the good fortune of total acceptance by the boys.

"Who could've guessed this?" Pete said to Kelli and shrugged his shoulders.

Kelli faced Cory. "Sweetie, calm down a second. What did you mean when you said 'I knew it' right after we told you what Chris' teachers said?"

"Well, Chris and I have been talking about how it would be really neat if we could be in the same grade. Since it would be dumb for me to go backward, we thought it would be better if he went up to my grade." Cory crossed his arms in front of his chest looking very smug.

Kelli just stared at him, amazed at how easy this was going.

"And when did you boys cook up this idea?" Kelli's asked playfully. She saw a big fat grin on Pete's face.

"Last year," Cory stated proudly with his chest puffed out.

Chris was silent, staring out the window as the car crossed the river on the way to Hilton Mills. He was listening, but wanted Cory to do all the talking and take all the credit. Besides, that old familiar feeling that he was being watched had returned.

"So, you boys have been planning this for some time?" Pete asked.

"Yes, sir. Are you mad at us? All we did was make sure that Chris learned everything he needed to move up. He was studying my math books a lot and I was also teaching him history."

"No, we aren't upset with you at all," Pete said as he swung the car into the driveway.

"Your father's right. Actually, we are proud of you both," Kelli said while noticing Chris' silent demeanor.

"Chris, sweetie, is everything all right? You haven't said much since we left school. We are not upset with you. Are you worried about that?"

"No, momma. I'm just tired, I guess."

As the car pulled up to the front of the house, Chris asked, "Can I go inside now? Tomorrow might be my last day in the third grade and it feels weird."

"Of course you can go in." Kelli reached over the seat and brushed Chris' hair off his forehead. We'll come back to your room in a little while to talk about tomorrow. Okay?"

"Yes, ma'am."

"You boys might want to hit the sack a little early tonight," Pete reminded them. “The fall season of Little League starts tomorrow after school. Playing this fall will be good for both of you. It’ll increase your chances of being drafted into the upper league next spring.”

“Yes, sir.” As soon as the words were out, both boys had their doors open and disappeared into the house.

Pete let out a sigh. “Well, that went easier than I thought. Can you believe that these boys had this planned? “

“Not really. Cory was right though,” Kelli said as she stared out the window, not making any effort to get out of the car. “The boys knew that the only way for them to be in the same class was for Chris to move up. They really thought this thing through; and all of this from an eight and nine year old.” She yawned and opened her door but hesitated. “I do want to check with Cory tomorrow to see if he is still as excited about this change as he was tonight.”

“That’s a good idea. Let’s see how the weekend fairs and keep an eye on how the boys are feeling,” Pete said as he closed the car door and headed up the walk with his arm around Kelli.

As their parents busied themselves in the kitchen fixing plates of apple pie, the boys were in Cory’s room getting their baseball gear ready.

“Is Ivan playing this fall? I know Alex, Gene, and Jay are,” Chris asked while smearing some mink oil on his glove.

“He said he was,” Cory replied as he held up his new bat. “Just look at this thing. I’m gonna knock some home runs out of the park.”

“Do like Dad says and just hit the ball.”

“No joke. I will.” Cory held the bat down. “Do you think we’ll get drafted next spring?”

Chris didn’t say anything. He kept his head down and continued rubbing the mink oil into his glove.

“Well?” Cory dropped his bat to the floor and stood there with his arms crossed. “You know something, don’t you?

Chris said nothing.

“Come on, Chris. We’re not supposed to keep stuff from each other.”

“Well, I’m gonna make it and I’m pretty sure you and Alex will too.” Chris set his glove down and looked up at Cory. “But I’m not getting a good feeling about the others.” He picked his glove up and held it in his lap.

“So what are we gonna do? We can’t tell them.” Cory sat down cross legged next to Chris.

Chris was quiet again.

“I think we are going to have to help them practice,” he answered.

"Like how?"

"You know. Work on fielding, catching pop flies, hitting, and stuff like that."

"How are we gonna help them?" Cory asked. "We're still learning."

"Sure we are." Chris started rubbing the oil into his glove again. "But this fall is when you and I are really going to improve. And practice always helps. We can make it like spring training."

"Ya got a good feeling on that?" Cory asked as he picked his bat up.

"Yep. We just gotta put the extra time in after school and we'll do great. We need to make sure the other guys are with us on this," Chris added as he put his glove down and watched his brother swinging his bat.

"I'm not sure how you always seem to know things," Cory said as he concentrated on his swing. "But you somehow do. Hey, are we gonna be pro baseball players?"

"I don't know. I've never thought about it."

"Are we gonna be rich? You had to have wondered about that."

"Not really."

Cory stopped swinging his bat and looked slightly exasperated.

"Well, have you thought anything about what we're gonna be like when we grow up?"

"I think I'm going to run for president or something like that."

"You're joking."

Chris was staring at his glove, not saying anything.

"I guess you're not joking." Cory started swinging his bat again.

"Cory?"

"What?"

Chris stopped working on his glove.

"I know we planned on this grade thing and all, but are you really okay with me moving up in school?"

"Sure." Cory stopped swinging his bat and looked at his little brother. "What the heck are you asking that for? We wanted this to happen. Right?"

"I know we did. But …"

"Stop it," Cory said as he cut Chris off in mid-sentence and sat down in front of him. "I remember you warning me about things when we first talked about doing this. You told me people might say that you're smarter than me. But we both know that we planned this and wanted it to happen."

"Yeah I remember. It's so we can do more things together and help each other. Remember that part?" Chris said as he looked at his brother with the utmost respect.

"I know that, man. As you said, we are always going to be there for each other. That's what Bros do."

"You got that right," Chris said as he stuck his hand out. Cory grabbed Chris' hand in the secret handshake. The same handshake that had become the symbol of the close friendships all the neighborhood boys had formed.

Watching from a probe that was attached to a curtain rod in Cory's room, Zenta turned up the volume on her speaker in case the boys followed up their conversation with anything more important.

"Let's get ready, Zenta," Xander said as he stood up from his desk and stretched his arms over his head. "We are supposed to report to Intervention Team training after Tish gets here to relieve us. And that should be any minute now."

"Doesn't it amaze you at all that Chris can manipulate any situation, but he does it without malice? His motive is always a higher good."

"Who's higher good? How is his grade advancement helping anybody but himself and the Savior Project?" Xander asked as he sat back down.

"So far his intuition has led him to make decisions that have not had any adverse effect upon others. And yes," Zenta's voice was rising, "all of this does help our mission, but Chris doesn't know that."

"All right now. Don't get so upset," Xander replied as he held his hands up in mock surrender. "Let's get ready to hand this over to Tish."

At that moment, the lab doors opened and Tish strolled in smiling.

"So how are my favorite team members?"

"What's got you so happy?" Zenta asked as she signed off from her session and spun her chair around.

Tish plunked down at the desk to the left of Zenta and began logging on to the system.

"Let's just say things are working in my favor." She looked at Zenta and Xander and continued, "Now don't ask me anything more about my mood because I'm not saying a word." She brushed a strand of hair off her forehead. "Just be happy for me." She smiled and turned back to her monitor.

Zenta looked at Xander and shrugged her shoulders.

"You just came from the Intervention Team training, right?" Xander changed the subject.

"Yes. Why?"

"I was wondering why they want us to take the training. I mean after all, we would have to be on base here directing any intervention that occurred. Besides, it's Jzet's team that would be on the ground, right? We're just the backups in case something happens to them."

Not looking up from her monitor, Tish explained what went on in training.

"Colonel Braaddy told us today that his new strategy was to have all available hands do more intervention training in case we have multiple scenarios that require us to insert teams." Tish stopped typing and faced the others. "Braaddy said that if we had a major intervention occur which required both of Jzet's teams, and another situation arose, we would need the ability to send out additional personnel. This training also includes pilots and ground teams so I think it's a good idea."

"Well, if Tish thinks it's a good idea," Xander said with a hint of sarcasm, "I guess we should all go along with it."

"That's not quite fair," Zenta quickly responded in support of her friend. "I agree with her."

"Sorry. I was joking." Xander held hands up again. "Zenta, let's go. We've got to be on time."

"Right." Zenta stood up. "Tish, is Hajeck scheduled to come in and review reports on this shift with you?"

"Why, yes he is," Tish replied cheerfully.

The change in Tish's tone was evident, but Zenta did not inquire as to why even though it was obvious. She headed to the door where Xander was already waiting.

"All right then." She winked at Xander. "We will see you later on."

The lab doors swished shut behind them.

While walking down the hall to the Itran, Zenta noticed that Xander's expression had changed. His cheerful banter was gone, his head hung low with his shoulders slouching as he walked.

"Everything all right?" she inquired.

"Yeah, sure," he said in a monotone voice. "Let's just get down to training."

17 – CONVERSATIONS WITH A BUG

Colonel Braaddy closed the door to the huge training center to lower the noise level coming from the hanger.

"All right," he began. "Everyone has been through intervention training. And I'm sure the time we've all spent aboard Intervessels has created many bonding opportunities."

"Not to mention things none of us wanted to know about other's personal hygiene," Xander added with muffled voice, his hand loosely covering his mouth.

The entire group laughed at that, even Braaddy. Everybody except Jzet who glared at Xander.

Braaddy saw this and quickly added, "Very good, Xander. He brings up a good point. Even though the Intervessel travels quickly from here to Earth, there have been instances where the two crew members had to stay on board the ship until they could discreetly exit to one of our safe sites."

This statement brought about a few coughs and snickers.

"Yeah Tuu," somebody mumbled loud enough for most everyone to hear. "Use soap next time."

"Hey," Tuu spoke up over the coughs and snorts. "We got called out in a hurry since there already was a team on the ground and command thought another was needed. I didn't have a lot of time to get ready." He examined everybody's expressions seeking support. "Don't you all remember that?"

"I remember gagging," Maczee said while laughing.

"That's enough for right now, everyone." He moved to the console next to the wall with the large viewing screen. He gestured to the chairs facing it.

"Everyone take a seat. We are almost finished with our yearly review so pay attention. I want to review the emergency bailout procedures one more time."

As everyone moved into the seats next to the console and sat down, General Jhall and Colonel Prahash, the Chief Health Officer, remained right where they had been observing the training.

"Have you ever been in one of these, Colonel?" Jhall asked while pointing to an Intervessel that was sitting in the middle of the training floor. The ship was in a hover state, floating as if on a cushion of air.

"No, I haven't, General," Prahash responded. "I prefer to let you military types perform your duties and I perform mine." He walked toward the ship. "But I am curious about it. Would you show it to me please?"

Jhall headed there walking beside Prahash.

"Tell me Colonel, have you found any issues with the crews and their ability to handle extended stays aboard these fully loaded vessels?"

"No, sir. This group, including the secondary backups, is in excellent condition. I would recommend any of them for a mission."

"Good," Jhall said as he opened the sliding side door of the Intervessel. "I've got a secondary backup who has been pestering me to let her go on a real deployment. I've explained to her that a deployment doesn't mean there will be an intervention."

Prahash stepped up into the ship. A slight smile canvassed his face as he said, "Let me guess; Lieutenant Tish."

"Very good, Colonel." Jhall was now in the ship standing beside Prahash. "How did you know?"

"She has been asking me to intercede on her behalf to be chosen for a deployment."

Jhall shook his head. "I can't imagine wanting to go and sit around for a week waiting for something to happen. But I know we've got to have a team on the ground at all times." He opened an overhead storage unit. "Who is scheduled to return this week?"

"Dlocto and Bal," Prahash replied as he poked around inside of the medical supply cabinet. "I overheard crew members talking about it. Do you know who goes out next?"

"Tuu and Maczee." Inspecting supplies, Jhall revealed what he was thinking, "The week after that we have Jzet and Aiko scheduled. I'm thinking that we should let Tish take Aiko's spot on this mission. It'll show the regulars that we have faith in the secondary units as well. How do you feel about that?"

"I agree."

"There is one thing that concerns me," Jhall said as he closed the storage unit's door. "The Savior is now fifteen years old. According to Colonel Braaddy, his size and strength are that of an adult."

"That is correct, sir." Prahash watched as the general inspected another compartment. "In his last health assessment we performed two months ago, the Savior was well beyond our planned expectations in both physical attributes and capabilities along with mental competences and abilities. His IQ is off the charts."

"That really wasn't any of our doing now was it?"

"No. The IQ issue is something we can't explain. He's just one of a kind." Prahash sat on one of the bunks feeling the softness of the mattress with his hands.

"Has he exhibited any of the skills associated with mind control and power?" Jhall asked.

"Not that we have observed. But his brain wave patterns show he has the capabilities." Prahash replied as he stretched out on the bunk. "He has exhibited a strong tendency to influence decisions of others. But he is not aware that he is using a very limited form of mind control."

Jhall closed the compartment he had been inspecting, and sat on the opposite bunk from Prahash.

"From the reports I have read, we have had a relatively good seven years of training since the Savior skipped a grade in his schooling at age seven. He's adapted well to being with an older age group and exhibited all of the leadership traits we had hoped for." Jhall paused for a moment. "What concerns me is that he might use his extraordinary skills in a pressured or stressful situation."

"I had that concern at one time," Prahash said as he swung his legs over the side of the bunk and sat upright. "Captain Zenta's suppression program is controlling the conscious state so that none of these extraordinary skills or abilities rises to the surface." Prahash leaned forward with his hands clasped in his lap. "When the Savior was 13 years old, there was an incident in a sporting event he was participating in. It happened in a baseball sport game."

Jhall smiled and said, "Earthlings refer to it as a baseball game. It's actually an interesting event to watch from a strategy perspective."

"I find it very boring. Anyway, he was playing the position of shortstop and another boy at the home base hit the ball on the ground near where the Savior was standing. He dove toward the place where he would be closest to the projected path of the ball. While diving, he stretched his arm out to catch it in the glove. By my calculations, it should not have been possible for him to reach the ball."

"What happened? Did he catch it?" Jhall asked.

"As the Savior was leaping toward the ball, its path changed slightly, as if bending toward his glove. He did catch it, then sprung to his feet and threw it to one of his teammates."

"Did anyone notice the change in path?"

"One of his other teammates exclaimed how lucky the Savior had been to make the catch. It appeared that all of the other participants attributed the change in the ball's path to something called a 'lucky bounce.' However, upon replaying the video from an X13 probe, it was clear the ball changed path while in the air."

"But no one saw this change actually happen, did they?" the general quickly asked.

"It was too fast for an Earthling eye to observe, and the ball was traveling very close to the ground. It was hit very hard by the boy with the bat."

"Did Chris exhibit any indication that he changed the ball's path?"

"None. But it was obvious that he did it by willing the ball to him. We concluded that he had no idea that he had actually changed the ball's path."

"That's good." Jhall leaned forward, elbows on knees. "I do have another concern and that is his physical power. That brings us to Lieutenant Tish being on an active intervention mission. Let's say we had to subdue the Savior. Would his outstanding 'fight versus flight' instincts overpower our team should he choose fight?"

"As we observed in the training today, a whole section was dedicated to preparation for any eventuality such as the one you just described. All team members carry Glaze capsules attached to the back of their right hand which can be instantly activated. The teams are prepared for such a situation."

"Good." Jhall appeared satisfied. "Let's inform the lieutenant of our decision and hope she will have a non-eventful mission. We'll send her two weeks from now."

Those two weeks flew by fast as the SP Lab was churning with activity. The development team was in crisis mode.

Zenta spoke to Xander without taking her eyes off her monitor.

"It's just our luck to have a situation happen on Tish's first intervention mission."

"Let's not worry about it," Xander replied while watching a different probe's view monitoring Chris' actions. "Let's just follow procedure and do our jobs. We need to free that probe."

"So Chris, you've been really bummed for over a week now. You're fifteen, man. Why are you acting like you're fifty? You look like you've got the weight of the world on your shoulders," Ian said, trying to get Chris to talk as he walked into the room.

Sitting in an orange beanbag chair in the middle of Alex's room, Chris hadn't even taken off his blue jean jacket. His troubled expression cast a shadow on the mood.

Ian dropped down on the couch against the side wall under the Dogs Playing Poker picture. He knew how to get information out of Chris.

"When did you get here to Alex's?" Ian began his questioning.

"I guess about ten minutes before you. Shoot, man. We both rode home with Cory. You know it couldn't have been that long," Chris said irritably.

"Calm down, killer. I'm just trying to talk." Ian continued, "You know we are pretty lucky to have this place to hang out. Alex's parents are the coolest. That's not to say our families aren't cool either."

"Yeah, I know. This really is like a second home." Chris lightened up some.

"That's for sure." Ian was staring at Chris, waiting for him to respond. "Is something bugging you?"

Chris chose his words carefully as he considered the irony of Ian's question.

"I've just been under a lot of stress recently. No big deal," he said as he turned his palm over slightly to check on the little mechanical bug taped tightly to the inside of his hand. He paused, saying nothing for a minute then continued, "Besides, who gives a rip anyway? You've always got your head wrapped around Shannon. I'm surprised you had time to come here today." Chris finally took off his jacket and threw it in the corner of the room.

"Don't give me that crap," Ian quickly replied. "You're forever hanging with Cindy." He let the quiet mellow his statement. "Man, talk about the kettle calling the kitchen black, or whatever that saying is." They laughed at Ian's total screw-up of an old adage.

"You are right. I haven't been hanging with you guys for a while," said Chris. "Being a sophomore is so different."

Ian chuckled. "You're making it hard. Just do your homework, pay attention, and it'll all work out."

Chris smiled half-heartedly and said, "Yeah I guess. Where's the fun in that?"

Ian didn't respond so Chris dropped his smile.

"I still think something is up, and you might as well come clean," Ian said. "None of us have ever kept anything from each other." Ian raised an eyebrow and leaned forward in his chair waiting for Chris to respond.

"I gotta go to the can." Chris stood up and walked out of the room heading for the stairs to the upstairs bathroom.

"You'd better tell me when you get back," Ian shouted. He sat there in the dim light for a minute, then got up, went through the rec room, and out the door to the small slate patio. He pulled out a cigarette and lit it. Inhaling deeply, he stared blankly at the boxwoods, lost in thought. Ian had seen a little black object the size of a bullet fall on the floor and roll under Chris' desk at school yesterday. It was the size of a horsefly and looked like one he had seen flying around Chris' house a year or so ago. When this thing hit the floor, it actually started to move on its own instead of just rolling. Chris had bent down and snatched it up so fast that Ian thought it weird.

"That's got to be what's bothering him," Ian said out loud. He went inside, sat on the couch, and put his feet up on a pile of motocross magazines that were on the plywood coffee table.

Chris came shuffling into the room and silently plunked down on the same beanbag chair.

"Fess up man." Ian was looking right at Chris.

The statement got Chris' attention. He had been trying to figure out if he should tell Ian about everything. As he rubbed the mechanical bug taped to his palm, he wondered again about Ian's choice of the word 'bugging'.

Chris had recently been noticing a buzzing noise around the house and saw one flying in such a straight pattern that he thought it unusual. Two days ago he was raking leaves in the backyard and heard one. He looked up in time and snatched it out of the air. He had some distant memory of holding one of these things but couldn't remember any details. He planned to keep this one close. When it was in his hand, it didn't try to get away.

"I'm really okay," Chris said blandly. "I've just got a lot going on." He was sure Ian would never believe him, even if he explained absolutely everything.

He's got to know something is up, Chris thought as he got up from his seat. *I am acting strange, I guess.*

Chris saw Ian gently pat his coat pocket and give a sly grin.

"What are you smiling about?"

Ian said nothing. He pulled a picture out of his pocket that he had drawn. It was a sketch of the small black object Ian had seen at school. He held the picture in his hand, not showing it to Chris.

"Why don't you set a spell?" Ian said with that last word coming out in his southern twang.

It always amused Chris when Ian showed his roots. But he didn't give his familiar grin this time.

"Look," Chris began. "I really have something important to tell you, but I don't think you'll believe me." He sat down and glanced at Ian, trying to gauge a reaction.

Ian then said, "Well, I've got something to tell you too. And it's all about you."

"What?" Chris paused to let his frustration pass. "What the hell kind of response is that? You've been asking me about stuff because you can tell I'm stressed out. You know something has been bothering me." He waited for Ian to say something but Ian just sat there with a Cheshire cat grin so Chris started questioning him.

"Is this about Cindy? My motorcycle? Did you do something to my motorcycle?"

Ian finally responded, "Hell no. It's nothing like that. Anyway, if what you've got to say is so important, you go first."

Chris stared at Ian like he thought he was nuts. "No way, man. I ain't telling you nothing till you come clean first. Did Sterling make something up about me again? I bet he's running around telling people that I'm doing drugs or something like that. He probably said I stole the band's candy bars. You know the hall monitors tried to pin that one on Cory and me."

"Are you serious?"

"I'm very serious. Do you know who did it?" Chris said thrusting his index finger at Ian.

"Alex and I never told you who heisted the candy bars, did we? We didn't know that the 'nerds' tried to pin it on you and Cory."

"Come on now. I can tell you did it." Chris countered. "Tell me. Cory and I were taken up to the principal's office and they said they had proof that we did it. Who was with you? Did you take them?"

Ian had his head down and was obviously trying to suppress a smile. Then he looked up at Chris and asked, "Do you wanna buy a candy bar?" He started laughing as Chris jumped on him and wrestled him to the floor.

"Come on man." Ian managed to say a few words as Chris tried to pin him. "We didn't know they were eyeing you guys."

"You should have told us," Chris said as he released his hold on Ian. "We're never supposed to keep stuff from each other. You oughta give us some of that candy."

"Don't worry, we will." Ian was still laughing. "Alex didn't want to tell you figuring that you'd be mad or something."

"I can't believe you guys did that," Chris tried to sound angry but realized that Alex and Ian hadn't intended for Cory and him to get involved. "I guess what ticks me off is that you were going to let us hang out there with all those nerds saying we did the heist."

"Honestly, we didn't know. Besides, they didn't have anything on you guys so it never crossed my mind. Sorry about that. We cool now?"

"We're cool. You guys still shouldn't have stolen those things."

Chris thought that maybe he should wait to tell Ian about the mechanical bug. Today just wasn't the right time. Besides, he was in a better mood now and knew he'd be eating some free candy momentarily.

Right then, the sound of the outer door to the basement rec room slammed shut catching their attention.

"Yo, yo, yo, boys." Alex's loud greeting filled the air. He poked his head around the corner and peered into his room saying, "So where're the girls?"

"Are you nuts?" was Ian's quick reply. "It's Thursday and we all have school tomorrow.

"That never stopped us before." Alex plopped himself down on one of the beanbag chairs.

"I don't know about you guys, but I got a ton of homework and dinner will be ready in about a half hour," Chris said as he got up. "Besides, what would y'all's girlfriends say?"

"He's got a point," Ian chimed in.

Alex kicked his shoes off, propped his feet up on the coffee table and put his hands behind his head.

"My Patti wouldn't say squat. You boys could use a few lessons on who's the boss."

"Crap." Ian got up from his seat and feigned a bored expression. "Here comes another lecture from the almighty Greek."

"I think I'm gonna duck out on this one," Chris added as he headed out the door. "See you boys tomorrow."

Alex's voice resonated over his shoulder droning on about ways to handle relationships with women. Chris glanced back and noticed Ian didn't make it out of the room with him so he kept going out the rec room door and onto the patio. A chill in the fall air forced a quick donning of his coat.

Walking across the street to his house, Chris decided it was time to find out what made this mechanical bug tick. A faint memory surfaced of him catching one as a toddler.

It must not have hurt me otherwise I'd have scars on my hands.

The one he had just caught had chewed, sawed, or cut its way out of any container he put it in, including a lead box. That's why he kept this one duct taped to the inside of his hand. He took one last look at his taped palm then bounded up the steps to the front door of the house and went in to get ready for dinner.

After the family meal was done, the table cleared with the dishes in the dishwasher, Chris claimed a heavy homework load and shut himself in his room. Planted in the leather rolling chair with the desk lamp on, he peeled back the duct tape on his palm.

"I'm keeping a hand on you at all times," Chris whispered out loud.

A knock at the door stopped the unwrapping. "What?" He re-secured the tape on his palm.

"Don't 'what' me. This is your mother." Kelli opened the door carrying a folded stack of laundry. "You could get your own laundry off the dryer you know." She crossed the room and set the stack on top of his dresser.

"Sorry, Mom. I'll get them next time."

"I thought you said you had a pile of homework? Don't stay up late working on it. Cory's homework is almost done. Try to get everything wrapped up so you can get to bed at a decent hour. Okay, sweetie?" Kelli said as she headed out the door.

"Sure, Mom. I've got to go and get something outta Cory's car."

Chris passed her in the hallway, was out of the kitchen and on the porch in a flash. He opened the screen door to the driveway, letting it slam behind him. Opening the passenger side door, he reached under the seat and grabbed an old beat up flashlight.

That should do the trick, he thought. *Uh oh, forgot the duct tape. There's some in here somewhere.*

He searched in the glove compartment and sure enough, Cory had a roll. Chris grabbed it and headed to the patio off the back of the porch. Hitting the light switch beside the door to the kitchen on his way through the screened in porch, the glow from the outside light on the side of the house lit up the round metal table on the patio. Chris sat in one of the chairs, turned on the flashlight, and set it down facing the center of the table. He began unwrapping the duct tape from his hand.

Ahh, here you are.

Chris held the black bug in his fingers now, observing it from different angles.

It feels like it's made of steel. Kinda looks like a bullet with a little bit of a bulge in the shell end instead of being flat.

He set the bug on the table with one hand ready to grab it in case it moved. He held the flashlight with his other hand. As Chris leaned closer to study it, four little legs popped out of the bottom of the device, thrusting it upward so that it stood with its rounded bullet end, or its eye, facing him. He jumped backward in his chair, almost dropping the flashlight. "What the ... ," Chris said out loud. He reached out and cupped his hand around it.

"Calm yourself and listen to me."

Chris heard these words, but there was no sound. They were in his head and the words were coming from the bug.

"What? Are you talking to me?" Chris said out loud.

"Yes, I am talking to you. Reach into your deepest memories and remember me from your early childhood."

The bug stopped talking while Chris' faint memory became clearer now. Suddenly he remembered everything. He caught one when he was in his playpen. And this was the thing that talked to him when he was a baby.

"You visited me all the time and taught me many things," he said out loud. "Your name is Zenta." Chris leaned forward in his chair with a stunned look on his face. "I haven't thought of you in ages. You're a probe. Why did you wait so long to reveal yourself to me?"

"I had to talk to you because I know it is your objective to keep me. That cannot be allowed. I am here to watch over you, to train you, and to prepare you for a great mission. You will not be permitted to contain me nor will you be permitted to remember any of this."

"Holy cow. I can't believe you can talk. You aren't really talking, but I can hear you in my head. This is so cool. And how do you suppose I'm just going to forget about all of this?"

"You have always trusted me. You must trust me now. This will not hurt."

"What do you mean this won't hurt? What are you planning on ..."

Chris felt strong hands grab him from behind.

"Hey!" He tried to break free of the grip. Whoever was behind his chair had their arms around him in a bear hug, holding him tightly against the back of the chair.

Chris was about to shout out when he caught a glimpse of a figure dressed in black just to his right. A gloved hand quickly covered his mouth and a hand held his head. Chris started breathing heavily through his nose, his heart pumping wildly. Attempts at raising his arms and standing up both failed. The figure to his right was staring right at him but Chris couldn't see a face. The grip around him tightened as he felt himself lifted off the ground, chair included. His mouth remained covered and a hand still pressed his head into the chest of the other figure.

Chris started to panic. Sweat was soaking his shirt as he struggled. The death grip around him made it difficult to breath. He tried to yell, but all he produced was some muffled sounds against the glove.

A female voice from the right side attacker was speaking something other than English. Chris realized he understood everything being spoken.

"Jzet, the capsule is ready to administer," she had said.

"Do it."

With his eyes now adjusted to the light, Chris could make out skin tight black clothing on what was definitely a female. Her head was shrouded in a black hood with a slits to see through. The light from the porch reflected off of piercing green eyes that bore right through him. The female kept one hand firmly on Chris' mouth pushing his head harder into the chest of the other figure. Then she snapped some kind of tube under Chris' nose with her other hand. A sweet aroma traveled up his nostrils. His vision began to blur, his head felt real light, and then everything went black.

Jzet set Chris and the chair down on the patio. He gently leaned him forward while Tish carefully laid his head on the table. They ran off into the woods toward the creek and all was quiet.

Ten minutes passed when the door from the kitchen opened.

"Chris! What are you doing out here?" Cory stepped off the porch and walked over to Chris.

"Hey. Dude. Chris. Wake up, man." Cory pushed on Chris' shoulder. "Get up. What the heck are you doing sitting out here? Are you drinking?" He pushed him again. "And what's with the flashlight and duct tape? You gonna go kidnap someone? Where's your coat? It's chilly out here."

Chris raised his head. His mind felt as if it was in a fog. He opened his eyes and everything was blurry. He stared at the table as he regained his focus. A roll of tape was there and a flashlight illuminated an empty table.

"I asked you what are you doing out here?" Cory playfully smacked Chris on his head.

"I dunno man. I guess I was just, uh, taking this stuff out to your car and sat here to think. I must have nodded off."

I really did nod off, Chris thought. He looked at the tape and light and wondered why he had them out there.

"I didn't realize I was so tired."

"Well get your butt up and get in the house. Mom's been asking where you are. Get to bed, man. Tomorrow's another day."

As Chris stood up, he said, "Yeah, tomorrow's another day. Crap. I didn't do all my homework. And wow, why are my arms and shoulders so sore? I feel like I've been wrestling or something."

18 – ALIENS EVERYWHERE

Bam!

The door leading into the kitchen from the screened porch slammed shut as Chris bounded into the kitchen. After dumping his backpack on the floor and throwing his coat on the barstool at the end of the island, he looked at the fridge then toward the pantry. With hunger in his eyes, he immediately went and opened the pantry door.

"Chris, how many times have I told you not to slam the screen door?" Kelli said from the dining room where she was folding towels.

"A lot. Hi Mom, and sorry 'bout that."

"Please try and remember. You're fifteen years old now. You know better than that." She finished folding the last bath towel. "How was your day?" She asked as she walked into the kitchen with a handful of clean dish towels. Her tone had softened.

"Okay." As soon as the word had left his mouth, three oatmeal cookies filled the void.

Without looking and using a mother's intuition, Kelli told Chris, "Don't ruin your appetite for dinner." She finished putting the towels in one of the drawers and turned to watch her youngest son stuff another cookie in his mouth as he poured himself a glass of milk.

"I wond ma," replied a mouth full of cookies as the milk glass was raised and the white liquid disappeared into a teenage bottomless pit. Chris set the glass in the sink.

"Rinse that and put it in the dishwasher," Kelli reminded him. "Don't leave it for me."

"Yes, Mother," came the monotone reply that all teenagers used to pacify a parent. "I gotta go call Cindy now."

"Where's your brother?"

"Doing something to his car." Chris' voice trailed off as he headed down the hall grabbing the phone off the small bookshelf then kicking the cord along the carpet so it would stretch down to his room.

"Don't stay on there too long," Kelli hollered down the hall. "Your father should be calling sometime soon."

A monotone 'Yes, Mother,' was faintly detected by Kelli.

In one swift leaping movement, Chris landed on his bed on his back while still holding the phone. He reached behind him and pulled his pillow up under his head as his other hand picked up the receiver. Holding the beige princess style phone in his hand, he used his index finger to punch in Cindy's number. It was busy.

Zenta adjusted the probe that was sitting on top of the curtain next to Chris' bed. She was trying to see the number he was dialing.

"He's calling Cindy," Zenta said to Tish as she maneuvered the probe a few inches down the side of the curtain.

"You'd better tuck that probe behind the sheet," Tish said.

"It's a curtain."

"I know that." Tish shifted in her seat to get closer to her monitor. "Did you see how much Chris ate when he got home from school?"

"He eats all the time and keeps growing taller. It wasn't that long ago that he was in elementary school."

"You're right. What's that saying they have on Earth? It's something like 'time is flying when you are having fun' or close to that."

"That sounds similar to it but might… wait." Zenta put her hand up. "Listen," she said while turning up the volume on her speakers. "I think Cindy answered the phone."

"Hello?" Cindy's soft voice was barely a whisper.

"Hey there, baby doll."

"Well, I thought you'd never call." The soft tone was replaced by scorn.

"Geez. Give me a break. I just got home from school."

"Yeah, sure. You and Cory got home then you filled your face before you called me," she said jokingly.

"Well, I was hungry."

"You're always hungry."

Right then, Cory came into the room.

"Are ya gonna say it?" Cory whispered.

Chris put his finger to his lips and mouthed the words, "I don't know."

"Is someone in the room with you?" Cindy asked. "You stopped talking."

"Cory came in to get something," Chris said while pointing to the door urging his brother to leave. Cory stood still with a smile on his face. "Hang on a second. He's trying to ask me something." Chris covered the mouthpiece with his hand.

"I don't feel right doing this," Chris said to Cory while shaking his head.

"Come on, man. You said you could convince anyone of anything and you took the dare."

"But I didn't know y'all would pick something like this. Gene is not even here to make sure I do it."

"I told him I'd watch ya. Hurry up now and get on with it."

"Well, get outta here for a few minutes then," Chris said waving Cory toward the door.

Cory left as Chris adjusted the pillow under his head and kicked off his tennis shoes. He uncovered the phone and began to speak.

"Sorry about that."

"Geez." Cindy sounded ticked. "What the heck did he want?"

"Nothing important. He left."

"Good. Now where were we?"

"Well," he started slowly. "I've got something really important to tell you. It's not bad or anything like that." He paused to see if she would respond. When she didn't, he went on, "It's kinda weird in a way."

"Chris Gates. Do you need me to come to your house right now? I was going to the library later tonight anyway."

There was a long pause.

Chris started wrapping the phone cord around his index finger to see how many loops he could get around it.

"Chris! Are you still there?" Cindy sounded uptight.

"Well," Chris started again. "I guess I can tell ya over the phone."

"All right then. Go ahead," she said calmly.

"Like I said, it's nothing bad about us. I mean, we aren't breaking up or anything like that."

"So, it's not another girl?"

Chris could see the tip of his index finger turning purple.

"Nah. Nothing like that."

"Well then, what?"

Chris thought this would be easy.

I shoulda practiced this.

Sudden shooting pain in his finger forced him to unwrap the phone cord.

"Well ...," Another pause. Cindy was silent. Chris then inquired, "Are you listening to me? You aren't saying anything."

"Of course I'm listening to you. It's really easy. You aren't saying anything either."

"Okay, okay." Chris reached into his pocket and got out a piece of bubble gum. "Do you believe in life on other planets?"

"Chris Gates. What the heck does that have to do with what you are telling me?" The sharp edge in Cindy's voice resurfaced.

"It actually does. Really it does."

"How so?"

"Just please answer the question." Chris popped the gum in his mouth.

"I never really thought about it but I guess it could be true." She paused, then asked, "Really, Chris. What does this have to do with what you were going to tell me?"

"You and I have been together for almost 5 months now, right?" Chris switched the receiver to his other ear.

"Yes."

"And we really want to be together, right?"

"Of course we do."

"And just 'cause I'm fifteen and you're sixteen doesn't mean we aren't mature enough to know about all kinds of things."

Silence.

"Well?"

"I wasn't sure if you were done. You didn't say 'right' at the end."

"Geez. Right?"

"Yes, Chris. Where is this going?"

"You know I always confide in you. And this stuff is weighing on me so much that I've just got to tell someone. This has been going on long before I met you. I hope I don't get in trouble for telling you this." Chris lifted his head from the pillow and saw his door slowly open with Cory's face showing through the gap, grinning ear to ear. Chris waved his arm to get him to back off. It didn't work.

"How would you get in trouble?" Cindy sounded concerned now.

"I've been told never to tell an Earthling any of this."

Cory had crawled into the room on his belly and was peeking around the bottom edge of the bed when Chris caught sight of the top his head and then his smiling face appeared. Chris motioned for him to leave the room, but Cory continued to crawl closer.

"What do you mean Earthlings? Is this some kind of joke?" Cindy asked.

Seeing that Cory wasn't going to leave, Chris continued.

"Oh never mind. I knew you would never believe me. I'll get in trouble if I tell you so forget it."

"No, sweetie. I'm sorry. Tell me. I'll believe you."

With Cory stifling a laugh, it was all Chris could do to keep a straight face. His reluctance to play a trick on Cindy had faded with Cory's continual prodding.

"All right then. I'm just going to say it and hope for the best. I've never told anyone this before so I'm really nervous." He waited a second or two. "I'm not from this planet."

There was a long pause. Cory was rolling on the floor with both hands covering his mouth.

"WHAT?!!!"

"I knew you wouldn't believe me." Never mind. Just forget it."

"No, wait. Are you being serious?"

"Look, I can get in a lot of trouble for just talking about this. Let's just forget the whole thing."

"Wait, Chris. Are you really an alien? No joke now. Really?"

"That's what I've been trying to tell you. But now you are going to break up with me and my superiors are gonna find out and make me go back home." Chris sat up in his bed now and was watching Cory trying not to laugh out loud. He continued. "I'll probably be put in prison. So please don't tell anyone."

Cindy wasn't saying anything.

"Cindy, are you still there?"

"Yes. I'm here."

"You do believe me don't you? Please don't tell anyone."

"I believe you and I won't tell. But I have a lot of questions."

Cory had gotten up on his knees and was next to Chris so he could hear Cindy's voice coming through the phone's ear piece. He raised his arms while looking at the ceiling in a mocking gesture of a religious type of hallelujah moment.

"What kind of questions?"

"Well, to start with, are you human?"

"Of course I'm human. Don't I look like it?"

"Yeah, but there are all those TV shows that have all kinds of weird beings from other planets."

"That's just TV stuff. I'm real."

"What color are you really or are you just wearing some kind of suit or costume?"

"Well, I did have my skin color changed. I'm really a light shade of blue."

Cory slapped both hands over his mouth and let out a muffled shriek.

At that moment, Kelli pushed the door open and stuck her head in the room.

"Chris, are you still on the phone? I told you not to be long. Your father is going to call." She surveyed the room with a quizzical expression.

Chris quickly covered the phone's mouthpiece.

"What are you boys up to?" She entered the room and stood with arms crossed looking at her sons.

"Nothing, Mom," Cory said while still on his knees. He had lowered his arms but obviously not before his mother had seen him in his 'praying' position. "Chris is talking on the phone and I was just looking for guidance."

As soon as the words left Cory's mouth, both boys busted out laughing.

"Well, just hurry up and finish with the phone," Kelli said with a wry smile. "You boys are up to something. I can tell." She backed out of the room keeping an eye on her sons.

Chris uncovered the mouthpiece.

"Cindy. You still there?"

"Yes I'm here. What was that? I could only hear muffled sounds. You covered the phone."

"I had to. Mom and Cory came into the room. Look, I gotta get off. Dad is going to be calling soon."

"I'll be by to pick you up after dinner. Tell your parents we are going to the library. We've got to talk. Okay?"

"All right. See you around seven."

"Okay. Love you."

"Love you too" Chris hung up the phone.

"Brilliant. That's all I gotta say, Bro. You pulled it off." Cory smiled as he put his hand out for the Bro handshake. "I don't know how you did it, but she bought it hook, line, and sinker."

"I guess," Chris said shaking Cory's hand. "But I'll have to undo it when she comes to pick me up."

"I know. But it's still cool that you did it. Wait till I tell Gene. I swear you can talk anyone into anything."

Chris shook his head. "I can't believe I took that dare from you guys."

"Well, that's what you get for daring us to put cherry Kool-Aid in the shower heads in the girl's locker room. One dare for another."

"I didn't think you guys would actually do it," Chris said while getting off his bed.

Cory laughed and added, "Let this be a lesson to you that you shouldn't dare people to do stuff."

"You got that right. I've really got to figure out how to avoid getting hammered by Cindy for pulling this alien stunt."

"Well," Zenta said, glancing at Tish. "That was a bit ironic, wasn't it?"

Tish was still looking at her monitor and shaking her head. She hadn't slept well the night before and was acting a bit punchy from being tired.

"How did he convince her that he was an alien? Either she likes him a lot or she's not very smart."

"I think it's a little bit of both."

"Well, I think she's pretty stupid."

"You sound like an Earthling when you say that," Zenta said, kidding her friend.

Tish held her hand up.

"Wait. Listen to the announcement coming from Troid, something about pilots reporting."

"Repeat. All front-line fighter pilots report to your respective units in the hanger at this time by orders of General Jhall."

"Wow," Tish exclaimed jumping up from her seat. "Something is going on."

"Seems that way," Zenta added while checking for any further details on her computer.

"We've got to find out what is happening," Tish said as she headed for the door.

"Where do you think you're going?" Zenta asked while motioning for Tish to sit down. "Only essential personnel are supposed to be in the Command Center."

"And what makes you think I was going there?"

Without a word, Zenta eyed Tish with a raised eyebrow and pointed at her monitor.

Tish sat down.

"We don't need to leave the lab to know what's going on. Father showed me how to capture the video and communications feed from the Command Center."

"Is that allowable?" Tish asked with heightened interest.

"Well," Zenta replied with a hint of mischief in her voice. "Considering the source, I'm willing to take my chances." She keyed in some commands. "There. We should start seeing what the Command Center sees."

Springing to life on Zenta's monitor were five Kahn Fighters lined up in a row, the middle one, Kappa 252, was carrying a large payload underneath. Twelve Reep fighters were lined up behind them.

"What is on the bottom of the middle Kahn?" Tish asked.

"It's the new meteor shaped nuclear bomb. I also want to get the video feed from the camera in the back of the Command Center that records all activity," Zenta said, leaning over to Xander's workstation and typing on his keyboard. "I'm going to use Xander's system so we can keep yours on the Savior." She moved her chair so Tish could have a better view.

The Command Center popped up on Xander's monitor with General Jhall standing next to the front screen manning his console. In the back of the center, Marsitta was at her communications workstation. In between them, the rows of regular workstations were filled with various personnel going about their duties with more individuals still reporting in.

The front screen was split four ways with the top left view showing the Kahn Fighters, the top right showed ten Reep Fighters near Mars, and the other two bottom views were blank.

"I would guess that we've detected aliens somewhere," Zenta stated nervously.

"It would appear so. It's been an alien kind of day," Tish added trying to ease the tension.

"Major Donac, are the Europa and Mars squadrons in place?"

"Almost, sir," Donac replied from his workstation on the furthest right of the front row. "We are waiting on a visual of the Europa squadron."

To the left of Donac were members of the Anti-Detection Unit; Jzet, Dlocto, and Callun. They were monitoring the data feeds being transmitted by the X5 Probes.

"Captain Maczee," Jhall bellowed into his microphone. "Is there a problem with one of your squadrons?"

"No, sir," Maczee replied. "We are waiting for Europa squadron to gear up. It appears they are just deploying their X5s."

"Well get them in line, Captain," Jhall barked. "We don't have all day."

"Major Jzet." Jhall turned his attention to the ADU personnel. "Do we have an X5 ready to do the weapons inspection?"

"Sir, the image should be coming up on my monitor momentarily."

"Captain Dlocto." The general was going down the line of the ADU. "How many probes do we have near the raiders?"

Dlocto fumbled with his keyboard and said, "Uhh. I'm still getting that data at the …"

"Captain!" Jhall yelled. "We've got Veloptor raiders in this solar system somewhere between Neptune and Saturn and we have yet to find out their exact location. Let's move it."

"Yes, sir."

"Command, this is Captain Maczee," she announced, breaking in on the exchange.

"Yes, Captain?" Marsitta answered.

"The Europa squadron is online."

The bottom left panel of the front screen now showed Eighteen Europa Reep Fighters slowly moving forward in unison, away from the X5 probe that was transmitting the video feed. Even at this distance from the sun, the light was bright enough to reflect off the sleek white Y shaped fighters.

"Command," Maczee's voice came through the speakers. "I am ready for X5 inspection of the meteor on the bomb rack."

"Affirmative, Captain," Jhall replied. "And please make sure your squadrons are online in time in the future."

"Yes, sir."

"General Jhall?" Dlocto hesitantly interrupted. "I have the necessary data on the raiders.

"Let's see it."

"Yes, sir. Please direct your attention to the four way view split on the front screen. The top left view shows the Kahns with an X5 moving in for an inspection of Kappa 252, top right is the Mars squadron, and the bottom left is the Europa squadron. The bottom right view is an X5 visual of the three Veloptorian raiders, two of the ships being of the Kreshtee series, single pilot fighters, small and fast with limited weapons. They are accompanying a Coorstar midsize fighter, crew of four, multiple weapons, slow, but highly maneuverable. The raiders are in a stationary position near Neptune."

"Thank you, Dlocto. Captain Maczee. Did you copy that information?"

"Yes, sir. We also have the image up on our screens."

The sun provided sufficient light to clearly see the Veloptorian fighters suspended in space. The Coorstar had a large pyramid rear section, the power complex, with three long tubes extending out to a clam shell shaped crew cabin holding the pilot and crew command area, weapons, and additional cargo space. The two, bird shaped Kreshtees were hovering around the larger Coorstar as if inspecting it. Some type of missile device attached to the bottom of the Coorstar.

"Captain Dlocto, get me an analysis of that missile type object on the Coorstar," Jhall ordered.

"Sir, that data is coming in from the X5 now. Uranium had been detected along with some other unknown materials."

Jhall looked at his second-in-command, Donac. Their eyes met each other's worried expression.

"Well, Major. It looks like we have a race on our hands. I don't think they brought a nuclear bomb to just show it around."

"I agree, sir." Donac answered. "Let's get them first."

"Agreed."

Jhall looked at the screen again, then turned to the ADU crew.

"Major Jzet," Jhall bellowed across the center.

"Sir." Jzet was prepared to be called on. "I am ready to do the weapon inspection."

"Proceed."

Captain Maczee's Kahn Fighter appeared in the top left of the screen. As Jzet guided an X5 probe closer to the Kahn, the nuclear meteor could be clearly seen attached to an external bomb rack. It was half the size of the Kahn Fighter. He maneuvered the probe around to all inspection points. The bomb mimicked space debris found in any galaxy, looking somewhat like a large baked potato.

"All attachment arms are secure," Jzet informed the center. "The release mechanism is set. The extra external light ring on the bomb rack is in sync with the Kahn's light ring. It's a go."

Zenta and Tish were still huddled around their monitors watching events unfold.

"I've never seen this weapon before. Is this the first time we've ever used it?" Tish asked.

"I heard that the weapons specialists built it in orbit about a year ago. It's been orbiting around the moon ever since. I saw some of the testing documentation"

"Why did we make the bomb look like a meteor?"

"By using a meteor shaped enclosure to conceal the weapon, we can send the bomb to its destination and not alarm the intended target as it approaches. The target will think it's a piece of space debris." She then pointed at the extra light ring on the bomb rack. "The Kahn fighter will release it at high speed so the meteor will continue toward the intended target. This negated the need for a propulsion system for the bomb."

"So will it deliver the weapon at SOD or SOL?

Zenta leaned back in her chair, relishing the role of knowing the inside information.

"Well, from what I've learned, the Speed of Dark is too fast to use for the bomb, so it will be released at the Speed of Light. But first, the Kahns will move closer to the intended target via SOD. The 252 will then do a short SOL burst and release the nuclear meteor. We want the Veloptors to detect it as space debris so that they won't be alarmed. The meteor will race to the target to be detonated by probe." She held up her hand. "Wait, General Jhall is saying something."

"Captain Maczee," Jhall began. "We are going to execute this maneuver exactly like the test runs. Short SOL run, release, drop out of SOL, then await orders. You and your squadron will be in the safe zone, but positioned close enough to go in if the meteor fails to detonate. The Europa and Mars squadrons will also go in if required. Have your GAIA Reep Fighters follow you to the launch site."

"Affirmative, General," Maczee answered. "Our cameras are on and we are ready to launch on command."

The front screen upper left view now showed a straight shot of space from the Kappa 252 camera. Clear open space awaited them.

"Major Donac," Jhall barked. "Are all systems a go?"

Donac checked and quickly replied, "Sir, yes, sir."

"Now, Captain Maczee," Jhall ordered. "Launch!"

Everyone saw a quick flash of light and the Kahns vanished.

The next view from an X5 traveling with the Kahns was of the fighters slowing to a hover. Captain Maczee's Kahn did a quick SOL burst and released the Meteor. It was dead quiet in the Command Center as all eyes were on the three Veloptorian fighters on the front screen. The fighters began to shift positions as the Kreshtee that had been hovering under the Coorstar moved to a parallel position with the others.

"Major Jzet." Jhall broke the silence. "Move the X5 probes back. It appears that the Veloptorians have detected the meteor heading their way."

"Yes, sir. There has been some communication chatter between the raiders. They only have short range radar detection so we should see …"

Jzet never finished his sentence. A bright flash filled the room for a brief instant. Those who had been looking at the screen quickly diverted their eyes or covered their face. This left most everyone blinking continuously to regain focus. Zenta and Tish weren't affected as much since their visual feed was on their smaller lab monitor.

"The X5 feed is gone," Callun exclaimed.

"The probes were obliterated along with the raiders," Donac said as he shook his head. "Isn't that a bit obvious?"

"Captain Maczee," Jhall said as he looked at the blank lower quadrant of the front screen.

"Already on it, sir. I've just flashed ten X5 probes to the last known coordinates of the raiders so we can blanket the area."

"Very good, Captain."

"General," Jzet said getting Jhall's attention. "We should have a visual and a data feed momentarily."

No sooner were the words out of his mouth when the blank quadrant on the front screen filled with thousands of stars and the faint image of Neptune in the background. The Command Center was silent.

"They're gone," Cullen said quietly.

"It worked," Marsitta said in a hushed tone.

"General Jhall," Jzet called out. "I have swept the area for any trace of the raiders. The only data I'm receiving aside from normal space elements is radiation from the meteor detonation and traces of iron and other material commonly found in Veloptorian fighters. With these amounts, I would have to conclude that the raiders were obliterated."

"I concur, Major," Jhall replied. "Major Donac. Your situational analysis, please."

"Sir, based on our intelligence, Veloptorian raiders are regularly lost in space due to the inaccuracies and deficiencies in their Magnetic Plate Splitting technology or Plating as they call it. Past history shows that the Veloptorian High Command never deploys rescue missions for lost ships."

A smile slowly spread across Jhall's lips. He typed a few words on the console keyboard, then faced the room and adjusted his headset microphone.

"Everyone was very efficient in conducting this operation. We have again proven that our soldiers and our technology will prevail in this ongoing war with the Veloptors." He paused as he scanned the faces of everyone in the room. "Finish your tasks, all squadrons are to return to base, and I'll expect a summary report by tomorrow for the Supreme Council. Dismissed."

"That was interesting," Zenta said as she switched the monitors back to their original views.

"How so?" Tish asked.

"There were no cheers or congratulations at all."

"Well, even though Command didn't treat it as a victory," Tish said as she stood up and walked to the water dispenser, "I am very glad we avoided detection by those raiders."

"I am too. We've had enough alien encounters for one day."

19 – IS ANY OF THIS REAL, OR NOT?

Chris could not figure out where he was. Even though the sun was shining brightly, and the water was crystal clear, he felt like he was in a fog.

The last thing I remember was going to bed.

He shook his head hoping the cobwebs would clear. He looked at the pounding surf washing onto the sparkling white sand and wondered how he got there. The captivating scene of the clear blue sky melding into the crystal clear waters looked familiar to him, but he could not remember having been there before.

"Is this a dream or what?" he asked out loud. Sitting on the sand with his elbows resting on his knees, he lowered his head not expecting an answer to his question.

"It's not a dream. You're really here, in a way."

Startled, he snapped his head to the right and saw Zenta sitting about five feet down the beach from him. His eyes froze on her.

"You look just like how I've seen you in my mind," Chris said, unable to break his stare.

Zenta smiled and leaned back with her hands in the sand. Eyes closed, head tilted up, her bronze face glowed in the sun.

Chris, stumbling over his words, asked, "How …? Where are …? How did we get here? And how is it ...?"

Zenta put her fingers to her lips.

"Shhhhhh. Don't say anything. Close your eyes, listen to the waves, and let your mind clear."

"But …"

"Shhhhhh. Close your eyes," Zenta repeated as she closed hers.

Chris continued to stare, but soon realized he should do as he was told. Leaning back with his eyes closed, it became clear to him why he was there. He was going to be facing a test but was unsure of what it was. The image of Zenta kept clouding his thoughts.

"Tell me what the test is," he inquired, his eyes open now and leaning forward.

"If you had waited," Zenta said as she got up, a hint of disappointment evident in her voice, "you would have known it."

"But why make it so difficult when you can just tell me?"

Walking by him, she touched her index finger to his lips and uttered, "You still need to learn patience. That is a big part of your test." She continued walking down the beach.

Chris scrambled to his feet and quickly caught up to her.

"Man, you walk fast. Are you in a hurry?"

"No." She slowed her pace. "We have plenty of time."

"So…," Chris started to say something but didn't know where to begin. "How did I get here? Where are we?"

"I brought you here with your mind and you picked this place. Do you remember where you were before you arrived here?" she asked as she headed up the beach to a huge palm tree.

"I'm pretty sure I was asleep in bed. I had finished a paper for school and was really tired."

"Be sure. Don't guess. Where were you and what were you doing?"

"I was asleep in bed."

"That's better. Don't guess at things too quickly. Take the time necessary to be sure of what you know, then trust that information. Always practice this skill and make it a habit." She stopped under the tree and sat down.

"So why did you bring me here?" he asked as he sat down next to her. He was enamored with her smooth bronze skin. The gentle wind blew her pure white hair off the shoulders of her skin-tight black and green uniform. He was mesmerized.

"Really, Chris, do you mean to tell me you can't figure that out? Don't disappoint me. You are highly intelligent. Stop letting your mind be clouded by outside influences and focus on the situation at hand. What would you be doing right now if I wasn't here with you? How would you be handling this; alone, waking up on a beach, knowing that the last thing you remember was sleeping in your bed."

"Actually, I'd unwind, catch a little sun, take a swim, then I'd go exploring." He stretched out on the sand, rolled over on his stomach and gazed up at her.

Zenta frowned.

"But seriously," he continued. "You are the outside influence that is clouding my mind. I've seen you in my head for years, but didn't really know or remember that until now. I'm having problems concentrating because you are so beautiful. I feel like I've known you forever." Chris rolled back over and sat up next to her, sand covered his shorts.

"Well, I don't know about forever, but we did meet the day you came home from the hospital. We talked for hours." Zenta paused, lost in thought.

"That outfit you are wearing is so sexy. Skin tight, black and green tiger stripes look good on you. It accents that forever tan. Are all the girls on Terlokya as pretty as you?"

Zenta flushed as much as her skin tone would allow. She glanced at Chris, paying attention to the broad shoulders and muscular build of the gawking teenager. But before she could respond, Chris asked another question.

"Do tigers on Terlokya have green and black stripes?"

"We don't have tigers. This is the fur pattern of a sentar. They are similar in size to your mammal, the horse. It has the body type of a tiger and the head of a bear with the swept back horns of a water buffalo. They are excellent mammals to ride in our mountainous regions and have also adapted well to the ice climate on the planet Cezzeck."

"That's so cool. Can you get me one of those?"

Zenta shook her head.

"Let's get back on subject."

Chris gave that big smile of his.

"Right. We were talking about how beautiful you are."

"Are you having a hard time focusing because of how I look?" she asked gesturing to herself.

"Yes."

"All right then," Zenta said as she stood up. "See if you can focus when I look like this."

Raising both arms above her head, Zenta brought them down in a sweeping motion around her body immediately transforming herself into a Veloptor. Its large reptile head shimmered with a bright shiny green hue under the intense sunlight. The nine foot tall creature made a hissing sound as it slapped its long, powerful tail on the sand, making a loud sound. As it reached toward Chris with a long four clawed hand, the armor it was wearing made a clanking sound.

Chris immediately swung a leg in a swiping movement at the feet of the creature knocking it off balance. The Veloptor's strong legs were not prepared for Chris' quick cutting swipe. As it hit the ground, it transformed back into Zenta. She effortlessly sprang up to her feet just as Chris did.

"What the heck was that all about?" he hollered, arms out in a self-defense posture. With his adrenaline going through the roof, Chris' breathing was rapid and deep from the quick exchange of action.

"Now that's focus. You reacted with immediate action to a perceived threat as if it were instinct. Do you know what that was?" Zenta asked.

"Yeah. It was a Veloptor." Chris stopped talking and with a quizzical expression continued. "What the heck is a Veloptor and how did I know it was called that?"

"Come on, Chris. Think and trust your mind. Don't make me tell you."

He thought for a second. "They are the enemy of all humans. On

Earth they were called Velociraptors or Raptors for short but they're extinct." He paused. "You taught me this."

"Yes I did. Earth was not the only planet where Veloptors evolved. I'm not sure why your ancestors changed the name and added 'cira' to Veloptor but you can only teach your children so much."

"Children?"

"Never mind about that. Most importantly, you passed the test."

Chris gave an excited fist pump into the air and kicked at the sand.

"Yay! I took the beast down."

"And you reacted just as you should. A real Veloptor would have killed you in an instant if you hadn't reacted so quickly."

"I guess you're right."

"Now do I have your real attention and not your eyes?"

"Yes, ma'am," Chris responded as he looked down.

"Don't ma'am me. I'm not your mother. And you kick pretty hard." Zenta started rubbing her leg where Chris had hit her.

"Oh, sorry. I didn't mean to hurt …"

"That's all right," she quickly said cutting him off. "It's good to know your strength. Let's walk down the beach and talk."

"Okay."

"Have you figured out why you are here?" She asked watching him for a change in expression.

Chris strolled along at a slow pace concentrating on thoughts and ideas he didn't normally process in a conscious state. He was aware of Zenta next to him but his focus was deep in his own mind, analyzing the current situation and evaluating it.

"You're going away … to Terlokya." Chris looked at Zenta with a sad expression. He felt as if his energy was draining out of his body.

"That is correct," Zenta answered as she continued walking.

Chris stopped in his tracks.

"Why? Why do you have to go?"

"Chris." Zenta turned and walked back to stand right in front of him. "I haven't been home in about eighteen years. Do you love your mother?"

"Of course I do. What does that have to do with this?"

Zenta didn't respond. She waited.

"Oh," Chris put it together. "You haven't seen your mom in a long time then, right?"

"It has been quite a while."

"So this is why you brought me here, to tell me this," Chris asked as he looked down at his feet while he squished sand between his toes. "Who will be training me now? Are you coming back? When?"

"One at a time," Zenta laughed as she held her hands up. "Tish will train you while I'm gone. I grew up with her. We are practically sisters and I trust her with my life, so I trust her with yours." Zenta put her hand on Chris' arm. "As for a return date, I don't know exactly when it will be, but I will be back."

"This is really going to change everything for me now," Chris said as their eyes met.

"What do you mean? Are you referring to my being gone? No, wait. You're talking about this meeting aren't you?"

"Yes," he answered. The rejection in his voice was evident. "I'm not sure what to believe anymore."

"Explain."

"Like, is any of this real, or not?"

"Oh, it's real. I know you aren't going to want to hear this but you will not remember anything about us being here," she said as she released his arm and took a few steps down the beach.

"How's that gonna happen?" he inquired as he followed her. "We actually meet for the first time so you can tell me you are going away. And to top it off, I find out that you are the most beautiful girl I've ever seen. Do you honestly think I'm going to forget this?" Chris kicked at the sand again.

"You know that I can't let you recall any of this in a conscious state. Do you remember the time you caught a probe and two individuals dressed in black visited you?"

Chris was silent as he walked along, his brow furrowed. Quietly he said, "Yes, I remember now. Why didn't I remember before?"

"We can't let interventions or training memories remain in your consciousness at this time. If you think about it, you'll know why."

Chris looked out at the blue ocean with its waves gently rolling in. He had never seen an ocean and beach so perfect. He knew this must be a dream, but a different kind of dream, one he had never experienced.

After a long pause, he answered, "I understand why. It's not my time yet. When will I be able to know all of this information in a conscious state?"

"That day will come. I'm not sure when that will be. There are many potential scenarios that could affect when it will happen. Besides, there is so much more for you to do here on Earth before you leave."

"Leave? Here?" Chris asked with a raised voice. He stopped walking. "Where am I going?" This was getting to be too much.

Zenta stopped and faced him. "Chris, you are destined for great things. You are the Chosen One. Don't think of it in terms of religion, although you will be prepared for the masses that will see you that way.

You care for your planet and believe in your people. It comes naturally to you. We have enlightened you regarding many different facets that come with those beliefs. You have a very influential future ahead of you. It can and will be very intimidating."

"The future doesn't scare me at all."

"I know it doesn't. That's part of your strength."

Zenta again reached for Chris' arm and held it gently. She studied his expression.

"Do you trust me?" she asked.

"Yes. I feel I've known you my entire life."

"You have. Our conversations have gone on longer and deeper than any others you've had, and any others I've ever had." She let her hand slide down to his and then held it. She turned and walked down the beach still holding his hand. "I care deeply about what happens to you. I will never let anything negative come into your life as long as I can help it. One day, you will travel and learn about other places. This will help you when it comes time for you to save your world."

"It sounds so far out," Chris said. "I mean, to think these things are gonna happen to me is hard to imagine." He looked down at their intertwined hands and his heart did a leap. His gaze then rested on Zenta's bronze angelic face. He sighed.

"What was that for?" she asked.

He thought about saying what he was feeling, but something inside him resisted that urge.

"This is just a lot to digest, that's all," he lied.

Zenta glanced up at him, studied his face for a couple of seconds, and then smiled.

"Maybe someday, Chris. Not now. We've got too much to do."

"What?"

She didn't respond but instead, revisited her main point.

"As I stated before, Tish will be handling your training and nothing in that regard will change for you. You will hear her voice at night. Your subconsciousness has been prepared about this upcoming change for a while so that your training could proceed uninterrupted."

"Then why did you arrange this meeting?" he asked as he felt her hand start to pull away. He held it tight so she couldn't let go causing her to stop walking and turn to him.

"Your mind is very strong, Chris. I had to make sure that your entire consciousness was in tune with the changes that are coming. Remember, I have been with you and watched over you since day one. You have a way of using your mind to influence situations and I had to be sure that my leaving would not jeopardize this project."

"Project? That's what I am?"

"No, not you. Your training."

He laughed. "I knew that. I just wanted to make you say it."

Zenta pulled her hand back and playfully smacked him on the shoulder.

"That's not nice to do," she said with a feigned mean expression.

"Ow." He reached up and rubbed the spot that she had hit.

Zenta's expression softened as she immediately raised her hand to touch his shoulder. Chris grabbed it.

"Have you ever been swimming in the ocean?" he asked as he pulled her toward the water.

"Chris Gates! You were faking an injury. That's not fair." She started to pull her hand back so Chris quickly reached out and caught her other hand. She half-heartedly tried to pull away.

"Well, have you?" He now had her stepping into the water.

"What are you doing?" she exclaimed. "I have boots on. All you are wearing is a pair of cutoff jeans." She started to offer more resistance. "You can't do this."

In one swift motion, Chris picked her up and cradled her in his arms.

"I am doing this. If you want those boots to stay dry, you'd better pull or kick them off," he said as he headed out into the surf.

"Chris Gates! Put me down." Zenta was squirming in his arms and kicking her feet but he held her tight. "Slow down and let me get these off," she said while yanking on her boots. She tossed them on the sand.

"How'd you get this water to be so perfect," he asked as he waded further in.

"It is how you see it in your mind." Zenta's resistance had subsided. With her arms around Chris' neck, she was smiling even though she was getting wet. The water was perfectly warm. "You know I could have stopped you from doing this."

"Even more interesting than that," he said as he let go of her legs and swept her against him, "was why you didn't."

Towering a good eight inches above her, he gazed into her eyes. Her face lifted up and they kissed, his lips covering hers in a long and passionate kiss.

"We can't do this," Zenta said as she looked away.

"But we just did." Chris turned her face to his and kissed her again. She offered no resistance.

"Chris, wait," she said as she spun around in his arms so her back was against him. She wrapped her arms around his. "You are mature beyond your years."

"I have the best teacher."

"Well, thank you. But I didn't teach you that." She felt totally at ease in his arms as he gently rocked her to the rhythm of the waves. "We must go now."

"No way. We can stay here a while longer."

"You know we can't," she replied as she leaned her head against his chest. "It's time for you to get up."

"I'll sleep in."

"You know it doesn't work that way." She turned around in his arms, facing him. "I don't want it to end either, but it's time. We will see each other again."

"Just one more." He closed his eyes to kiss her again.

Beep. Beep. Beep.

Chris opened his eyes and thought he saw a fly or something buzz by inches over his head. He was disoriented. His alarm was beeping loudly causing further confusion. He saw '7:05 AM' flashing on the clock.

"Are you gonna shut that thing off?" Cory stumbled into Chris' room complaining. "It seems like it's been going off for hours."

Chris swatted at the clock on the windowsill and knocked it to the floor.

Beep. Beep. Beep.

"Shut that thing off, man," Cory said irritably.

Chris fumbled around on the floor for the clock and finally hit the right button.

"What's wrong with you? I've never heard your alarm go off for such a long time. I banged on the wall like forever. Are you okay?"

"Yeah, I guess," Chris said as he sat in bed rubbing his eyes. "How long have I been here?"

"What? What are you talking about? You've been here all night, unless you got up in the middle of the night and went somewhere."

Chris was still confused. "I feel as if I was somewhere else. Must have been a dream. Wait, it was obviously a dream, but I can't remember anything. It was bright, though."

"It was bright, huh? Well get your butt in gear, sunshine. We gotta go to school." Cory huffed and walked out of the room.

Tish reached through an opening into the mind chamber and removed the electrodes from Zenta's forehead. She hit the button to open the entire cover.

"Come on, dreamer. Time to get up," Tish said as she reached under Zenta's arm to help her sit up. "So how was it?"

"That was not how I expected it to go," Zenta said as she shook her head.

Tish pulled up a chair and sat down.

"What do you mean?" She brushed Zenta's hair out of her face. "Did something go wrong?"

"Not really. Yes. No." She lowered her head. "I don't know."

"Come on. Tell me."

Zenta climbed out of the chamber.

"I was able to test him. He reacted to the threat as expected and he'll be fine with the change in training while I'm gone."

"Well, that's good. This is what you needed to find out, right?" Tish asked as she stood up and walked to the door.

"He kissed me."

"He what?" Tish's jaw dropped as she walked back.

"He kissed me." Zenta was too embarrassed to look her friend in the eye. But she had always told Tish everything. "He swept me up in his arms, carried me out into the waters of the ocean, and kissed me."

"What kind of kiss?" Tish inquired excitedly.

Zenta rolled her eyes and said, "THAT kind of kiss."

"Oh my. Now what?"

"I don't know. His power to influence is amazing." Zenta shook her head like she was trying to clear everything out. "But we need to keep this between us."

"All right. I won't tell."

Zenta went over to her chair and sat down.

"Tell me this," Tish said as she sat on the edge of her workstation. "Would you do it again?"

"With no hesitation," Zenta quickly replied.

Chris was fumbling around in his room trying to piece together school clothes. A knock on the door by his mother interrupted his lack of progress.

"Chris, you need to hurry it up a bit." Kelli looked at her youngest son in his disheveled state. "You need to put on some decent clothes for school. I don't think cutoff jeans are appropriate."

"I know Mom. I slept in these. I'm trying to find my jeans now."

"Well, find another gear too, sweetie."

"Okay, Mom." Chris closed his door after his mother had left. He reached into the pockets of his cutoffs, as he habitually did with all pants, to check for anything in the pockets before taking them off. Shoving his hands in his pockets, he felt something at the bottom of the right one. Rubbing a finger around didn't quite tell him what it was so he pulled the pocket inside out and was surprised to see sand sprinkle out onto the floor.

"What the …?"

20 – LAST BASEBALL PRACTICE

Always the jokester, Chris carefully put a liberal amount of eye black on the inside, front rim of Gene's baseball cap. It was a sunny day so most of the team would be bringing eye black to the field to use under their eyes. Chris was alone in the locker room. The musty aroma of dirt, leather, and sweat filled Chris' nostrils. High school locker rooms were notorious for compounding their smells into one big monstrous odor. Jefferson Academy's baseball locker room was no different. Chris put the top back on the tube of eye black, stuck it in his gym bag, and hung Gene's cap right on the hook under his name plate; Gene Hudson - Pitcher.

Chris spun around at the sound of the locker room door opening. Cory came in and started stomping his metal cleats on the concrete floor to get some of the mud out.

"Hey!" Chris hollered. "Aren't you supposed to do that outside before you get that crap all over the floor?"

"What?" he asked while still stomping.

"I said ..."

"What?" Cory repeated himself. "I can't hear you with all this noise." He smiled, stopped stomping, and sauntered over to Chris.

Chris turned to his locker and stared at his name plate; Chris Gates - Shortstop. It hadn't really sunk in yet that next Tuesday was the last regular season game before the league tournament.

"So what's happening?" Cory asked as he hung his jacket in his locker which adjoined Chris'.

Chris picked up his glove and covered his face with it as he breathed in the leather fumes.

"Ahh, the real smell of baseball is right here in my glove."

"Are you okay?"

"I'm just preparing myself for the end of the season. Four years of high school baseball just flew by." Chris closed his eyes and reminisced about his time on the Patriots baseball team. They went undefeated last year and were state champs.

There will be a lot of pressure to repeat. He let that thought roll around in his head for a bit.

It had been a lot of fun. There was the rush after class to get to practice, wearing the school jacket with the big letter J on the front, pep rallies, the fans cheering them on, playing a game you love, all the little details about having played a high school sport. It was just about to end. Even the old locker room here at Jefferson with its smell, look, and feel would be just a memory. Graduation has a way of ending comfortable habits. He was going to miss playing baseball for Jefferson.

"It's hard to believe the season is almost done," Cory said shaking his head.

"I know what you mean. I'm missing it already," Chris added. "But ya gotta admit; it's been a great ride."

"I still can't believe you started at shortstop when you were fourteen," Cory added shaking his head.

"Well, we both made the team when I was thirteen and you were fourteen."

"Yeah, I remember. You coulda started then if it weren't for that senior, what's-his-name."

"Hey. He was a good guy. His name was Mac and he taught me a lot of stuff." Chris took another whiff of his glove. "It's a game and it's been fun."

"It sure has, especially playing on the same team with our best friends, all the girls thinking we're great, and beating everybody in the state. You're kinda lucky considering you're gonna play at the next level."

"Maybe. We'll see. I know I'll always have these memories."

But it looked like Chris would have every opportunity to continue playing. Standing at 6'4", college scouts were drooling over his coverage ability, not to mention his switch-hitting skills. Having been elected co-captain by the team for the last two years also showed leadership skills.

"What's your best baseball memory?" Cory asked.

"These lockers," Chris replied jokingly. His locker didn't really look like a locker at all, but more like a stall. It was a framed section of a wall from the floor to ceiling with framed mesh dividing each stall. There were hooks inside to hang clothes, a shelf at top to put books and things, and a shelf below for cleats. Seniors had the best lockers; the ones closest to the showers or the front door. Juniors and sophomores had the island ones in the middle of the room. Freshmen were lucky if they got a locker. Between every five wall lockers was a window set high on the wall. This provided plenty of natural light without needing the glaring overhead florescent lights.

"Are you nuts? You call these lockers?"

"I'm just kidding. I'm really going to miss playing for Jefferson."

"Oh you know you're gonna be playing for some university next year or get taken in the draft," Cory said as he rubbed Chris' head messing up his hair.

The conversation halted as the door suddenly swung open and Ian burst through, looking left then right. His eyes were wide as he scanned the room as if searching for something or someone.

"Over here," Chris hollered. "Anyone behind you?"

"Nah. Did you do it"?

"Do what?"

"What are y'all talking about?" Cory asked.

"You don't wanna know," Chris replied patting his brother's shoulder.

"C'mon on you idiot. You know what I mean." Ian walked to Gene Hudson's locker and gently lifted Gene's cap up off the hook. He spied the eye black on the inside rim and a huge grin broke out on his face.

"I can't believe you'd do this before one of our last practices. And everyone always thinks it's funny when it comes from you. If I tried that, I'd get my ass kicked," Ian said as he shook his head.

"Really?"

"You always get away with pulling pranks. Like when you filled in the recessed letters on the stone pillar out front with clay."

"What are you talking about?" Chris was grinning.

Cory smiled, knowing what was coming next.

"Don't be stupid. You know what I'm talking about. The pillar that has 'Thomas Jefferson' on it. Remember? You filled in 'Thomas' and then painted 'George' over it. People who weren't from around here that drove by thought the school was named after George from the Jefferson's TV show. What a riot everyone had with that. But noooooooooooo. Did Mr. Special get in any trouble?" Ian waited for Chris to say something but he just grinned, so Ian answered his own question. "Of course not. How do you get away with this stuff?" Ian shrugged his shoulders and put his hands out.

"Just lucky I guess." Chris gave his best 'aw shucks' look.

"You have been lucky," Cory jumped in. "You seem to get away with a lot. But we all did stuff and none of it was really bad. They were just harmless teenage pranks."

Ian added, "Sure but it also helps to be popular with everyone wanting to be your friend and girls crawling all over you. And it doesn't hurt that you're the town's famous sports hero."

"You know, kindness can go a long way even if it's just having a kind word, a helping hand, and a smile for everyone," Chris said.

"Yeah, yeah, yeah. That's all fine and good. So how do you explain all the girls constantly throwing themselves at you?"

"Hey now. I never took advantage of anyone," Chris countered both hands up.

"Ian, you didn't seem to mind when girls latched onto you after Chris ignored them," Cory added.

"Okay then, enough of that. So are you going to do anyone else's hat?" Ian changed the subject.

Ian barely got the words out when the door flew open and guys started pouring in. The locker room started to fill with teammates. Everyone was talking at once as they all got ready for practice.

"Hey!" Alex yelled above the chatter. "Who's got my cleats?" Everyone could hear clangs and thuds as he threw things around trying to find his cleats. "When I find the SOB that took 'em, they'll be facing a rat tail."

Someone yelled, "Look on top of your locker you moron!"

He looked up. Sure enough, that's where they were.

"If I find out who called me a moron, you and I are gonna tangle," Alex hollered back.

"Shadduppp!!" a chorus of players shouted from every part of the locker room. Bantering prevailed. Being Friday, the guys were excited about the weekend.

Chris began chatting with David Smith about next week's game when Gene started yelling above the locker room buzz.

"All right, Patriots!" Gene put his cap on and stood up on his bench. He had his practice jersey on with his glove under his arm and was ready to go. Slowly, he looked around the room at everyone. Being one of the co-captains along with Chris, the players were expected to listen to them whenever they spoke.

"We'd better have a really good practice today, 'because Stafford is coming after us next week." Gene paused to let his words have an effect. "They would like nothing more than to knock us off our pedestal. We're number one and we need to show it. So let's practice our hardest and give it one hundred percent." He adjusted his cap on his head, exposing a very black forehead. "Who's with me?" A few cheers and yells went out. "Come on, Patriots. Let's hit the field!"

Gene jumped to the floor, jogged to the locker room door, and ran out, followed by a bunch of the team, some snickering, barely able to contain their laughter. A few of them shot smiling glances toward Chris as they headed out the door.

Chris was watching the guys still around him and laughingly said, "Why do they always assume it was me who did it?"

David looked right at Chris with a cockeyed grin.

"Because it's always you who does these things," David said as he got up. He patted Chris on the shoulder, and made his way to the door.

Chris and Ian were the last ones to head out to the practice field. The sound of their metal cleats scrapping against the pavement echoed off the nearby buildings. Chris pulled his mini binoculars out of his bat bag, and stopped at the fence. He searched the field where the girls' field hockey team was practicing.

"What the heck are you looking for?" Ian said.

"Come here and get a gander at Jessica. She's wearing the shortest shorts I've ever seen."

"Lemme see man." Ian went to the fence and took the binoculars from Chris. He put them up to his eyes and looked out to where the girls were doing team drills.

"Wow. She does have on short shorts. How did you know about this?"

"She told me she was going to be wearing them today." Chris waited a bit for Ian to get a good eyeful and then said, "You'd better give those back to me or you'll never leave this fence." Chris grabbed the binoculars.

"Yeah, I've seen enough. We'd better get going. Don't wanna make coach mad."

As they jogged to the diamond, Chris glanced at Ian and smiled, not too much though. He didn't want Ian to think something was up.

Rounding the fence to the practice field, Coach Hrica's booming voice could have been heard over cannon fire.

"Gates! Johnston! Get your butts in gear and get on the field!" he yelled from the pitcher's mound. The rest of the team was standing around him in a circle, their equipment still in their hands. Chris and Ian hustled out on the field and joined the other players. A few of their teammates glanced at Chris and Ian and a few of them did double takes when the caught sight of the rings around Ian's eyes. Coach Hrica began talking about the upcoming tournament.

"Now listen up you guys," the coach began. "Every team in our conference and state tournaments will be gunning for us." The coach stopped talking because of the snickering from the players around Ian, who was oblivious to what was going on.

Ian looked at Alex who was trying as hard as he could to not laugh.

"What?" Ian asked to everyone as he looked from face to face trying to figure out what was so funny.

Gene piped up from the other side of the circle, "Y'all need to shut up while coach is talking." He took off his hat and waved it at Ian.

"Yo, Ian! Keep it down." Gene then saw that Ian had rings around his eyes and started laughing while Ian was laughing at Gene's black forehead. The whole team busted out in hysterics except for Coach Hrica. He stood on the pitcher's mound with his arms crossed, tapping his foot. The Coach was an imposing figure, powerfully built, an athlete who had been coaching for years. He also knew he had a tight knit team. The distraction was actually a good thing, lightening the mood somewhat. But now it was time to show who was boss.

"Well, well, well," he said loudly while waiting for the laughter to die down. "I guess we have a jokester in our midst." A lot of heads turned toward Chris, as did Hrica.

"I wonder who could have done this." With a slight smile he bellowed, "Gates! Give me five laps!"

21 – MAJOR INTERVENTION

"We're the Virginia Athletic Conference champs!" Alex hollered at the top of his lungs while standing on one of the benches in the locker room.

"Yeah! We're number one!" Gene, Jay, and Chris yelled together.

The chaos in the Jefferson Academy baseball locker room bordered on insanity. Even though the team was expected to win the conference regular season and the tournament, the boys were jumping around and yelling like this was their first championship.

"Bring on the state tournament!" Cory screamed.

It wasn't even close. Jefferson had beaten every team in the conference tournament by at least seven runs. It was nice that most of the Jefferson baseball team had returned this year so the hitting power was there again. And for the second time, they rode the pitching arms of Ian and Jay along with the gloves and bats of Chris, Alex, Gene, and Cory.

It had taken the team a while to get to the locker room after the final game. Throngs of students, parents, the press, and a number of college scouts had mobbed the boys after the big win. Being the defending champs, along with having one of the best baseball facilities in the state, Jefferson was able to host the conference tournament and the large crowds that accompany such events.

Inside the locker room, Chris sat in front of his locker pulling off his cleats. Across from him, David was babbling about next week's state tournament.

"So the newspapers are saying that the Potomac Generals are favored to win it all. These reporters are nuts. It seems that none of those buttheads have watched us play. We crush teams like Potomac."

Gene had just walked up to his locker and joined in the conversation.

"Now David, let's not get too cocky."

"I agree," added Alex as he plopped down next to David. "Gene's right. We've been winning this season 'cause Coach kept us focused on our game plan and didn't let us get caught up in the media hype. What do you think, Chris?"

"Well, if you must know," Chris answered as a smile slowly spread across his face, "I think we're going to crush everyone in the tournament and win it all."

"That's what I'm talking about!" David yelled as he jumped up from his seat. "I'm with you Chris!" He slapped him on the shoulder.

"Hey, watch it, man."

"Sorry. I'm just pumped." David sat back down.

"That's cool. Stay pumped," Chris said with a smile.

"Well, Chris," Alex countered. "Why did you just jump into the hype, as coach says?"

"I just know we're going to win. So let's act like it. We can stay focused, but I feel that if we have confidence in ourselves, it will go a long way in helping us win it all."

Alex looked down, obviously mulling this over. The boisterous atmosphere in the locker room faded into the background as the boys waited for Alex's answer. Being the oldest, his opinion always carried weight with the others.

"Okay. I'll go along with that. Let's just agree to be confident in ourselves and focused on winning it all."

Chris jumped up and yelled, "That's it!"

"Hey, guys," Cory interrupted as he came down the aisle to his locker. "I don't know what you all are talking about, but we just won the conference championship and we've got to celebrate."

"He's right," David added. "We can add to this later. Let's get cleaned up and go party."

"You said it! It's party time," Alex declared clapping his hands together.

The boys did plan on celebrating that night by attending a big party.

After they had finished showering and changing, Chris, Alex, and Ian walked out of the locker room ahead of everyone else.

Ian immediately started planning. "So here's what's up. Alex and Cory are going to drive us all home so we can get ready for tonight and then drive us to the party."

"How is it you get to volunteer me to drive everyone around?" Alex asked.

"You always do."

"And it costs gas. Got some dough?"

"I'm sure we can pool some change together. Here comes Jay and Cory. How 'bout you Chris?"

Chris gave a cockeyed look to Ian. "You know Cindy is coming to pick me up."

As they were walking across the parking lot, Jay chimed in, "Don't you ever want to just hang with the guys?"

"Sure. Once your legs look as good as Cindy's."

"Mine already do," Cory stated in a high falsetto voice.

"Back to the gas subject." Alex brought the conversation around to the most important issue, money. "The needle is on E and we don't go unless there's dough."

Jay and Ian tossed their equipment in the trunk of Alex's restored 1971 silver Capri when Gene came running up.

"Hey gang. Party at Zack's cottage tonight. His Ps are out of town and everyone is gonna be there. Oh yeah, Alex, here's that fiver I owe ya."

"Talk about karma. Now it's party time, boys," Alex said as he climbed into the driver's seat. Ian and Jay got in the other side, with Jay in the back.

Cory, Chris, and Gene made their way to Cory's Plymouth Charger.

"We'll see you boys at Alex's house around nine!" Cory hollered at the speeding Capri as he threw his equipment in the trunk. "You and Cindy gonna meet us at nine, Chris?"

"I'll head on over to Alex's with you and she can meet us there. I'll call her when we get home."

Cory squealed the tires leaving the parking lot as the boys headed out to prep for a night of fun.

As nine approached, everyone was arriving at Alex's house.

"Yo, Chris," Jay yelled across the backyard.

"I'm busy," Chris hollered while getting a soda out of a cooler. He handed it to a tall blond girl standing next to him.

"Look you twit. You-Know-Who is gonna be here any second," Jay said with his arm wrapped tightly around a girl wearing a Jefferson cheerleaders uniform. He accidently spilled some drink onto the girl's skirt.

"Watch it, big boy."

"Don't worry," Jay replied as he stumbled a bit. "You won't melt."

Chris turned his attention back to the blond.

"So, Becky, are you coming out to the party tonight?

"I thought I might if you're going," she said with a sly smile as she put her arm around Chris' waist. "Are you talking about the one at Zack's cottage?"

"Well it's actually Zack's parent's cottage, across the reservoir from the Rock Store."

"The store where some of us are able to buy beer?" Becky purred as she winked at him.

"That's the one. The cottage is not that big, just four rooms, but this place is really secluded." Chris put his arm around Becky's shoulders.

"So," Becky whispered in a sultry voice as she put her other arm around Chris' waist. "Tell me exactly how far down the reservoir road this place is so I can meet you there."

"Sure thing." He tapped Jay on the arm. "Yo, Bro. Remove your lips from that girl for a second."

"What? Can't you see I'm busy?" Jay answered.

Jay's girl shot Chris a mean look.

"My name is Amy, Chris. I'm not just some girl. We're in Chemistry class together," Amy said as she stomped her foot.

"Sorry, Amy. No disrespect intended," Chris apologized and winked at her eliciting a giggle.

"Jay, would you say that Zack's cottage is about a quarter mile off the main reservoir road?"

"That sounds about right. It's down an old gravel road and really hidden by the trees. It's just past the other end of the bridge. A lot of great parties have happened there.

At that moment, Cory walked up and tapped Chris on the shoulder.

"Bro. Listen here. I got something I need to show you in the car."

Chris turned and looked at Cory, his arms now wrapped around Becky.

"What? It's gotta be now?"

"Yeah, now. Sorry, Becky. Can I borrow my brother for a sec?"

"Sure, Cory. Only if you bring him back." Becky's silky reply made Cory do a double take at her expression. The way she stared at Chris showed that she obviously thought he belonged to her for the night.

Cory grabbed Chris' shirt and pulled him away. As they stumbled down the slight incline from Alex's patio to where the cars were parked, Chris pulled his shirt sleeve from Cory's grasp.

"What is wrong with you?" Chris said to his brother frowning. He reached the pavement and started pulling on his shirt sleeve to try and get some of the wrinkles out. "Man, you stretched out the neck on this thing by yanking on it like that."

"I was gonna ask what is wrong with you?" Cory said glaring at his little brother. "If Cindy had driven up while you were hanging all over Becky, she would have had a cow. And you know I'm right." Cory kicked his shoe against the tire of his car trying to get dirt out of the treads of his Nikes. "We could have a disaster like we've had before when she's suspected that you were with another girl."

"I can't help it if all these girls want to be my friend," Chris said as he gave that famous smile and headed toward the patio.

"Hold on, bro. That ain't it."

Chris turned around.

"What do you want me to do?" he exclaimed, shoulders shrugged and hands up in the air. "I'm not married to her. I'm foot-loose and fancy-free." Chris rocked back on one heel and pushed off with his other foot, effortlessly spinning himself. He stopped spinning and faced Cory, arms crossed and smiling. "What?"

"You amaze me," Cory said shaking his head. "You get all the girls all the time, but some day you're gonna get caught. You know it."

The sound of a car coming down the street had both boys checking it out.

"Speak of the devil. You lucked out again." Cory patted Chris on the shoulder as he left to go up to the patio. "I'll take care of Becky for you."

"I bet you will."

Everyone was beginning to head to their cars as Chris walked over to Cindy's Celica.

"I'm so excited about tonight," Cindy said as she popped out of her car and ran to Chris, jumping into his arms. He easily held her then set her down. "You drive." She handed the keys to Chris. He gave them right back.

"You start out. I'm still a little bushed from the games today. I'll drive us home." He took her in his arms, and gave her a kiss, then opened the car door for her.

"Oh, Chris, I love you so much."

Chris just nodded and gestured toward the door. After she slid into her seat, he closed the door and walked around to the passenger side.

I really don't want to get that serious right now, he thought. *But I guess she's already there.* He climbed in and off they went following a line of cars heading across town for the reservoir bridge.

On the way, Chris and Cindy saw that some of the boys had stopped off at a rock store to get food and drinks. Cindy guided the Celica over the bridge. She hugged the shoulder of the bending road that veered left and then took a sharp turn to the right.

"Chris, the dark sky is so pretty with just a few rays of light left." Cindy looked at Chris to see if he was listening. "Chris?"

"Yes, it's cool. But watch out for this hairpin. It's really dark here. The driveway to the cottage is only a few hundred feet on the right."

Cindy slowed and began to navigate the hairpin. It curved hard around an embankment that sloped down on the right about twenty-five feet into a gully which lead to the reservoir. Chris glanced ahead and saw the deer.

"Watch out!" he screamed.

But Cindy didn't see the doe jump from the left shoulder onto the road. She jerked the wheel to the right while slamming on the brakes, causing both of them to snap forward, hitting their heads. The car left the road careening down the embankment. The front right tire hit a large boulder pushing the corner up into the air, rolling the car over onto the driver's side as the vehicle plummeted down the gully. Loud screeching of metal sliding across rocks and debris filled the air. No more than a few feet from the reservoir's edge, the car came to a stop on its roof.

As the spinning wheels slowed, an X13 Probe appeared and began zipping from window to window peering in at the occupants. Nothing was moving with the only sound being the engine. The probe stayed right outside the passenger window facing Chris for a few moments then flew back up to the main road turning left toward the reservoir. No cars were coming across the bridge. All was quiet. The probe hovered for a couple of seconds then spun around and flew up the road about 200 hundred yards to a large tree on the left shoulder. A loud creaking noise began to resonate from the base of the tree. Bark and splintered wood shot out from around the lower trunk. The tree began leaning over the road, snapping away from its base and landing with a crashing thud across the road. The probe turned at the sound of a car coming across the reservoir bridge. Two loud pops occurred within fractions of a second and the car veered sideways sliding to a stop, blocking both lanes. The probe then faced the field across from the gully, as if waiting.

The engine was still running as Chris' head twitched. He moved his arm and felt his face. It was wet. Confusion set in, but he didn't panic. He tried to see his hands in the dark, but his vision was blurred.

Where am I?

He realized he was hanging upside down, in a car, Cindy's car. It all came back in a rush … the reservoir, the deer, and the noise.

"Crap!" he shouted. "Cindy! Cindy! Baby! Can you hear me?" Reaching over, he felt her still buckled in her seat, not moving. He felt for a pulse on her neck.

Thank goodness.

He grabbed the latch on his own seatbelt and released it. Even though he was injured, Chris had a moment of clarity right as the buckle was released.

Shouldn't have done that …

Pain blasted through his head as it hit the roof, his body crumpling down afterwards. Ignoring the agony, he swung his legs around and stuck them out the window so he was lying on his back.

I've got to get myself under her before I release that belt.

He immediately caught the smell of gas. His mind raced.

My God, should I shut the car off or not?

Something deep in his mind said yes so he reached up and turned it off. The motor sputtered and coughed till it finally quit.

Now I gotta get her out of here.

He slid himself under Cindy. With a hand supporting her head, he released her seatbelt and she slowly slid down onto his chest. He maneuvered her body so that she was next to him, then wiggled himself out the passenger window.

Why am I so wet? And why does my neck hurt? He was sitting outside of the car now.

I feel so dizzy. He fell backward, put his hand on his neck and felt something jagged slice his hand.

What the hell is stuck in my neck? His nostrils flared.

Oh God, the gas! Forgetting about his neck, he spun himself around. From his knees, he reached through the window, put his hands under Cindy's arms, and pulled her out. From a crouching position, he slid an arm under her back and one under the crook of her knees, picked her up, and stumbled away from the car.

I am so dizzy. I'd better set her down before I drop her. As he was putting her down, he blacked out.

Across the road from where the probe was watching, a large, dark, twenty foot long cylinder descended out of the night sky and hovered in the field about twenty yards from the edge of the road. The Intervessel's side panel slid open and two black clad figures jumped out hitting the ground in a full sprint toward the road. Floating behind them was a sphere with antennas protruding from its surface.

"You go to the occupants and I'll start on the vehicle," Dlocto quickly told Tuu.

"Yes, sir."

They crossed the road and scrambled down into the gully with the sphere right behind them. Tuu immediately knelt beside Chris and Cindy. He activated his medical scanner which hummed as he moved it over their bodies. Dlocto reached through the window of the car and attached a small square box to the interior roof.

"Captain Zenta." Dlocto spoke into his mic.

"I'm already moving the sphere." Dlocto heard Zenta's voice in his ear piece. "And Dlocto, let's dispense with the ranks for right now. Time is critical."

"I agree."

The sphere moved over the car, which then lifted it off the ground. Floating three feet in the air, the vehicle rotated right-side up and remained suspended. Dlocto attached another small box on top. After picking up various car pieces and parts that were strewn around the ground, he placed some inside and put the rest on top of the car as it began to vibrate. Dlocto then went to check on Tuu's progress.

"Tuu, what is the status?"

"I'm still evaluating. There is blood everywhere but there doesn't appear to be any life threatening injuries. They were both wearing their seatbelts which appears to have saved them."

"Which one is worse?"

"It appears to be Chris. He has a small object lodged in his neck. Cindy has a small gash on her head."

"Can you tell what the object is?" Dlocto said pointing at Chris' head. "It appears to be some kind of glass."

Tuu touched the end of the object in Chris' neck. "It is a glass type substance. Zenta, are you viewing this? Should we extract it at this time?"

Zenta had been watching the entire medical inspection on her monitor in the SP Lab.

"Tuu, adjust your camera."

He adjusted the controls to the camera attached to the side of his mask. "Is that better?"

"Yes. Troid says it is a piece of the rear view mirror. Do not extract it until you have a coagulation body patch ready."

Dlocto reached into a pouch on his hip, pulled out a patch, and handed it to Tuu. Firmly griping the piece of mirror in Chris' neck, Tuu pulled the glass out and secured the patch on the wound in a simultaneous motion.

"It is secure. Two streams of blood shot out." Tuu held his scanner over the wound. "The patch is slowing the blood flow, but he has lost a significant amount. I am not sure how he had the strength to pull the girl out of the car." Tuu handed the piece of mirror to Dlocto who tossed it into the vibrating car.

"They are ready," Tuu declared.

"Zenta, send the pods down." Dlocto checked on the progress of the car as he talked to Zenta.

She keyed in the proper commands. "The pods have been released. Have all car parts been placed inside the car?"

"Already done," Dlocto replied.

Across the road, two dome covered stretchers floated out of the ship. Both moved quickly across the road and down the gully.

"The pods are here, Zenta," Tuu stated as he stood up. "Let's place Chris into one first." He knelt down by Chris' head and put his hands underneath his shoulders, while Dlocto held Chris' legs.

"Open pod," Tuu commanded as he and Dlocto laid Chris in one of the pods. They repeated the same procedure for Cindy.

"Colonel Prahash," Zenta announced, getting the colonel's

attention for an update. "The vehicle's occupants are now in the pods."

"Thank you, Zenta," Prahash replied from his station in the base Medical Center. As the Chief Health Officer of GAIA, it was his job to oversee any health emergencies that involved Earthlings and Terlokyans. He busily entered commands into his computer. The pod's dome coverings closed and both filled with a cloudy vapor as the beds glowed red. Robotic arms could be faintly seen through the vapor moving over the occupants.

Dlocto returned to the car. He adjusted a control on his handheld device and the vibration of the car slowly came to a halt. The Toyota Celica appeared unscathed. Still hovering in the air, Dlocto directed the sphere up the gully with the car suspended underneath it.

"Colonel Prahash, is the health realignment procedure completed yet?" Dlocto inquired as he stood next to the pods.

"It is ninety percent complete," Prahash replied. "I am going to move the pods up to the road. The procedure should be completed by then." Both pods floated up the gully. "Remember to glaze them."

Now on the road, Dlocto had the sphere lower the car to the pavement. He then guided the pods to each side of the car.

"We will place Cindy in the car first," Dlocto said as he opened her pod expelling vapor. The red glow faded out. They placed her in the driver's seat. With her hair neat and tidy, the light blue summer dress absolutely spotless, she looked exactly as she did before the accident. Appearing asleep, her breathing was shallow and even as Tuu glazed her. They repeated the procedure with Chris.

Tuu removed the box from the top of the car while Dlocto leaned over Chris to buckle the seatbelts. He checked Chris' neck where the mirror had penetrated his skin and asked, "Are you receiving this image, Zenta?"

"Yes. I don't see any trace of the wound. Your mission is complete. Clear out."

Tuu and Dlocto guided the sphere and the pods off of the road to the Intervessel, loaded them, climbed aboard and took off into the night.

Everything on the road was quiet as the probe flew inside the car and hovered in front of Chris' face. As his face began to twitch, the probe flew out of the window. Chris' eyes popped open. He stared straight ahead.

What just happened?

He touched his face, his neck, and his clothes. I'm okay. He looked at Cindy. She appeared to be asleep.

She's so beautiful. Was the deer a dream? I thought we hit it. Why are we sitting in the middle of the road with the engine off? What happened?

A car horn blared causing Chris to jump in his seat. Cindy woke with a high pitched shriek.

"Will you move that thing out of the road?" The horn honked again. "What the heck are you guys doing just sitting there?"

Chris looked in the rear view mirror and saw Cory leaning out his window yelling at them.

"Geez. We had some old lady with two flat tires blocking both lanes on the bridge. We get her out of the way and then find you guys here. Ya gonna move that thing? Party time is wasting away." Cory pulled his head inside and blew the horn again.

Ian leaned out the passenger window and yelled, "It was sweet of you guys to wait for us, but why didn't you walk down and help us?"

Cindy looked at Chris. "Chris, what the heck is going on? Last thing I remember was swerving to miss a deer. Did we hit it?" Cindy's eyes began to tear up.

"No babe. We must have missed it. Everything's all right now. Start the car up and let's get down to Zack's before Cory blows the horn again."

"But what happened?" she asked as she started the car and slipped it into gear. "I could've sworn we hit that deer."

"I'm not sure what happened. I thought we did too. But here we are. Let's forget about it for now. Don't tell the rest of the gang about this until I've had a chance to figure this out. Okay?"

As they drove down the gravel road to the cottage, Cindy shot Chris a quick glance and said, "That was just weird. Let's not think about it."

"Good idea." Chris wasn't sure about anything right then.

I'm sure we hit that deer.

He was positive there was an accident but there isn't a scratch or dent anywhere. His neck started aching so he reached up and rubbed it.

22 – TAKING ONE FOR THE TEAM

Chris began to stir out of his drug induced sleep.

I gotta get up, he thought. His throat hurt and was as dry as salt. He tried swallowing, but it felt like a reverse dry heave.

Did I get drunk? He ran his hands through his hair. *My head is throbbing. What have I done?* He raised his right hand and rubbed his eyes. He opened them but everything seemed blurry. *I'd better get up and get some water.*

He put his hands down onto the sheets, scrunching the material in his hands, feeling the texture.

These feel different. Almost like motel sheets. Where the hell am I?

Then his full bladder got his attention.

Oh man, I need to pee. When he tried to move his legs, searing pain immediately radiated out from his left knee, encompassing his entire body. It felt like someone was slicing open his leg with a rusty hacksaw.

"Aaaaarrrrgghh!! What the ..."

It all came back to him like a storm rushing in over the horizon. He was in the hospital and had surgery to repair his knee. The memory of the loud popping sound of his ACL tearing rang in his head.

That third baseman jumped on me, the fat pig. I bet he got up afterward and laughed at me, while I was on the ground in agony. I'll kill him if I see his fat ass again.

"I see you're awake," a voice from the dark spoke. Chris' nurse had come into the room. "I heard you say something so I came in. It's a little dark in here. Do you want me to turn on some lights?" She adjusted the brightness of the bed side lamp.

"I don't care. I can't see, my throat hurts, I gotta pee, my knee is killing me, and I'll never play ball again. Can you give me some medicine to put me to sleep? I don't want to be awake."

"Well if your knee hurts, I can give you something for that. My name is Lisa and I'm the nurse on duty tonight." She studied Chris, his disheveled blond hair, the frown, the total look of despair. "You can go ahead and pee. You have a catheter in."

"Great," Chris said as he lifted up the covers and peered down below.

"You've been out of it for some time now."

"How long has it been?"

"You came out of surgery at six. You were in recovery for a while. Don't you remember being there?"

"No. What time is it?"

"It's almost midnight. The recovery room nurse said you were awake and talking right after surgery. Do you remember talking to someone named Terri? She said you were babbling all kinds of gibberish." Lisa checked his vital signs.

"I don't know a Terri and I don't remember being awake. If you're not going to give me something to sleep, why don't you go and harass other patients?"

Lisa ignored Chris' brush-off as she readied his IV to add pain medication. "We have a light floor tonight. Besides, it's late and I'd rather harass you." She smiled as her eyes fell on his muscular arms. "Why do you say you'll never play ball again? What were you playing when you got hurt?"

"Baseball. I was playing baseball."

"What happened?" Lisa released the pain meds into the IV. "Your knee should start feeling better now." She waited for Chris to respond. When he didn't, she prodded again. "Please tell me how your knee was hurt. It might be good to talk about it." She focused intently on his face.

Chris looked at Lisa for the first time. Her voice sounded so sweet to him, but he realized things were still blurry and he couldn't see her face clearly. "Do you have anything for my eyes? I can't see a thing."

"Yes, just a sec." Lisa went into the bathroom and ran warm water over a clean washcloth. While she was in the bathroom, a small bug flew out from under Chris' bed to the top of the metal IV stand, attached itself, and changed to silver.

Lisa brought the washcloth back and stood next to Chris' bed. "Lay your head on the pillow." He did and Lisa gently rubbed his eyes.

"That feels better." Chris opened his eyes and could see. "I feel so fuzzy." He stared at Lisa. "Wow. You're a knock-out. I love blonds with beautiful faces. You're gorgeous. You're a model, right? No, wait. I know. You're an angel, aren't you?" Chris felt light headed. "What did you put in my IV?"

"I gave you medicine so that you would think I was beautiful. How is your level of pain?"

"A whole lot better now that I've seen you."

"So if I looked like the wicked witch of the west, you'd still be in a pissy mood?"

"I dunno." Chris was thinking about his knee again. He moved his leg ever so slightly. The pain had eased up some. "You've sure helped me by being here though." His expression changed from the drugged, goofy grin to one of sadness.

"Why don't you tell me what happened now? I really want to know." Lisa adjusted his pillow and sat on the edge of his bed. She picked up his hand and held it in both of hers. “Come on. Spill the beans. I bet it won’t be as bad as you think.”

“It is bad. I’m done … finished. I can’t play ball again. Every single major southern school had a scout there checking me out. Me! No one is going to offer a scholarship to a cripple.” Chris closed his eyes, lifted his head and slammed it against the pillow. When he began to raise his head again, Lisa reached over and held her hand against his forehead.

“That will do nothing to alleviate the problem.”

“What?”

“Trying to bash your head on a pillow. Let me get you a board or a brick.”

Chris chuckled. “Okay. Get me one.” He opened his eyes and looked at Lisa. Her eyes were a deep blue, accented by her blond hair. “Gosh you’re beautiful.”

“You said that already. Now how did you hurt your knee?”

“You look too young to be a nurse. Are you one of those candy stripers or something?”

“That’s funny, big boy. I’ve already completed my two year degree and am going to the University next semester to get my undergraduate degree in nursing. I skipped a year of high school. Now will you tell me what happened?”

“Okay. Here’s the whole story. We were the defending state champs and playing Potomac High in the state title game. It was the bottom of the ninth inning, score was tied five to five, there were two outs, and I was up to bat and had to get on base. I was the winning run.”

“You play for Jefferson, right? You guys have been in the paper and on the news.”

“Yeah, I used to play for them. This is my senior year. It’s all over now. I’m finished … done ... crippled.”

“They fixed your knee you know.” She wondered if that statement registered with him. “Tell me the rest of the story.”

“Well, I worked the count to full after having two strikes on me. You know what that means, right?”

“Of course ya big lug. You were batting and had two strikes but got the pitcher to throw three balls.” She smiled and continued. “I like baseball. I used to play softball in high school. Go on.”

He glanced up at her and continued. “So the count was full and the next pitch was right down the pike. I smacked a liner to the wall between center and left. I was busting ass. As I rounded second, the third base coach was waving me on to third. I glanced to the outfield while motoring around and saw that the center fielder had bobbled the ball so I kept going. He must have had a rocket arm, ‘cause he threw a rope to the third baseman. I knew I was up a creek when I saw the ball hit his glove right as I was tucking in my right leg for the slide. Everything then seemed to go in slow motion. I looked at his face and he had a big evil grin. Then, all of a sudden, I saw his eyes close and he fell on me to tag me. He just passed out. I know it. I felt my left leg buckle up as he fell forward onto me, then I heard a loud pop. Light and pain was all I could see and feel. I was screaming as I tried to push my right leg out and roll out from under him. He wouldn't get off me. The pain caused me to black out. Then I woke up here."

"Wow. That's awful. You don't remember anything after that?"

"All I remember is waking up here and realizing that I'll never play baseball again."

"Is baseball that important?" The dim light glimmered off the tears welling up in his eyes. She squeezed his hand.

"That was a big part of my life." He gazed into Lisa's eyes for a couple of seconds then continued. "That was my ticket to college and beyond. Baseball made me somebody special. Now I'm just a cripple."

Lisa's eyes started to tear when she saw him trying not to cry. When he turned his head away from her and pulled his hand from hers, his tears started flowing as if someone opened up a spigot. She leaned forward, grabbed a shoulder with one hand, put her other hand behind his head, and pulled him to her. He buried his head into her shoulder and started sobbing.

"My life is over," he cried. "I'll never have another chance at being somebody special again."

"Don't say that." Lisa held him against her, rocking him and rubbing his back while he continued to cry. "You already are somebody special. I can tell. Other good things will come along. You're a powerful young man with your whole life ahead of you. You'll be surprised at what life has in store for all of us."

With his head still on her shoulder, he managed to say one more thing before succumbing to a drug induced sleep. "I'd like to believe you. But I've always been afraid of failure. And that's what I am now."

"You're not a failure. The pain medications they have you on right now can act as depressants. Things will get better. You'll see." She held him for a while, gently rocking him in her arms. Lisa felt him go limp at the same time her pager began vibrating. She lowered him onto the bed and brushed his hair off his forehead then left the room.

"Wake up, Hon," Cindy said as she gently pushed on Chris' shoulder. "It's nine o'clock in the morning and time to wake up."

Chris began to stir. He opened his eyes but the face in front of him was blurry. He saw blond hair.

"Is that you, Lisa?"

"Who the hell is Lisa?!?" Cindy said with great volume.

That really woke Chris up.

"Cindy. Hi baby. When'd you get here?" He worked at pulling himself up in the bed to a sitting position. He failed.

"Answer my question. Who the hell is Lisa?"

"Cool down, girl. She was my nurse from last night. Don't get so uptight."

"Well, you looked all goofy when you said her name."

"I'm on frickin' pain killers, for Pete's sake." That made him mad. "If all you're gonna do is give me a hard time, then you can split." He tried to roll over and face the window in his room, but didn't have much luck.

"I'm sorry, baby. You know how I don't like other girls hanging around you," she purred sweetly as she sat down on the edge of his bed, bumping hard into his left knee.

"Ow, damn it!" Chris yelled.

She jumped up.

"Wow. I barely touched your leg."

Chris sat up fast and put his hands on his knee as if to rub it, but thought twice about that move.

"I'm sorry, baby," she said with a concerned expression. "I didn't mean it. Is that the leg they operated on?"

"Do you mean to tell me you don't even know which knee I hurt?" Chris' hands still hovered over his knee. "It was the left one." He grimaced with pain. "Jeez that hurt like crap. Watch it please."

"Didja think I did it on purpose? I told you I was sorry," she huffed. "I'm going home if you're going to treat me like this."

Chris flopped back in his bed, eyes closed tight, fists clenched.

"Look," Cindy began. "They fixed your knee. I heard the doctor tell your mother. So I don't really see why you have to act like such a prick."

"A prick? I've lost any chance of ever playing ball in college and you haven't shown me one bit of sympathy for that."

"Is that all you can think about? Playing ball?" Cindy had her hands on her hips and her eyes wide open.

"Have we just met or something? I've played ball ever since we've known each other. You thought it was so great to be dating the big baseball star in town. And now you act as if that part of my life meant nothing."

"That's all done with. Now we can focus on us." Cindy put on her cute face acting as if she had just given the perfect response.

"I can't turn it off like that. Baseball was a big part of my life and my future."

Just outside the room, Lisa was standing there as Dr. Hall, Chris' orthopedic surgeon, walked up behind her.

"Miss Haskett?"

She jumped.

"Oh, hi Dr. Hall."

"I thought your shift ended at 7 AM?"

Lisa put her finger to her lips and took Dr. Hall's arm leading him away from the doorway.

"Sorry, sir, but there's a commotion going on in that room right now."

"What do you mean?" he asked with a puzzled expression.

"It appears that Chris' … uh … the patient's girlfriend has arrived and they are having a bit of a tiff, you might say."

"Well then. What do you suggest we do?" he asked as he put his hands out. "And why are you still here?"

"The day nurse called in sick so I was asked to stay until they could pull someone from another floor."

He shot her a quick sympathetic look.

"I do need to see how he's doing."

"That's exactly what I think would help defuse the situation. But I wanted you to be prepared for what you're about to encounter."

"All right then. Let's go in," Dr. Hall said as he headed to the room.

"I'll be in there in a few minutes. I need to get some dressings."

Lisa headed to the supply room while Dr. Hall went into Chris' room.

"Well young man, how are we today?" Dr. Hall asked as he alternated between flipping pages of the chart and peering over his glasses at his patient.

Chris noticed his doctor was very tall, at least as tall as he was. That, coupled with his slightly graying hair surrounding a handsome, sharp featured face and the fact that he was a doctor, gave him an air of authority that was needed in the room. The obvious tension weighed everything down.

"As well as can be expected," Chris answered, eyes darting back and forth between the doctor and Cindy.

The good doctor ignored the conflict for the moment.

"Have you been fully briefed on the procedure I did on your knee?"

"Not since I've been awake."

"Well, we did a full ACL reconstruction…"

"I'm sorry to interrupt," Cindy blurted out. "But could I have just a minute with Chris before you go into this long explanation of what was done?"

"Well," Dr. Hall began. "I think that …"

"Cindy." Chris had both his hands in the air as if he was stopping traffic. "Stop it. This is my knee, my future, and I want to know everything about it. So please be quiet."

"All right then." Cindy picked up her small bag she had placed in the chair. "I hope you and your 'future'," Cindy made quote marks in the air, "enjoy each other."

"Fine."

"Fine then. Goodbye," and out the door she went.

A few minutes later, Lisa ran into Dr. Hall as he was coming out of Chris' room.

"Miss Haskett, you were right," Dr. Hall said while putting Chris' chart in the holder. "That was a tense situation."

"Sorry I missed it but I got called into another room," Lisa said as she breathed a sigh of relief. "How did you handle it?"

He explained as they walked to the nurse's station.

"I tried talking to the patient, but I was interrupted by the girlfriend, I think her name was Cindy, and I couldn't really get a word in edgewise. Chris then shut her up and she left."

"He did what?"

"He told her to keep quiet so he could listen to me explain the ACL procedure. The girlfriend appeared offended and decided to leave. She seemed quite self-centered. Do you know them?"

"No, I just met Chris last night. I didn't meet Cindy. From what you've said, I'm glad I didn't have to."

"Well, the young man is going to be fine. As with all young patients, they don't realize that time is the best medicine. That and making sure they follow through with their physical therapy. Please try and emphasize that to him."

"He's being discharged this afternoon, right?"

"I'm not sure yet. As you are aware, we attempted to do the repair arthroscopically, but there was too much damage to other areas that also needed attention. So I had to open him up. I'm thinking I'll keep him here one more night."

"Thanks, Dr. Hall. I'll go change his dressing now."

"I've already removed the old one so half the work is done."

"Sure. That was the easy half," she replied with a smile.

They both laughed as she headed to Chris' room.

"So how's Cal Ripken?" Lisa asked as she set her dressing tray on the table next to the bed.

"Very funny," Chris responded sorrowfully. He was lying on his back staring at the ceiling.

Lisa proceeded to clean his knee and prepare it for the new dressing.

"Anything interesting up there?"

No response.

"You know, Dr. Hall is the best on the east coast in ACL reconstruction."

"So? It'll never be the same." Chris was now staring out the window.

"Well, actually it can be. You have to trust him when he tells you that in time, and with your physical therapy, your knee will heal up as if you never injured it."

The door to the room flew open and banged against the wall. Lisa spun around and stood face to face with Cindy.

"Would you please leave the room?" Cindy said loudly, not bothering to introduce herself. "I have a few words for my ex-boyfriend." She started bobbing her head from side to side trying to look around Lisa at Chris, insinuating that she was in the way.

"Hi. I'm Lisa. It's nice to meet you. I'm Chris' nurse for this shift," Lisa replied totally ignoring Cindy's rude manner. "While I would like to accommodate you, I can't leave right at this moment. I'm in the middle of changing his dressing. I'll be done in a few minutes."

"Fine then," Cindy responded through clenched teeth. "I don't care if you hear this." She walked around Lisa to the other side of the bed. Chris didn't even acknowledge her presence.

Cindy said nothing as she waited for a response from Chris. When none came, she launched a tirade.

"I just thought you might want to know how the game ended," she began. Ice seemed to hang on every word. "They carted you off the field so I know you didn't see or hear any of this."

Chris continued to look out the window totally ignoring Cindy. Lisa deliberately took her time applying the new dressing.

"After that guy fell on your leg, you somehow pushed your leg forward and it touched the bag. Their third baseman had dropped the ball. You were safe."

Chris stared blankly at the window.

Cindy continued, "After you were taken away, Ian replaced you on base. Then Gene came up to bat, got a hit and Ian scored. Jefferson won and y'all are state champions. Again. That winning run would have been you. You won the game for Jefferson."

Lisa glanced at Chris and saw that his eyes were closed.

"I think he's gone to sleep," Lisa said as carefully as she dared. She had finished the dressing and was packing the tray to leave.

Cindy glared at her.

"You keep out of this." Her wrath went back to Chris. "Wake up, Chris. Don't you have any appreciation for what I just did, as mad as I am at you? You had better thank me for this."

His eyes remained closed.

"Chris Gates! Wake up."

"I'm sorry," Lisa quickly jumped in, "but I'm going to have to ask you to leave. The patient is obviously tired and visiting hours are not until …"

"Don't get your panties in a bunch, missy." Cindy stomped to the door. "I was just leaving." She turned for one parting shot at Chris. "And I hope you have great luck with your baseball career."

She stormed out with a tug on the door to try and slam it. She failed.

Lisa stood flabbergasted, the dressing tray in her hands, staring at the slowly closing door.

"Thank you," Chris whispered.

Lisa studied Chris' face for a second. His eyes were still closed and his face expressionless.

"You're welcome," she whispered and quietly left the room.

The charge nurse, Collette, looked up when Lisa approached the nurse's station.

"So…," Collette began watching Lisa over the top of her glasses, "when is that blond hunk of a baseball player being discharged?"

"Who?"

"Don't give me that 'who' crap. The whole floor has been talking about that boy."

Lisa acted uninterested as she gathered paperwork together around her workstation.

"He's just a patient."

"Really?" Collette set her glasses on her desk and leaned back in her chair. "Is that why you had no problem staying past the end of your shift?"

"For your information," Lisa said with an air of coyness, "I was asked to stay over."

"I know. I was just teasing you."

"Did you hear about the commotion his girlfriend caused?"

"I heard all about it. You'd better head home and get some sleep if you want to see him again. They've pulled someone from another floor and you're supposed to rotate to second shift tonight."

"What makes you ...?"

"Stop it girl. I can see it in your eyes. Get on home so you can get back here."

"Most importantly right now, he needs a friend," Lisa said.

"But that's beside the fact that he's easy on the eyes."

That elicited a giggle from Lisa as she grabbed her stuff and left.

Later at the start of second shift, Lisa arrived for work and scanned her patient clipboard. It was 4:05 PM. and Chris had not been discharged. She turned to one of the other nurses.

"Do you know if Chris Gates had any visitors this afternoon? He had a rough morning."

"We heard. His girlfriend broke up with him," the nurse said as she checked the visitor's log. "He's had a bunch of people in to see him all day long."

"I need to check on him."

"Sure you do, girl. Isn't he kinda young for you?"

"I don't know what you are referring to." Lisa felt her face flush so she acted as if she was searching for something at her workstation. "Besides, I'm only nineteen. Just because I finished high school early and ..."

"Yeah, yeah, we've heard it all before: shining star going for the big degree. Blah blah blah."

"I'm just saying that Chris finished his high school a year early too. We have something in common."

"Well, with his gloom and doom attitude and your peppy outlook, you appear to be opposites."

"He's in need of a helping hand right now."

"Make sure that's all you give him, sweetie. We're watching out for you 'round here."

"Thanks," Lisa said with a smile as she picked up her stethoscope. "I'm going to do my rounds."

"And get that boy to take a bath," the nurse added.

"Okay." She headed to Chris' room. She knocked twice, didn't hear an answer, so she pushed the door open and peeked in.

It appeared as if Chris hadn't moved since the last time she was there. He was still on his back staring at the window. The curtains were drawn shutting out the afternoon sun.

Lisa noticed the huge baseball trophy surrounded by bouquets of flowers on the far table. Cards littered the table next to the bed. There were quite a few extra chairs in the room.

"Wow. It's like a dungeon in here. Those flowers need some light," Lisa declared as she opened the curtains letting in streams of light.

"I like the dark," Chris mumbled without moving his eyes. "It fits my mood."

Lisa ignored his morbid response.

"I guess you had a big crowd in here today," she said while standing in front of his window, hands on her hips. "Have you had a shower or bath today? I'm sure you need one."

"That's pretty bold to say. Do I smell or something?"

"No silly. Let's get some of these bath towelettes out of your closet and get started."

"So you're going to bathe me? I'm not crippled ya know." He watched her move around his room.

"Well, it's so nice to hear you say that," she said as she opened one of the packages. "So now you realize that you will be back to your normal self. That is after healing time and physical therapy help fix things, right?"

"You tricked me." The morbid tone returned.

"Not so fast with the sad voice." Lisa had already started wiping an arm down. "I thought I heard a hint of brightness a second ago."

"It was fake."

"I don't think so. I can see through you, Mr. Gates," she said as she put the wipe down. "Lean up so we can get that gown off. You need a new one and we've got to get you cleaned up."

"That's all I'm wearing. I don't think you want to go there."

"I'm a nurse. You don't have anything I haven't seen before."

Caught off guard by her boldness, Chris retreated.

"Well, can I keep the covers up then?" he asked as he took off his gown. "I'll do the below area."

"Now you're talking. Cooperation is the key." She finished his back then pushed on his shoulder, forcing him down on the bed, and proceeded to clean his chest."

"Hey, what's up with that? I can do this."

"I hear ya, but I don't see any effort."

He quickly grabbed the towelette from her and continued.

"Are you a real nurse? You look too young to be doing this. What are you, seventeen or eighteen?"

"You asked me that yesterday. Great drugs, huh? But I am the real deal. I finished school early and got a jump on college. As a matter of fact, I went to your crosstown rival, Monroe."

"You went to Monroe? When did you graduate?"

"Two years ago. I just got accepted to the University so I can get my four year nursing degree. My parents and I moved here my sophomore year. I skipped my junior year."

"Wow. A real go getter." He lifted the covers and started doing the below area. He paused and looked at her. "Don't be watching me right now. These are my privates."

"Like I said earlier, I've seen it all. And anyone as handsome as you has surely had all kinds of girlfriends so I'm sure you've seen it all too."

A sad expression washed over his face. His cleaning slowed.

"Sorry. I didn't mean to strike a nerve. I know it was rough this morning."

"It had been brewing for a while. Sure, I saw other girls, but Cindy and I had been dating on and off for more than two years. We've been fighting a lot 'cause she knew I was going off to college soon and she didn't want me to go." He thought about what had just been said. "I guess I'm not going anywhere now." The cleaning stopped.

Lisa sat on the edge of the bed.

"Listen Chris, I won't beat around the bush. Your recovery isn't going to be easy. It's going to take a lot of work on your part. I know you can't see the light at the end of the tunnel, but with these types of injuries only time and physical therapy will get you back to normal. You have to trust me."

Chris just sat there, blankly staring as if he was in a trance.

"Look at me." She reached over and touched his face.

He looked up.

"You've got to believe me. You are stronger than this. I know it. Picture this moment as the ultimate test. This is a 'can you come back from this adversity' type of test." She held one of his hands in both of hers. "I'll make a deal with you."

"What's that?"

"I'm going to give you my phone number and if you ever feel down like you can't go on with recovery, you call me and I'll help you through it. Deal?"

"Sure."

"Do you mean it? I'm serious now."

"Yeah, I'll do it."

"Okay then. Let's get this bath done and start your future."

23 – A TRIP HOME

Zenta hooked the latches on her last bag. She sat down on her bed and looked around her quarters. Running her hands over her white velvet bedspread brought about a sense of gloom. Her throat tightened as she thought about leaving her home of almost twenty years. She looked in the mirror and adjusted her dress uniform.

I'll only be gone a year at the most. Did I just calculate time based on Earth and not home? I'm going to have to start thinking in Terlokyan time.

Even though she knew the project was in capable hands, anxiety reared its ugly head. She thought about her conversation with Xander in the lab last month.

"He's not responding to anyone," Xander said not taking his eyes off his monitor. "Not even his brother. Can you believe the way he reacted when the entire baseball team came in to see him?"

"I watched the whole thing too," Zenta answered from the adjoining workstation. She was also glued to her monitor.

"I can't even tell if he's upset about losing his girlfriend. It appears that the only person capable of getting through to him is his nurse. What's her name again?" Xander asked.

"Lisa Haskett."

"Look at this," Xander said pointing at his monitor. "She's giving him a bath."

"I'm watching the same things you are." Zenta's voice had a cutting edge to it.

"Sorry. I'm just commenting."

"It's not necessary."

"Have you thought about whether this particular test may be too tough for him to cope with at this age?"

"His physical age may be seventeen, but his training along with his advanced maturity and high intelligence makes this the perfect test for him." She turned away from her workstation. *I need to keep convincing myself of that.*

Xander stood up and stretched his arms over his head.

"I know that when we extract him, we will fix any past physical injuries and defects. But to injure him on purpose to see if he can ..."

"Look," Zenta said while pulling off her headset and slamming in down on her keyboard. "You were in the meetings when we decided which challenge was best. Everyone agreed that testing Chris on his strength, desire, and ability to fight through situational hopelessness was the best option."

Xander was startled by Zenta's outburst, but continued his questioning.

"I know that. But to injure him, take away baseball, and then have him lose his girlfriend, well, this could be too much for him. I mean he just turned seventeen."

"That was unforeseen."

"To make it worse, you're going home to Terlokya next month. Have you thought about delaying that?" Xander asked as he sat down.

"I can't." Zenta moved her chair to face Xander and paused to gather her thoughts. "I haven't told anyone this. The only ones who know about this are my father and Tish." She bit her lip. "The reason I have to go home now is that my mother is sick."

"I'm sorry, Zenta," Xander said quietly as he put his hand on her shoulder. "Will she be all right?"

"We're not sure. Father told me I need to go," she said closing her eyes.

"Well, the Planet Transport will be here in a few weeks. They haven't moved up the schedule so she can't be that bad."

"You're right. I'm sure I'll get there in time to see her if anything dire is happening. I'd rather stay here during this test, but ..." She didn't finish her sentence.

Time has sure passed quickly since that conversation.

Taking note that most everything in her quarters was still in place, she picked up her bags and headed out the door. In the corridor, she caught sight of Tish.

"Are you going to the lab?" she yelled while trying to walk fast. She was struggling with both of the heavy bags.

Tish spun around and happily replied, "Yes, I am." She walked back to Zenta. "Let me carry one of those for you."

Zenta handed her the duffle bag.

"So you were going to let me leave without saying goodbye, so long, get lost, nothing?"

"On the contrary, my dear," Tish said smiling at Zenta. "I was going to the lab knowing you'd check in there before leaving. Being on the 80th floor has its advantages."

"I don't know about that. We're next to all of the labs and the Command Center."

"True. But our quarters are a lot nicer than the ones on the lower floors except for those on the 60th floor."

They stopped at the door to the lab while Zenta put her bag against the wall.

"Let's leave these outside the lab so they aren't in the way. I can't stay long anyway."

Tish complied and opened the lab door.

"When do you report to the transport?" Tish asked as she spotted Xander.

"In an hour," Zenta replied as she went to her workstation.

"Hello Xander, or should I say goodbye?"

"I guess goodbye, at least for a year or so." Xander got up and gave Zenta a hug. "We're going to miss you."

"Xander." Tish tapped him on the shoulder. "Have you heard from Zenta's replacement, Gunstot? I know he got off the transport last night when it arrived."

"I heard that when he got here, he immediately went into briefings with the Supreme Commander, Colonel Braaddy, and Major Jzet. I haven't seen him but he should report here soon. But before anything else happens, take a look at this," he said pointing to the image on his monitor.

Chris was alone, sitting in an orange beanbag chair in the middle of Alex's room. Next to him was a beverage can but Zenta couldn't make out the label. She checked the monitoring stats and the time there was 11:10 AM.

"What's he drinking?" she asked.

"Uhh," Xander began glancing at Tish, then Zenta. "I believe it's the alcoholic beverage called beer."

"He'd better not be drinking alcohol," Zenta stated through clenched teeth as she glared at the image. She watched as Chris picked the can up and drained it, and then threw it across the room. Zenta fumed. "How long has he been doing this?"

"Zenta," Tish began. "We know you've been busy for the last two weeks having to prepare to go home so we haven't bothered you. With Lieutenant Aiko filling in, you haven't been at the lab. But Chris has been on a downslide ever since he was released from the hospital."

"Is he doing his physical therapy?" Zenta inquired.

"He went twice," Xander replied. "Most of the time he just sits in Alex's room and drinks."

"Well, this is unacceptable. I'm not going to be able to go home now," Zenta said as she whipped around and stomped toward the door. The door opened as she got there and Sohan's large frame filled the space. She took a step back. He was wearing his military dress uniform.

"Zenta. I knew I would find you here." Following Sohan were Braaddy, Jzet, and Gunstot. "I thought you might want to meet the newest member of the Savior Project team before you leave."

After the introductions and niceties were finished, Zenta pulled Sohan aside.

"Father, I have a real dilemma," she began. "It seems that the Savior is not responding to the challenge as well as we expected."

"Why? What data is leading you to this conclusion?"

"He is not showing the drive and determination to overcome this setback that he has exhibited before in past challenges. He is not doing his physical therapy and he has started drinking alcohol."

Sohan's brow creased as he thought of his response.

"Tish came to me yesterday with her concerns about this."

Zenta appeared surprised and glanced at Tish who was instructing Gunstot on workstation operations with Xander.

Sohan continued, "It is my firm belief that a major underlying cause of his depression is the lack of companionship due to his female friend abandoning him."

"I don't know about that, Father," Zenta said in an exasperated tone. "Their relationship had grown stale. I've researched Earthling teenage relationships and have found that it is rare for these early boyfriend and girlfriend interactions to last very long."

"Exactly," Sohan emphasized his point by thrusting a finger in the air. "I have instructed the team to foster this budding relationship between his hospital nurse; I believe her name is Lisa. From the data Tish has shown me, the nurse appears to be the only person that he interacts with on a deeper level."

"She what!?" Zenta exclaimed in a loud voice garnering everyone's attention in the room.

Sohan looked taken aback by Zenta's outburst. "Did you not understand me?" he asked.

Zenta quickly composed herself.

"Yes, Father. I'm not sure if the distraction of a girl …"

"Supreme Commander," Tish was asking for Sohan's attention. "Sorry to interrupt, but could you please help us explain the details to Gunstot concerning the extraction sequence?"

"Absolutely. Excuse me, Zenta," he said touching her arm. "I'll be back after this."

After Sohan joined Xander and Gunstot, Tish took the opportunity to go over to Zenta who was fuming.

"Before you say anything," Tish began hesitantly, "I did this for the sake of the project."

"Tish, really? I don't think Chris can afford the distraction of a girlfriend right now. This nurse doesn't appear to be his type." She was avoiding eye contact as she spoke.

"Zenta, listen to yourself," Tish replied firmly. "You can't even look me in the eye when talking to me." She waited to give Zenta a chance to make eye contact. When that didn't happen, she continued.

"Search within yourself. You need to put your feelings aside and think of what is best for Chris. We know that he's all alone right now and Lisa is the only person he is responding to. We've got to do something different because we are losing him."

Zenta continued to avert her gaze.

Tish went on, "I'm sorry this is happening, but if you really care about him, then you know we have to do this … right?" She waited for Zenta to respond.

"You're right," Zenta mumbled, finally looking up at her friend. But her expression wasn't one of understanding.

Tish smiled and put her hand on Zenta's shoulder. "Remember that we always watch out for each other. Okay?"

"All right, but step out into the corridor with me for a minute." Outside the lab, Zenta launched into a tirade.

"You, most of all, should know exactly what all of this means to me and why I feel the way I do. I've put my whole life into this project and now because of some little teenage witch, it's falling apart. Plus, I've got feelings for Chris now. The worst part is that I can't be here to fix any of this. I expected more support from you."

Tish fired right back. "You're being totally unfair. All I did was make sure the project stays on track, and for that to happen, Chris must recover. Our best chance right now is Lisa. If you continue to let your personal feelings get in the way, then there will be no Chris for you to return to."

Zenta was shocked that her best friend would not take her side. A look of sad but truthful realization spread across her face. She walked away from Tish, not wanting her to see the tears welling up. After a few steps down the corridor, she stood in silence for what seemed an eternity. Finally she wiped her eyes and turned around.

"I get it. I don't like it, but I get it. I did let my feelings get in the way," she said as she walked back to Tish. "Thank you for doing the right thing. And I'm really sorry."

"It's fine. We have to focus on Chris so that everything is normal when you return. I promise that will happen."

At that moment, the lab doors opened and Sohan came out.

"I wondered where you both disappeared to." He was all smiles, unaware of what had just transpired. "Now let's get down to the hanger so we can board a shuttle to the ship."

Zenta stared at her father in disbelief. “You just said ‘we’ didn’t you?”

“Yes I did. I’ll be returning home too. I’ve been away almost as long as you with only those short and infrequent trips home. This is only your second. Considering the current circumstances at home, I thought I would go with you. The Savior Project is in good hands.”

Zenta checked to see if anyone else was in the corridor besides Tish. Seeing no one, she jumped up threw her arms around her father’s neck.

“Father, this is the best news that I’ve heard in a long time.” She let go and dropped down. “Mother will be so happy to have both of us home.”

“Yes, I know,” Sohan said as he readjusted his uniform looking a bit uncomfortable at the show of affection.

Zenta looked at Tish. “Did you know?”

“Yes, but he swore me to secrecy,” she said grinning.

Sohan checked his Trace.

“We’d better get to the hanger. Planet Transports wait for no one.”

Tish ran down the corridor shouting over her shoulder, “I’ll get an Itran.”

Sohan looked at his daughter and said, “Give me one of your bags and let’s get down to the shuttle.”

“Where are yours?”

“Already there.”

The Itran took less than twenty seconds to arrive at the hanger from the farthest most point on the 80th floor. Waiting at the Itran door next to the hanger were four Supreme Guards, also known as SGs. These guards, all officers, are charged with escorting the Supreme Commander whenever he travels. In Terlokyan military circles, they are known as the best of the best.

“Well, Father,” Zenta said as she eyed the SGs while getting off the Itran, “it has been a while since we’ve traveled together. I had forgotten you had escorts.”

“Part of the job,” Sohan responded. “Lieutenant,” Sohan directed his attention to one of the SGs, his rank clearly displayed on his collar. “Please take the captain’s bags and put them on the shuttle with mine.”

“Yes, Supreme Commander,” the guard replied without a hint of emotion. He took Zenta’s bags and carried them as if they were feathers.

“I haven’t seen these guards around. Where do they stay?” Zenta asked as they headed to the shuttle.

“They came in on the transport. SGs are unconcerned where they are deployed. Their preparation is detail specific and they are always ready for any contingency."

Walking quickly across the tarmac, the three approached Dagar DS-D613, the shuttle that would take them to the Planet Transport. All personnel came to a ramrod straight position at the sound of General Jhall shouting, "ATTENTION! Supreme Commander present!" Everyone snapped a quick salute, and held it until Sohan returned it.

"At ease." Sohan extended his hand to Jhall who shook it heartily.

"Safe travels to you, sir," he said quickly. "I wish I was going with you."

"Likewise. Your time will come." Sohan looked inside the shuttle and spotted Donac in the pilot's seat.

"Major Donac! It's good to see we'll be in good hands."

"Yes, Supreme Commander," Donac replied after a quick salute. "We want to get you and the captain aboard the transport safe and sound."

Sohan then asked Tish, "You are riding in the Dagar with us, are you not?"

"Sir, there doesn't appear to be any room. All seats are taken and the cargo area is at capacity."

Sohan again peered inside the shuttle and shook his head saying, "I believe you are correct." He paused and then said, "You're a Dagar pilot, correct?"

"Why yes, sir. But that seat is occupied," she replied gesturing to the seat.

"Well, who is in the copilot's seat?"

Zenta recognized who it was and said, "That would be Lieutenant Aiko."

Tish interrupted, "Sir, this really isn't …"

"Nonsense." Sohan leaned inside the Dagar. "Lieutenant Aiko, would you please step outside?"

The lieutenant came out onto the ramp, his eyes darting from face to face. "Yes, Supreme Commander?" He nervously snapped to attention and saluted.

"At ease, Lieutenant. Would you mind if Lieutenant Tish replaced you as copilot? I would like her to accompany us to the transport but there isn't any room."

Aiko appeared relieved. "Why of course, Supreme Commander. I would be honored to give up my seat. Thank you, sir. I mean Supreme Commander." Beads of sweat had formed on his forehead but now the tense expression was gone.

Sohan then bellowed, "Major Donac, we've had a change in copilots. Would you please bring Lieutenant Tish up to speed on the flight preparations?"

"Yes, Supreme Commander. Welcome aboard, Lieutenant. Come on up and let's get started."

Tish situated herself up front while Sohan and Zenta buckled themselves in their seats. After another round of salutes, the shuttle lifted off and exited the hanger through the top of the base.

"Major, please give me a quick status update," Sohan asked as he put his gloves on.

"Yes, Supreme Commander. Colonel Dobbie is in Command of Planet Transport Mover One with Major Qwan serving as second in command. The light ring was assembled yesterday and is fully charged. The Dagar placement and launch team is off to the right of the transport. All we need to do is get you on board."

"Looks like we'll be underway shortly," Sohan said to Zenta as he patted her on the leg.

Rarely did Sohan show any public father-daughter affection. He always treated Zenta as any other soldier under his command. Not that the SGs would have noticed. They sat perfectly straight in their seats with their eyes straight ahead, Pulsars in their laps.

"Supreme Commander, we are heading for the right side front bay which is bay number two," Donac announced from up front.

"Thank you, Major."

Zenta stared out her window at the transport as they cruised alongside passing bay eight. The ship's call letters, PT-P438 were each bigger than the Dagar they were on.

"Father," she said not taking her eyes off the transport, "it never ceases to amaze me how big these Planet Transports are. We are only coming up on bay six."

"That's why they are called Planet Transports. A fleet of these could just about move a planet's worth of people and material. The use of a single transport for resupplying GAIA works perfectly."

These ships were the large workhorses of the Terlokyan military. The sheer size of a Planet Transport necessitated that their servicing, in regards to being loaded and unloaded, occur on the dark side of the Moon so they avoid detection from Earth. Their use in the transportation of resources from mining operations to the resupplying of colonies, outposts, and bases make them highly efficient due to the vast amount of material they can transport. Designed in the form of a caterpillar, an egg shaped front housed the command and control operations of the ship. Attached were large octagon shaped sections that were detachable. Some were for material transportation; others were for ship operations as in docking bays and crew quarters.

The sight-seeing was interrupted by Donac's voice.

"Planet Transport, Pi, four, three, eight, this is Dagar Shuttle, Delta, four, one, three, requesting permission to come aboard via bay two. We have the Supreme Commander on board."

The speaker crackled, "Dagar Shuttle, Delta, four, one, three, this is PT Mover One flight control. Permission granted. General Dobbie and the crew of Mover One are honored to have the Supreme Commander come aboard. Bay control will guide you in."

"Lieutenant Tish," Donac said as he tapped her arm rest. "Have you ever landed a Dagar on a PT before?"

"No, sir," she responded. "But I'd sure like to try."

"Then you have the controls."

Tish adjusted her mic and took the controls. She lined the Dagar up as the bay door began to open. As she approached the entrance, bay control instructed Tish to proceed along the light line and occupy dock one. Tish maneuvered the Dagar along the lights and placed the ship in the front most slot. Noticing activity at the dock, Tish gave a heads-up to Sohan.

"Supreme Commander, just so you are prepared, outside on the loading dock is a color guard and a contingent of officers," she announced.

"Thank you, Lieutenant." Sohan was busy gathering his things when he leaned over to Zenta and quietly said. "It's to be expected but I do detest these ceremonies. I view them as a waste of time."

"I know," Zenta responded. "But they really aren't for you as much as they are for your people to show their appreciation for everything you do."

"I suppose."

The door to the Dagar opened and there stood Colonel Dobbie at attention. Medals and battle decorations adorned her uniform. Her white hair was cropped at the shoulders and framed a hardened, high cheek-boned face. Behind her, aides and officers formed a gauntlet leading to the loading dock entrance.

"Attention," barked the Colonel. "The Supreme Commander is now on board."

Everyone saluted.

"At ease," Sohan said as he stepped onto the dock. "Colonel Dobbie. How is my favorite PT Colonel?" He extended his hand.

"I'm fine, Supreme Commander. It is a pleasure to have you on Mover One," she replied giving him a firm handshake. "I don't mean to rush you, but if we are to make the rendezvous at planet Kekter for a load of Costine, then we need to hurry and flash. Would you care to join me in Operations?"

"Yes, Colonel. Let's make it happen," Sohan said as he gave a quick wave to Donac and Tish. Then they walked down the gauntlet, both lines of aides and officers at attention and saluting.

Zenta quickly ducked inside the Dagar and ran into Tish who was exiting to say goodbye to her.

"Oh, I'm going to miss you," Zenta said through beginning tears as she hugged Tish.

"Me too," Tish responded. "Seems like we just got together again and then you have to go."

They both were sniffling.

"But you'll be back before you know it," Tish consoled. "Besides you are about to flash and that's always a thrill."

"I guess," Zenta sighed. "Traveling at the speed of dark never thrilled me as much as everyone else." She looked around for her bags and realized the SGs had taken them.

"You'd better get in there." Tish pushed her toward the door and right into a Supreme Guard.

"Captain," the SG said in a monotone voice. "The Supreme Commander sent me to bring you to the bridge. We are about to flash."

Zenta and Tish hugged again before Zenta exited.

Donac fired up the Dagar, secured the proper permissions, and exited the bay of the transport. He maneuvered his shuttle behind the placement and launch team, a short distance from the light ring.

"Get the flash shields while I tune into the launch frequency," Donac said as he hurriedly tuned the radio.

As they both attached their flash shields to their helmets, the speaker crackled with activity.

"Mover One flight control, this is the placement and launch team. All systems are go. We launch on your command."

"This is flight control, roger that. I await the Colonel's count and command."

Donac and Tish watched as the huge light ring in front of the transport came to life blazing a lighted path in space that went on forever. The ship, glowing as if it were pure energy, was now positioned with its front section just inside the ring.

Colonel Dobbie's voice came through the speaker, "Three, two, one, FLASH!"

The light ring went dark and Planet Transport P438 vanished.

24 – THE SKIDS

Chris crunched another beer can and tossed it on the floor of Alex's room just as Ian walked in.

"Hey," Ian said as he sat in one of the bean bag chairs across from Chris.

"Hey."

"How long ya been here?" Ian asked.

"Since yesterday."

"Been to your physical therapy or PT or whatever you call it?"

"Nope. Been drinking."

"You do know that it's eleven in the morning, right?"

"Didn't you hear that Budweiser is the breakfast of champions?" Another huge gulp went down.

Ian looked at Chris' unkempt hair, dirty face, and wrinkled shirt.

"Why don't you go home and get yourself together? I know you've got a PT session this afternoon. I'll go with you."

"What for?" Chris chucked another empty can into the plastic trash barrel, and then leaned back with his hands behind his head. "It doesn't matter anymore."

"It matters to a lot of people, so it should matter to you."

Chris stared straight blankly ahead. Then he reached for another beer.

Ian started in again, "Before you open that, hear me out." He stood up. "You have got to snap outta this. Alex is running one of his dad's restaurants, and all you've done all summer is sit, sulk, and drink. Cory and Gene are at college while you're doing nothing to further your education. Jay and I start at Jefferson next week." He paused to let it all sink in. "So what are you going to do with all of us moving on?"

Chris tried to jump up, but his weak knee caused him to fall back into his seat. When he finally got to his feet, he launched into his own tirade.

"Damn it, Ian. You have no idea what I'm going through. I feel …"

Ian interrupted. "I don't know? We don't know? What the heck are you talking about? We've been watching you for the past three months. It's eleven o'clock in the morning and you're drunk. I don't wanna see that. We grew up together for Pete's sake," he exclaimed while throwing his hands up in the air. "You wrecked your knee. No fault of yours. Your girlfriend dumped you, but you've always said you didn't care if she hung around or not. And because of your knee, baseball is on hold."

“On hold?” Chris was yelling now. “On hold for what? Shouldn’t you have said done?! That would have been the appropriate word. Do you think anyone wants a player with a blown out knee? Cory told me how fast those baseball scouts left the field after I got hurt during the championship game. I’m done. I can face it. Why can’t everyone else?”

Chris limped toward the door to leave and Ian grabbed him by the arm. Chris spun around and swung his fist at Ian but lost his balance. He landed on the floor instead.

“Wow, man,” Ian uttered quietly. “I never thought I’d see the day …”

He didn’t finish his sentence. Instead, he stepped over Chris and left.

After a few minutes, Chris whispered in a drunken stupor, “Don’t leave. Please don’t.” Making no effort to get up, he continued whispering, “I can’t believe I just did that.”

Thousands of miles away on the Moon, Tish’s eyes were tearing up while sitting at her workstation.

“Look at him,” she said to Xander between sniffs. “We’ve failed him and Zenta is not here to fix it.”

Xander, watching his monitor, saw Chris try to get up off of the floor but couldn’t keep his balance. He fell down again.

“We’ve done everything to get him to respond and nothing has worked.” Her voice quivered as she watched the drunken spectacle. “I can’t figure out how to get him and Lisa together. I really believe that will solve this.”

Xander spoke quietly, “Pull yourself together, Tish. If Gunstot walked in here right now and saw you, what would we say to him? ‘Oh it’s nothing, Gunstot. Tish just stubbed her toe’.”

“That’s the least of my worries right now. None of it matters if we don’t fix this,” Tish said as she pounded her elbows on her keyboard and put her head in her hands. “Short of sending the intervention team down there, glazing him, and delivering him to Lisa’s doorstep, I don’t know what else to do.” She watched Chris on her monitor. “Look at him. He can’t even stand …”

“What did you just say?” Xander quickly asked.

“I was trying to say that he can’t even stand up.”

“No. No. Before that.”

Tish looked puzzled.

“I don’t know. I was being facetious about sending in an intervention team and …”

“That’s it!” Xander shouted. “That’s exactly what we’ll do.”

"Xander, we can't send in a team for something like this. Colonel Braaddy might approve this but Jzet is in charge of the intervention teams and you know his feelings about this project. We have to get his approval before Braaddy will okay it." She turned back to her monitor. "Oh my. What's he doing now? He has left Alex's and from the direction he's heading, I'd say he's going to Jay's house. He can barely walk."

"Listen to me, Tish. This current situation could be considered an emergency," Xander explained. "We put our case together and then take it to Braaddy first since it is somewhat unorthodox." Xander had moved his chair to where he was practically sitting on top of Tish. Excitement vibrated in his voice. "Tish, you've stumbled on the perfect solution."

Looking away from her monitor, Tish asked, "Do you really think Braaddy will go for it?"

"Not only do I believe it, I want to take it one step further and volunteer us to do the intervention."

"You are farrook. That will never happen."

"No, I'm perfectly sane. Braaddy has his problems with Jzet so I really think this will work. We can label it as a live training mission for me. You've already been on one so you've got mission experience."

"Well," Tish said as she shook her head in disbelief. "If this is what we're going to do, let's start putting our case together."

Chris knocked on the door and Jay answered.

"Man," Jay exclaimed as he stared at Chris. "You look like crap and reek of beer. What are you doing here this time of day?"

"Sorry 'bout that. I was hoping you could take me into town so I can go to PT."

"Where's your car?"

"I can't drive with this knee of mine."

"I guess I can take you. Are you going like that? Why don't you go home and change 'because you really stink,"

Chris tripped on the threshold coming in the house but caught himself. Standing upright he slurred, "Suuure would be nice to do that, but my mom is home and I really don't want to see her."

"Yeah, that's probably a good idea. I wouldn't want to see you either. Come on down to my room," Jay said as he headed to the stairs. "You can grab a shower and I'll lend you a tee shirt and some sweats."

Carefully maneuvering down the stairs, Chris responded, "Thanks, Jay. Do you know where David Smith's place is on 17th Street?"

"Sure, why?" Jay asked as he got a towel out of the closet. "You know he's hanging with a bad crowd now. Those two guys he's living with are into drinking and drugs."

"I heard," Chris said as he went into the bathroom. "I just want to talk to him about how he's totally let go of his baseball and his college dreams." He closed the door and started the shower.

"Good," Jay yelled through the door. "Maybe that'll help you figure out what you want to do."

Kelli got to the kitchen phone from the dining room by the second ring, "Hello?"

"Hi. This is Lisa Haskett, Chris' nurse from the hospital where he had knee surgery. Is this Mrs. Gates?"

"Yes, it is," Kelli said, wondering why Lisa would be calling. "What can I do for you?"

"Well, while Dr. Hall was on rounds today he received a call from Chris' physical therapist. Normally those calls go to his office, but the therapist was having trouble contacting the doctor. One of the nurses I know called me. I'm no longer working there since I'm in nursing school."

"I see," Kelli said still sounding puzzled.

"Mrs. Gates, according to the therapist, Chris hasn't been to any of his appointments in over a month."

Kelli's mouth opened to speak, but nothing came out.

"Mrs. Gates?"

"Yes … Yes. I'm here. I just … are you sure about this?"

"Ma'am, I'm only passing on what the nurse told me. I just thought you should know. If Chris wants any chance of getting his knee back to normal, he's got to do his PT."

"I know, I know," Kelli was flabbergasted. "I don't know what to say, Lisa. I thought he was keeping his appointments." Kelli sat down on the kitchen stool, shaking her head. "I'm going to make sure he goes from now on. The only problem is that he's never home. He's so depressed about his knee."

"Mrs. Gates," Lisa's voice rang with concern. "Here's my phone number. I want to help out if I can."

"Just a second. Let me get some paper. All right, I'm ready."

"It's 434-555-2735. Please call me if you need me."

"Okay I will. Thank you, Lisa."

Jay slowed down on 17th Street and pulled over to the curb in front of David's house.

"Hang here a second, Jay. I'm gonna go in and see if he's here."

"Okay." Jay turned the car off. "What time is your appointment again? It's twelve o'clock now."

"At two o'clock," Chris lied. "I'll be right back."

Chris hobbled up the walk and stairs, limped across the porch and knocked on the door. It opened.

"Well, well, well," David's smiling face met Chris, beer in hand. "If it isn't Jefferson's fallen jock. I heard you've been pounding brewskis for a while."

Chris waved his hand in a downward motion. "Yeah, well, let's keep that down right now." Chris quickly glanced over his shoulder. "David, can I hang here for a bit?"

"Sure." David looked around Chris and saw Jay in the car. "Let's get Jay in here and down some brews."

"Nah, man," Chris pleaded as he put his hand on David's chest and gently pushed him back into the house. "Let's keep him outta this."

"Okay, man," David said as he put hands up in mock surrender. "Whatever you say, captain. Hurry up and get in here. We got a case of beer to drink."

"Cool, thanks." Chris spun around in the doorway and was heading for the stairs when he said, "I'll be right back."

He hobbled down to Jay's car and leaned on the sill.

"Hey, man," Chris used a fake upbeat voice. "I'm gonna hang with David a bit and talk about the future. He'll give me a ride to therapy so you can head on home."

"You sure?" Jay had no reason to not believe Chris. He looked up to him like a big brother and would never expect him to lie. "I don't mind hanging out if you need me to."

"Nah, I'll be okay. Thanks for bringing me into town."

"No problem." Jay started the car. "Call me if you need me." He put his hand out for the Bro handshake.

Chris hesitated for a second, knowing he had just lied to one of his best friends. But he grabbed Jay's hand and shook it anyway. "Thanks again."

Jay drove off and Chris stumbled inside.

Gunstot, his eyes glued to his monitor, watched as David handed Chris another beer.

"Tish and Xander," Gunstot hollered to the others in the rear of the lab. "We have to do something. Chris has consumed six alcoholic beverages and is opening another."

Tish and Xander, huddled together in the back of the lab, didn't acknowledge Gunstot's statement. They were putting the finishing touches on their intervention plan for Braaddy and time was of the essence.

"That should do it," Tish said as she picked up the notes. "Wait, have you ever flown an Intervessel?"

"Just in the training area. Did you fly one when you were on your training mission?" Xander asked.

"Yes. It's so easy to fly."

"Well, I've flown one around base during training so I would assume I'm qualified. I will eventually have to in a real mission."

"Right. I say the plan is done so let's go."

Tish and Xander both stood up and were face to face with Gunstot who was standing on the opposite side of the back row of workstations.

"We must do something," Gunstot pleaded with his hands in the air. "He is drinking too much."

The other two looked at each other. Tish spoke first.

"I know we need to help him. We've been trying to come up with something. Do you have an idea?"

"No I don't. You are the experts." He walked back to his workstation. Spinning around, he pointed his finger at the other two, and said, "Even being new, I can see that an intervention is needed here."

Xander nodded at Tish. This time he spoke first.

"That's what we were thinking, Gunstot. Great idea."

Tish walked over to her workstation and sat down.

"I'll go get Braaddy," Xander said as he exited the lab.

Both Tish and Gunstot silently observed Chris on their monitors while they waited for Xander to return. Finally, Tish broke the silence.

"So, Gunstot," Tish began her inquiry. "How do you think Jzet will respond to an intervention request considering the circumstances? It's not exactly a life or death situation."

Gunstot turned to Tish with a stern look in his eyes and said, "Are you farrook? It's very possible that if we don't intervene, Chris could suffer an alcohol poisoning incident." He pulled his headset off in frustration and tossed it on his keyboard. "If Jzet denies this request, then he is working from a different agenda. He …"

Gunstot was interrupted by the lab doors opening with Braaddy and Xander striding in. Tish and Gunstot jumped to attention.

"At ease," Braaddy barked.

"Colonel Braaddy," Gunstot began, "what an honor to have …"

"Cut the crap," Braaddy interrupted as he stood next to Tish's workstation. "What's this I hear about requesting an intervention?"

"Sir," Tish took the lead. "It appears that Chris has not responded well to the injury challenge. Xander and I have written up an assessment with an intervention proposal. Chris is indulging in self-destructive behavior and is avoiding our planned resolution to the situation."

"And exactly what is the situation? Wait. Gunstot, you're the newest member of the team here. I want you to give me your assessment."

Gunstot gulped and said, “Well, sir, Chris is consuming large amounts of alcoholic beverages. He has now started associating with irresponsible and immoral individuals who are encouraging these destructive acts.” Gunstot’s tone grew with confidence as he explained his viewpoint. “Furthermore, these alcoholic beverages alter his mind to the point that even when we get a rare opportunity to get an X13 probe in next to him while he is asleep, communication with his mind is impossible.”

Braaddy smacked the back of the chair he was standing next to.

“Well then,” he said, clapping his hands together while looking at all three. “I’m absolutely positive that this project team I’ve assembled has a solution.” He crossed his arms on his chest. “Well? I’m waiting.”

“We …,” both Xander and Tish spoke at once.

“I’ll explain,” Tish said putting a hand on Xander’s shoulder. “We have decided that an intervention is necessary to extract the Savior from the house he is currently staying in and deliver him to the residence of Lisa Haskett. She was Chris’ nurse when he was in the hospital for surgery and appears to be the only person who has the ability to alter his behavior.”

Braaddy put a hand on his chin and lowered his head, obviously pondering what he just heard.

“I’m familiar with Lisa Haskett. I suppose all the details have been worked out in your report.”

Xander handed Braaddy the documents that he and Tish had written up.

“Good,” he said as he started flipping through them. “I’ll review these on my way to see Jzet. If the analysis comes up with convincing evidence of this self-destructive behavior, then we’ll have to take action immediately.” He headed to the doors.

“Sir,” Xander stopped him. “Tish and I would like to be on the intervention team.”

“Not together. One of you can, but I need experience in the lab with Gunstot if we approve this intervention.” The lab doors opened. “You two decide who goes,” Braaddy said as he departed.

A dark, moonless night had settled in around the house on 17th Street. David and his roommates were asleep in their bedrooms while Chris was passed out on the living room couch. Beer cans covered the coffee table and littered the floor.

An Intervessel silently drifted down through the trees into the middle of the backyard. As the side panel opened, Xander clad in black attire, hopped down onto the dewy grass followed by Dlocto. Not making a sound, they made their way to the side porch that led to the kitchen. Both of them heard Tish’s voice over their ear pieces.

"This side door will take you into the kitchen. The immediate doorway on your left takes you into the living room. Based on what I'm seeing right now, Chris is laying on the sofa right under the big bay window that has the view of the street. The street lights are on, but no one is out there at this time. I'm not sure if the probe's heat sensor readings on Chris are correct. The data says there are two people in the same location. Wait." Tish entered a command. "Switching to the probe's infra-red." She adjusted her monitor. "We've got a problem."

"What?" asked Xander?

"Chris has a female lying with him."

"That's not a problem," Xander interjected. "We'll glaze her like a cheap donut and move her out of the way."

"That's affirmative," Tish replied with a slight snicker. "But cut the unnecessary remarks and proceed in."

"I thought it was funny," Dlocto said into his mic as he heard Gunstot in the lab laughing in the background.

"Cut the chatter," Tish said firmly.

Xander held a small device against the lock of the door and a red spark shot out. The door opened effortlessly. Dlocto went in first and moved quietly into the living room followed by Xander who quickly checked the other hallway for movement. Dlocto glazed the girl, who shook her head from side to side. Then he glazed Chris.

"He didn't even flinch at the Glaze," Xander whispered into his mic. "The girl sure did."

Dlocto and Xander gently lifted the girl and laid her on the floor.

"I'm sure he's had too much alcohol," Tish responded. "Bring him out the same way you came in. I'm checking outside the house now to make sure it's clear."

They picked Chris up and carried him out of the house.

"If Lisa Haskett's house has moved, we're in for a surprise," Xander said quietly as he lifted Chris up into the ship.

"I don't like surprises," Dlocto said quickly. With everyone inside the Intervessel, he closed the door. "Are we still going to 14th Street North?"

"That's affirmative," Tish acknowledged.

"Take us to that address, Xander. We'll deliver our package to the front step, knock on the door, and then get out of there."

25 – THEY MEET AGAIN

Bang ... Bang.

Lisa sat up in her bed. She rubbed her eyes not wanting to believe someone had just knocked on her front door. She looked at the clock: 2:00 AM in big red text glared at her. She brushed a few strands of hair off of her face and felt something move against her leg.

"Don't worry, Otis," she said to her six month old puppy, which was curled up on the bed beside her. "I'm sure it's those kids playing 'ding-dong ditch' again." Leaning over to the night stand, she turned on her lamp. "It's two o'clock in the morning. Geez." She looked at Otis who slowly stretched his legs, gave a big yawn, and rolled his head toward her. His sleepy eyes momentarily opened then closed.

"Well then. You're not watchdog material and obviously, you're not interested in getting up." Lisa gently patted Otis's head then ran her hand through his shiny black fur. "I'll be right back. I'm just gonna take a peek out the window," she said as she flipped the sheet off her and swung her legs over the edge of the bed.

Lisa tip-toed quietly into the hall and then went into the dining room. Her eyes were now adjusted to the darkness. She parted the front window curtains ever so slightly. Staring at the front stoop with only a modest glow of light coming from the street lamp, there appeared to be some clothes piled on the steps. But when the pile raised an arm up, she quickly went to her front door and opened it a crack. Peering out, she saw the crumpled form of Chris on the stoop lying on his back with both legs extended down the two steps. He had his left arm up in the air as if signaling for someone. She figured he had been hitting the storm door with his hand.

Bang … Bang …Bang.

Lisa swung the heavy wooden door open and suddenly realized she had on nothing but a tee shirt and panties. She quickly closed it.

But he's hurt, she thought to herself.

She opened it again. Chris had dropped his arm down on the stoop.

"Crap." Lisa closed the door and ran to her room to get a pair of sweatpants, then made a quick trip to her bathroom to gargle some mouth wash. Running out of her room, she slowed in front of the hallway mirror to examine her hair.

"What a mess." She used her fingers to straighten it a bit. "Oh, the heck with it."

Opening the door again while flipping on the outside light, she looked through the glass storm door at Chris. From the way he was waving his arm again, it became apparent that he was dying or drunk. She guessed the latter.

Lisa opened the storm door and said in a calm matter-of-fact voice, "Well, it's about time you came to see me."

Chris rolled his head on the concrete stoop to where he could somewhat see the source of the voice. Unable to distinguish between the two upside-down profiles in the two doorways, he muttered, "Sure, baby. Ya gonna help me in? I seem to have lost my balance."

"Of course you did. I'm going to get something that will help you get up. You stay right there. Okay?"

"Yesh, baby," he slurred. "I be here."

While Lisa disappeared into the house, Chris dropped his arm down onto his chest.

"Where the heck am I?" He raised his head up and looked out onto the street. "They changed David's street. That's just great."

At the sound of the door opening, he laid his head down and looked up toward the light only to be greeted by a pitcher of cold water right on his face. He quickly sat up, eyes burning, his face, hair, and tee-shirt totally soaked.

"Hey!" Chris turned and saw who his assailant was. "I know you. What the heck did you do that for?" He shook his head, water flying off his near shoulder length hair. "How'd I get here?"

Lisa stood in the doorway, arms crossed, smirking at him with the empty water pitcher still in her hand.

"So, you missed me?"

Chris checked out his surroundings. Leaning to one side, he got up to his feet, obviously favoring his left leg. His head was a little clearer from that face drenching.

"Really," he said, "how'd I get here?" His eyes finally rested on Lisa who was still smiling and asked, "What time is it? And why did you do that?"

"One thing at a time," she began. Pushing the door open further, Lisa ordered, "First, get in here."

Chris limped in and stood in the front hallway while Lisa closed the door.

"Second, keep your voice down. My roommates are asleep."

"Roommates?"

"Do I need to get another pitcher of water and wash out your ears?" she asked sarcastically, gesturing to the couch in the living room. "Third, it's two o'clock in the morning."

"Wow. For real?" He shook his head and sat down. "Two o'clock in the …"

"Are you going to repeat everything I say?"

"I'm just trying to understand what's going on."

"Do you even know what day it is? Or the date?"

"Sure. It's March something."

"Wow. That's precious. You got the month right."

"What? Why are you …"

"Never mind." Lisa cut him off while setting the pitcher on the coffee table. "As for how you got here, I have no idea." She tossed him a towel that had been draped on the back of the chair and sat down. "Call before you come visiting next time." Leaning forward and making a sniffing sound, she added, "When was the last time you had a shower? You stink."

"It's nice to see you too." Chris rubbed the towel over his head. "Seriously, I don't know where I am."

"You're in my living room."

"Duh. Where is your living room? Wait … don't answer that." He tossed the towel onto the couch. "It's in your house."

"You learn fast."

"So, where is your house located in the city?"

"It's on 14th Street."

"That's only three streets from where I was on 17th. It's not that far."

"Which house on 17th Street?"

"I dunno. I think its 325 or something."

"Well, I'm on the north end of 14th and 325 is on the south end 17th. So it's a bit of a hike."

"That's okay. I can do it."

"Do what? Walk back there? You're not going anywhere, bubba." She stood up. "You're going to take a shower and then get some sleep."

"But …"

"No buts. However, you can get your butt up and hop into the shower. I'm going to get you some towels and I've got a huge pair of gym shorts you can wear that I used in a skit. They should fit you."

Lisa helped Chris get up and into the bathroom.

The next morning, Lisa readied herself for class. She had looked in on Chris who was sleeping soundly on the couch. After grabbing a quick bite to eat, she sat on the edge of the couch and gently shook him awake.

"Chris, wake up for a second."

He opened one bloodshot eye and said, "Headache."

"I'm not surprised. I've got some aspirin in my bathroom and a toothbrush for you. You need to get up and move into my room. I don't want my roommates freaking out by finding a stranger sleeping in our living room."

"Do I hafta?"

"Yes. I have to go to class."

"Class? You're in school?"

"Yep. I'm in the University in the Nursing School."

"That's cool." Chris rubbed his eyes. "How'd I get here?"

"We discussed this last night. It's a wonder you made it anywhere as drunk as you were. You really must have missed me."

"Yeah, that's it." Chris put both hands on his forehead. "Can you get the aspirin for me?"

"No, I don't think so. You'll get it yourself when you are in the bathroom. You need to suffer from this hangover headache a little longer so that maybe, you'll change the path you are on. I can help you with that, as I told you before."

"What?"

"Never mind. I've got to get to class so you've got to get up and go to my room."

"I just wanna lie here and suffer."

"Stop stalling. Get up, big boy and move it," she ordered while prodding him along.

With Chris finally asleep in her bed, Lisa went to class.

The spring of 1984 brought about the usual seasonal changes. April showers had passed and May flowers colored the city. The chill in the air had warmed and the days were longer providing opportunities for growth. Chris had seized one of those opportunities and was riding his bike back to Lisa's house from PT.

I had forgotten how riding a bike could be so much fun and good for you, he thought as he pedaled along Hessian Road. The wind felt good on his legs. He looked down at the huge scars on his left knee.

I'm never sore from PT anymore. The scars didn't bother him; rather, he used them for motivation. *They will be a good reminder on how I almost lost everything.*

He stopped at the intersection of Rugby Blvd and Coiner Avenue.

I really should do it now. I've put this off long enough. David is sure to be home.

Coiner Avenue led to 14th Street which was straight ahead. Rugby led to 17th Street

He took a right on Rugby.

After two knocks, the front door opened.

"Hey there, buddy boy," David said as he stuck his hand out. Chris grabbed it with a good tight grip and gave him a hearty handshake. "Come on in the house. What the heck have you been up to? You disappeared a couple of months ago leaving Becky what's-her-name lying on the floor."

"I guess I did." Chris closed the door and followed David into the living room. It was cleaner than the last time he remembered. "Are your roommates here?" He plopped down on the couch.

"Nah, it's only four o'clock. They don't get off work till five. I got off early." David sat in the chair opposite Chris. "Wanna a beer?"

"Nope."

"Nope? What's up with that? Last time you were here, you drank everyone under the table." David stood up. "I'm gonna get one. What happened to you anyway? You split in the middle of the night, and I haven't heard from you in months. You were practically living on my couch."

"Wait, David. Hold off on getting that beer," Chris said as he jumped to his feet and held his hands out, gesturing toward the chair. "Have a seat for a sec. I want to talk to you."

"Sure, man." David came back from the hall and sat down. "What's up?"

"Well, I tell ya," Chris barely got the words out and started to choke up. He swallowed hard, controlled it, and continued, "I was in a bad way when I showed up on your door step a few months ago."

"You ain't just whistling Dixie there," David chuckled. "I've never seen you like that."

"So why didn't you stop me?" Chris had a pleading look in his eye.

"You're a big boy. You were our captain. I wasn't going to tell you what to do."

David stood up again and Chris knew where he was going.

"Let's go outside a sec. I want to show you something." Chris popped up off the couch so fast, it surprised David.

"Well, okay." They headed to the door. "Your knee seems to be a lot better. You're moving around like the old Chris."

"I am the old Chris," he said as he stepped out into the sun drenched front yard. He walked over to his bike. "Check it out, man."

David got on it. "Wow. This is a Viscount ten speed road bike." He bounced up and down on the seat. "Cool. Where's your car?"

"I don't need it. This is part of my comeback. I've been riding this baby to PT."

"From your house?" David stared at Chris like he was crazy. "You're nuts. That's at least fifteen miles from here."

"Nah, man. Not from my house. I've been staying on 14th Street."

"Really? Whose place is that?"

"No one you know; just someone who's helping me out." Chris checked David's expression to see if he was going to pursue that any further. He quickly changed the subject. "You still got a bike?"

"Yeah," he said as he lifted his feet and tried to balance, "at the parent's house. But one of my roommates has a Viscount out behind the house."

"You know that Cory, Alex, and Gene are all in college and they're riding bikes every day to and from class."

David was still trying to balance without touching the ground. "That's gotta suck."

"Not really, according to them. They love being in college." Chris watched David wobbling back and forth. "Why don't you take it out on the street and see if you can still ride one?"

"All right."

Chris followed David as he pushed the bike out into the street, hopped on, and started riding around.

"Hey," David hollered through a big grin, "I can still do this."

"Of course you can," Chris said smiling. "I bet you can still play ball too"

David put the brakes on and the tires screeched to a stop.

"Playing ball is done for me. I didn't get any pretty scholarship offers like the rest of you guys." The good demeanor was gone.

"Oh yeah, right." Chris threw the attitude right back at him. "Look at the great offers I got. None!"

"Well, you were gonna have one until your knee blew out. You had an excuse. I just wasn't good enough."

Chris walked up to him and put his hand on his shoulder.

"You are good and I should know. We played together. If you had the chance to play college ball again, would you take it?"

"You mean walk on to a team?"

"Better than that, man." Chris checked to see if he really had David's attention. "Do you remember Lin Hrica from Jefferson?"

"Sure. He was our coach."

"Ian and I are going out to LA next fall and play for Northrop University where Hrica is the head baseball coach," Chris said proudly and playfully punched David in the shoulder.

"You're going to LA?" David's jaw dropped.

"Inglewood, actually. But that's like a suburb of LA." Chris could feel the good energy flowing.

"No way."

"We are. Why don't you come with us? They have a great engineering program. I remember last year you talked about looking into programs similar to it."

David was quiet, just sitting on the bike staring blankly downward, obviously thinking. He scuffed his right foot on the ground and then looked at Chris.

"So what are you and Ian going to major in?"

Chris slapped David on the back and said, "I'm gonna be in the business school focusing on business information systems and statistics. Ian is going for a degree in mechanical engineering." He again put his hand on David's shoulder. "So you'll go with us?"

David got off the bike and started walking it up into the yard.

"Well, it beats the heck outta staying in this place with a bunch of guys I don't know that well." He nodded his head toward the house. "Can't see that I have anything to lose. Yeah, I'll do it." This time he punched Chris in the shoulder. "Where do I start?"

About an hour later, Chris was putting his bike up on Lisa's back porch. He went into the kitchen and found Lisa rummaging through the fridge.

"What's happening?" he cheerfully asked, sweat dripping from his chin due to his fast ride from David's.

"Nothing much. I was looking for the mustard for the burgers, but it looks like we're out." She turned to see him. "How was PT?" she inquired as she sat down at the kitchen table.

"Awesome. And to boot, I finally did it." He started prancing around the room like a proud peacock.

Lisa giggled at the sight. "Did what?"

"After PT, I rode over to David's and spilled the beans on what I've been up to."

"And?"

"Have we got room for one more for our Friday cookout?"

"David said yes to your idea?" Lisa screamed jumping up from her seat into Chris' arms.

"He sure did. He wants to go to Northrop with me and Ian."

"Ian and me," she corrected.

"You're going too?" he joked while hugging her. "That's so awesome." He was still holding her in his arms, her feet in the air.

"Put me down you big goof." She pushed gently on his chest.

"Okay." He put her down and sat down at the table. "Ya know, Lisa, I hope you never tire of hearing me say how grateful I am to you for helping me out. I mean, I can't imagine where I'd be right now if it weren't for you."

Chris stared at Lisa, whose back was to him at the moment. She was wearing one of his old practice jerseys, barefoot, and had on short, cutoff jeans. Her movements were swift and deliberate while at the sink washing dishes, but to him, she was graceful and beautiful.

"Well, big boy, you're the one who showed up on my doorstep. I didn't bring you here." She looked over her shoulder and smiled. "You must have realized you needed to change."

"Well, I don't remember how I got here, but it doesn't matter. You and your roommates were so cool to let me crash in that extra room in the attic."

He got up from his chair and headed to the back door.

"You're paying your way so take credit for it." She put some dried plates in the cabinet above the sink. "I mean after all, being Jefferson's assistant baseball coach is not anything to sniff at. It's paying your bills."

"Yeah, you're right. It really helped finding out about Coach Hrica being at Northrop." He clapped his hands together. "I'm gonna scrape down the grill and then ride down to the store on Grady to get some mustard." He reached out and smacked her on the butt.

"Chris Gates!" Her head snapped in his direction with a fake frown on her face. "You know better than that."

He let go of the door handle and covered the two steps over to her in one hop. Grabbing the dish towel, he stood behind her and removed her hands from under the running water, dried them, and held them in one of his. He gently turned her to face him.

"I know I've asked you a million times, but I'm gonna keep on asking. Can we start dating now?" he pleaded in a real serious voice. "After all, I've done a complete 180. I've cleaned up my act. I'm heading off to college, and I'm looking forward to my future now. I want you in it."

Lisa reached up and put her finger on his lips. "Shhhhhh. We've talked about …"

Suddenly, Chris stumbled backward. His mind reeled with visions.

Wait, he thought to himself as his vision clouded. *Where am I?* He was seeing all white. He heard a female voice in head.

"Chris! Chris! Are you all right?"

He felt his shoulder hit against the cabinet. Someone was holding his arms. He knew he was being moved and pushed into a chair. But he couldn't see.

"Chris! What's wrong?"

The female voice was louder now.

Who is that? Why can't I see?

Whack! Chris felt a sharp sting on his face. He could see clearly now. Lisa was standing in front of him and had just slapped him. He reached up and put his hand on his cheek.

"Ow. What'd you do that for?"

"What was happening to you?" she asked in a panicky voice. "Your eyes glazed over, you started stumbling around, and you kept mumbling something about sand. Are you all right?"

"I think so." He rubbed his face. "I'm okay." He got up. "Maybe I stood up too quick before or something. I was real dizzy."

"I dunno. Why don't you sit down and rest a bit."

"Nah, I'm fine, really. Do you hear a buzzing sound, like a fly or mosquito or something like that?"

"No, why?"

"I thought I heard a bug. Maybe I'm just hearing things."

"That's really weird. I'm gonna keep my eye on you."

He got up and opened the door. "Promise?" That sly, playful grin had returned.

"Yes. But there is no way you are going to the store alone. We'll go together."

"Okay." He started out the door but stopped. "Hey, I didn't get your answer when I asked about us dating."

Lisa had gone back to the sink but wasn't answering him. She glanced up.

"We'll talk about it."

"Yes!" Chris yelled with excitement as he pumped his fist in the air and stepped out onto the deck. "Woo-hoo!"

On the ride to the store, Chris slowed his bike down as they approached the market. Lisa noticed and slowed down too. Glancing at Chris, she asked, "You okay? You're slowing down."

"I'm fine. I wanted to ask you something." He pedaled along slowly in the bike lane riding next to Lisa. "Is the only reason we can't date is because of the rule against boyfriends living in the house? Honestly, tell me now." Chris kept looking ahead and then at Lisa to see her reaction. He could tell she was really thinking on this.

"Well …," she began. "Oh look. We're here." Lisa pulled her bike up next to the store and got off while Chris did the same. "You wait here with the bikes so we don't have to lock them up. I'll get the mustard."

"Wait," Chris said as he reached out and touched her arm. "It is really important that I know. Please tell me."

"Why? Why do you need to know this right now?" Lisa pleaded as she faced him.

"I've just got to know," he said as he put his hands on her

shoulders, "because I've fallen head over heels in love with you."

"Chris," She searched for words. "I …,"

"Shoot straight," he said firmly. "If it hurts, I'll recover and will always be grateful to you for what you've done for me. I won't backslide. I've got too much to do now. Besides, even if you say no, that doesn't mean I'll give up."

He gazed into her beautiful blue eyes surrounded by that sweet, pretty face. He touched her soft, wavy blond hair.

"I won't ever give up hope."

The pleading in Lisa's eyes softened as she put her arms around him.

"Chris, uh …," she cleared her throat. "I could fall for you so easily. Maybe I already have."

Their heads turned as an elderly couple came out of the store and shuffled past them.

"Greetings," the man said, nodding in their direction. His wife, stooped over from age, smiled at them.

"Good afternoon, ma'am, sir," Chris acknowledged as he and Lisa stepped away from each other.

"Oh don't let us interrupt you." The lady's raspy voice was almost a whisper. She looked at the man, then took his hand and said, "Isn't young love beautiful?"

"Almost as beautiful as ours," he replied almost out of earshot as they continued on their way.

Chris and Lisa turned back to each other and hugged.

With her cheek pressed against his chest, she whispered, "I've been hurt before. I don't want to ever feel that again."

His lips were pressed against her hair as he held her tight. He whispered back, "I could not, nor would I ever hurt you."

She lifted her head up and looked at him.

"I know what you're like. You're big, strong, popular, and smart to boot. You're honest too. But I also saw how many girls came into the hospital to see you. Word must have traveled fast when your girlfriend broke up with you because the floodgates opened. You don't remember I'm sure. Depression and narcotics have a way of doing that. You're what they call a 'ladies' man. You can't help that you're the entire package."

"I don't care about any of them. I care …"

Lisa put her finger on his lips, just like before.

"Don't. I know what you're going to say."

She lowered her finger and put her head back on his chest.

If this is heaven, I don't want to leave, he thought.

Lisa interrupted his dreamy thoughts.

"I know you are destined for something really big in this life," she continued.

"How do you know that? I'm just a normal average guy."

"No, you're far from that."

She lifted her head off his chest.

"Tell ya what," she began while looking into his eyes. "You're going off to college in a few months, all the way across the country in LA. That'll be Hollywood heaven for you: girls, girls, girls. But if you're serious, and up for it, then let's agree that neither of us is going to date anyone else. We're both going to remain single."

"What? I'm sorry, but my heart was melting just then while I was holding you. What do you mean?"

She stepped back from him, but still held his hands.

"I promise to not date anyone else unless I clear it with you first."

"Okay, I guess. But…"

"Ahhhhttt. No buts." Lisa had the finger coming up, but Chris beat her to it by putting his own finger over his lips.

"You got a nice butt," he muttered through his partially closed lips.

"Chris!" She playfully stomped her foot, trying to act serious. "Do you promise to …"

"Shhhhhh." This time Chris had put his finger on Lisa's lips. "I get it. I promise not to date anyone else unless I clear it with you first."

She gazed up into his eyes. "Really?"

"Really." He cocked his head. "Does this mean we are officially not dating now?"

"Yes. It's official." She quickly stood up on her tip-toes and kissed him.

He was shocked. "You kissed me." He reached for her but she had spun around and made a beeline for the store. "Wait" He followed her. "That was our first kiss. This is important."

Glancing back at him while opening the door, she said, "We need to buy the mustard and get our butts home. Everyone will be there soon. You wait with the bikes."

A couple of hours later, throngs of people were milling about in the backyard at the cookout. Chris had gone around front to meet Ian who had just pulled up to the house.

"My man," Chris said as he bounded barefoot, down the front walk to Ian's car. "It's so awesome for you to come." They shook hands.

"I don't know about this, Chris," Ian said nervously while eyeing the house. "Who's here?"

"Lisa and her roommates are here, of course, and a bunch of their friends from school. There are some really fine looking women here."

"See, that's the thing that bothers me. I don't know any of these people."

"You know Lisa and me. You've met her roommates. What's the problem? Come on. Let's go hit the cookout."

"You may feel comfortable around all these people, but I'm seventeen and I've never hung out with a college crowd. Don't you feel the least bit intimidated?" he asked, not budging from the side of his car.

"I'm seventeen too. We're both almost eighteen. And who's going to intimidate you? If anything, they should be intimidated by us. We're Bros and nobody tops that," Chris said with emphasis as he patted Ian on the back. "Besides, we're going to Northrop out in LA in the fall, so we're college boys now. And," he stepped back and play-acted swinging a baseball bat, "we're going to be college baseball players."

"Maybe you feel that way, but I'm still in Jefferson. That's just high school." Ian lowered his head and crossed his arms, frowning slightly. "I mean the couple times I've been over here, well…, Lisa and her roommates are knockouts, man."

"Look Bro," Chris leaned up against the car next to Ian and put his arm around his buddy's shoulders. "If you get in a conversation with any of these beautiful girls and they ask about school, talk about Northrop and how you're gonna be playing baseball in LA next season. It's all in how you package the message, my man."

Showing some spunk now, Ian smiled and got up off the car and clapped his hands together. He looked at the house. Music drifted around from the backyard.

"You're right. I may not be as smooth as you in thinking these things out before hand, but ya only gotta tell me once." He was smiling. "Now, what's that surprise you told me about on the phone?"

Chris popped up off the car, and looked up the street to the next intersection. He spotted David about a block away from the corner heading toward Lisa's house.

"Speak of the Devil," he said tapping Ian on the arm and pointing at the fast approaching bicyclist.

Ian saw who was on the bike and said, "David Smith is coming to this thing? I haven't seen him in almost a year. What's up with him being here?"

"Ask him yourself," Chris answered.

David braked, squealing the tires and fishtailed to a stop.

"What's happening boys? Am I late?"

"Just in time, buddy." Chris pointed to the porch. "Stick your bike up there."

Ian gave David a pat on the arm.

"David Smith. Great to see you." David shook Ian's hand.

"Same." He put the bike up and asked, "Are the burgers and dogs ready? I'm starved." He cupped his hand to his ear after hearing the music and smiled. "Are the women here yet?"

"Boatloads." Chris winked. "But you have your priorities mixed up. You asked about the food then the girls."

"That's 'cause I'm hungry."

"So how do you know this crew, David?" Ian asked.

"I've been hanging out here a few times over the past couple of months. Chris invited me to the cookout because you were coming and the three of us need to make plans."

"Plans?" Ian quizzically looked at both of them.

David glanced at Chris. "You didn't tell him?"

"Nope," Chris answered smugly. "You tell him."

David raised his hands in the air and shouted, "I'm going to LA with you guys and play for Northrop!"

Ian's jaw dropped. "You are?" He draped his arms around both of the boy's shoulders and jostled them. "When did this come up?" Ian's voice exuded excitement.

"A while ago," David answered. "Chris talked me into it."

"Absolutely," Chris continued. "The three of us are gonna play ball together again for Coach Hrica."

"Wow!" Ian jumped up in the air. "This is gonna be so cool!"

"You got that right." David rubbed his hands together. "Now, how about some food?"

"All right. Let's go have some fun, boys," Chris said gesturing toward the backyard. They followed the sound of the music to the cookout.

Far away in the lab on Base GAIA, Tish pulled off her headset, reached over, and patted Xander on the arm.

"We did it," she said smiling broadly at him.

"We sure did. We are back on course."

26 – CALIFORNIA CHALLENGE

General Jhall and Colonel Prahash sat in the front row of the base theater watching the opening ceremonies of the 1989 California Independent College and University World Series tournament. The theater was quite elegant for being on a remote Terlokyan base. One would think they were in a very refined opera house on Earth. The Terlokyans were strong believers in the arts and held quite a number of events from plays to movies to educational lectures in the theater. There were even weekly showings of a famous science fiction television program from Earth.

"Why must we suffer through this baseball extravaganza?" Prahash leaned over and asked. "You know I detest these Earth sporting events."

"Because the Savior is playing," Jhall responded. "This affair is the cumulative event for all the time and effort that our soldiers and the Savior himself have put forth to overcome adversity." General Hall slapped his own knee for emphasis. "It was a dark time just four years ago."

Prahash nodded in agreement.

"It was an amazing turnaround considering the severity of the challenge," the Colonel added. "But many of us believed a problem never existed. Chris Gates had to be put to the test and we knew he would pass it."

Both Jhall and Prahash were surprised to hear a voice enter the conversation from a seat behind them.

"We were lucky," Jzet said leaning forward. "If it hadn't been for that nurse he would have failed the challenge: that and the fact that we had to send an intervention team down there to save him from his own destructive behavior."

"I'm not a believer in luck, as you well know, Major," Jhall responded. "And if I remember correctly, you were opposed to the intervention. But now we will never know what might have happened had we not intervened."

"Nothing would have happened," Jzet stated adamantly. "He would have failed."

"There isn't a …"

"Excuse me, General. I would like to respond to the Major on this."

"By all means, Colonel Prahash," Jhall replied with an air of disdain as he turned and gave Jzet a stern look.

"Major Jzet, it is not a well-kept secret that you detest this whole project."

A smile slowly spread on Jhall's face.

"As a matter of fact," Prahash continued, "I'm not sure why you are involved with the Savior Project considering how you continuously try and undermine it."

"How dare you ..." Jzet said jumping to his feet.

Jhall stood up and spun around so fast to face Jzet that the Major's mouth was still open to speak when the general cut him off. Towering above Jzet's six and a half foot frame even from the downward slant of the theater floor, Jhall's show of quickness had the battled hardened major back in his seat fast.

"You will not speak to a superior officer in that tone or in that manner! Don't you ever forget that. You are dismissed!"

"But ..."

"I said you are dismissed, Major Jzet!" Jhall yelled and everyone in the theater was now watching the confrontation.

Jzet lowered his head and left the theater. His departure elicited a few cheers and some applause.

"As you were," Jhall bellowed out to the others present and then sat down.

"Well then," Prahash said. "That certainly quieted things."

"Where were we?" Jhall totally ignored Prahash's statement. "I believe we were discussing how the Savior had passed this latest challenge." Jhall pointed at the screen. "Behold. The teams are now on the field. And there's the Savior." He paused for a few seconds, admiring the crystal clear picture. "I must say that whoever is in the Savior Project Lab operating the X13 probes is doing an excellent job getting these views."

The screen in the front of the theater was split with the left side showing a view of the baseball field from the upper area of the Palm Springs Stadium. All of the teams were standing in their various lines facing toward the American flag flying near the outfield fence. The right view of the screen was from the ground looking up showing Chris between David and Ian. The boys were taking their hats off and getting ready for the National Anthem.

"What a unique view of the three boys. It is a benefit to be able to have the probe hide in the grass and transmit the image from that position," Prahash commented.

"Indeed."

"I really can't understand your fascination with this Earthling sport. It appears to me that players spend more time standing around expelling saliva from their mouths and touching their reproductive organs than actually playing the game. And this is not taking into account that they put various substances in their mouths, like seeds and tobacco, to increase their saliva flow so they have to, how do they say it, 'spit' more." Prahash scrunched up his face and shook his head.

"Well, my dear Colonel, you must pay more attention to the strategy employed by the managers of the team," Jhall said chuckling a bit. "It is similar in that regard to the Earthling game of chess."

"That, I would disagree with, my good man," Prahash said while shaking his head again. "The game of chess is one of the only civilized contests I have found on this planet. It has been a challenge to find others of equal stature."

"I can see that I'm not going to win you over on this argument."

"Please, don't waste our time. And speaking of challenges, I am surprised that you never commented on the significance of the Savior's discipline and self-control in relation to his commitment to the female Earthling, Lisa Haskett. That was a challenge unto itself."

"When was this, Colonel?"

"It was reported in one of Lieutenant Tish's yearly evaluations. I believe it was the report for the 1988 year. When I read it, I felt it revealed one of the true self-control characteristics that we sought in the Savior's development. I was intrigued by this so I researched the detail from that year and added my observations."

"I must have missed that. I see so many reports, as you well know. But I would like to hear more about this," Jhall said as he then pointed toward the screen. "Look now. The opening ceremony is finished and the teams playing in the first contest are ready."

"Yes, yes. I see that. I'm not sure I can sit through an entire baseball event. There will be three days of these contests."

"Well you must see the first one. The Savior's school, Northrop University, is competing against Marymount College."

Just then, Colonel Braaddy came down the aisle.

"General Jhall and Colonel Prahash, may I join you?"

"By all means, Braaddy," Jhall responded as Braaddy scooted by them and took his seat. "And let's dispense with the ranks for right now and enjoy this contest. It's a big day for the Savior."

"Indeed it is," Braaddy added.

"By the way, I'm glad you are here," Jhall declared. "Prahash was about to enlighten me on Lieutenant Tish's 1988 yearly project evaluation. The good Colonel said he added his observations that revealed some interesting characteristics about the Savior."

"I do recall the report," Braaddy said. "I missed your observations, Prahash, so I would like to hear them too."

"Very well," Prahash began. "As I stated earlier, the Savior has shown remarkable discipline and self-control characteristics that we all agreed were essential. The Savior's time at Northrop provided us with an additional challenge."

"That being?" Jhall asked.

"As we are all aware, Chris Gates has developed a relationship with the female Lisa Haskett, although a very guarded one from her standpoint. She did not want to enter into a commitment with him due to his perceived reputation."

"Perceived reputation?" Jhall asked. "Do you mean his popularity amongst the female species?"

"I'm not sure if perceived is the correct word," Braaddy added.

"True. However, Lisa Haskett was worried that Chris would be tempted to be with many different females since there is an abundant supply of supposed beautiful ones in the city of Los Angeles. So they made a pact with each other not to become involved with their respective opposite sex while they were apart from each other."

"It must have worked," Braaddy replied. "She is there at the tournament in California."

"From the standpoint of not breaking that vow, it was a success. But where the challenge came in was when it became a strong test of his will and self-control."

"How so?" Jhall asked. "Give me an example."

"Gladly. I specifically noted this occurrence in my observations. An event occurred during the month of December in 1988 when all students at Northrop were taking tests for the end of the four month teaching session. Chris was studying for these tests in his apartment with his other two friends, Ian and David.

It was unusually warm for southern California on December 10, 1988. The drought had persisted all year so it was a hot and dry day. Chris was sitting at his desk in front of the window fan, barefoot and clad in cutoffs. He flipped over the notes he was reading and continued highlighting material.

"Come on guys, that's it," Ian said from the couch wearing only his boxers. Papers and books littered the area around him. Tossing his text book on the coffee table, he exclaimed, "We've been at this all day. I need a break and a beer." He got up and walked out to the kitchen, stepping over a pile of dirty laundry.

"Fine," David added. He was planted in the decrepit excuse for a La-Z-Boy. "I think I need one too. How about you, Chris? We've been studying for eight hours straight." He stretched his arms over his head.

"I dunno, man. My Systems Analysis final is tomorrow morning. You don't know what this class is like."

"You've told us all about it. You've studied enough for the entire class. I don't know why you feel you have to ace everything. I'm happy with Bs."

Ian came back in the living room with three beers.

"Here ya go," he said handing one to David. "Chris, think fast!" Ian shouted as the can sailed through the air toward Chris' head. He reached up and caught it.

"Wow. I guess I'm having a beer. Do we have any chips?"

"Hey you two," David interrupted. "I forgot to tell y'all that Cory called last night while you were at dinner. And guess what?"

Silence prevailed as Ian and Chris were both taking huge gulps of beer.

"Great interest, morons," David kidded. "I'll tell you anyway. He's gonna marry that girl he met at college this past August."

"What?!" Chris blurted out, spilling beer down his chin. "He's what?"

"That's cool," Ian jumped in. "What's her name again? Diane something?"

"Diane Costas, and he said they're planning to get married at the end of next summer after they graduate. He's bringing her home for Christmas break so we'll get to meet her. Don't tell your parents, Chris. They don't know anything yet. He wants to tell them during the holidays."

"Okay. Looks like I don't know much about it anyway. He should've called me."

"He tried but you weren't here."

"Right. I gotta call him." He wiped his chin with his hand. "How about them chips, Ian, you chump."

"Geez. I'll go check," Ian said over his shoulder on his way to the kitchen. Then the phone started ringing.

"Hey!" David yelled. "Get the phone while you're out there.

"Duh," came the reply.

"Chris, listen up. We should go out to eat. I gotta get away from these four walls." David plopped down on the couch.

Chris leaned back in his chair and took a swig of beer.

"Yeah, I'm hungry for sure."

"Hey David," Ian yelled from the kitchen. "It's Casey on the phone for you."

"Can ya bring it in here? The cord will reach."

Ian came into the living room, beer in one hand and phone receiver in the other while he kicked at the tangled cord to get it to reach the couch.

"Here you lazy butt." Ian tossed the phone on David's stomach.

"Thanks. Hi Casey."

Chris got up and went to the old beat up television which sat on a red milk crate. He turned it on then picked up a beer can from the floor and stuck in on one of the rabbit ear antennas. The other one was already adorned with a can. Nothing but fuzz came up on the screen so he smacked the right side and a picture appeared. The local news was on.

"I sure wish we had cable," Ian said while stuffing his face with a handful of chips.

"We can if you pay for it," Chris replied as he jumped on the La-Z-Boy.

"Okay, we'll see you tonight," David said as he took the phone receiver to the kitchen. "Guys, guess what?"

"You're gonna get me another beer?" Chris asked.

"Sure, but seriously. Casey and a bunch of her friends are going to the Cathouse up in Hollywood tonight to see … wait for it …"

"Just tell us, man," Ian whined as he threw a pillow at David.

"All right. Aerosmith is supposed to stop by and jam. But more importantly, if you weren't paying attention, Casey is gonna be there with a slew of her friends."

"Awesome!" Ian shouted. "I'm in. Chris, you in? Casey's going."

"I dunno, man. I've got a final tomorrow. You guys don't have yours until Monday."

"Come on, Chris. Casey Wilson has had the hots for you since she got to California and you know it," David teased. "You don't have to hit the sack with her. Just go dancing. Make the girl happy. She's been following you around like a puppy for two years." David shrugged his shoulders as he went for more beer.

"She ain't no dog for sure," Ian added. "And her friends are knock-outs." He took a beer from David while another beer was tossed at Chris.

Chris caught it and asked, "Why can't I get my beer handed to me like everyone else?"

"Screw that," David said while pushing on Ian to sit up on the couch so he could sit down. "You going or not? Come on ya wussy."

"All right, I guess," Chris reluctantly answered while running his hand through his long wavy hair. "But just for a while. And we get to leave when I say. Agreed?"

"That's cool, man," Ian said excitedly as he jumped up. "We gotta get cleaned up and get something to eat first."

"Okay then. Let's get this show on the road," David declared with a clap of his hands.

At about nine o'clock that night the boys were searching for a parking space just a block from the Cathouse. Chris was behind the wheel of the old blue Plymouth Duster that the boys had bought together when they first arrived at school. The car resembled something out of a demolition derby with each corner having a number of dents which accented a fading paint job.

"No spaces, man," David said from the back seat.

"There's a car pulling out now," Chris said gleefully.

"You're always lucky like that," Ian added. "And only a block from the club. Cool."

The boys hopped out of the car and headed for the Cathouse. Blue jeans were the evening's attire. Ian and David sported Northrop tee shirts and tennis shoes while Chris wore sandals and a black, Trax nightclub shirt from a club back east.

"Wow. Check out the line to get in," David observed. "It's gotta be fifty people long."

"Yeah, well, I guess we wait like everyone else," Chris said.

At the end of the line were a group of friends they knew from Northrop and Pepperdine. Willie Haislip, a teammate and the first baseman on the Northrop baseball team jumped out of the crowd at the boys.

"Hey you guys! And wow. Here's Chris, the ultimate jock, out on the town. This is awesome. What brings you all out tonight?" Willie asked.

"Nuttin really," David answered calmly. "Except that Aerosmith is supposed to show!"

"I know, man. This is gonna be so cool," Willie said excitedly and with great volume.

While they were talking, two of the girls from the group meandered to where Chris was standing.

"Hi. I'm Mandy and this is Rhonda. We go to Pepperdine." Mandy practically attached herself to the side of Chris then stumbled slightly in her tall high heels. She straightened up and leaned into him, pushing her breasts against his side.

"Howdy, girls. I'm Chris and this is …"

"I know who you are," Mandy purred while batting her eyelashes. "I've heard a lot about you." The aroma of beer was strong. "Do you like my outfit?" she asked not taking her eyes off him. "I just got it today."

Chris gave her white mini-skirt and very revealing top the quick once-over.

"It's really nice. I bet it'll keep you cool in the club."

"Let's hope so."

Rhonda had now plastered herself to Chris' other side. She took the end of the bright red scarf she was wearing, that did little to cover the skimpy shirt she had on, and lightly whipped it against his face to get him to notice her.

"Hey, big boy. How about my outfit?" Rhonda breathlessly asked.

"I like how you painted your shorts on," he replied eliciting giggles from both girls. "Those boots look really cool too."

"Hi," Ian announced finishing Chris' attempted introduction. "I'm Ian."

"Sure you are," Rhonda replied, not taking her eyes off Chris. "I've seen you play baseball before. You're awesome."

"Thanks," Ian said while shaking his head at being ignored.

The slight to Ian was too much for Chris, but his polite gene was still in control.

"Well, girls," he said while putting an arm around each one. "You'll have to excuse us for a minute while we go say hi to some people up ahead. It's been a while since I've laid eyes on them so I gotta take care of that." He gave that famous smile. "Y'all save our spot in line with you, okay?"

Mandy and Rhonda had their arms wrapped around his waist and their eyes locked onto his face.

Mandy finally said, "Absolutely, Chris. We'll wait right here for you." As he stepped away from them, Rhonda appeared to have a little trouble wanting to let go but Chris eventually freed himself. Reaching around Mandy, he tapped Ian on the shoulder interrupting his conversation with another girl in the crowd.

"What?" came the annoyed response.

"Come on and grab David 'cause we've gotta go see someone further up the line."

"What are you talking about?" Ian said looking like he had just seen a purple pig.

"Just get him and follow me," Chris said as he took off up the street.

He walked on the edge of the sidewalk avoiding the mass of people that were supposed to be in some semblance of a line. As Chris snaked his way through the throngs, a voice rang out from the crowd.

"Yo, Chris. What's up?"

"Timmy! It's you, man," Chris replied while giving the guy a high-five. "Hey, we play Palo Alto in the first game of the season and we're gonna whip your butts."

"Don't be so sure, big man," Timmy laughed. "We'll be swinging for ya."

"Then bring it on. Let's talk more inside."

Almost at the front of the line, Chris was greeted with a commotion.

"Sorry, but I can't let you in yet," said the huge fellow to the couple at the head of the line in front of the club entrance. "We are real close to capacity right now and I have to wait for someone to leave."

"Come on, man," the guy said. "Here's ten bucks to let us in. I'm sure you can use the money."

The club bouncer, some called him the gatekeeper, swelled up his six foot five inch frame with his bulging biceps straining his poured on club tee-shirt and put his face within an inch of the smaller guy. The guy's girlfriend looked up into the giant of a man's glaring eyes and moved behind her boyfriend.

"I told you already that …"

Chris tapped him on the shoulder.

"Excuse me, but how much is …"

"Can't you see …," the bouncer whipped around but stopped in mid-sentence once he saw who it was. "Chris Gates! Man, I never thought I'd run into you again."

Chris didn't recognize the guy for a second then it hit him.

"Jessie! You ol' dog. Whatcha up to? I forgot that you worked at this club." They clasped right hands and gave each other a chest bump with an easy back slap.

Ian and David had gotten there and were watching.

"Man, I was hoping to see you again one day. So, how's the great baseball star? I've read a lot about you in the papers," Jessie said with a big smile and a hand on Chris' shoulder.

Chris noticed Ian and David behind him.

"Jessie, my man. Let me introduce you to a couple of real close friends, Ian and David. They're also on the team."

"What's happening, guys," Jessie said as he high-fived the boys while towering over them. "I recognize you from your pictures in the Times."

"Nice to meet you," David replied. "So where did you meet this character?" he asked referring to Chris.

"Man, let me tell ya. It was late at night and I was broke down with a flat on the Santa Monica Freeway in a freak downpour. My jack was missing so I was just standing there getting soaked not knowing what to do. Then out of the darkness comes Chris pulling up behind me in a blue piece of crap he called a car. He got out in that rain, got his jack, and helped me change the tire. I was wondering to myself if this idiot, white, college boy knew what he was doing 'cause we were next to a bad area of LA. I could tell by his accent that he wasn't from around here. Anyways, after we finished, we went to my place, I introduced him to my boys, and we drank till the sun came up. That is one trusting SOB you got there."

"Wow, Chris, you never told us about that," Ian exclaimed. "When did this happen?"

"About three months ago. Wasn't a big deal. Someone needed help." Chris answered.

"That's my man!" Jessie said playfully punching Chris' shoulder. "You said you were gonna call so I could get you down here to the club."

"Sorry. School, exams, what can I say?" Chris was a big strong guy, but he was small next to Jessie. "But I'm here now. Does that count?"

"Yeah, that's cool," Jessie said still wearing that big smile. "Hey, you guys wanna go on in?"

"How much is it?" David asked.

"Nothing for my man, Chris here," he said patting Chris on the shoulder. "You all go on in. I'll catch up with you later."

"Thanks, Jessie," Chris said exchanging another round of high-fives. "You 'da man."

"Nah. That's you," Jessie replied opening the door for them.

"Hey," the guy at the front of the line protested. "Why did you let them in before us? We were here before they were."

Jessie swelled up to his full size as he glared at the guy.

"Did you hear anything we talked about or are you as deaf as you are dumb? That's my friend. I don't know you. If you have anything else to say, I'll make sure you say it at the end of the line."

The guy's girlfriend finally spoke up. Looking right at her boyfriend, she said, "Will you please shut up?"

Inside the club, the boys slowly made their way through the sea of people toward one of the bars. Loud thumping techno-rave music, the latest craze, blared out of speakers everywhere in the dim, smoky club. As they pushed and bumped along, Chris saw all the posters and pictures of famous rock stars plastered on every wall. It was tough moving. People stood shoulder to shoulder talking, drinking, or watching the packed dance floor.

Finally saddling up to the bar, David got the bartender's attention and ordered three drafts.

"Easy, hotrod," Chris exclaimed as Ian handed him a frosty mug. "I didn't say I was gonna drink anything. I might just have a ginger ale or something."

"A what? Come on you dweeb," Ian had to practically yell to be heard above the music. "You're at the hottest nightclub in LA, the Cathouse. You're surrounded by beautiful women, we got in for free, and you think you maybe should drink a soda? Get real, man."

"He's right, man," David added. "This place is wicked."

"All right," Chris said giving in. He took a big swig from his mug.

At that moment, a high pitched squeal was heard.

"David!" Casey and her friends had found the boys. She was bouncing up and down like a little girl who just got her first Barbie doll. She gave David a hug. "Ian!" He also got a big hug. Then she stopped bouncing and stood in front of Chris. "Hi, Chris. I'm so glad you're here." Like lightning, she stood up on her tip toes, wrapped her arms around his neck pulling his face down, and planted a kiss right on his lips.

Chris was returning the kiss somewhat, but he couldn't get her to stop. To dodge an awkward moment, he picked her up; all hundred and ten pounds of the little five foot five inch blond. This caused her to squeal in delight. Then he gently set her down.

"Whoa, girl. That was some greeting," Chris said tasting a cherry sweetness in his mouth.

"Sorry," Casey said, putting her hands on his chest. "I'm just so happy that you came."

While she stayed glued to him, staring up with goo-goo eyes, he couldn't help wonder how he was going to resist this beautiful creature. It appeared that most girls that night had dressed provocatively and Casey was no exception.

David leaned over to Ian and said as quietly as he could, "How come I didn't get a greeting like that? And why do girls always fly to him like flies on a … shucks … I don't know the rest of that adage."

"I don't think that is one, but I know what you mean," Ian replied.

Casey's friends were now milling around the boys and drinking beer when the talk turned to dancing.

"Let's dance," Casey said grabbing Chris' hand and pulling him toward the dance floor. He resisted.

"Why don't we wait a while …"

That effort failed as David and Ian pushed Chris along behind Casey so he had no choice but to follow her through the mass of partiers. Totally surrounded in the middle of the dance floor, Casey was already moving to the music. Chris finally joined in while trying desperately to avoid eye contact with Casey who was zeroed in on Chris' face.

"I am so happy you finally came out to party with me," she said sweetly as she put her arms around his waist.

The music was so loud that Chris barely heard her. He smiled, pointed at his ear and shook his head thus killing the conversation.

A couple hours later after more dancing and beer, Willie and his group finally made it in and found them at the bar. The party atmosphere had intensified as the evening wore on. The Pepperdine girls approached Chris while he and Casey sat on barstools. Casey wasted little time in making it obvious that she had her hooks into Chris for the evening. He had done his best to not encourage her and to distance himself, even making numerous trips to the restroom, all to no avail. Keeping his distance without appearing rude was not his forte. For a brief moment, they were left alone. Chris had a feeling that something was about to come up. He was right.

"Chris?" Casey spun her barstool so she faced him and then put her hand on his leg.

"What's up, Casey?"

"I'm feeling a little tired. Do you think you could take me home?"

Her apartment was a couple of blocks down from his place so it really wasn't out of the way. But from the dripping sweetness of her request, Chris knew she was angling for something else. Then an idea struck him like lightning.

"Sure, Casey. I was thinking about heading home anyway."

"You were?" Her eyes widened as she sat up straight in her seat. She grabbed both of Chris' hands and said, "That's wonderful. I was ..."

Chris cut her off before she could say anything more.

"Yeah, I've got a final exam in the morning and I really didn't want to be out too late." He stood up. "I'm gonna tell David to make sure he and Ian have another way home."

Casey looked a bit confused but Chris figured his idea was the best way out of this particular predicament. After checking, Willie said he'd give David and Ian a ride since he also lived close by. Ian gave Chris a hard time as he was leaving.

"What a lame excuse," Ian chided Chris. "You could just tell us that you're going home with her."

"It's really not like that, man," Chris replied while checking to see if he was out of earshot of Casey. It didn't appear to be an issue. She was happily chatting with her friends although she occasionally snuck a quick peek at him. He turned around and leaned on the bar next to Ian. Facing the mirror behind the bar, he could covertly observe Casey. It must have been the moment his back was to her that she locked her dreamy gaze on him, eyes moving up and down his backside. He shook his head a couple of times, then spoke to Ian.

"Casey mentioned she wanted to go home and you know I've got that final tomorrow."

"Whatever you say, Bro. But you can't fool me."

"Ian, look at me," Chris said straight-faced.

"What?"

"Do you really believe that I would screw things up with Lisa?"

"I dunno, man," Ian said shaking his head. "Casey's pretty hot, but I know you have to go." He patted Chris on the shoulder and winked. "You've got that BIG final tomorrow."

"Shut up you twit. I'll see you later at the apartment." He drained his mug and started toward Casey.

"Yeah, sure. See ya tomorrow sometime," Ian laughed as he turned back to the bar and picked up his beer.

"You ready to go?" Chris said to Casey.

"I sure am," she purred as she hopped off her barstool and took his arm. "I'm so tired."

Those words poured out of her with such enthusiasm that Chris knew he was going to have a tough time getting out of this without hurting her.

After making their way through the crowd and out the front door, Chris chatted with Jessie, making plans to get together. On the way to the car, Casey lifted her hair off the back of her neck.

"Boy, it's hot. Aren't you burning up in those long jeans?" She let go of her hair and grabbed his hand. "You've got to have some shorts in the car you can change into for the drive to my place."

Holy crap. We haven't even gotten to the car yet.

"Nah, I'm okay. Once the car is moving with some wind coming in we'll be fine."

Chris got the old Duster out onto the freeway heading to Northrop. Casey had planted herself so close to Chris that there wasn't enough room to shove a toothpick between them. She had one hand on his leg and her head on his shoulder.

"Uh, Casey, can I ask you a question?"

"Sure. Anything for you."

Oh boy.

"If you had a boyfriend and y'all were at different schools, let's say they were on opposite coasts, would you ever cheat on him?"

"Never. I would be faithful. I know it would be a long distance relationship but we could always talk on the phone, write letters, and during breaks we would be able …"

"Got it. Cool. Now for the next question."

"Okay."

Chris glanced out his window at the passing cars as he carefully thought of the correct wording for his next question.

"Would you expect your boyfriend to remain faithful to you even though there would be a lot of temptation to, let's say, stray?"

"Are you thinking about going to grad school back east, Chris? If you are, I know we can make things work. I mean I know we've just started …"

"Casey. Stop."

"What? Did I do something wrong?"

Chris caught a quick glimpse of Casey. With her lower lip sticking out and downcast eyes, she looked as if someone had just run over her new Barbie doll. He glanced up in time to see the Northrop exit sign so he flipped on his turn signal and took the exit.

"No, you didn't do anything wrong. And this is all hypothetical. If you were in the situation where your boyfriend was clear across the country, would you expect him to remain faithful to your relationship?"

"Are you leaving California when you graduate next May?"

Geez.

"Casey, this has nothing to do with me."

Wait.

"All right, Casey. Let's say it is us. You're here in LA and I'm all the way across the country on the east coast. Would you expect me to remain faithful to you if we were in a relationship?"

She lowered her head, not saying a word.

"Well, yes. I would hope you would be true to me."

"Would it hurt a lot if I cheated on you?"

"It would absolutely kill me. I would be devastated."

Chris took a left onto Aviation Blvd. and realized the clock was ticking for him to wrap this up before getting to her place.

"Well, I want you to think for a minute about us being in a relationship and you finding out I cheated on you. Think about that feeling." He waited a few seconds as he saw her staring straight ahead, her brow creased, lost in the thought. "Now tell me, how would you feel?"

"I would be really hurt. I don't think I could handle it."

"So, what if I told you I have a girlfriend in Virginia and she would be just as devastated if I cheated on her? What would you say to that?"

"Do you have a girlfriend?"

"Yes, Casey. I've been telling you that since the first day we met. You just didn't want to hear it." He pulled up into a parking space in front of her apartment building and turned off the car. An icy silence filled the air.

"I guess it wouldn't be right for us to do anything then," Casey said very softly. "Right?" She looked up at him with tears welling in her eyes.

"Oh Casey," he said as he put his arm around her shoulders. "I'm so sorry. I've never given you any indication that I wanted to be anything more than friends. I guess my message just didn't get through."

She rested her head on his shoulder and sniffed a few times.

"I guess I was trying so hard to win you over that I never listened to that part. But you're right. It wouldn't be right for you to cheat on her.

What's her name?"

"Lisa. She is so special to me, Casey. I wouldn't be here in school ... heck, I don't think I'd be alive if it weren't for her."

"We'll, she's gotta be really special to catch someone like you." Another sniff. "She is one lucky girl 'cause you are the sweetest and most polite guy I've ever met. And that's all in addition to you being a hunk."

"A what?" Chris asked with a chuckle trying to lighten the mood a little.

"A hunk. Good looking. Hot. Easy on the eyes." She let out a giggle. "Get it? You're the real thing. And I'm just sorry that I never had a chance."

"Let me walk you up to your apartment."

She looked at him.

"Nothing more than that, Casey. It's that polite thing I got going on."

"Okay," she said wiping her eyes. "I guess I shouldn't expect anything less."

Chris jumped out and even ran around the car to open her door.

"Wow. Lisa really is lucky." She got out and stood next to him. "Chris Gates, you are so different."

He put his arm around her and walked her to the apartment.

"What do ya mean?"

"I dunno. I can't put my finger on it exactly. It's beside all the other stuff I said." She stopped in front of her door. "I mean you really are someone special." She stood up on her tip toes and kissed him on the cheek. "I think I've had a very enlightening evening. Actually, I know I have. And it was fun too Thank you."

"No, Casey. Thank you for being so understanding. I'll tell ya, if it weren't for the fact that I'm in a relationship, I woulda dated you in a heartbeat."

"Really?"

"For sure. You are special too. Can we still be friends?"

"Well, you're someone I want to keep in touch with. Friends for life?"

"Deal. I'll see you tomorrow. You've got a final too, right?"

"Yep." She opened her door and then turned to face him. "Good bye, Chris Gates. I'll see you tomorrow." She winked and closed the door.

"Well then," Jhall said after Prahash finished his account of the event. "That didn't appear very easy for him to do."

"It wasn't," Braaddy added. "I've seen the video of that night in the club and he was definitely attracted to her. That took sheer discipline and will power. Wouldn't you agree?"

"I think love may have played a part too. It would appear that the Savior has chosen a mate for the future," Prahash said.

"I concur," Braaddy answered.

"So, what do we call a test like that?" Jhall asked Prahash.

"I'd call it the California Challenge," Prahash answered. "And I'd say he passed."

"Indeed."

27 – GLORY RETURNS

From the pitcher's mound, Ian looked over his shoulder at Chris and winked his right eye twice.

It's going to be a high fastball, Chris thought. That was Ian's signal for that pitch. Noticing how the batter was standing in the box, Chris knew the guy was going to try to go up the middle.

I got this. If Ian can hit his spot, I'll get to the ball.

Cal Tech was down one run thanks to David's grand slam in the last inning. The score of the California World Series Championship game was Northrop University 6 and California Institute of Technology 5. It was the bottom of the ninth inning with one out and runners on first and third. Ian had a full pitch count at three balls and two strikes.

From his shortstop position, Chris had effectively shut down the middle of the infield for the entire game. But a hit into the outfield, or through the infield, would at least tie the game if not win it outright for the Beavers. The runner at third base would have to be held there.

Chris looked up into the stands, easily zeroing in on his family. Cory and his parents, along with everyone else, were on their feet. His eyes locked on Lisa who was watching him, smiling. He saw her holding the medal of her necklace which sent more adrenaline rushing through him adding to an already over-flowing abundance.

He bounced up and down on the balls of his feet. If Ian didn't hurry up and pitch the ball, Chris felt as if he'd explode. Suddenly, chills began to flow through his body even in the eighty degree heat. Everything seemed to slow down and move at the speed of a turtle. Chris shook his head as if something was in front of his eyes. He watched Ian take forever in what appeared to be a long-drawn-out windup to deliver the pitch. The ball floated out of his hand toward the batter.

What's going on?

As the ball approached the plate, the batter looked like he was moving his bat through a vat of molasses. A snail would be the winner in any race here.

CRACK! The ball blasted off the bat and then lazily sailed to Ian's right as he tried in vain to reach for it with his glove, but was too late. The ball traveled like it was on a rope three feet above the ground, slowly shooting in a straight line to the outfield grass.

I gotta dive. Chris felt like he was running in water. Taking one step to his left, he launched himself horizontally toward second base, his gloved hand extended as if making a one handed dive into a pool, body fully stretched out.

WHAP! The ball slammed into Chris' glove forcing his wrist to snap backward. He squeezed his glove around the ball. Out number two.

"ARGH!" Chris yelled as he hit the ground, unable to break his fall. In one fluid motion, he flexed every muscle in his body springing himself up from a prone position and pulling his knees underneath him. The ball had already been transferred from his glove to his right hand. Before his knees even hit the ground, his arm was already cocked back ready to fling the ball to first base. As he spewed up a cloud of dust from hitting the dirt again, he fired a bullet to the first baseman who stretched out to receive the throw.

THWAP! The sound of the ball hitting the pocket of Willie's glove came a split second ahead of the Cal Tech runner's extended arm as he desperately tried to get back to first base. Right on top of the play, the black clad umpire's tightly squeezed fist moved up and down while sweat whipped off his face. He looked skyward and bellowed "You're Out!", thus ending the game and sending the fans into a roaring frenzy. Still on his knees, Chris watched his teammates leap into the air screaming ecstatically. Things were now moving at normal speed but Chris still didn't react in time as Ian came diving onto him starting the traditional dog pile. Chris managed a quick glance up at Lisa before being covered by his teammates. Her beaming smile said it all.

Almost an hour after the game had ended, and the trophy ceremony completed, the Northrop locker room was in a spirited flurry of chaos. Sitting in front of his locker, Chris soaked in all the excitement. He heard someone scream, "It doesn't get any better than this!" Another said, "We are the champions!"

We did it, Chris thought as he sat down in front of his locker. *We are the best of the west.*

Northrop University had just won the 1989 California Independent College and University World Series tournament. All of the independent leagues, comprised mostly of small to mid-size schools, played a single elimination tournament to crown the best in California. This year's 'California Series' was held at the Palm Springs Stadium right next to LA and home to the Palm Springs Angels, the class A affiliate of the California Angels (now the Anaheim Angels). The Northrop baseball players were ecstatic to have won the tournament on such a big stage and it showed by the celebration in the locker room

Celebratory beer foam hit David Smith right in the face, stinging his eyes. He shook it off and laughed while shaking up another beer. He chased Willie down one of the isles and cornered him right as he popped the top of a pressure filled can right as Willie popped his. Beer flew everywhere as both of them tried to drench each other. The rest of the team was also in on the action with spewing soda and beer flying in every direction.

Chris saw Ian pushing through all the players that were standing close by, trying to get to his locker that was next to Chris'. The guys were drenching each other with Gatorade, water, beer, and anything else they could put their hands on. Ian laughed as someone dumped a cup of beer on his head. He shook his head spraying Chris in the process.

I am going to have to take one heckava shower before I go out to see everyone. Or should I run out and see them now? He stood up as Ian finally sat down in front of his locker.

"Man, how great is this?" Ian said loudly over the boisterous crowd as the boys high-fived each other. "Did you see all the families outside of here?"

"Nah, I was one of the first ones in here after the trophy ceremony. Too many people were crowding around."

"Well, Lisa's out there and you also got a lot of pro scouts outside wanting to talk to you."

"Really? I guess I'd better go back out. I'll get to the scouts after I see Lisa." He sat down and searched for a towel to wipe some of the beer and water off of him.

Chris' entire family was outside the locker room along with Ian's and David's. He had really been surprised that Lisa had made the trip out there to see him graduate and go to the tournament. He thought back to when he met everyone at the airport.

"Man," Ian said while staring wide eyed out the huge windows in the LAX terminal. "I've never seen so many planes in one place."

The words barely left his lips as someone jostled into him as they passed by. A small herd of a family, two adults with five kids in tow, continued bumping their way through toward their intended destination. Ian barely noticed as he continued watching the flowing sea of silver, blue, and other multi colored planes, all with black tires and heated exhaust fumes stretching across an endless expanse of concrete.

"I know," Chris said in an excited voice looking down the long corridor of bobbing heads darting in and out of various airline alcoves, all just arriving or trying to get into the air.

Ian peered at all the overhead signs.

"Are you sure we're at the right gate?" he asked.

"No not really. I just picked a gate that said flights would be arriving from Cape Town, South Africa. I heard their flight got diverted and they would be on one of these."

Ian looked surprised for a split second.

"You're full of crap." Ian looked up at the gate sign again. "That's so bogus, you twit. We're at the right gate." Ian continued looking out of the window.

"Yeah, well, why did you ask? I fooled you for a sec, though."

"Sure you did." Ian kept standing up on his tip toes looking down the wide hallway. "I'm just stoked about seeing everyone."

The boys saw a United Airlines jet pulling up to their gate. Considering it was time for the flight to arrive, they assumed this was it. Their eyes now locked onto the opening of the cattle chute that funneled arriving passengers from their sardine can into the huge filtering barn of a terminal.

"David had better hurry up and get here. Do you think he was able to get the team van?" Ian asked as he sat down on the ledge in front of the window.

"I sure hope so. He's cutting it close either way." Chris sat down next to him.

"Well, I hope he got it. We're gonna have a tough time getting anything into the old Plymouth Duster."

"No problem. We'll just pull out the magazines and blocks of wood. Then we can fit three or four people in the back seat with three in the front."

Ian punched Chris on the shoulder.

"We can't do that you twit. That stuff holds the front seats up. Besides, I can see our mothers trying to get in the car through the windows."

Chris started laughing at that mental image.

"I can see them asking why the doors are tied on with ropes."

At that moment, David came running up out of breath. "Are they here yet?"

"Not yet," Chris said still laughing about their car.

"What are you laughing at?" David asked.

Ian stood up. "We were just talking about the Duster. Did you get the van?"

"Sure did." David high-fived Ian. "I'm glad the main LAX entrance is just down from Northrop or I'd have never found it. This place is so big. So how many do we gotta carry?"

Chris' fingers started flying out. "With Ian's mom, my three, and your parents and little brother and sister, well, that's eight. Maybe you shoulda gotten a school bus or something."

Ian asked, "Is Lisa coming?"

"Nah, she had to work." Chris said dolefully as he looked out the window.

"When was the last time you saw her? Wasn't it during Christmas?"

Chris shook his head. "Don't you remember? She had to be at her parents for Christmas and we didn't get to see each other. Her aunt was sick or something so she couldn't get back to town."

"No big deal. You'll get to see her after the tournament and graduation."

"Yeah, sure." Chris pointed at the jet. "We need to move closer to where the chute comes up to the gate. People are getting off."

Rushing from the tunnel was the first class crowd with a young mother pulling her whiney chocolate covered seven year old son ahead of a pack of neatly dressed business suits followed by an assortment of high dollar riders. The normal passengers came next led by an overly large fellow carrying his entire wardrobe which no doubt ate up the overhead space along with two seats. More nameless, faceless people passed the boys as they waited for their loved ones.

"Is Cory gonna stay with us?" David asked as he kept his eyes on the tired, stressed out herd flowing by.

"I hope so. We aren't too far away from the Holiday Inn near La Tijera Blvd," Chris answered.

"Ian!" David shouted. "There's your mom."

Dressed in a denim pants suit, Ian easily spotted his mother followed by David's parents, wearing expressions of relief as they dragged along his two younger siblings. An elderly couple shuffled along behind them. Chris caught sight of Cory popping his head up from behind them. Barely visible down the tunnel's ramp, Chris could just make out his parent's faces in the rush to the gate. Chris was so excited to see Cory come trotting up to him that he didn't pay attention to any other passengers, especially the blond girl walking behind Pete.

"Bros!" Cory yelled as he ran to his brother and buddies, leaping into their arms. After handshakes and a few back slaps, Chris asked Cory, "So where's this new girlfriend, Diane?"

"She couldn't come. She's already planning our August wedding," he said shaking his head. "What'd I get myself into?" They all laughed.

Faces brightened as the boys quickly turned their attention to their individual families, mothers first, of course. Ian hugged his mother, Helen, and lifted her off the ground. David was engulfed by his family with all four of them trying to touch him at once.

"Mom," Chris said as he reached for her getting the warm embrace he had so missed. Then he glanced up and said, "Dad." He stuck his hand out which Pete playfully swatted away as he reached his arms around his wife and son, embracing them both. A blond head slowly became visible over Pete's shoulder. The world stopped for Chris as his heart skipped a beat.

"Lisa!" he shouted.

Pete and Kelli joyfully released their son.

"Chris!" Lisa shrieked. She jumped into his arms and buried her face into his neck and shoulder as he held her in the air in a tight embrace. "I've missed you so much."

Then they kissed, like never before. Lisa had both hands on the back of Chris' head, her fingers intertwined in his blond curls. Their surroundings faded into nothingness as Chris' pulse raced to the heavens. Tears of joy streamed down Lisa's cheeks, meshing between their skin as their lips continued their connection. Cory finally had to tap his brother on the shoulder.

"Yo, Bro." Tap, tap. "Yo, you two, time to come up for air." Cory raised his eyebrows and looked up while tugging on Chris' Northrop practice jersey. "All eyes are on you so stop the lip-lock."

No response.

"Chris, this is your Mother," Kelli said as she put her hand on her son's shoulder.

Chris immediately put Lisa down and they stepped apart from each other. Chris averted his eyes and nervously smoothed his long, wavy locks while Lisa sheepishly glanced down and ran both hands through her long hair to straighten it. Both looked totally embarrassed.

David's younger sister, Kathy, stifled a giggle, leaned over to her little brother Karl and said loud enough for everyone to hear, "This isn't awkward at all."

"I'm sorry, Mrs. Gates," Lisa said blushing profusely while smoothing her light blue sundress.

"Sorry, Mom," Chris said guiltily glancing up at his mother. "It's just that ..."

"It's all right, Chris," Kelli said as she slipped her arm around Chris' waist and pulled him next to her. Then she put an arm around Lisa's shoulders. She walked them away from the others as the families had begun to chat amongst themselves.

"Look, you two," Kelli began, "I know it's been a while since you've seen each other, but could you please try and refrain from that type of display? With David's siblings here ..."

"Mom," Chris interrupted, "it's cool." He peeked at Lisa who still had her head down in embarrassment. "We haven't seen each other since last summer."

"Oh my," Kelli was shocked. They stopped walking. "I thought you two …" She looked at Chris, then Lisa. "Christmas?"

"No, ma'am," Lisa said, with an almost desperate air about her. "I was at my aunt's so we didn't get to see each other."

"Thanksgiving?"

"Mom, I didn't come home for Thanksgiving last year, remember?" Chris revealed.

"Gosh, that's right," Kelli recalled while nodding her head. "I remember now. Well, then, that explains it all." She released them both. "I'll tell you what. You two head to baggage claim and start getting the bags. I'll go and get the others and we'll follow you down." She caught their eye and added, "Eventually." Kelli turned and walked away.

Chris and Lisa looked at each other in disbelief.

"Chris?" Lisa began. "Did your mother …,"

He put a finger up and said, "We were told to go to get the baggage. Let's not disappoint anyone." He grabbed her hand and pulled her toward the escalator.

Breaking into a grin and looking like a little teenage girl on her first date, she lurched ahead of Chris pulling him behind her. He jumped in front of her on the escalator, spun around, and put his arms around her waist while she draped her arms around his neck interlocking her fingers, capturing her prey.

"Where were we?" Lisa asked, batting her eyelashes seductively.

"I was just about to tell you that I have something for you."

They reached the bottom of the escalator and stepped off walking hand in hand toward the baggage claim area.

"Well," she began and suddenly pulled him out of the foot traffic to a shallow alcove with water fountains. "What is it?" She stopped talking as they embraced and kissed again.

"I've missed you so much." Chris stared lovingly but intently into her eyes.

"I missed you more."

"You know this has been killing me almost four years now. I have remained faithful and true to an agreement to not date anyone. I'll be coming home in a few days and all I can think about is you."

"You're all I think about too. This hasn't been easy for me either. There are so many things I want to tell you."

"Me too."

Lisa's expression changed to one of thoughtfulness.

"You know you have some decisions to make even before you come home," she began. "Your mom showed me some of the letters from pro baseball scouts. They'll be everywhere at your tournament. Plus there's the possibility of graduate school that we wrote about."

Chris looked away for a couple of seconds with a furrowed brow as he formulated a response.

"I'll tell you how I see it. If we are dating with a serious commitment, any big decisions have to be made together."

"I can see that as a possibility."

"Really?" Chris' eyes lit up with excitement.

"Really," she said with the loving look returning to her eyes. "Now what was that about something you wanted to show me?"

He started fumbling around trying to dig something out of the pocket of his shorts.

Lisa gleefully watched as Chris pulled out a small, black, worn out velvet bag.

"I've been carrying this around with me every day since I got it last August. It makes me feel closer to you."

"What is it?" Her eyes were sparkling.

"I wanted to give this to you at Christmas to protect you in your travels, but since you were at your Aunt's house, we didn't get to …"

"Chris, this is killing me." She was bouncing up and down barely able to contain her excitement. "Hurry up and tell me what it is."

"Okay. I know we need to walk before we run. And I don't want any chance of you saying no to me about anything so …" Chris could tell Lisa was excited by the way she was clinging to his arms and squeezing them. This was besides the fact that she couldn't hold still. He opened the bag as covertly as he could, and poured the contents into his palm.

"Chris Gates." Lisa was about to explode. "What have you got there?" she said while trying to see what was in his hand.

"Like I said, I don't want you to say no." He opened his hand exposing a sterling silver Saint Christopher's medal. On the front, the imbedded turquoise image of the patron saint of travelers gleamed in the light.

"In high school," Chris began slowly, "guys would give a St. Christopher's medal to a girl if they were going to date exclusively. This was to protect her in her travels when they were apart." He paused as his face flushed. "I want this to be more than just dating so I'd like to ask you to be, well ..." He stopped again stumbling on his words. "I was scared that if I asked you to be engaged that you would say no." He gulped. "So will you be engaged to me to be engaged? Kind of a pre-engagement?" He held up the medal. "I really want to begin our lives together."

Lisa stared wide-eyed at the medal, then at Chris.

"Oh, Chris." Her eyes were watering. "Yes." She took the medal out of his hands and jumped up into his arms, flinging her arms around his neck as he held her, the side of her face pressed against his.

"Yes. Yes. Yes." She pulled her head back and kissed him.

"Yes. This is perfect." She squeezed him so tight.

"Wait," he said in a slightly raspy voice. "You're choking me."

"Oh. Sorry." She released her hold and slid out of his grip to the floor. She opened her hand and stared at the medal, then jumped into his arms again. "I love you, Chris Gates."

"Wow. I love you too."

"Dude." Ian punched Chris in the shoulder again. "Chris!"

Chris looked up from his seated position in front of his locker. "What?"

"Man. Where were you? I've been standing here talking. You zoned out or something."

"I was just thinking …" He stood up. "Wow. Sorry about that. Got lost in thought."

"Come on, man. Let's go out there and see everyone."

Chris rubbed his hands together. "All right, let's go."

As the boys pushed their way through the throng of cheering teammates to the locker room door, David caught sight of them.

"Where y'all going?" he yelled.

Ian pointed to the door and David fell in behind them.

The rush of lights, cameras flashing, and the multitudes of milling people greeted the boys upon opening it. Their coach, Lin Hrica, was in the middle of the pack of microphones, reporters, and fans giving an interview. His stocky frame attired in a coach's baseball uniform stood out in sharp contrast to the mostly mild and meek news people that surrounded him.

"… and if it hadn't been for the hitting of our batters and the stellar play of our infield, I don't think we could have kept this pace up. I mean with a sixteen team tournament, you have to win four games in three days to be champs."

"Coach." A reporter from the crowd shoved his mic a little closer. "Henry Moore with ABC Sports. I understand the reason for the big crowd is that you have a big pro prospect on your team, which is highly unusual for a club team at a university not known for sports. Care to comment on that?"

"Well, it is tough job at Northrop trying to get any headline time with our Takraw team doing so well." That elicited a few chuckles. "But baseball is a team sport, and all my boys played a big part in our run to the championship."

The coach glanced to his right and saw the three boys standing by the locker room entrance.

"And here are three big reasons we were able to make this run,"

Hrica said as he raised a hand up gesturing for the boys to join him.

Chris started shaking his head no, but Ian grabbed him by the arm and plunged into the crowd followed by David. Moving through all the people, Chris' head was on a swivel as he tried to spot Lisa and his family. Right as they reached their coach he spotted Lisa with Cory near the archway leading out onto the field. Wearing sunglasses, she was waving at him while standing up on her tip-toes, her blond hair glowing in the sun giving off a golden aura around her angelic face.

Hrica reached out and pulled Ian and the others next to him.

"Let me introduce you to the Virginia contingent of our team. Ian Johnston is our number one pitcher. David Smith, one of our outfielders but more importantly, our grand-slam cleanup hitter. And last, but far from least, is our shortstop, Mr. Shutdown, Chris Gates."

Having been thrust into the limelight by the introduction, Chris immediately had a slew of microphones shoved to within inches of his face. He shielded his eyes from the sudden brightness of the video cam lights. The intensity of the light, coupled with all of the sunlight streaming in both ends of the stadium's covered locker room area, blinded him somewhat.

"Chris!" A newspaper reporter was the first to get his question in. "You've been on the sports pages a lot. How many Major League teams have contacted you?"

"I don't know. Coach keeps us away from all that."

Another reporter asked, "Can you tell us what you thought when you hit that three run triple in the seventh inning? And do you think that's what quieted the bats of the Cal Tech Beavers?"

"I feel that the real turning point of the game was when David Smith hit his grand slam. That broke their spirit."

A guy from the back shouted, "How did you feel when you caught that hit up the middle and threw out the runner trying to get back to first to win the game?"

"I'm just thankful Willie caught the ball. If he hadn't stretched out as far as he did, the runner would have beaten my throw. And Ian Johnston deserves the credit for delivering a pitch that kept the ball in the infield."

Chris kept looking from face to face as the questions kept pouring in.

A woman wearing a Dodgers baseball cap asked, "Why did you boys come all the way out to California to play college ball? Don't they have baseball back in the hills?"

Laughter emanated from the crowd.

"We wanted to play for one of the best college coaches out there," Chris answered.

"Mr. Gates, Henry Moore with ABC Sports." Henry moved his mic in front of the others while puffing his chest out in self-importance. "Have you spoken with any of the pro scouts yet? I chatted with Phil Martin, a scout with the New York Yankees, just a few minutes ago and the Yankees are very interested in talking to you. They feel you will be one of the first players picked in the draft."

"I ..." Chris tried to speak, but more questions came at him. The woman reporter asked another question.

"Is this a new style with the eye black smeared down your face? It looks a bit intimidating. Is that the reason you did it?"

Other questions about his eyes were asked as Chris realized how that happened. In the second inning when he was in the dugout, he had wiped the sweat off his face, forgetting that he applied eye black under his eyes before the game. The black mess was smeared down his face like war paint. He decided to change the subject.

"Let's not lose track of how we got here." Chris was speaking over all the questions now. "As Coach Hrica said, Northrop played as a team all season. No single player was more important than the teammate next to him. We functioned as a unit and every player deserves credit for winning today. Ian and David will answer some of your questions now. If you will excuse me, I've got to go see my family and my beautiful girlfriend over there."

Cheers and applause erupted from the locker room entrance as Chris pushed through the crowd. He glanced in that direction and saw the rest of his team looking at him with goofy grins, excited faces, and expressions of support. Loud yells and positive hand gestures were fired at him from this motley crew, most of them still in their dirty uniforms. A few shrill whistles elicited a smile from Chris as he reached the edge of the mass that had been surrounding him. He reached up with both hands and ran down the gauntlet of his teammates slapping high-fives.

Chris felt a pat on his back, turned and looked into his father's eyes.

"Son, I've never been more proud of you in my whole life than right now and not from the way you played. It's from what you just said. You shared the glory and credit with everyone." Surrounded by Lisa and his family, along with the rest of the Virginia group, Chris reached for his dad and gave him a big hug. Pete wrapped his arms around his boy.

"Ahh, Dad. I had a great example to follow. I love you."

"I love you too, son. Now go see that girl of yours."

Chris and Lisa's eye met. All the noise died away and everything became silent. His vision was filled with the love of his life and all he could think of was how wonderful things were. He was going home soon with the girl of his dreams. His life was really coming together.

No one had noticed the small, black object attached to a drain pipe above the throng of people. It sprouted some wings and flew over to a light fixture on the opposite wall.

Tish adjusted the control stick, moving the X13 probe on the fixture to get a better view of the people below. She then leaned back in her seat and yawned.

"I'm tired. We've been monitoring this event non-stop for almost a week now. I'm glad it's done."

"Me too," Xander agreed. "This has been an eventfully long observation period with graduation and the baseball tournament." Xander stood up and reached for his drink. "But they were some good games."

"Yes they were. I like baseball now. I had to spend some time studying it to fully understand it. There appears to be ample time to stand around with a lot of spitting and scratching going on."

"Do either of you know who is on the Planet Transport that came in?" Gunstot inquired from the adjoining workstation.

Tish answered, "With all that we've had going on here, I didn't even hear that one had arrived."

"It flashed in about three hours ago," Gunstot said.

"Hey," Xander said from the rear of the lab. "Maybe Zenta is on this one."

"Sure she is." Tish's replied sarcastically. "That would make her almost six years overdue."

"Okay then." Gunstot got up and walked to the lab door. "I don't want to hear this speech again. Would anyone like something to eat? I'm going to the mess hall."

"I'd come with you to avoid the speech too but she," Xander gestured toward Tish, "would probably stab me in my sleep if I didn't stay and listen to her complain again."

"I have not been complaining." Tish stomped her foot. "She was only supposed to be gone two years at the most."

"I'm leaving now," Gunstot said as he went out the door.

Xander came back up front and sat at his workstation.

"Go ahead, let's hear it." He pulled off his boots.

"What now? Are you going to undress in here?"

"Come on. Spill your beans or your guts or whatever they say on Earth."

"The correct saying is spill the beans, I believe. And I don't think that's the right one to use for this situation anyway." She rocked back in her seat and put her feet up on her desk. Glancing at her monitor, she watched Chris and Lisa holding hands while walking on the baseball field.

"I just think it is totally irresponsible for Zenta to be away from the project for so long. I mean four years or more past your return date is a bit much. Don't you agree?"

"You've asked me this a thousand times and I've told you a thousand times that we don't know the details of what has been going on. We all know her mother died but we are isolated from personal details unless it is of an absolute need to know." He picked up one of his boots and threw it back down. "I need to shower and change my uniform."

"Yes you do."

"Hey, I've been here for two days straight."

"So have I but I don't smell like you do." She checked her monitor. "It appears the families are discussing going to their respective quarters."

"Good. Maybe we can get some rest now. Did you hear if Chris discussed plans to attend graduate school for advanced education or play baseball with the professionals?" Xander finally put his boots on.

"All I heard was that Chris and Lisa were going to make that decision after they got to Virginia."

Xander stood up and headed to the lab doors.

"I've got to go clean up. Gunstot will be here shortly. You don't mind if I run to my quarters real quick, do you? I'll bring you something to eat."

"You go ahead. I'm going to write up the summary of today's events."

"All right." As the door opened Xander found himself face to face with Zenta all decked out in her dress uniform, her long white hair showing six more years of length.

"Xander!" Zenta squealed, dropped her bag, and engulfed him in a huge hug. Gunstot was right behind her.

"It's so good to see you," she said resting her head against his shoulder.

"It's so very good to see you, too," Xander said as he released his hug. "Welcome back." With his hands on her shoulders, their eyes met. "It makes me very happy to see your smiling face again. We've missed you."

Gunstot broke up the little reunion.

"Tish!" he yelled overtop of Xander and Zenta. "Guess who I found wandering the halls?"

Tish was already up and rushing toward them.

"You'd better back away from him and give me a hug!" she shouted, almost on top of them.

Zenta gently pushed Xander away to clear a path just as Tish got there. Two long separated 'almost' sisters began sobbing as they held each other.

"Oh, I'm so glad to see you," Tish cried.

"Me too," Zenta said through tears while hugging Tish.

Xander and Gunstot looked at each other.

Shaking his head, Xander said, "I don't get it."

"No male ever will," Gunstot replied.

They all came in the lab and sat in their seats along the first row. Tish and Zenta scooted their seats together so close that they might as well been Siamese twins.

"So tell me …," they both spoke simultaneously and laughed.

Tish nodded to Zenta. "You first."

"All right. I'm sure you are all wondering what happened that caused my delayed return by four years."

"Really, has it been that long?" Xander said sarcastically.

"Stop it." Tish reached over and slapped him on the arm. "Go ahead, Zenta."

"Well, things have not been easy. Mother was really sick when I got home." She paused and looked down. "I'm sure you heard that she died a year ago."

Tish put her hand on Zenta's knee. "We did hear and I'm so sorry."

"I'm sorry for your loss, Zenta," Xander added.

"Yes, from me too," Gunstot said.

Zenta didn't respond right away, looking as if she was on another world.

"Thank you. It's been a while now so I've gotten past it, somewhat. Her death really affected Father … and me. But you might say he hasn't really gotten over it yet." She lowered her gaze and closed her eyes as she suffered through the horrible memory.

She looked up with a pained expression.

"We also suffered a surprise Veloptorian attack on Cezzeck right before I was scheduled to leave."

"What happened?" Tish and Xander asked in unison.

"We heard about it but not many details have filtered down," Gunstot said with concern. "Tell us about it."

"It started about a year ago. Their ships have been plating in and out of that solar system. Then they attacked all at once. Cezzeck's far moon was captured and we haven't been able to dislodge them so we're in a stalemate. We are just spread too thin."

Just then, Xander's Trace went off.

"I'm being summoned to the hanger. It seems there is a

preliminary briefing for those of us going home on the transport." He stood up. "I've got to go down there. Tish, fill me in when I get back."

Gunstot got up. "I'm going to go down with him and see if anything came in on the transport for us."

"That's a good idea," Tish replied. "One of us will brief you."

After they left, Tish said, "I forgot that Xander was going home when you returned. I guess I blocked it out."

"Well, you're next in line."

They sat in silence for a few moments.

Zenta finally asked, "How is Chris?"

It took Tish over an hour to tell everything that had transpired covering the almost six years that Zenta had been gone. On Terlokya, Zenta had read the briefings and updates that regularly came in for the Supreme Council and Sohan. But they only gave summaries of occurrences, never any detail. After Tish finished, ending with the part about Chris and Lisa becoming a committed couple, Zenta sat with her head slightly bowed in stony silence.

Tish put her hand on Zenta's knee again.

"I know what you are feeling."

Zenta glanced up and met Tish's gaze.

Tish then continued. "I'm sure this hurts here." She put her other hand over her heart. "But you have to be happy with the fact that Chris is as strong as ever, both mentally and physically. His mental capacities far exceeded our initial estimates." She waited for some kind of response. When none came, she added, "You have to also realize that anything Chris is doing now on a social level is all unimportant compared to what his true mission in life is. He is bigger than all of this. And so are you."

Zenta finally spoke.

"I have wondered for quite a while how I would react to hearing exactly what you have told me. Logically, I knew the only way for him to get back on track was for this relationship to develop. I don't believe he needs to be in a relationship to be able to exist, but he needed this one to move past the knee injury. And I've accepted this as the optimal outcome for him and for the project."

"It's the best thing that could have happened considering all the circumstances. We could have lost him," Tish added.

"I don't know about that, but thank goodness we never had to find out." Zenta then patted Tish on the knee, got up from her seat, and said, "Now let's celebrate our reunion. I got us a little something." She reached into the case she had carried in and pulled out an ornate translucent red bottle that had a plain, blue, label wrapped around it.

"Is that what I hope it is?"

"Only the best. It's the finest Bonzoon made in the capital. I paid a fortune for this bottle and it was worth it." She proceeded to pull out two pearly white ceramic goblets and placed the flat bottomed cups on her workstation.

"Have you had any yet?" Tish asked with an air of anticipation.

Zenta sat down again and poured just a tiny amount in each cup.

"I had a cup with this amount in it two days ago," she answered and winked. "But not from this bottle. I felt like the universe was mine."

They raised their cups and clinked them together.

"To the next chapter," Zenta declared.

"Onward."

28 – PLANNING FOR THE FUTURE

CRACK! The seagulls scattered at the sound of the bat connecting with the pitch on that early February morning in 1990. The hit turned heads of the Yankee coaches at their Tampa spring training facility. They watched the ball sail over the outfield fence on an unusually warm, winter day.

"Okay, Chris. That's enough hitting," Yankee scout Phil Martin said as he waved Chris over to the dugout. "Grab your glove and get out there at shortstop. You're about to be peppered with grounders so look sharp. There are a lot of important people watching today." He pointed to the press box way up behind home plate. "The Boss is in there. I want you to show them what I saw out in California."

Lisa was also watching, sitting with Pete in the lower area of the stands right above the dugout.

"I'm still bummed that I couldn't fly down yesterday with you two," he said as he adjusted his hat to the rising sun.

"You didn't miss much," Lisa replied. "We were given a tour of the facility and met the coaches and some of the players."

"That's a lot in my book. I would love to have met any of them. I mean after all, this is the best team in baseball."

"They were really friendly to us. Not what I expected from big sports stars."

They sat silently for a while as they watched Chris take some easy grounders. The hitting stopped momentarily while one of the coaches gave instructions to the batter.

"It sure is warm," Pete said as sweat formed on his brow. "I'm glad I brought a pair of shorts."

"Me too," Lisa added. "I'm not used to warm weather in February."

"So when will you two set a wedding date?" Pete asked as he reached under the seat to get his water bottle. "As I said earlier, Kelli was pushing me to find out anything while we're down here." He wiped his brow with the back of his hand and then took a drink of water.

"Now, Mr. Gates," Lisa began without taking her eyes off the field. "With all we've got going on, we're just not sure …"

"Lisa," Pete had a hand up. "I thought we were going to drop the 'Mr. Gates' stuff. It's Pete or as I've told you, I'm okay with you calling me Dad, too. Hint, hint."

"All right, Pete," Lisa said laughingly. "The Dad part will come, all in good time."

“Look. They’re hitting harder ones to him now,” Pete noticed.

The grounders were being stretched out on each side of Chris, becoming more difficult to get to. He laid out horizontally to his left and snared a ground ball, quickly got to his feet and threw to first base. The next hit was to his right which he backhanded while letting his momentum turn him 180 degrees. While still in the air, he whipped his arm, throwing a bullet to first.

“Yeah!” hollered a coach from the dugout as two other coaches clapped their hands together with one yelling, “Wow” and following it with a shrill whistle.

“Did you see that?” Pete asked as he tapped Lisa with the back of his hand while keeping his eyes locked on his son.

“I call him ‘art in motion’ when he does stuff like that,” Lisa said, still mesmerized by Chris’ athleticism.

After another half hour, Chris was standing near the batter’s box with Phil while they talked with the coaches. Lisa and Pete had walked down to the last row at the bottom of the stands and leaned on the rail trying to hear the conversation.

“Can you make out what they are saying?” Pete asked in a hushed tone while leaning over to Lisa.

“Not really.”

“I heard someone say Columbus.” Pete cupped a hand on his ear.

“Chris told me Phil mentioned that management is concerned about the lack of a good shortstop in Columbus. That’s the reason for this special assessment,” Lisa said.

“Is that what you really want? For him to play a level below Major League Baseball? That’s still pretty high up on the baseball food chain, but it’s a tough life. I know you two talked about him completing his Master’s degree so he could teach at a high school.”

Lisa didn’t respond right away. She glanced down, obviously thinking about what to say.

“Well,” she slowly began. “I told Chris it’s a once in a lifetime opportunity. I don’t want us to have any regrets about this decision. I’m just glad that he got the fall semester of grad school under his belt.”

“Me too. This is mighty big of you, Lisa. I mean you both are putting your future of being together on hold while this happens.”

“I know. Oh look,” she said seeing that the group was breaking up. “They’re done. Let’s go down on the field.”

Chris and Phil were walking toward them while the coaches headed to the opposite dugout.

“Hi Dad. Hi Babe. Sorry it was so boring,” Chris said wearing a big grin.

After everyone exchanged pleasantries, Phil turned to Lisa.

"Well now, Lisa … how is Chris' future bride to be?"

"What?" Lisa said as she blushed. "What in the world are you telling him, Chris?"

"Don't blame the boy, ma'am," Phil said patting Chris on the back. "You're all he could talk about this morning. I was afraid he would be distracted by having such a pretty girl here watching him."

Lisa's face was red as a beet.

"But he surprised me," Phil continued. "Or should I say I really wasn't surprised. This boy was in a zone out there; fully engaged. And the coaches noticed that." Phil was smiling at Chris, who was wearing his best 'aw shucks' look.

"Do you want to tell them or should I?" Phil asked Chris.

"What? What?" Lisa was hopping up and down with excitement. "Tell us."

Chris was looking down, obviously embarrassed about the attention.

"Well …" he began. "I … uh …"

"Oh heck," Phil interrupted. "Since we'll be getting to know each other better, I'm going to spill the beans."

Lisa let out a little squeal and had her hands clasped together in anticipation of what was coming.

"It looks like the coaches feel our boy here is ready to compete for the shortstop position out in Columbus Ohio."

Before the last words were out of Phil's mouth, Lisa had jumped into Chris' arms. He caught her effortlessly as if she were a pillow.

"Whoa, girl,"

"What do you mean, whoa?" she asked. "This is so great. Pete, isn't this great?" She slid out of Chris' arms and gave Phil a hug. "This is so wonderful. I can't stand it!"

Pete slapped high fives with Chris and Phil.

"So, Phil," Pete began as he joined the others. "When does he have to report?"

"He needs to report here in a couple of weeks with the rest of the rookies," Phil replied as he placed his hand on Chris' shoulder. "So you'd better get on home and wrap stuff up. You've got a long season ahead of you. And remember what the General Manager said; always be ready for a call to come up to the Majors, or as they call it, the Show."

During spring training, Chris impressed the coaches to where they tagged him as the new starting shortstop for their Triple A franchise. A few months into the grind of the 1990 season, Chris had settled into the routine of being an everyday player. Endless bus trips and revolving hotel rooms took a bit of the luster out of the heady world of being a pro player. As a starting shortstop, he did occasionally get a couple of days off which he spent at home with Lisa, family, and friends. In June, he got called up from Triple A to the Majors for a game in Detroit. He managed to hit a towering home run his first time at bat, played two error free innings, and showed his athleticism with a few unbelievable plays. The next day, he was sent back down to Columbus due to lack of space for him to be on the permanent Major League roster. His performance made the sports pages along with the television sports news programs. Chris was being referred to by New York sports-talk-radio commentators as the future shortstop. His Columbus coaches kept reminding him to be ready for the next call to the Show and that he'd probably stay in the big leagues.

In early August, Cory and Diane's wedding date was the big event that had everyone really busy. Chris managed to get a few extra days off before the big weekend. He and Lisa were in the living room at the Gates house in Hilton Mills discussing that evening's rehearsal dinner with Kelli, Cory, and Ian.

"All of this is happening so fast," Cory exclaimed with his hands up in the air. Sitting on the couch between his mother and Ian, he sighed and leaned over with his head between his knees. His shoulders shrugged up and down while fake sobbing sounds bellowed out. He looked up; his eyes saddened as if someone had just run over his cat. "It's already Friday and the dinner is tonight," he said, again raising his arms up in a pleading gesture.

"Hey, you're the one who wanted to get married right after college," Ian said as he smacked Cory on the back.

"Yeah," Chris chimed in from his comfortable position; lying on his back in the middle of the center area rug between the two couches. His bare feet were propped up on Lisa's lap as she sat on the other couch across from the others. "You should have waited."

"At least we picked a date," Cory countered. "Unlike you two dweebs who don't even own a calendar."

"Hey," Lisa spoke up. "Be nice."

"Well," Kelli said, standing up. "We aren't getting very far here. We are still waiting for Diane and her mother to get back from the hairdresser and it appears hunger is causing us to stray off subject." She headed toward the kitchen. "I'm going to fix lunch for everyone so you all go wash your hands."

"Yes ma'am," was the collective response.

Kelli was halfway to the kitchen when the phone rang. She picked up the extension next to the television.

"Chris," she said holding the receiver out. "It's for you."

"Who is it?" he asked from his prone position.

"Mister, I am not your secretary," Kelli said with feigned seriousness while holding the receiver out. "But I think you'll want to take this. It's one of your coaches."

Chris was up in a flash taking the phone from Kelli's hand.

"Hello?"

The dead silence allowed the coach's voice to be the only sound in the room.

"Yes, sir." He glanced up and saw everyone staring at him. He waved his arm, hoping they would all disperse, but to no avail. Nobody budged.

Now the center of attention, Chris tried to keep a straight face. His eyes closed as the message from the voice registered deep within him. Different scenarios with varying outcomes raced through his brain.

Why this weekend?

Time seemed endless as he finally came to the realization of what he must do before ever uttering a word.

"Yes, it's this Saturday."

Ian whispered to Cory, "I'd give a dollar to hear the other side of that conversation."

"I'd give ten," Cory replied.

"I understand, sir. I can't do that." With those words, Chris felt his future cloud over. Waves of uncertainty washed over him like a pounding surf… then relief.

"I know, sir. I really do appreciate it. … No, sir, I don't have any other brothers. … I'm glad you understand."

Concerned expressions changed to ones of hope; except for Cory.

"Yes, sir. You're sure they are okay with this? … Please let me know otherwise, okay? … Yes, sir. … Thank you, sir. … I'll see you Monday."

It felt like it took forever to hang up the phone. He knew everyone would want answers. He turned and saw anxious faces and worried looks. Lisa was standing in front of him with hands clasped together.

"Well?"

"What?" Chris said flashing that famous smile, arms out, shoulders shrugged. "Coach is just checking on me."

"Bull crap," Cory said.

Chris met his brother's eyes and saw Cory's jaw clenched as if a fight were brewing.

"Tell us what that really was about, dear," Kelli said.

"That was it, wasn't it?" Lisa asked.

"What 'it' is that?" Chris dodged the question.

"You know," she replied. "You were being called up to the Show, right?"

"You mean the Majors?" Ian asked.

Chris kept the smile.

"Yes. But Coach understood what is going on and said that in situations like this, the guys up in the big office understand family matters like this," he explained.

"And you're sure he said it was okay to go to my wedding?" Cory asked. He came up out of his seat like lightning, his voice quivering. "The last time you were called up, you were told that the next one would probably be permanent, right?"

"Yes, but Coach said there was no problem. Things like weddings are acceptable excuses to miss games."

"But this isn't just some game. This is the call you've been waiting for. You can't just miss it." He took two shaky steps toward Chris. "This is the Majors." He stopped and threw his hands up getting ready to say something but Chris cut him off.

"Will you listen to me?" Chris stared right at his brother with eyes of steel. "Saturday is one of the most important days of your life. I'm going to be the best man at your wedding so there is nothing on this Earth that will keep me from doing that."

"Well then," Cory yelled at him, veins protruding from his neck. "You must be under someone else's control 'because no one in their right mind would give up a chance to play in the Majors."

Chris felt shivers roll through his body. The always open doorway of wordless communication between the brothers had slammed shut with those words. Action was needed. He went to his brother and wrapped his arms around him. It felt like he was holding a cold statue. He stepped back.

"Look Bro," Chris began. "I want to be in the Majors as bad as you want it for me. But this is your wedding." He bent down to look up into Cory's lowered face. "If Coach had said I should go, then I would have asked you to make sure it was all right before saying yes." Cory remained motionless.

Lisa was wide-eyed with every muscle in her body tensed up as she watched the exchange. She had never seen the brothers act this way. Kelli stood stone faced as she witnessed the heated exchange between her sons.

Chris, still bent over, grabbed Cory's arms and gently pulled on them, keeping his eyes locked on his brother. Their eyes finally met.

"I'm …," Cory swallowed hard. "I'm sorry I said those things." He reached for Chris and the brothers hugged.

"I'm sorry too, Bro. I know you were just watching out for me."

Tears rolled down Lisa's cheeks as she went over and put her arms around them. Kelli and Ian followed suit. The group hug was the perfect antidote. All was good.

Cory and Diane's wedding dawned to a perfect day and came off without a hitch. At the reception, held at the Farmington Vineyards, Cory relished being the center of attention, but never missed an opportunity to be with the Bros. Diane was absolutely stunning in her wedding dress, her beautiful, long brown hair seemed to vibrate against her white gown. She too enjoyed the attention of the boys along with all of the wedding rituals. From cutting the cake, to the first dance, she glowed. Everything was flawless. Chris fulfilled his role as best man and Cory and Diane were very appreciative of his sacrifice. The newlyweds left for their Aruba honeymoon as life returned to normal in central Virginia.

Another call to the Majors never came during the rest of the summer. Chris continued to shine for Columbus through the end of the long, grinding season. Arriving home totally worn out after the last game was played, Chris was in time to begin the fall semester of grad school.

Chris and Lisa got an apartment together in town and settled into a routine. Lisa was working at the University's main hospital while Chris went to grad school there and worked part time at Jefferson as an assistant baseball coach. They made that little one bedroom place their sanctuary. Tucked away on the middle floor of an old former plantation house, the happy couple was inseparable. And with Otis to look after, it was as if they were a little family.

One early Saturday afternoon, Lisa came in the apartment from getting the mail and stood behind Chris who was at the kitchen table, various papers with scribbled notes were spread across mounds of books as he worked on a research paper. Lisa tossed a magazine on the chair next to him.

"There's your Northrop Alumni Magazine." Her face did a slight twitch as she looked at the next item. "Who's Casey Wilson?"

Chris looked up at her.

"Who?"

"Casey Wilson. She sent you a postcard from LA." Lisa let the 'A' linger on her lips longer than normal. "She says she's now in grad school there." Lisa squinted at the little print on the card and moved to the window for sunlight. "Says here that she read about you in the papers and you're the talk of the school. Next is some blah blah blah about classes."

Lisa stopped. ‘Then she writes, “I hope you and Lisa have somehow managed to make a life together with you playing baseball and all. It’s got to be tough but you can do it. Hang in there. Your friend for life, Casey.” She crossed her arms and looked at Chris, smiling slightly. Her eyes rested on his broad shoulders, his head down, the pencil still moving.

“Were you listening to me?”

His head snapped around.

“I’m so sorry, sweetheart. I was just trying to finish this one note.” His cheeks flushed red. “Yeah, right. Casey. ... Well, she was this girl out at Northrop.”

“She’s not a girl anymore?” Lisa quickly said, batting her eyelashes.

“What?” Chris scrunched up his face. “No. I mean yes. She went to Northrop and had a crush on me.” He patted his lap for Lisa to come sit. She complied and he proceeded to tell her the story. Lisa kissed him on the lips when he finished.

“You should write back,” she said as she gathered up the rest of the mail. “And make sure you tell her hello from me.”

Chris watched as Lisa put away the pots and pans from the dish rack from their small kitchen counter. She slowed her movements and looked at him.

“What?” Smiling she asked, “Why are you watching me?”

He stood up and enveloped her in his arms. The warmth of her gaze radiated deep into his heart. Butterflies were taking wing in his stomach.

“You amaze me, you know that?”

“No I didn’t.” She pecked him on the lips. “Tell me more.”

“You are so understanding and trusting.” He gently rocked her from side to side, his eyes still locked on hers. “You do know that you are the only girl for me, right?”

“And you are the only boy for me.” She rested her head on his chest, enjoying the swaying motion and the beating of his heart.

“I want to ask you a question, Miss Haskett.”

“And what is that, Mr. Gates?”

“I was wondering when you would like to become Mrs. Gates.”

The corners of her mouth turned up but she didn’t move her head.

“Is this a marriage proposal, Mr. Gates?”

He kissed the top of her head.

“Why yes it is, Miss Haskett.”

The world slowed for Chris as he watched that angelic face turn toward him, her eyes fluttering shut, her lips slightly parted and uplifted to him. His vision clouded over as he kissed her, feeling a vibrant energy course through his every fiber, her body almost vibrating in his arms. As the fog lifted and their lips parted, his eyes opened to a smile.

"Whenever you want to … Mr. Gates."

"Well then. In that case, I'd like to take my bride-to-be out to dinner tonight and put our plan together. Sound good?"

"That sounds wonderful."

The Virginian, their favorite restaurant on the Corner, was packed that evening. Fortunately, the crew knew the happy couple and was able to find a booth in no time. Chris surprised Lisa by getting down on one knee and officially proposing to her in front of the cheering staff and the clapping patrons. Her eyes sparkled as he opened a little velvet black box exposing her new engagement ring. The rest of their time there was heavenly spent lost in each other's eyes, the outside world far removed from this evening's bliss.

After returning to their apartment, the planning phase went out the window as a bottle of champagne topped off the evening and the engaged couple fell into each other's arms, their lovemaking strengthening their already deep bonds of affection.

The next morning, Chris awoke to the aroma of bacon and eggs. He shuffled into the kitchen to find Lisa at the stove, humming a tune, and looking as beautiful as ever. Wearing one of his baseball jerseys, she smiled at him. His knees weakened and pulse quickened as he noticed she had not buttoned up the front. He wrapped his arms around her as she spun effortlessly around to face him.

"Good morning, beautiful." He pecked her on the forehead.

"Good morning to you, sunshine," she replied

He felt her heart rate rise to meet his. Feeling his chest about to burst, he guided her over to the table.

"What are you doing? I was going to fix …"

"I know you were. Since you fixed it, I can at least serve it," he said as he gently sat her on one of the kitchen chairs. "And you might want to fix the front of that jersey or we'll end up in the other room with a cold breakfast awaiting us."

"After we eat," she said as she complied.

With breakfast finished, Lisa reached across the table and cupped Chris' hand.

"So what happened to the planning part of last night?" she asked as she winked at him.

"Oh, I don't know." His curly blond locks framed his flushed face. "I thought we did some pretty good planning for the future, don't you? I think we should go do some more planning."

"Is that what we're going to call it now?" she said as she squeezed his hand. "But seriously, we should pick a date and figure out what has to happen before then."

"Okay, then. I've been giving this a lot of thought."

Over the next half hour, Chris explained his vision of the next year. This spring, he wanted to try and make the Major League roster. He told Lisa that if he made it, he felt they should get married in the summer of '92 since his professional career would be laid out. He surprised her when he said that if he didn't make the Majors during this next season, he wanted to finish grad school and begin his non-baseball career.

"Lisa, I know what it's like to spend hours on bus rides, sit in hotel rooms, play in front of sparse crowds, and always wait for the phone to ring. I talked to some guys in Columbus that have been waiting for five, six … some of them have been waiting ten years for the call. They miss their families for six months of the year. I don't want to be one of those guys. I want us to have a life together."

Lisa looked into his eyes and saw determination and fire. Leaning forward in his chair, intensity burning in him, it was obvious he had thought this through.

"If this is what you want …" She checked for any hint of wavering. Seeing none, she continued. "Then I support you if you are absolutely sure about this."

"I'm sure. I've been able to do what most guys dream of. I played for the best team in baseball. I got to play at Yankee stadium. I even hit a few home runs. I think that's a lot."

"Then I'm with you," she said as she reached up and caressed his face. That brought a huge smile.

"So either way, we should set a date sometime in the summer of '92 and get married so we can really start our lives together. How do you feel about that?" he asked.

She got up, unbuttoned the jersey, and sat on his lap.

"I feel I can hardly wait for the summer of '92."

After that, they proceeded to do more planning.

29 – TIE THE KNOT

During the spring and summer of the next baseball season, Chris occasionally got called up to the majors but was always sent back down after a few days. With countless veterans on the roster, and none of them set to retire, permanent space just wasn't there.

When the season was over, Chris negotiated with team management, since he was at the end of his two year contract. The team declined to meet the contract figure he requested through his agent, so he told them he was going to take the year off and complete his graduate degree. They agreed but retained contractual rights to him if he came back.

That fall, Chris and Lisa announced to everyone their intention to get married the next summer. A June date was picked and the usual wedding preparations ensued. Chris took heavy course loads each semester so he could graduate the following May and received an immediate job offer from The Jefferson Academy to teach computer science.

The big wedding day arrived suddenly amidst the hustle and bustle of everyday life. On the afternoon of the ceremony, the air conditioner was humming in the background of the vestry as Chris peered through the crack in the door to the sanctuary. Small beads of sweat formed on his forehead which he wiped away with his sleeve. Cindy Leathers, his ex, was strolling around in the sanctuary.

Her blond hair had been done at a hairdresser for sure, Chris thought. *Why would she get so prettied up and come to my wedding? Man, she's still a knock-out.*

At a little over five feet, Cindy had always appeared small next to Chris's six foot four inch frame. He ran his hand through his tangled locks and nervously pulled at the collar of his shirt as if he was suddenly being strangled.

Far away in the SP Lab at Base GAIA, Tish was watching Chris on her monitor while she chewed on a red licorice-like piece of rubbery candy.

"Get up and come see this," Tish said to Gunstot while giggling and attempting to keep her snack in her mouth.

Gunstot was sitting to her left with his head on his desk.

"Chris is peeking out a door at his old girlfriend and he doesn't have any pants on."

"I don't care," Gunstot replied from his slumped position at his workstation. His head was buried in his arms that were draped across his keyboard.

"Come on. This is funny."

"No. I'm sick of watching all these pre-wedding activities."

"Really? This is what we've worked for; getting these two married."

"I know that," he said raising his head up. "But all this is just making Zenta difficult to be with."

"In what way?"

"She is never happy, always short tempered, and very moody. She is too depressed to be around."

"I hadn't noticed," she lied.

"Of course not. You two are like sisters."

Gunstot got up and walked to the viewing platform underneath the large ceiling window.

"Platform console: rise." The control console and handrails rose from the floor. Gunstot pushed the button to raise the platform. At the same time the roof covering opened and a starlit night greeted him.

"What are you doing?" Tish asked.

"I am taking a break. This wedding has depressed me too." Gunstot stared out into space noting how lucky he was that he had a perfect view of Mars. They hardly ever saw it from this vantage point. "Why couldn't we have just let him play baseball?" He looked down at Tish. "If we had done that, maybe this wedding would have been postponed or not happened at all."

"You know the answer to that," she replied while stretching her arms over her head. "It was decided that he should be guided to a leadership career and that would have been difficult with him playing baseball."

"How's that again?" Gunstot angrily asked from above.

"You were there when the decisions were made to manipulate things by interfering with a few catches; by sending probes to influence the coaches to fill the rosters with other players … it sure didn't leave a lot of room or even a chance for him to move up."

"I remember not agreeing with any of that."

"It was what was needed. It doesn't look like Chris has any regrets from what he has said. It's already done so there is no going back."

"Whoever made that final decision must have been farrook." Gunstot shook his head as he watched two Reep Fighters fly out into space.

"That would be Colonel Braaddy so you can take that up with him," Tish said. "Besides, it looks like Chris wants to be a family man anyway. Now get down here and do your job."

"Oh all right."

"Who are you looking for?" Cory asked the question without even looking at what his younger brother was doing. He was still trying to figure out how to put his cummerbund on. "It's way too early for anyone to be out there."

"How do you know I'm looking at anything in particular?" Chris stepped away from the door and walked back to where Cory was standing. "I'm just checking to see if anyone's in the church yet."

"Bull crap. You saw somebody out there." Cory pulled off the cummerbund and threw it on the soft maroon carpet. "What in the heck is a cummerbund used for anyway? Is it just to cover up a belt?"

"It keeps your shirt clean when you're eating dinner at the reception." Chris opened the gym bag which was sitting on the table adjoining the huge mahogany desk. "Ready for a shot yet?" He pulled out a bottle of Jack Daniels along with two shot glasses and set them on the table. Chris looked to the opposite side of the desk where a huge bookcase was built into the wall, hundreds of books lined neatly on the shelves.

"I wonder if Father Donavon has read all of these books?" he asked.

Cory totally ignored his question and said, "Don't you think you'd better put on some pants? What if someone comes in? Besides, I can't handle your boxers with those hearts on them." Cory picked up the cummerbund and tried to put it on again. After another attempt, he threw the soft velvet-like piece of fabric down in disgust. "And you never told me who's out there." He went to the vestry door, ducking under the ornate glass chandelier that Chris had hit earlier.

"Cindy is out there, you dog. I knew she would find a way to come to your wedding. And what is she doing walking around with Brian the dork boy? Who invited them? There is no way your bride-to-be would invite your ex. Right?"

"Hold on man, too many questions at once." Chris remembered why Brian was there and refreshed Cory's memory.

One night a few months ago when he and Lisa were out bar-hopping, they ran into Brian up around the University. Brian had cornered them in a booth and acted as if he was an old pal of Chris'. They had both gone to Jefferson but didn't hang out in the same crowd. Chris heard that Brian was trying to date Cindy, not that it bothered him, but on that night, after a couple of hours and a few beers at the bar, Lisa ended up inviting Brian to the wedding.

"Does it bother you that she's here?" Cory asked.

"I don't care one bit. I didn't invite them," Chris mumbled as he poured out some bourbon into the two shot glasses. "Lisa invited Brian.

And why do you still call him dork boy?"

Cory walked to where he dropped his cummerbund and picked it up. "Brian was called dork boy in high school, so I will always call him that. Besides, he really is a dork. He's still chunky and has the same spiked hair. Did you check out Cindy's hair?" Cory let out a shrill whistle. "I can see why you always go for blonds."

"What do you mean I go for blonds? Change that to 'went'. I'm done with that. Lisa is the only one for me now."

Chris walked over to Cory and handed him a shot glass full of Jack.

"Cheers."

"Cheers."

They both downed their shots. The bourbon burned Chris's throat on the way down. He grimaced slightly, grabbed Cory's glass, and went to the table to fill them again. He was careful not to spill anything on the fine linen.

"Man, I can't believe it took you to the ripe old age of twenty-five to finally get married," Cory said as he grabbed his glass and plopped down on the couch under the window. "But seriously dude, how long do you think Cindy has been dating Brian?"

"I don't know and I don't care."

Cory downed his shot and shook his head. "And put your damn pants on."

"Hey don't sweat it. I've decided to get married without pants."

Cory snorted some bourbon up through his nose at that one.

Chris chuckled too. "What are you worried about? We got here early on purpose so we could hang out and not be rushed."

Chris went to his tuxedo bag that was hanging on the door-jam of the closet, removed the pants from the hanger, and laid them across the closest chair. "No one is supposed to show up for another half hour." He pointed toward the door to the sanctuary and said, "Except for the two out there now."

Chris searched in the bottom of his bag. "Do you have my black socks?"

"Check my bag. But really; does it bother you that they're dating?" Cory started fiddling with the cummerbund again.

"I wish you'd stop with the Cindy crap. Hey, these blue socks would look great with a black tux. Did you bring my black ones?"

"Yes I did. They must be in the car. I'll go get them, but we need to talk more on what we're going to do about Cindy when I get back. Lisa's going to be mad when she finds out your old girlfriend is here." Cory slipped out the other door to the vestry office that led out to a side street.

Chris sat on the couch with another shot in his hand, thoughts speeding through his mind.

This is gonna suck big time. With Cindy out there, I might screw up my vows.

A sudden loud knock on the outside door caused Chris to spill some bourbon on his leg. “Damn it, Cory.” Chris got up and went to open the door. “Why’d you lock the door you fool?” Opening it, he found himself looking right into Lisa’s eyes.

“I guess it must be bad luck to see the groom instead of the bride on a wedding day judging from what you’re wearing,” Lisa said as she pecked him on the cheek. “Where are your pants?” She looked around the room and saw his pants on the chair. “And you called me a fool.”

She took the shot glass out of his hand and downed the bourbon. “That’s good. I think I’ll have one more.” She went to the table and poured another shot.

Chris stood there dumbfounded as he stared at his future bride. She was absolutely stunning. Her tanned golden skin glistened and was accented by her little pink halter dress. Beautiful blue eyes twinkled with intensity, and her perfect cheek bones were surrounded by the most gorgeous blond hair he had ever run his fingers through. This was the girl who had saved him from the depths of depression. He dreamed of their future together; homes, children, their life. He felt so alive around her. And with all of those wonderful thoughts, the best he could say was, “What are you doing here?”

“I have to get ready at the church too, silly.” She downed her second shot. “I’m getting married today.” She set the glass down. “Oh I almost forgot. I met your old girlfriend out in the church.”

Chris gulped.

Lisa walked up to Chris and kissed him. “Did you know she was here?” She reached up and put her arms around his neck pulling him closer.

He thought about saying no but he had never lied to Lisa and knew he never would. “Cory and I both peeked out and saw her walking around. If you want me to go out there and tell her she should go, I’ll have no problem with that.”

“Without pants? That’d look real sharp,” Lisa said rolling her eyes. “I think we can leave Cindy alone. I don’t care if your old girlfriend is at our wedding. After all, you’re marrying me, not her. I’m not the one who’s going to have regrets. Are you?”

Chris smiled and pulled her closer to him. “Nah. Everyone in that church is going to be watching the luckiest guy in the universe marry the smartest and most understanding girl found anywhere. You really do rock my world. Marry me, please?"

She tightened her arms around his neck and as he held her close. He noticed a sprinkling of light freckles across her nose that the sun had brought out. He wanted to kiss each one.

"I'll marry you anytime," she replied and pulled his head down while he covered her mouth with his in a pulsating kiss.

His heart raced like a horse straining for the finish line.

Finally coming up for air, Lisa took a step back and said, "Wow. Let's go elope right now."

"I'm … ah … with you on that." Chris felt disoriented but so alive.

"Cancel that. You don't have any pants. Besides, I have to go and meet everyone who's helping me get ready. When's Cory coming ba ..."

Cory came crashing through the door.

"Chris! Lisa's car …" Cory spotted Lisa and stopped in his tracks as if he had stepped in glue. "What's up, Lisa?" He brushed his hair off his forehead and strolled over to the table.

"Cory, is something wrong with my car? You started to say something about my car when you stumbled in here," Lisa batted her eyelashes at him, a hand on her hip, and her head cocked to one side.

Cory fumbled his words, "Nope. Your car is okay. Nothing wrong there. I just went out to the car to get some socks." He tossed a pair on the table and poured a shot. "Then I was just … uh … going to … um …"

Lisa walked to where Cory was and patted him on the cheek. "It's okay, Cory." She looked at Chris and saw a twinkle in his eye. "We have an extra guest at the wedding. The more the merrier, right boys?" She winked and slipped out the side door.

Chris' eyes followed her swaying hips under her flimsy sundress as she walked away. "I really love that girl."

Cory wiped his brow. "Whew. You want to tell me what just happened here? I mean I felt like I was walking into …"

Chris cut him off, "Don't sweat it, dude." He sat on the couch next to his brother, sliding his arm around Cory's shoulder. "All is good, Bro. We need to finish getting ready. The boys should be here any sec."

"Man, you should be so thankful to have a girl like Lisa. Nothing shakes her. She is so steady with your relationship. I really believe she can handle any tough problems that might come your way."

Thinking about her made Chris feel stronger as if he could conquer the world.

Chris finally put on his pants as the rest of the guys, Jay, Gene, Alex, and Ian, showed up looking like southern gentlemen in their gray tuxedos.

"Boys, one last toast, and then we need to put this stuff away,"

Cory informed the others. “Father Donavon will be here in about five minutes.” He raised his glass. “To Chris and Lisa. I bet their marriage will last the longest of all. The best to both of you.”

“Here, here,” came the collective response. They slapped down the empty glasses as Father Donavon walked into the room.

“Greetings, gentlemen. I'm so glad to see you all together.” The boys immediately lost their casual attitudes as the man who had guided most of them spiritually since childhood walked in. He was a tall man with graying temples who instantly commanded respect with his stature and calming presence. He warmly shook hands with each of the boys, his sincere smile reminding every one of them of a time when he had been there for a word of advice or a needed reprimand.

“I can tell you all have toasted the day.”

The boys avoided his knowing look and stammered as they looked off in various directions.

“Not to worry. Even I have been known to indulge in spirits on special occasions. But now I need a few moments with the groom and best man. The rest of you need to report to the front of the church and prepare for guests. I believe Mrs. Gates stopped by the front foyer and inquired why none of you were at your stations.”

Cory handed the gym bag to Ian. “Okay, guys. Y'all better cut out and do your thing. We don't want my Mom bent out of shape. Not on this day.” He nodded and finished with, “We'll be seeing ya coming’ down the aisle.”

“Gotcha,” Ian said as he grabbed things that needed to be put in the car while the rest of the boys dispersed.

Alex slipped through the vestry door into the church with Gene right on his heels. There were a few people sitting in the pews and some standing around in the aisles of the dark colonial era church chatting while waiting for formal seating to begin. As Alex opened the darkly stained, wormy chestnut door to the foyer, he hit Cindy right in the back of the head, knocking her two steps forward away from Brian. Alex stopped dead in his tracks, his jaw dropped at the surprise bashing, thus causing Gene to run into him.

“Ow!” Cindy yelled, spinning around while putting a hand on her head, eyes burning with fire. “Watch it you pri … oh … hi Alex. I have been wondering where you guys were.”

Alex’s calm, Greek demeanor almost flew out the window as a tirade of questions from Cindy flooded his senses.

“Have you seen Chris? Where is he? Is he in the vestry with Cory? Is he coming up front?”

“Cindy.” Alex put his hand up. “Stay right here and Gene will answer your questions." Alex turned around to Gene, and mouthed the words, "Keep her here."

Gene nodded.

Alex left and Gene opened with, "Now that was a pile of questions." He paused for a few seconds, reaching his hand under the back of his collar to pull out his brown curls while staring at Cindy. "Did you get your hair done differently? It looks great." She blushed. Gene then slapped Brian on the shoulder. "How are ya, man? Long time no see."

"Likewise." Brian grabbed Gene's huge hand watching his disappear. He shook it as if Gene was a long lost friend.

"So, Brian," Gene continued. "What have you been up to?"

"Cut the crap." Cindy said in a raised voice. "Where the hell is Chris?" The pretty little southern belle smile vanished, replaced with the cold hard steely look of a Confederate general.

"Why do you want to see him?" Gene asked.

"I just want to wish him the best before he gets married." She looked up at Gene and Scarlett-O'Hara-at-the-barbeque miraculously, and suspiciously, resurfaced. "After all, we spent quite a few years together before he broke up with me."

"I believe you broke up with him."

"But he went off the deep end and started treating me like I didn't exist." A pouting lower lip appeared.

"Cindy, do you remember that those were some hard times for him? His whole future went right down the toilet with that knee injury. His baseball scholarships were yanked, recovery took a long time, and you left him."

"I left his ass 'cause he was totally ignoring me and drowning in his own little pity party."

Gene inhaled slowly, straightening up to his full six foot two inch frame.

"You left him when he needed you the most," he responded barely moving his lips.

Brian fidgeted and finally blurted out a high pitched plea between clenched teeth. "Both you guys need to nip this. Look around."

Cindy and Gene stopped. All eyes of the dozen or so guests in the foyer were glued to the pretty young woman, with steam coming out of her ears, quarreling with the stern faced handsome young man in the gray tux. The only sound now was that of the church aging.

The front door suddenly swung open. Chris and Cory's mother, Kelli, stepped into the foyer. Gene quickly put his arm around Cindy, pinning her to him, and then turned her to face Kelli.

"Mrs. Gates. How are you? You do remember Cindy, don't you?"

Through pursed lips from a forced smile, Kelli replied, "Why yes I do. It's been a while. How have you been, dear?"

Almost six inches taller than Cindy, Kelli, impeccably dressed in a lavender dress that matched the bridesmaid's gowns, towered above her, eyes focused and blazing.

"I've been fine, Mrs. Gates." Cindy swallowed hard and cowered. "I hope you have been doing well. This is a big day for you."

"Yes, it is. Someone outside just mentioned there was a bit of a tiff in here. It is my intention to make sure everything goes smoothly. Isn't that right, Gene?"

"You bet, Mrs. Gates. I was just about to seat Cindy and Brian."

"Hi, Mrs. Gates. I'm Brian." His voice sounded shaky.

"Of course you are, dear. Gene, please take Cindy and Brian to their seats. Alex is seating people now and needs your assistance." She looked at Cindy. "I hope you enjoy the ceremony. Perhaps we'll run into each other at the market sometime. We'll catch up then." She shot a quick glance to Gene then walked away.

Before Cindy could say anything more, Gene spun her around and quickly moved through the door into the sanctuary. Brian sheepishly followed.

White roses and pink tulips bunched with lavender filled the historic church with the ambiance of spring and new life. Lisa loved these colors and had an arrangement on the end of each pew. Chris, let the women of the family make all the decisions about the wedding decorations. He had learned from his friends to just agree with whatever had been suggested. Chris's job was to make sure he had the ring and to be at the church on time.

As Cory came into the vestry, he heard Father Donavon giving Chris his final words of advice.

"Do not let Cindy influence your thoughts about the journey ahead of you. I have counseled you and Lisa. We've discussed Cindy. She is a part of your past. Lisa is your future."

Chris nodded. "I know, Father. She truly is my soul-mate."

"Excellent, my boy." Father Donavon turned to Cory. "Good. You're back." He checked his watch. "It is time for us to go. I just heard our queue on the organ." He put a hand on a shoulder of each of them and looked at Chris. "Are you ready, my son?"

The gleam in Chris' eyes sparkled with desire. "Let's do it."

Father Donavon glanced back from the doorway and said, "As you boys always say, let's do it."

The music, the people, and the pageantry swallowed Chris up. He was a deer in the headlights as he and Cory moved to the right side of the altar stairs. Chris looked out at the sea of people that filled the pews, seeing a mass of featureless faces. Focusing on the front row, the beaming expressions from his parents and grandparents became clearer. Taking a deep breath, he smiled and nodded to friends and relatives. Then his eyes met Cindy's. Her beautiful hair surrounded glistening eyes and down turned lips.

Is that a tear rolling down her cheek? He looked away.

The music changed and down the aisle came Alex, Ian, Gene, and Jay escorting the bridesmaids, separated by the rhythmic beat of the music. Guests waved or winked as the procession progressed. The dark wooden paneled walls seemed to brighten from a barrage of camera flashes.

After each couple separated and took their respective places on each side of the aisle, Chris caught Cindy's saddened eyes, her long face looking like someone who had lost something.

I'm leaving her behind. She's hurt, but I didn't mess things up. She left me when I needed her most. Cory's right. I should be so thankful. He closed his eyes as visions of Lisa filled his head.

Chris snapped back to reality when the Bridal Chorus from Lohengrin by Richard Wagner began to play. Lisa, advancing on her father's arm, met his eyes, sparking a feeling within him of her being inside his soul. He wanted to run down the aisle screaming I DO! I DO!

Cory nudged Chris with his elbow and whispered, "Good choice, Bro. She's definitely the one."

As Chris watched the girl who saved him from destruction, rekindled his life, and gave him purpose, he whispered back to his brother, "I am so lucky."

All the monitors in the lab at Base GAIA had been showing the wedding festivities throughout the day. Tish watched her monitor as Chris and Lisa danced slowly at the reception. During the song, they kissed as if the world had stopped just for them. Tish glanced at Zenta to see if she had seen them.

She had. Her shoulders slumped as if her spine was jelly, her head bowed. Strands of her beautiful white hair fell forward hiding tears that dropped ever so slowly onto her leg. Her whole body appeared deflated and rocked with a sob as she turned her head toward the wall.

Tish and Gunstot watched as Zenta, with one hand on her chest, slowly removed her headset and got up. Looking as if it took great effort to even move, she gradually made her way out of the lab without saying a word.

30 – PERFORMANCE, POKER, AND POLITICS

Zenta pulled on the collar of her dress uniform in hopes of loosening it.

This constricting feeling is driving me insane.

"Is there a problem, Major?" Colonel Braaddy inquired quietly to avoid anyone else on the Dagar hearing his question.

"No, sir. It's that I'm not too particularly fond of these dress uniforms." She glanced across the aisle at Hajeck and Donac to see if they heard her, not that she cared. There were quite a few simultaneous conversations occurring amongst the receiving delegation. "This high collar is choking me."

"I don't care for them either, but we don't have a choice." He pointed out the window at the FALK as he continued. "Supreme Council members expect us to be at our best and Councilor Dienong demands perfection."

As the Dagar approached the huge War Carrier, Zenta watched one of the bay doors open. Surrounding the bay were six launch portals for Reep Fighters. She turned in her seat and looked out the window behind her to catch a glimpse of the Battle Cruiser, the TRAZ.

"He's my least favorite councilor," Zenta said as she caught sight of a couple Dagars from the placement and launch team. "I'm sure he's had Admiral Kaioc and his entire crew on the TRAZ jumping at his every word. And now he wants to have the receiving delegation pick him up from the FALK. If this is any indication of his well-known controlling behavior, then I am dreading his review of the Savior Project."

"Everything is in order so I'm not worried. I am more concerned with getting Dienong and his party in and out of here so we can get back to work."

"How long will it take for the FALK to build the outpost for the new Titan squadrons?"

"Not long. Military Command has decided to keep a carrier in our solar system on a yearly rotation cycle until we extract the Savior. The FALK is the first. It's also carrying the new squadrons for all the outposts, plus three new ones for us." Braaddy smiled. "That's a lot of firepower."

"I hope we'll never need it. I assume Dienong will return to Terlokya on the TRAZ right after the review?" Zenta inquired.

"Correct. The sooner, the better."

Within an hour of arriving on base, the ten representatives from the

People's Legislature were seated around the long, oval table in the Council Communications room with Dienong at one end and General Jhall at the other. Colonel Braaddy and Zenta were to Jhall's left, and Hajeck, who had recently been promoted to colonel, along with Xander were on Jhall's right. Jzet sat as close to Dienong as possible. Others were seated at the table and around the outer wall of the room.

Dienong raised a hand and the room fell silent. He stood up, his robe making a rustling sound.

"Major Marsitta." Dienong's high voice had a raspy quality to it. "Are we ready to connect Sohan and the rest of the Supreme Council?" He smiled and gestured toward the wall communications screen.

"Yes, Councilor." Marsitta faced the communications workstation and keyed in the appropriate commands. The huge screen lit up with life sized images of Sohan and the other Supreme Council members.

"Greetings, my fellow Terlokyans," Dienong said with a slight nod of his head.

Everyone in the room rose to their feet.

"Greetings, Councilor," Sohan replied. He was standing in front of his seat at the podium to the left of the Supreme Council bench. The council members remained seated. "You may begin when ready."

Sohan managed a quick glance at Zenta. They'd only had a few conversations since she left Terlokya six years ago.

"Thank you, Supreme Commander." Dienong looked down the long table at Braaddy.

"Ahem. Colonel Braaddy, we've read the reports on the change with the Savior's career path; from the original plan of him becoming a leading sports figure to one of a political nature. Currently, it is Earth's summer season in their year 2003 and twelve years have passed since his sports career was halted. The council has been provided with additional information indicating that no progress has been made in regards to the Savior's political career. Would you please enlighten the council as to the current state of this new plan?"

Dienong sat down without a change in his expression.

If eyes were weapons, Braaddy and Zenta would have burned holes through the smiling Jzet. Everyone knew he was the source of the additional information. Braaddy jumped to his feet.

"Supreme Commander, Supreme Council members, and fellow Terlokyans, it is an honor to update you on Terlokya's most important project." Braaddy surveyed the participants with intent interest evident in some and doubt in others. Looking smug, it was obvious Jzet had won Dienong over to his way of thinking, which was his belief that a Terlokyan should lead Earth.

"The change in the Savior's career path was necessary due to uncontrollable variables in the sports game the Savior was participating in. Our research indicates that many athletes in the game of baseball are ingesting medications that Earthlings refer to as 'performance enhancing' drugs. While my project team is confident that the Savior would never bow to any pressure to ingest these drugs, his superior performance could lead others to conclude that he did. This would lead to a tarnished image due to guilt by association. With this additional information, the decision was made to guide the Savior to the second career option; politics."

Braaddy noticed Sohan's beaming smile and the long faces of Dienong and Jzet. He continued.

"While I'm of the opinion that twelve years is insufficient time to bring the Savior into the political arena on Earth, others on the Phase 3 Savior Development Team believe the timing is perfect. We also benefited from this career change in that it gave us the opportunity to implement the second challenge for the Savior; his ability to make a life altering self-sacrifice. I am now going to let Major Zenta present these details." Braaddy nodded to the audience and gestured toward Zenta. "Major?"

Zenta stood and scanned the expressions in the room. She knew that for this presentation, it was a benefit to be the Supreme Commander's daughter. Her dedication to the Savior Project was unquestionable. She had, so far, dedicated her adult life to this.

"It gives me great pleasure to provide the details of this change in the Savior's career path and the positive results from the second challenge. As many of you know, three challenges were developed to test the Savior in overcoming severe personal adversity, his willingness to make an extreme self-sacrifice, and the third challenge is his ability to create a following amongst his fellow Earthlings. This new career path will provide a better opportunity for the third challenge." She checked her notes to give everyone time to digest that information.

"As expected, the Savior passed the first challenge of suffering a severe injury. He rehabilitated himself to an even better state than before."

"The Savior met and passed the second challenge by sacrificing what was to be a most promising career in the sport of baseball. His sacrifice of notoriety and popularity along with future monetary gain was more than we could have hoped for."

Zenta went on to explain about Chris forgoing a possible Major League baseball career with its guaranteed financial independence and choosing to continue his education and start a family.

"As for changing the Savior's career path, Colonel Braaddy explained the reasons behind it. When the decision was made, we helped guide the reshaping of the Savior's life. He had to become a family man, essential in his employment, and an influential, well-known figure in his community and surrounding areas. We took advantage of his name recognition. His decision to forgo the sports career brought him more notoriety. Intervention is less frequent since the Savior's ever expanding interest is to involve himself in social and political issues and find solutions."

During the next half hour, Zenta provided details of Chris' life from starting a family to his employment as a teacher and baseball coach at the Jefferson Academy. At Jefferson, he was in a position to have a positive influence on young minds leading to his popularity among adult parents. Positive affirmations around the room gave evidence that Zenta had changed everyone's opinion to a positive one as she told of the birth of Chris and Lisa's children. Taylor was born in June of 1999 and Michelle born in August of 2002. She gloated over his love and dedication to his wife and children even though deep inside, it still made her heart ache.

"As you can see, this change has had numerous positive outcomes. The Development Team now feels it is time for the Savior to launch his new political career by announcing his desire to seek office. He has built a solid family foundation, secured two advanced education degrees, established a multitude of influential professional relationships and is well known because of this. Well established political insiders have been pressuring him to seek political office. The Savior realizes that he will have to be the one to make changes in society."

Zenta felt it was time to close so Braaddy could take questions. She checked and when Braaddy nodded, she took a deep breath and exhaled slowly.

"Supreme Commander, Supreme Council members, and fellow Terlokyans, you are fortunate to be here at the time when the Savior will be announcing his political intentions during your stay here. It has been an honor to have presented you with this information. Thank you."

Zenta sat down to applause that increased in intensity as Colonel Braaddy stood up for questions. He raised his hands after a minute and things became quiet.

"We appreciate the positive feedback." Braaddy glanced at Jzet, who was staring blankly at the table, shoulders hunched over, not moving a muscle.

Dienong was no fool and saw the writing on the wall. He looked intently at Braaddy, hanging on every word, giving every indication of total support.

"Are there any questions?" Braaddy asked.

Sohan stood up, but Dienong rose quickly and said, "Supreme Commander, if I may?"

"By all means," Sohan replied with a bit of concern evident in his voice.

"Colonel Braaddy. I must commend you on a job well done. By all appearances, your efforts and those of your team are fully supported by the Supreme Commander and the Supreme Council. I do not believe there are any questions." He looked at Sohan and his fellow council members who were all smiling and nodding in agreement. "Well then Colonel, carry on and let the Savior's political career begin."

Back in Virginia, December was just a few days away.

Wow. 2003 has flown by. It's already time for the annual Bros Poker party, Chris thought as he drove home from work. He fiddled with the BMW's radio, switching between the sports stations.

It's only two weeks away and there's still so much to do.

Chris wondered why Jay hadn't responded to his emails. "I'm gonna call him." He pulled out his cell phone.

"What's up, man," Jay answered.

"Hustling home as fast as the car in front of me will allow. Hey, why haven't you responded to my email about the party?"

"I need to respond? How many years have we been doing this?"

"Lemme see ..." Chris racked his brain. "For the last twelve years, always the second Friday in December, in the old carriage house on the Forest Hill Plantation. What's your point?" They laughed.

For this annual get together, the guys met shortly after work. Their wives had grown accustomed to this ritual, some referring to it as childish activity. But it had become a tradition and had achieved a level of sanctity never to be touched or altered for any reason. It was totally harmless fun.

"My point is that I haven't missed one in twelve years," Jay said.

Chris could hear the 'gloat'.

"Forgive me, Bro. I've always handled everything for this event which, by the way, will be the 13th Annual Plantation Christmas Poker Party."

"Whoopee. Bring your money so I can win it," Jay chuckled.

Another call was coming through. Chris checked and Cory's number popped up on caller ID.

"Look, Man. Cory's calling in. I'll call you sometime tonight."

"Cool. Later."

Chris took the call.

"Cory, my man."

"Dude. Have you got everything ready for the big game?" Cory asked excitedly.

"Man, can you believe it's just two weeks away? I hope there's enough time to get it all together. What are you and Diane doing tonight? We got the pizza-movie gig."

"Looks like the same at our house. The kids have been clamoring for it all week. But tomorrow night we're having Alex, Julie, Ian, and Shannon over for game night. Diane already talked to Lisa and y'all are coming. We're going to dump all the kids in a pile downstairs, load 'em up with movies and popcorn so we can own the upstairs."

Chris whipped the Beamer into another lane to avoid a car drifting into him. "Moron!" Chris shouted through closed windows.

"Gee, if you don't wanna come, you don't have to call me names," Cory teased.

Chris turned his radio off. "Sorry, dude. A freakin' dumbass musta just got his license from the liquor store and is out for the first time. What'd you say before?"

"Just stuff about Saturday night. Lisa must have told you about it, right?"

"She probably did. I've just been preoccupied with this political thing I've wanted to talk to you about."

"Go for it."

Chris backed the car into the garage then hit the door remote to close it. "Hang on a sec." The garage door made a clanking sound as it lowered. "I just pulled in."

"All right. What's up?"

"It's about entering politics. I can't believe I'm considering this. Everyone says I have great ideas so why can't others just listen to me and then act on them? And I hate wearing suits. Oh the heck with it. Let's talk about it this weekend."

"Sure thing. We'll hash it out then. You know how to reach me. Just open the window and yell. Ya know?"

"I know. Later, dude." Chris loosened his tie and looked at the stuff in the passenger seat that had to be carried in. Sighing, he let his thoughts wander.

He glanced up at his rear view mirror and caught site of the hallway door to garage slowly open and then close. He eyed a little shadow on the floor as Taylor came around the back of the Beamer. Chris watched in the side mirror as his little boy, already dressed in his footed pajamas, tip toed up to the driver's side window. Chris quickly grabbed the newspaper so he would appear to be preoccupied.

"BOO!" came the shrill little voice.

"Ahh," Chris yelled looking startled. "You scared me." He quickly opened his door and picked up his squealing four year old. "Come here, boy!" He gave him a hug and blew a raspberry on his neck.

"Daddy! Daddy! That tickles!" He giggled while Chris held Taylor against his chest and jumped out of the car.

"How's my little man?" he asked while cradling Taylor.

"Good." Taylor giggled again. "Rub noses."

Chris rubbed noses and asked, "Where is everyone?"

"Mama's upstairs with Michelle. Did ja get pizza?"

"I sure did. I got the kind with liver and onions."

"You did not."

Chris put Taylor down and opened the rear door to get the pizzas out. "Can you carry these upstairs little man?" he asked while carefully laying the boxes on Taylor's arms.

"Daddy, I always carry them." With the pizzas safely secured, Chris opened the hallway door and Taylor headed for the stairs walking very carefully.

Chris gathered up his stuff, grabbed the flowers and wine from the back seat, and hustled down the hall.

"Dad-deeeeeeee." Chris was met at the top of the stairs by his year and a half old daughter, Michelle. She was bouncing up and down a few feet from the top, arms out-stretched toward her daddy, her fingers opening and closing.

"Pick me up. Pick me up," she squealed.

"How's my Sweetpea?" Chris inquired of his little one. Setting his things down on the dining room table, he picked her up and held her high over his head.

"How big is Michelle?"

"Dis big," she said as she raised her hands up.

Lisa had come into the great room and went to greet Chris.

"Hi, sweetheart. How was the drive home?" She gave him a kiss.

"It was okay." He handed Michelle to Lisa and picked up the flowers from the table. "How was your day?" he said as he finally noticed what she was wearing. "Wow!"

"Wow what?" Lisa replied batting her eyes seductively. She used her free hand in a sweeping gesture from her black and white zebra striped top to her skin tight white pants. "You like?"

"More than that," he said as he put his arms around her and Michelle. He kissed Lisa causing Michelle to push on her daddy's shoulder.

"Kiss me too, Daddy."

"Okay, Sweetpea." He gave her a peck on her forehead then a raspberry on her cheek.

"Daddy! That tickles me."

"It's supposed to, silly." He held up the flowers. "Look at what I got for Mommy and you."

"Pretty," Michelle said clapping her hands together.

"Yes, they are. What's the occasion?" Lisa's eyes flickered with excitement. She put her hand on Chris' arm and gave a squeeze.

"I thought I'd better stay on my toes and get you something to show my appreciation for all you do before some other dude comes along and sweeps you off your feet."

"That sounds like a good reason to me," she said while walking out to the kitchen with the flowers. She set Michelle down and got a vase from the pantry.

Chris then handed Michelle the two movies he had picked up at the video store.

"Daddy. I wuv dinsors." She ran and jumped on the couch.

"That's dinosaur, Sweetpea," he corrected her. "That's the Land before Time movie."

Taylor quickly joined in as he came into the room.

"That's my favorite movie." He sat down next to Michelle. "Daddy, put the movie in please."

Chris bunny hopped to the entertainment center eliciting loud giggles. He turned on the television and VCR and put the movie in. With everything adjusted, he walked into the kitchen where Lisa was putting pizza on plates for the kids.

"After we get the kids settled in, let's go talk about this political stuff. Do you remember Jon Dover from that summer gig I had in his print shop when I got back from California?"

"Vaguely."

"Well, he's on the city council and he's the guy who's been leading the effort to get me to run for the senate. He's hosting that meet and greet event next week to introduce me to the political kingmakers." He got the corkscrew out of a drawer and opened the wine. "You know the changes we'd like to see in government. Well, this is a big step to seeing those things through." He picked up Taylor's plate.

"If anyone can change our government, it's you," she said convincingly. She carried Michelle's plate to her and put her juice cup on the coffee table. Chris did the same for Taylor.

"Sit next to me, Daddy," Taylor mumbled through a mouthful of pizza.

Chris looked at Lisa and said, "I guess we'll be talking later." They both shrugged, grabbed some pizza, and sat on the couch for pizza-movie night.

Two weeks later, Cory bounded up the stairs at the old carriage house. Shaped like a small barn, the 19th century era house was still in perfect shape. Originally built to hold four carriages, it was too small for modern cars. Two mid-size farm tractors and other farm equipment took up the space now. To the left of the two huge barn style doors was the entrance to the stairway leading up to the living quarters.

"Beer here," Cory said as he put the case of Budweiser on the counter. He opened the case and got a couple cans out. "Ahh, cold beer." He tossed one to Alex.

The upstairs room of the carriage house had its own little kitchenette in the living area. The rustic appearance was enhanced by the natural wood color of the pine board walls. Once the living quarters for the farm manager, Junior Henderson, it was unoccupied ever since he got married and moved to one of the adjoining properties. Being an old high school buddy, he made sure the guys had access to the place each year for the big game.

"That beer won't be cold for long unless you put it in the fridge," Ian said sarcastically from the couch as he wiped barbecue sauce on his jeans.

"So is Junior gonna join us again this year?" Alex asked as he opened his beer.

"He only came to the first one" Gene quickly replied while biting on a chicken wing. He wiped his face with a napkin and then wiped his hand on Alex's flannel shirt. "We invite him every year and he turns us down." He grabbed another wing. "Oh well. At least David said he was coming again. It was kinda cool getting him involved last year."

Alex laid a chicken bone on Gene's shoulder without him knowing.

Chris went to the fridge for a beer. "I agree." He stopped off at the counter for a slice of pizza.

"Hey," Ian hollered from his reclining position. "Bring me one of those too."

Chris handed the slice to Ian as he sat next to him.

Everyone heard the downstairs door slam shut and the stomping coming up the stairs.

"Boys!"

"David!" came the chorused greeting.

Gene got up and slapped him on the back. "Grab something to drink and eat. We're just stuffing ourselves before the game begins."

"Sounds good."

Everyone refilled their plates and planted themselves around the spacious room.

"Well, guys," Chris got everyone's attention. "I've decided to go ahead and run for Al McDonald's senate seat."

"You what?" Alex blurted out from his barstool at the counter causing part of a chicken wing to fall out of his mouth. "I knew you were thinking about it, but, wow. That's a heck of a thing to take on."

"Well, I've talked to some of you guys about it." Chris set his beer on the coffee table. "Not one of you said it's a bad idea." Everyone nodded and mumbled positively. "There are a lot of community leaders and people around the state who have told me that I have fresh ideas and I've shed new light on previous initiatives."

"You mean like recycling?" Ian asked.

Cory jumped in. "Not just recycling, dude. Although, I feel that everyone could put more effort into environmental programs. The bigger issue is about finding alternative sources of energy. Tell 'em Chris."

"Cory's right." Chris leaned up and put his elbows on his knees. "America is too dependent on oil and coal. Add the fact that most of the oil producing countries don't like us very much."

Gene coughed at that statement. "That's because we're always going around and telling other countries what to do."

"True." Chris stood up now. "But think about the possibilities if we developed the industries for solar and wind energy. America would be less dependent on others and would own all the clean energy technology. We need to make the investment in today's dollars versus tomorrow's."

"You've been on the state and local news enough about this issue," Ian added. "With your past talks about it, a whole lot of people know you, so you have good name recognition."

"You said government debt was something you wanted to take on," David chimed in.

"We, as individuals, can't keep borrowing money without it coming back to bite us in the butt. The government keeps borrowing while we send cash overseas to some countries that are corrupt and we never know if that money reaches the people that need it. We don't know where that money is going. Why are we sticking our nose in areas of the world where the people don't want us? Who died and made us the world police?"

"You got that right!" Alex shouted. "Get the heck outa Greece!"

Gene tapped him on the shoulder. "We're not in Greece, idiot."

Alex scrunched up his face. "Yeah, you're right. I think I'll have another beer."

"Tell 'em the big thing that makes you different," Cory said excitedly.

Chris stood up. "The point is, is that we have to balance the budget. So we use a combination of cutting expenses and raising taxes."

"That won't get you elected when you use the 'T' word," Ian piped in.

"Tough choices to make. But we have to do it. The infrastructure of the country, like roads and parks, is crumbling. But I think the one big thing that will make me different is that I want to take us back to viewing politics and government the way our founding fathers did." Chris walked to the center of the room. "Politics was never meant to be a profession. When our union first formed, you served your government for a short period of time and then returned to your original profession. So I'll do what I can in one term and then come back to teaching and coaching at Jefferson. And I won't take any corporate campaign donations, only donations from individuals. I want to fix campaign contributions and lobbying."

"You sound like all those buttheads on the campaign trail," Alex razzed Chris.

"Maybe, but I'm going to stick to my word and actually change things. I'll meet with citizens, not lobbyists. That's who I represent. We, as citizens, have to take our government back from the career politicians."

The guys all looked around the room at each other and appeared to be in agreement.

"Are you still planning on being an independent?" Gene asked.

"I'm not joining any party. My message is that I'm a citizen who is going to represent the citizens of my state and serve on their behalf in our federal government. All of those things I've talked about are possible to do in one term. I'm going to use the media to get my message out there."

The guys were silent for a minute, not moving much, obviously thinking.

Ian spoke first, "You do have the face that people somehow remember. Maybe it's that charisma of yours. Ha ha ha."

All the guys were laughing now including Chris.

"It certainly wasn't all the partying he did. He always hid in the background," Alex added eliciting more laughter.

"Yeah, and that great baseball career that skyrocketed." Gene jumped on the 'get Chris' bandwagon.

"Hey, hey, guys," David hopped off his barstool with his arms raised. "Ya gotta give Chris credit for pursuing the game as far as he could. You have to admit: he was good."

"Was?" Chris asked jokingly from his seat on the couch.

"I can't help it if you turned down a chance to stay in the majors," David said shrugging his shoulders. "That puts your baseball career in the past now, bub."

Cory got up from his seat.

"I know y'all are teasing now, but everyone here knows the real reason Chris isn't playing Major League ball," Cory stated with an air of seriousness.

"Sure. We all know he picked family first. He's a regular saint," Alex teased as he went to the fridge for another beer.

Gene got up and started rubbing his hands together as he walked to the card table. "Well at least he's still got it on the softball field. He's the best damn pitcher in the league and I'm glad he's on our team."

"So will you guys be on my team when I start changing this country?" Chris asked while taking a seat. "Are you all with me on that?"

"You know we'll do anything for you, Chris," Alex said as he sat down next to him. "We may kid around with you, but that's 'cause you're one of the Bros. Somehow you've always been right about stuff and I know you'll be right on this too"

Back in the Savior Project Lab, Zenta leaned forward on her workstation and yawned.

"I wish I could play that game," Gunstot said as he watched the card game. "Every time we've tried playing it here, I never win anything."

"It takes practice," Zenta told him. "Besides, Xander never told you all the strategy for the game."

"Really? Well, that explains a lot. I didn't know there was strategy."

Zenta smiled. "Never trust Xander when it comes to gambling."

"Thanks for the late advice. Speaking of gambling, looks like your plan to get Chris into politics worked."

Zenta got up and started to walk around to loosen up. "It wasn't easy. In nightly education sessions, I had to use his disdain for politics as motivation to get him to want to change it."

Gunstot looked surprised. "He can't change the whole political system in one six year term."

"True. But he'll have such a powerful message and leave such a lasting impression that everyone will know and remember him. Plus, he'll be planting the seeds of change"

"That sounds like it might work."

"It had better."

31 – THE LIMELIGHT AND THE FIREFIGHT

With Lisa by his side, Chris waved to the roaring crowd from the stage as cameras clicked and people yelled his name.

"Run again, Chris! Please!"

"Give us another six years!"

"We need you!"

Chris and Lisa's eyes met for a moment, and that recognition of having made the right decision was evident in their smiles. He waved again to the crowd.

The stage on the steps of the historic Rotunda in the heart of the University was filled with dignitaries, academicians, politicians, and friends. All were convinced they could coax another run for the Senate out of him. The pressure was overwhelming.

Dressed in his usual khakis, tie, and dress shirt, Chris stepped next to the podium as if he was going to speak. It drove the crowd into a frenzy doubling the decibels. Exams hadn't started so students were spread throughout the crowd. The entire length of The Lawn was covered with people, almost two football fields worth. April 2010 had brought a breath of warm weather to the community and their favorite son had come home from Washington D.C. to share his decision.

The University's President, Gordon Stinson, put his hand on Chris' shoulder and took the lead at the podium. He raised his hands to the cheering crowd and spoke into the microphone.

"Welcome to the University of Virginia, home of one of our Founding Fathers!"

Hearing those words caused the crowd to roar to the heavens. Throughout his initial campaign and while in office, Chris hammered home the theme of returning to the founding principles that Jefferson, Adams, Franklin, Washington, and others used to create our country.

With President Stinson holding his hands up for calm, the crowd settled.

"Thank you. Thank you. What a welcome this has been for one of our own."

The crowd started up again but President Stinson quickly restored quiet.

"We'll be here all day." He waited to make sure the crowd had settled. "I know you didn't come to hear me speak, so I'll be brief. I am pleased to have Senator Chris Gates, representing the Commonwealth of Virginia and its citizens, here today to announce his future plans." Stinson turned and gestured toward Chris who was standing a few feet behind him with his arm around Lisa. Taylor and Michelle stood in front of them.

"Chris has served the Commonwealth in such a way that I'm sure Jefferson would have voted for him." Stinson had his hands up to ward off the cheers.

"Since I know it will take him some time to quiet everyone down again, and if you haven't already met him, let me introduce Senator Chris Gates."

A decibel meter would have shattered from the deafening crowd noise. All of the national and state wide news organizations were in front of the stage with cameras rolling. News teams were having trouble relaying their commentator's live coverage. Even foreign news groups were present in case Chris said what everyone wanted to hear.

Chris stood at the podium surveying the crowd. There wasn't an inch of space anywhere. The balconies of all the historic Pavilions were filled to capacity. Balloons and signs floated over the crowd. Children rode on their parents shoulders. Blue jeans and tee shirts stood next to dresses and three-piece suits. This was truly a following. Chris put his hands up and the crowd immediately fell silent.

"Please run again," a woman shouted from the front. "We love you."

"And I love you too." Chris held a hand up so that only a minor roar occurred.

Flashing his trademark genuine smile, Chris began to chuckle.

"I just realized something," he said while reaching up and adjusting the mic. "I've got to use," he gestured quotation marks, "those words that make everyone crazy."

Laughter spread through the crowd.

"So y'all need to bear with me and not make this longer than necessary." He paused and looked at the crowd.

"Our Founding Fathers ..."

That's all it took. As was the case with every crowd he spoke to, the moment those words left his mouth, things erupted. What he had accomplished in creating change and awareness in government was just short of miraculous. By referring to the way the founders of the United States had structured the country, these three words had taken on a new meaning for change.

He put his arms out as if he wanted to embrace everyone.

"Come on y'all. Let's try again." With order restored he continued.

"Our Founding Fathers, some who stood on these very steps, would be proud of you. You are the ones who again have embraced the ideals that they laid out more than two centuries ago. I only reminded our country of those ideals. We don't need political parties to achieve change. We need citizens."

He paused, letting that sink in.

"We're smart enough. We used common sense and stopped listening to the political rhetoric that used to dominate the news."

A few cheers started but when his hands went up, the voices died down.

"Think about what we've done."

Chris removed the microphone from the stand, loosened his tie, and walked to the edge of the stage.

"Now remember that we did this together. First of all, we pointed out to the rest of our representatives that we were tired of being in debt. Why did Washington keep cutting our domestic programs but kept giving aid to other countries? I do care that some of those countries are our friends, but none of us are able to feed the neighbor's family when our family is starving. We have to be strong before we can make others strong."

A few hoots and cheers came from the crowd. Chris walked back and forth across the stage as he talked about his successful environmental programs and how our country was now making the needed investments in alternative fuel sources since fossil fuels had a finite life. Other accomplishments listed were many. One was political attack ads. Instead of disagreeing on issues and attacking the 'messenger' of the idea, politicians now presented their differences to the newly formed Citizens Committees who would give input from the voters. Campaign contributions from big business were now shied away from by candidates who wanted the support of the masses.

Chris had the crowd fired up after talking about his achievements during his time in office.

"But the one thing that has eluded me," he stood up straighter and pointed at the crowd, "and has eluded you … and that is term limits."

The crowd was stone, cold silent.

"The only ones who can make term limits a reality … in other words … vote on it to make it law, are the very ones in office who would be voting themselves out of a job. Having been around these career politicians in Washington for the past six years, I can tell you most would be lost without this job. That's the problem. It's a job to them, not service to us."

The crowd clapped at that statement. Chris turned around to make eye contact with Lisa. They again exchanged a wordless understanding of what had to be done.

The crowd grew silent as they hung on his every word.

"I'm a school teacher and a baseball coach."

"Go Coach!" a youthful voice yelled.

Chris recognized one of his high school players in the crowd. "Go Scott!" he yelled back.

"That's what I do for a living. All I did is what Thomas Jefferson did; and that was to serve our nation as best as I could." A few cheers were heard but quickly ended as everyone nervously waited to hear his decision.

"We didn't achieve our goals when it came to term limits. This is a big part of getting back to what our Founding Fathers planned for us. Being elected to political office means to serve your country, not turn it into a career. From what I've learned, the only way we are going to have term limits, is for the voters to make it happen. We should only elect candidates that are going to push for term limits and set an example to everyone else." He stopped and looked out at all the yearning faces. "Someone has to start. If I can't get the career politicians to hear what the citizens are saying, then I can still lead you, but only by setting an example."

He lowered his gaze for a couple of seconds to ready himself.

"To be true to my principles and yours, which we received from our Founding Fathers, I cannot possibly run for another term."

The groans echoed everywhere.

Chris held the mic down and let the crowd vent for a while. Shouts of, "Run again anyway!" reverberated. Chris held the mic up and continued.

"Look. We have the power. Six years ago, I came to you with a message and ideas. You believed in me and sent me to Washington to make those ideas bear fruit. We almost batted a thousand, didn't we?"

A few shouts of, "We need you!" were heard.

He raised his hands. He knew he had to instill something in the people.

"Okay everyone. I've got a new idea." He glanced down at all the media people and their equipment camped right in front of the stage.

"Could I ask you wonderful media people to clear a little path up to the stage," he said gesturing to the center area in front. News anchors and camera operators looked at each other then back at the stage in disbelief as if Chris had just spoken to them in Chinese. He gestured again. "Come on you guys. I really need a path here so I can have access to the audience. You can keep filming whatever you want. But I have to have this area clear in front for a few minutes. Think of it as a parting of the media sea," Chris said moving his hands simulating an opening.

With much head shaking and mumbling, the media people right in the center began picking up their equipment, wiring, and whatever else to open the center. This caused a chain reaction with all of the news crews having to move to their right or left to accommodate the shifting tide.

Melissa Howard, a reporter for Channel 29 News, and her cameraman, Lance Utley, had been in the middle. They shuffled along with the others scooting a couple of feet to their left, but she lagged behind to try and secure space close to the middle.

"Lance," Melissa was trying to get his attention without being too loud but it wasn't working. He was lugging two bulky cameras, a stand, and pushing an equipment case along the ground with his feet.

"Lance!" That got his attention.

"What? Can't you see I'm busy right now with all this crap?" He glanced at her and saw she was only carrying her microphone. "You could have at least offered to help move something."

"Don't go too far. We want to stay close to the middle."

"Geez. Did you hear me or is that all you're good for, barking orders?" Lance threw the stand down and set the extra camera on the equipment case. He looked behind him and saw an Italian news crew yelling at each other. Speaking in Melissa's ear, Lance shouted, "I hope you're happy now."

"Lance!" She pushed him away and pointed at Chris. He was sitting in a chair near the edge of the stage. "Get your camera ready to film this. I have a feeling this is going to be a one-of-a-kind speech." Melissa held her mic out to capture what he was about to say.

"That's not so bad now, is it?" Chris asked then looked out to the crowd. "Tell you what; do you think everyone in the first fifty rows or so could sit? It's a beautiful day and the ground is warm and dry."

People began moving about like animals in the wild trying to beat the grass down. They eventually started sitting and appeared relaxed now.

"There. That's better," Chris said showing his big smile. "Nothing like having a chat with five thousand friends." That brought some laughter.

Melissa leaned toward Lance and whispered, "Are you getting this?"

"Sorry. I was filming those birds up in that big tree." He had his camera on Chris.

"I know you all were hoping that I was going to run again. And now that you've heard me out, I'm sure you understand why I can't. I would like to finish the things I said I was going to do. But this last one, term limits, is going to take a lot of work. If we all vow to only elect candidates who guarantee they will serve only one term, and also make term limit reform their top priority, then that's who we want to nominate.

Regardless of political affiliation, we would all know which candidates should be considered for nomination. After that's established, we can see where they stand on the rest of the issues."

Chris watched as people conferred with those around them seeking affirmation.

"But what you just did is not enough." He received puzzled stares. "Talking to your friends or relatives next to you about this is not enough to make sure we follow through. Let's take an additional step."

He pointed to a young man near the front wearing a backpack, most assuredly a student there.

"Young man, would you come up here please?" The student sprung up from his seat and came right up to the stage.

Then he pointed to the left at an older gentleman in a suit, standing by one of the pavilion columns. "Sir, would you please join us?" The fellow nodded and sauntered up to the stage.

Next he pointed at Melissa. "Young lady, would you come join us too, please?"

She covered her mouth then pointed at her microphone. "I can't ... I'm with the news ... a reporter ... here." She was fumbling her words. "With all of these news people … here."

"Nice one," Lance whispered as he focused his camera on Melissa. "Get up there."

Chris insisted. "I know you're with the media. We won't hold that against you. Please join us."

The crowd cheered for her to join the others. She finally relented.

President Stinson leaned over and whispered to Lisa, "Was this planned?"

"We never know what he's going to do. It seems he's driven by another power."

Back up front, Chris got up from his chair and sat on the edge of the stage.

"Thanks, everyone." Chris turned his attention to the young man, "Hi. Tell us your name, where you're from, and if you lean to the left or right." Chris held the mic in front of him.

"I'm Adam Gordon from NOVA. I'm a third year student here and I lean to the left."

"Thanks, Adam." Looking at Melissa, he asked her the same thing.

"Hi. I'm Melissa Howard. I'm from the county here and I work for Channel 29 news. I would say I'm in the middle."

"Thanks, Melissa." Chris repeated the process for the older gentleman.

"Thanks, Chris. I'm Weldon Hastings. I own the Springhouse

Publishing Company in Alexandria where I live. I graduated from here in 1958 so it's nice to be back." Applause rippled through the crowd. "I would say I lean to the right."

"Thank you, Weldon." Chris remained seated, his legs dangling over the edge of the stage.

He spoke to the crowd. "There you have it. Including me, we have four distinct individuals covering the whole political spectrum. Now we are going to form political watch teams. Listen how we do this because I want everyone else to do this too." He looked at the three in front of him.

"Adam, you and I will be a team. Weldon and Melissa will be a team. What we're going to do is exchange contact information: phone and email. We'll stay in touch loosely but when it comes to any election cycle, we'll check in with each other to make sure the candidates that are in the race are term limit supporters. If they aren't we'll discuss what our next step is. Most importantly, we are committed to only supporting term limit candidates." He surveyed the crowd to gauge a response. An aide passed Chris pens and paper. "Thanks, but let's do this for the environment too." He pulled out his cell phone. "Okay, let's exchange."

After a couple of minutes, Chris stood up. "Thanks, guys," he said, nodding to the other three. Then to the crowd, "All right now. You saw what just happened. I want each of you to seek out someone close by that you don't know. Try for diversity in your selection. Exchange info and form a team." He clapped his hands. "Come on people. Let's do this."

Everyone in the crowd began talking and exchanging information. Even those on stage were doing it. News people were doing the same.

Melissa said to Lance, "What's your problem? Why aren't you doing this?"

"The English can't vote in colonial elections."

"Oh. I forgot you're a Brit."

"Pay attention," Lance said pointing at Chris getting ready to speak again. "Get your mic up."

"As I look out over this sea of faces, I'm hoping I've spotted some of our future citizen politicians. Stay in touch with your fellow team member. Spread the word on forming political watch teams. We've got roughly 5,000 people here. If each of you tells just one person, we've got 10,000. If those 10,000 each tell one person, well, you can see how fast this will spread. Big changes start with the smallest of efforts." He saw heads nodding and a few high-fives in the crowd. Everyone became quiet as Chris stood up and walked back to the podium.

"This has been great, but it's time for me to go. I do want to thank each and every one of you for coming out today and for your support during these past six years."

A few cheers rang out.

"But I still have another nine months as your senator. I plan on making those months as productive as I can. It has been an honor to serve you."

People started a 'We want Chris' chant.

"Thank you and I'll see you around."

With that, he put the microphone in its stand on the podium and waved to the crowd. Lisa came up beside him, slipped an arm around his waist, and also waved. The cheers and applause were overwhelming. Chris turned and shook hands with the people on stage, then walked down the side stairs toward the media.

Cory, who had been standing in the background on stage, came forward and thanked President Stinson.

After exchanging pleasantries, the President noticed Chris talking to the Italian news crew and asked, "Is he speaking to them in Italian?"

"Yes, sir, I believe he is. He feels it's better to communicate to foreign nationals in their language."

Stinson was surprised. "How many languages does he know?"

"All of the major ones and a few others from what I've been able to keep up with. He has a real knack for picking up new ones."

"Really? Where did he learn so many?"

"Well, high school, college, graduate school, and then on his own. They just come easy for him."

"Impressive. I'm sure that has served him well and will continue to do so. He's a unique individual."

Cory, nodding his head, replied, "That he is. Thank you again, sir. We'll be seeing you around."

"My pleasure," Stinson replied as he watched Chris. "I'm sure our paths will cross again."

Much later at the Gates' home, Chris and Lisa were sitting on the couch watching the Eleven O'clock News. Chris' speech was the leading story.

"Are you going to miss the limelight?" Lisa asked as they watched the news coverage.

"No, not really. What I'll miss is a way to communicate to the people. I managed to turn the media into a conduit for a message of change. I've planted the seeds. Let's see if they grow."

Chris glanced up at the ceiling.

"Did you see that?" Lisa asked.

"No, what?"

"The camera man moved his camera and filmed a bird in a tree while you were talking."

"Probably more interesting." Chris looked around the room.

"What are you looking for, sweetie?"

"I wonder if we left a door or window open somewhere."

"Why?"

"I keep hearing this buzzing sound, like there's a mosquito in the room or something."

"I'm sure it's just a fly. Oh wow, check this out," Lisa said pointing at the television. "Someone filmed you speaking Italian to that news crew."

On the moon, the SP Lab was humming with activity. The entire Development Team, along with a few extra technicians and some senior officers were sitting at every available workstation.

"All right, everyone," Colonel Braaddy said as he got up from his seat. "You heard the Savior. Changes have been made and the seeds have been planted. Good job, everyone." He turned to Zenta.

"Major Zenta, he has another nine months in the Senate. We'll give him a year to get settled back into his private life since that's how long we'll need to prepare for the extraction. So when he returns home, launch Phase 4 preparation."

Braaddy barely finished speaking when Major Marsitta's voice came across the base intercom.

"Attention. There has been a detection breech. Repeat: a detection breech. All fighter pilots report to the hanger immediately regardless of primary assignment. All Anti-Detection Unit members report to the Command Center immediately. All senior officers are needed in the Command Center."

Xander stood up and addressed Braaddy.

"Colonel Braaddy, sir. I have to …"

"I know Captain. Get down to the hanger."

Xander headed to the door right on Hajeck's heels. Tuu and Bal also left.

"Sir." Lieutenants Aiko and Johono stood in front of Braaddy. "We need to report to …"

"Hurry up and get down there. You have your orders."

Out the door they went.

Braaddy sat there with Zenta, Tish, and Gunstot, the only ones left in the lab. He looked down and shook his head.

"For the life of me I cannot figure out why two GAIA squadron leaders didn't immediately head out to their squadrons. This is their secondary assignment, not their primary."

"I'm sure it was out of respect to you, sir," Zenta said.

"What does Xander fly?" Gunstot asked.

"The Reep," Braaddy replied. "And Zenta, what are you still doing here?"

"With all due respect, sir," Zenta answered glancing up from her monitor. "I figured the launching of Phase four would supersede …"

"You heard the announcement, Major. I've got to report too. Let's move it." Braaddy stood up to leave for the Command Center.

"Yes, sir." Zenta got up and followed Braaddy out the door.

Gunstot looked surprised.

"I knew she flew the Reep but I didn't think they would have her deploy on something like this. Has she been checked out recently?"

"Last month," Tish replied not taking her eyes off her monitor. "This is such bad timing with the launch of Phase 4. I just wish she didn't have to go."

"I agree."

Zenta finished donning her flight suit, grabbed her helmet, and slammed her locker shut. Exiting the locker room into the pilot's ready room, she was bumped by Hajeck, head down and barreling through to get to a seat.

"Sorry," he mumbled, then looked up and saw who it was. "Oh Zenta, I didn't recognize you with the gear on. Been a while since we've had a scramble, hasn't it?"

"Yes. What have you heard?" she asked as they sat down to await Colonel Benswear, flight operations commander.

"Just that a large contingent of Veloptorian raiders entered the solar system near Pluto. I was in a hurry to get ready so I don't have all the details." They sat in the second row. "I did manage to speak with Benswear on the way down. He's assigning you to the GAIA's reserve squadron that will be deployed around Mars."

Zenta's mood soured, her shoulders slumped as she stared blankly ahead.

"That means no combat."

"There's a good reason for this. You are much too val …"

"Cut the chatter and give me your attention," Benswear barked from the front stage as he stood at the podium. He was a no-nonsense flight ops commander. Years of running battle hardened squadrons led to a very gruff manner. "Troid, bring the leaders of the outpost squadrons online to the side wall screen."

Full size screens covered the left side wall as well as the front wall behind Benswear. A four-way split appeared on the side screen showing the outpost commanders from Mars, Europa, and the newest outpost located on Saturn's Moon, Titan. The fourth view showed General Jhall, who was observing the briefing from the Command Center.

"It appears our Veloptorian friends have decided to pay us a visit," Benswear began as he turned to the front screen which showed Pluto. "From what the ADU culled from X5 Probes, this research fleet has approximately fifty midsize Coorstar fighters. These are accompanied by twenty or so single pilot Kreshtee Fighters. They are guarding a small contingent of research and supply ships so they are not here on a minor probing mission. It appears their intention is to conduct a thorough search of this solar system. ADU calculated that they used space plate slipping, or as the Veloptors call it, Plating, to arrive at the outer edge of this solar system. As you can see, they are currently canvassing Pluto."

Video feed from an X5 Probe filled the front screen. A large rectangular ship floated in orbit with small triangular bird shaped Kreshtee fighters streaming around it. Other ships could be seen in the background. Squadrons of Coorstars flew in formation in outer orbital paths.

Benswear continued, "What you see here is one of five research vessels that are performing the canvassing." He waited for the pilots to take in the visual. "Everyone knows the difference between the smaller Kreshtees and the larger Coorstars," he said while pointing at some on the screen.

"Now pay attention because this is the important part of the mission. The key targets are the Coorstars that have these tube shaped devices on each side."

A diagram of a fully equipped Coorstar appeared on the screen.

"These particular Coorstars with the extra tubes carry the nuclear spheres used to create the mini black holes that split the seams between magnetic plates so that their ships can perform Plating, which is their high speed space technology. We have to make sure these particular ships are destroyed to cut off any escape attempt. The overall goal is total annihilation of this research fleet. Their home planet is used to losing ships due to the instability of Plating. So we must have the Veloptors conclude that this particular fleet met its demise through an accident."

Benswear stopped talking to survey the room. Puzzled expressions would be a red flag. He observed positive looks with adrenaline filled fidgety movements. The veteran pilots were calmer, some slouched in their seats, others ramrod straight but with confident eyes. Rookies looked somewhat nervous, but once buckled in their fighters; their intense training would see them through. Everyone wore the same style gray and black flight suit, black boots and black gloves. Silence now prevailed.

"We are using the standard tandem of an attack Kahn accompanied by a Reep wingman. All squadrons are set up for this. Are there any questions so far?"

Hajeck's hand went up.

"Yes, Colonel Hajeck."

"Colonel, what pre-emptive measures will we take before we attack?"

"Thank you, Colonel; I'm glad you asked that. As everyone should know, we keep a carrier orbiting Europa. An hour ago, the CURC left Europa and flashed in behind the planet Uranus. As soon as all our squadrons are in flash position, Admiral Craymack of the CURC will launch two nuclear meteors within seconds of each other, one for each side of the planet. The goal is to take out as much of their fleet as possible. Any more than that might impact Pluto's orbit. Immediately after detonation, the CURC will flash in X5 Probes for quick visual assessments. Based upon these results, attack coordinates and detonation damage reports will be sent to all pilots. More questions?" He spotted Lieutenant Johono's hand up.

"Yes, Lieutenant?"

"Colonel, how long has the enemy fleet been in this solar system?"

"Based on the data I've received from Command, we detected the raiders immediately on the edge of the system as they plated in. The Veloptor fleet then zeroed in on Pluto. It has been about fifty minutes since detection so we've gotten our squadrons ready and our pilots briefed during that time. The only thing left to do is get your butts in your ships. Any other questions?"

Seeing no hands, Benswear ended the briefing.

"That's it. Everyone check your Trace for your exact assignment. Good luck and fly forcefully."

The room became a mass of noise with pilots shoving chairs back and scrambling for the hanger.

"I just did a quick read of my assignment," Zenta said as she and Hajeck both stood up to head to the hanger. "You were right. I'm being held back." They fell in behind the rest of the pilots as they shuffled through the doorway into the hanger.

"I know you are disappointed," Hajeck consoled. "But this is for the good of the project. We can't let anything happen to you."

"I guess." Her long face showed her frustration. They bumped into Xander on the way out.

"What squadrons are you assigned to?" he asked, his voice somewhat jittery.

"Well," Hajeck replied. "Lucky for me, you are my wingman in Maczee's First GAIA Squadron."

They both looked at Zenta who replied with zero enthusiasm. "I'm in Fifth GAIA Squadron, the reserves." She checked her Trace again. "Oh no. Major Kainel is the squadron leader."

They all stopped walking as Hajeck grabbed both of them by their arms.

"Zenta," he began as he faced them. "We know that Kainel has been harassing you since he arrived six years ago. Xander and I have always shielded you from him as has the rest of the SD team. I've made it very clear to him that you are not interested in his advances and for him to cease. Nothing is going to happen to you out there and if it does, Kainel will answer to me. Are we clear?"

"Yes. And thank you. You two should go to your squadron. Mine is here. Fly forcefully."

The three put their arms around each other, put their heads together for a moment, and then split up.

"You too," Xander said quietly as Zenta walked away.

About fifteen minutes later, Major Maczee's voice resonated through everyone's speakers.

"Command!" Maczee said loudly into her mic. "All squadrons have checked in and are in flash position."

"Affirmative, Major," Jhall replied as he visually confirmed that on the Command Center screen. While looking at the bridge of the War Carrier, the CURC, on his monitor, Jhall spoke to the Admiral in Command.

"Admiral Craymack, you may launch the meteors when ready."

Craymack's voice crackled over the speakers.

"Thank you, General. Missiles away! X5s are ready to flash after detonation."

All eyes were on monitors and screens as the calm scene of Veloptorian ships orbiting Pluto turned into a bright flash of light. Then there was nothing but blackness due to the obliteration of the X5s from the nuclear explosion.

Staff in the Command Center watched on the left half of their huge screen as four probe launchers on the CURC directed beams of light toward Pluto.

"Probes away!" Craymack announced and the launcher lights went out.

All screens and monitors came to life showing images of Pluto with debris orbiting the planet. Zipping in and out of view were Kreshtees and Coorstars.

"Fighters prepare to launch!" Jhall barked into his mic. "Colonel Benswear, have all coordinates been sent to the squadrons?"

"Yes, sir," Benswear replied from his workstation on the second row.

"Then let's go."

"Launch fighters!" Benswear yelled.

Xander glanced out his left window at Hajeck's Kahn as he flipped his lights on to flash to Pluto. He set his Magnetic Field Realignment speed to engage at full once he came out of the flash. Maczee's voice blasted out of his speaker.

"Flash!"

Her voice command was the launch trigger. It turned off the SOD lights and in an instant, Xander felt his body push into his seat. His vision flickered for a fraction of a second then suddenly; he came out of the flash hurtling toward Pluto at full MFR speed. A pack of Kreshtee fighters were right in front of him. He shot a quick glance out his window and caught a glimpse of the right wing of Hajeck's Kahn.

"We made it, Xander," Hajeck said via ship to ship communications with Xander.

"Yes, sir, we did."

"Look ahead and get ready! Our target is that group of raiders. Stick on my wing. We're going to do a down, left-right roll, under up."

"Yes, sir," Xander replied, his voice quivering slightly. Beads of sweat had already formed on his upper lip.

Hajeck dipped his Kahn down, banked left, then right, and pulled his stick back so that he would come up under the five raiders he was tracking. Xander stayed glued to his right wing matching Hajeck move for move.

"Okay, Xander. Open fire!"

The laser cannons on both fighters blasted streaks of blue though the group of Kreshtee raiders hitting three of them as Hajeck and Xander tore an opening in the middle of their group. Xander instinctively ducked as his Reep passed through exploding debris.

"Yeeowwwweee!!!" Hajeck excitedly screamed into his mic as he and Xander banked their fighters to come around for another pass at the two remaining raiders. "Let's get 'em again!" Hajeck felt himself sink into his seat from the G forces due to the tight turn. He checked Xander who was matching his every move.

The Kahn and Reep chased the two Kreshtee fighters as they tried to flee the superior weaponry of the Terlokyans.

Hajeck's scream had startled some in the Command Center when it came through the speakers.

"A little unorthodox of the Colonel, wouldn't you say?" Jhall asked Benswear while sitting next to him at an adjoining workstation in the

Command Center.

"I don't care how he does it or what he yells," Benswear replied not taking his eyes off his monitor. "He's one of the best and he's highly effective."

"That is true," Jhall agreed as he observed the action on the front wall screen. He watched as pairs of Kahns and Reeps ripped apart the remaining Veloptorian raiders. The overwhelming firepower of the Terlokyans was making for a quick resolution of the situation. Maczee broke Jhall's concentration as her voice came across the speakers.

"Terks! I just saw a Coorstar with tubes!" she yelled, adrenaline fueling her voice. "Let's hunt it down and any others like it. No escape for these contes!"

Meanwhile, having destroyed the other two Kreshtees they were chasing, Hajeck and Xander were in pursuit of two Coorstars, one with tubes.

"Stay on target," Hajeck commanded as they both fired their lasers taking out the Coorstar without tubes.

Xander's ventilation system in his flight suit was not keeping up with all the perspiration his body was pumping out. Ignoring the wet feeling, Xander remained glued to Hajeck's wing. He marveled at the sleek gracefulness of the much larger Kahn. Even in combat, the fighter was a spectacle to behold. Shaped like a flattened, snub-nosed teardrop, the two large laser cannons in the middle of each wing gave it a fierce look that had to frighten any enemy. The sight and sound of a large explosion next to Xander's right wing snapped him back to reality.

"I've been hit!" Xander yelled noticing two Kreshtees on his radar that must have snuck up on them. Flames shot out of the right side of his fighter. He and Hajeck had been too intently focused on the Coorstar, coupled with the fact that Xander had been distracted for a few seconds. That's all it took to make a mistake. Xander's Reep violently pulled to his left so he throttled back to avoid Hajeck, barely missing the rear of the Kahn as the Reep vibrated uncontrollably.

"Xander! Flash out of here!" Hajeck yelled as he watched Xander veer off to the left out of control. "Can you deploy your lights?"

Hajeck stayed on the Coorstar since it was the one with tubes. His laser cannons were firing wide open. He could not pull out since the mission priority was to eliminate detection possibilities at all costs. The Kreshtees stayed on him, letting Xander limp out of the fight. They were protecting the Coorstar.

"Trying … to … regain … control." Xander grimaced as he fought the stick to straighten his fighter. He needed to match the coordinates on his screen so he could flash back to base. "Can't … seem … to …" He flipped the switch to deploy his lights. They popped up and turned on.

Jzet, sitting at his workstation in the Command Center, directed an X5 Probe toward Xander's crippled fighter. The screen up front showed the Reep shaking as its lights deployed. Everyone watched as Jzet's little brother fought for control of his ship.

"Flash!"

The Reep vanished.

"Get me another wingman!" Hajeck yelled. "Now!"

"Captain Kainel!" Benswear shouted into his mic. "Get a Reep out there!

"Yes, sir," Kainel answered. "Squadron, who's ready to flash?"

"I am!" Zenta quickly said while deploying her lights. Before anyone could respond, she locked onto Hajeck's coordinates, leaving just one thing to do.

"Flash!"

Her lights went out and Zenta's Reep was gone.

A view on the Command Center's front screen showed Zenta's Reep disappearing as Xander's crippled ship flashed into view, flames billowing out of the right side.

"Get the rescue Dagars over to that Reep, now!" Benswear ordered. "Major Kainel, what's the idea of letting Major Zenta go into battle?" Benswear was standing as he bellowed into his mic. Sweat was pouring off his face, blood vessels protruding on his neck.

"Sir, the Major said she was ready. She flashed out of here so fast that I didn't have time to say anything," Kainel pleaded.

"Too late to do anything about it now, Colonel," Jhall said as he continued watching the action. "Focus on the battle."

"Yes, sir."

Zenta came out of the flash about two hundred yards off Hajeck's left side. She immediately opened fire on the two Kreshtees that were trailing the Kahn, blasting them to smithereens.

"All clear, Colonel," she said calmly into her mic.

With the threat removed, Hajeck did a quick rolling maneuver for a better angle and fired his laser cannons taking out the tubed Coorstar.

"Thank you, Zenta," Hajeck said, quite relieved at being saved. "I didn't think I'd see you today."

"You requested a wingman so here I am."

"Did you see Xander?" he asked as he banked his Kahn toward Pluto. Zenta was tight on his right wing.

"No. I was gone before he returned."

"He's in a Dagar and heading to base." Maczee's voice resonated over their speakers. "It appears he's our only casualty so far."

"That's good," Zenta said as she watched Aiko, in his Kahn, and his wingman Runba, chase down two Kreshtees turning them into fireballs.

"Attention, squadrons," Benswear announced to everyone. "I am receiving an all-clear-signal. All fighters form on your squadron leaders and return to your bases. First GAIA Squadron will remain to clean up the site. Good job, everyone. Command out."

"Zenta."

She checked her communications panel and noticed that a secure channel was open to her and Hajeck from the Command Center with Jhall on the other end.

"Yes sir, General Jhall."

"While I will commend you on your dedication and performance in battle, I was under the impression that you were instructed to remain with the reserve squadron near Mars."

"With all due respect, sir; I was never told not to answer a distress call. Captain Kainel asked who was ready and I said I was. I concluded that the situation called for immediate action and I was ready to flash. So I did."

"Very well, Major. But I think you, Major Hajeck, and I will need to discuss this further when you return to base ..."

Zenta's radiant feelings drained.

"… over tall glasses of my finest Bonzoon."

Zenta tried to speak. "Uhh …"

"Major? Did you understand me?"

"Yeeowwwweee!" Hajeck screamed into his mic. "We read you loud and clear, General. We'll find you the moment we get back to base. Thanks."

"You're welcome, Colonel Hajeck," Jhall said somewhat surprised at Hajeck's outburst. "Safe returns. Jhall out."

Hajeck and Zenta banked slightly to the right as they fell in behind the rest of First Squadron to begin their sweep of the area. Kahns and Reeps up front could be seen blasting any debris they encountered.

"Well, Zenta," Hajeck said through their ship to ship channel. "That was a surprise."

"Yes it was."

"This has been a big day all around, hasn't it?"

"It really has, Hajeck," she replied. "While the Savior has been in the limelight, we end up in a firefight."

32 – NEVER-NEVER LAND

Chris finished tying the laces on his cleats while still pondering his future. It seemed too good to be true that he could slide back into his old life without a hitch.

I hope I made a difference, he thought as he packed the minivan with softball equipment. He picked up the duffle bag full of bats and put it next to his gear.

"It amazes me that every year you always get stuck with hauling the equipment," Lisa said from the doorway of the garage.

Chris jumped slightly. "Wow. Didn't know you were back there spying on me." He leaned over and gave her a kiss.

"I wasn't spying. I was just watching my handsome husband, all decked out in his softball uniform getting ready for the first game of the season."

"It's just a jersey, sweetheart."

"You still look good in it."

"Are the kids ready?" he asked as he enveloped Lisa in his arms.

"They are. Looks like you're ready too." She wrapped her arms around him and slowly ran her hands up and down his back.

Chris pulled her closer and they kissed. Her mouth was so warm, the caress of her lips so soft. He tasted tentatively with his tongue, and Lisa opened her mouth with a soft, low moan.

"Mom, Dad, stop that mushy stuff," Taylor said as he pushed past them into the garage.

"Yeah. Gross," Michelle added as she came out of the hallway following her brother.

Startled and embarrassed, Lisa blushed profusely while Chris quickly changed the subject.

"You kids ready to watch your old man play ball?"

"You're not old, Daddy,' Michelle replied playfully as she climbed into the van. "You act like a big kid most of the time."

Lisa swatted Chris on the butt and smiled at him. "Let's go, kid. You have a game to play." Then she whispered in his ear, "We'll do some planning later."

The next day, Chris was sitting in his office at the Jefferson Academy when his phone rang. Gordon Stinson was on the line.

"Senator, I hope you are doing well."

"Thanks, Gordon, I am. But I'm not a senator anymore. I'm just a school teacher."

"The word 'just' is not one that I would associate with you. Did Vice President Winslow call you?"

"Yes he did. How did you know?"

"He's an old friend of mine. He touched base with me to see how receptive you would be to reentering politics but this time on a bigger stage."

"What did you tell him?"

"I said that I highly doubt it, that you are a man of principles, and once you've made a decision, you stick with it."

"Well, thank you. That's pretty much what I said. I really don't have any desire to be his or anyone else's running mate in the next election. Besides, I've been out of the senate for a while now and when you're out of sight, you're out of mind."

"On the contrary, my boy. Your name comes up everywhere in politics and business, even in academic circles now. That's another reason I'm calling. There's a new technology firm that is interested in talking to you about doing some consulting work for them."

"I would be more than happy to talk to them," Chris replied.

"I'd also like to open a dialogue with you about an adjunct faculty position here in the College of Arts and Sciences."

"Do you have someone in mind that you need my opinion about?"

"Quite frankly, your opinion won't be necessary. However, your acceptance will be."

"I'm not sure I follow you."

Chris did follow him though. He knew the moment he picked up the phone that it was Gordon calling him about opportunities. It never ceased to amaze him how he could sense future events. They made plans to get together.

"I'll tell you what, Chris, why don't we meet next week for lunch? What's on your calendar for next Wednesday?"

"I'm free. Where would you like to meet?"

"Carrs Hill at noon?"

"I'll see you then."

As he hung up, his cell phone rang. It was Ian.

"Ian, what's up?"

"Nothing. Just wanted to see if you were okay after last night."

"What do you mean? I'm fine."

"You sure? You were as pale as a sheet when you came in the dugout after the fourth inning talking about trees buzzing."

"Gene heard it too," Chris countered. "So did Alex."

"Well, they're just as whack as you. But seriously, I didn't hear anything and the look on your face last night worried me."

Chris remembered everything. It was the bottom of the fourth inning with two outs and he had pitched a pretty good game. Dave Heidelberg came up to bat and was egging Chris on with some chatter when a buzzing sound began in the woods behind the left field fence. David must have heard it because he kept looking over there. Alex and Dave kept glancing in that direction. Chris went ahead and pitched. Dave hit it right to Cory at shortstop and was thrown out at first.

"Chris?"

"I'm here. I was just thinking about last night. It wasn't a big deal."

"It sure looked like it when you came in the dugout and said that stuff."

"What'd I say exactly?"

"It was something like, 'there it is again.' I take it that you've heard this before?"

"I dunno, Ian. I can't remember. Like I said, it's no big deal." Chris glanced at his watch. "Hey man, I gotta run. Talk to ya later?"

"Sure thing. Take care."

That evening at home, Chris came out of the kid's rooms after tucking them in for the night. Lisa was in the kitchen packing lunches for the next day.

"What did you read tonight?" she asked.

He sat at the kitchen counter. "I didn't read. I told them one of my stories."

"Kinda figured that," she said as she pushed a plate of the leftover celery sticks and carrots over to him, then set a container of dip on the counter. "Was it one of your space stories?"

"Not this time." He bit off some celery. "Actually, I told them my version of Peter Pan and the Lost Boys. It's a story that I'd love to write a book about."

"Uh oh. I feel another project coming on."

"Don't worry. I won't start that just yet. I have many things I want to write about but I'm not ready to put pen to paper." He shifted uncomfortably on his barstool and stirred his celery around in the dip.

"Hey, I wanted to ask you if you heard any strange sounds coming from the woods last night at the ball game."

"No, why?" she asked as she sat across from him and got a carrot.

"You didn't hear anything like bugs buzzing or chirping or anything like that?"

"Didn't hear a thing. Did you?"

“Yeah. Some kind of buzzing sound. David and Alex heard it too. It was really strange.”

He finally ate the celery.

“It was probably Cicadas. They can be quite loud. They come out this time of year, right?”

“I’m not sure it was them. It sounded different. No big deal.”

“Is that all you wanted to say about last night?” Lisa asked glowingly.

“Well … uh …” Chris’s face flushed slightly.

“What’s this now,” Lisa said smiling. “The famous Chris Gates is at loss for words?”

“No and I’ll reserve comment … and action for a little later.” He reached across the counter and cupped her hand in his. “I also wanted to tell you about a call I received today from Gordon. He talked to me about an adjunct faculty position and some consulting work for a new Technology firm.”

“Chris that’s wonderful.” She gave his hand a squeeze. “Tell me, what did he say?”

“Well, he didn’t come right out and ask me. It’s the way he said things and then invited me to lunch at Carrs Hill next Wednesday.”

“That sounds positive. You know your intuitions always turn out to be right. So do you think he wants you to teach computer science?”

Chris yawned. It was close to ten o’clock.

“I have a feeling it’ll be languages.”

“Languages? Why?”

He stood up from his seat. “Something Cory mentioned after my speech at the University last year.”

Lisa leaned on the counter and held her head up with her hand while looking at Chris.

“Do you miss being a senator?”

Chris thought about the question for a few seconds.

“No, not really. I miss making things happen. I would have preferred doing things while remaining unknown. I think I could have accomplished more in the background. The media was unrelenting. I like being an ordinary guy.” He yawned again.

“Well, just remember that sometimes the media can be used for good too,” she said as she stood up and took Chris’ hand. “Besides, you are far from ordinary. You look tired, sweetheart. Let’s go to bed.”

“Sounds like a plan.”

“Well, we can do that too.”

Later on, with his head on the pillow and Lisa spooned against him, Chris drifted off to sleep with thoughts about his future playing in his head.

Someone else had other ideas about what should be going on in Chris' head. An X13 probe detached itself from inside the overhead light cover and flew down to Chris' pillow.

In the SP Lab, Zenta keyed a sequence of commands into her system. Afterwards, she got up and went to the mind chamber in the rear of the lab where Tish was waiting.

"Are you ready for this? You can't have a repeat of your last meeting," Tish said as she readied a probe for Zenta's forehead.

Zenta hit the button to open the cover.

"I'm ready this time. There will not be a repeat of the last visit. The only goal for this mission is to prepare Chris' subconsciousness for the extraction." Zenta climbed into the chamber. Tish attached the probe to her forehead and closed the cover.

"You'd better remember that," Tish said into her mic. "I wish there was another way to do this besides the Mind Meeting Method, but there isn't." She typed a command at the chamber keyboard and a gentle hum began.

Zenta's voice came through the speaker.

"I can feel the vibrations."

"Remember, this is the first time using the enhanced imagery software so you don't have to become anything unless you want to," Tish reminded her. "Just make sure you don't create more than you can control. Are you certain you need to spawn three Veloptors for this meeting?"

"Yes, I need to test him."

"Can you handle being with him again?" Tish asked. "I can go instead if you want me to."

"I can do this. Besides, according to the plan, the meetings are to be limited to only one individual having mind interactions with him."

"I know. But ..."

Zenta had raised her hand. "It's starting. See you in a minute."

Chris watched sand squish between his toes. He looked up and saw the waves gently rolling onto the fine, white sand. The shadow of the palm tree he was sitting under danced on the sand. Either direction down the beach was an endless paradise of palm trees gently swaying in the breeze with dazzling blue surf rippling back and forth. The bright sun forced him to squint when he looked at the water.

How did I get ...

Chris didn't finish his sentence. He took in his surroundings.

I've been here before, he realized as he felt his mind expand.

Noticing his cutoff jeans, he got to his feet.

These are just like the ones I wore last time I was here.

He walked a couple of steps toward the water. Looking to his right, he saw two sets of footprints in the sand.

Those are Zenta's and my prints from last time. It's like we were just here.

He closed his eyes and breathed deeply, opening his senses to everything.

Zenta is nearby. I can feel her.

A loud hissing sound snapped his train of thought. He immediately launched his body in a diving motion to his left. As his hands touched the sand, he grabbed fists full of it while a loud slapping noise thundered out. He tucked his body and rolled into a summersault. Springing off his feet further to his left, he fired both handfuls of sand toward the source of the sound. Flying through the air into another summersault, he caught a glimpse of a huge Veloptor that had dropped some type of object and was reaching for its eyes. Chris hit the ground running, heading straight into a thick grove of palms, hurdling fallen trunks as he put as much distance between himself and the reptile.

Why am I running? This has got to be Zenta testing me again.

Loud crashing sounds caused him to look to his left. Another Veloptor was running parallel to him about twenty yards off.

How did she recover from the sand in her eyes so quickly? Boy, she's fast. What's that in her hand?

The Veloptor raised some type of weapon in its clawed hand. ZIP! ZIP! Red streaks streamed through the air, inches from his face. He turned in time to see another blast of red slam into his shoulder sending him tumbling to the ground.

Barely a sound left his mouth as he rolled back up to his feet and kept running. Feeling his shoulder and checking his hand, he was surprised to see blood.

"She shot me, the witch!" Glancing to his left, the creature was matching him step for step so he veered off to his right. More crashing sounds came from behind him now. A quick turn of his head released a flood of adrenalin as he caught sight of another Veloptor right on his heels.

Where in the heck did that one come from? This can't be Zenta doing this.

Scanning ahead, he saw the perfect tree that was leaning away from him.

I've got to time this perfectly.

Slowing his pace to let the Veloptor gain a few steps, he proceeded to run up the tree and flipped himself over so that he landed on the back of the surprised reptile. He quickly wrapped his arms around the monstrous head of the creature and pulled to one side in a quick snapping motion to break its neck. He heard a pop, then he crashed to the ground; alone.

"Where are you?" he yelled.

The sound of more rapid footsteps grabbed his attention. Springing to his feet in a full sprint, he slowed down when he heard a familiar voice.

"Chris! You can stop now."

He stopped to catch his breath and realized he felt fully energized. While jogging toward Zenta's voice, he was surprised to find out how close he was to the beach.

I could have sworn I ran farther than that.

As he weeded his way through the trees he finally saw Zenta standing under the palm where he had been sitting. She was shaking her head and rubbing her eyes. She was even more beautiful than he remembered.

"Nice shot," she said while shaking sand out of her hair.

"Sorry about that. I didn't even stop to think about what was happening. I just reacted to the sounds and situation."

"That's what you're supposed to do," she said in between a few coughs. She looked up at him. "Why did you think to throw sand and run?"

"It was the only weapon available. After the sand, I ruled out the option of climbing this particular palm tree due to the fact that it was too far from another tree to make a jump, so I ran."

He thought for a second about how his mind was recalling every detail from his situational analysis. It had happened so fast.

"Well, at least I correctly guessed your response. Others predicted that you would climb."

Chris looked up at the palm. Reevaluating it now, since there was unpressured time to study it, he saw he made the right choice. He could not have jumped to the next closest tree.

"You shot me," he said with a hint of irritation.

"Yes and no. I didn't actually shoot you; the program did."

"The program?"

The testing program used to gauge your progress. I was the first Veloptor you encountered, but I used the program to generate the others."

"That's just great. I still got shot. I've got to put something on …" He glanced at his shoulder which was perfectly normal; no blood, no wound.

Zenta watched him as he analyzed the situation. In a split second, his expression was one of satisfaction; already in possession of the answers without ever having to ask questions.

"So what brings you to these parts?" he calmly asked.

Zenta saw that playful, confident smile. She touched her chest.

"You haven't changed at all. Except that your reactions are perfect."

"Great. And might I add, that's a heck of a way to greet someone when you haven't seen them in years. Are you here to tell me you're going away again because I didn't know you had returned."

"You're still a …" she paused for a second, "what do you all call it … a smart ass?"

"Wow. The compliments start." He sat down under the palm. "Come sit next to me. We have a lot to catch up on."

She complied.

"Do Terlokyans ever wear anything but those green and black uniforms?"

"You know the answer to that."

"I know. That was called 'being facetious'." Chris mimicked quote marks with his fingers. "I can teach you things too you know."

"I'm sure you can," she said as she scooted closer, unable to take her eyes off him.

"You look exactly as you did last time," he said leaning back on his hands.

Zenta noticed his lean, hard abdomen muscles and his still youthful looking tanned skin. She felt her heart flutter.

"So do you."

"Bah. I know I look thirty-some years older. I'm starting to show gray hair. I'm getting these little wrinkles at the edge of my eyes." He pulled on the skin under his eye to show her. "But you don't look a day older. How is that?"

"It's where I'm from. Our environment and our technology allow us to live very long in an almost ageless state. I'm really not that much older than you in Terlokyan years." She looked away from him to stop her budding desire.

"I need to tell you why we are here," she began.

"Can I get some of that Terlokyan ageless cream?"

Zenta frowned.

"I have some important information for you. You are going to be leaving your home for a while."

"When?"

"Very soon."

"Can I tell them?"

"Think."

"Yeah. Right. So why tell me?"

"We've found that your subconsciousness will need this information during the actual event so that critical adaptation feelings will quickly reach your conscious."

"Why not just use a probe?"

"A stronger imprint is established when there is a mind meeting."

Chris stretched his legs out and leaned against the tree.

"I need to take advantage of this time to work on my tan. You are so far ahead of me," he said as he closed his eyes.

"Must you always joke?"

"I'm trying to break the ice here. You're being so serious and all I can think about is what happened last time."

Zenta leaned back on her hands.

"That should never have happened. I was out of line to have allowed it."

Chris quickly popped up onto his knees and faced her.

"But it did happen and we both wanted it to. Whether you know it or not, we are destined to be together. You always tell me to search my mind. Well, I'm telling you to search your feelings."

He stood up, reached down, grabbed her hands, and stood her up. He held her in his arms.

"Obviously it was a successful search," he observed as their eyes met.

"Chris now is not the time," she said looking away. "That's one thing we do not have. Things are moving quickly so you must be ready. We'll be coming for you."

"What? Who?"

She stood up on her toes and kissed him on the cheek.

"Wait ..." he pleaded as he felt himself slip away.

Chris sprung upright in bed so fast; his momentum caused him to roll forward slightly. He rubbed his eyes. It was still dark. The nightlight in the wall illuminated Lisa, still sound asleep next to him.

I was dreaming. I know it. But I felt like I was somewhere else, but where was it?

He lay back down.

Whatever just happened, it felt real. There was someone there. I know it. Maybe if I go back to sleep, I'll find out.

He tossed and turned and he tried in vain to recall the dream.

I've dreamt it before. I know it.

As he entered that state between being awake and asleep, never-never land, he felt as if he was bathing in the warmth of sunlight. Then he dozed off.

33 – SAVIOR EXTRACTION

Up in the ship's operations center, or Ops for short, Colonel Dobbie nervously paced behind the high-back seat of her command console. Her ship, Planet Transport Mover One, was having a damage assessment performed and she was none too pleased.

"Get me a detailed status report immediately, Lieutenant!" she barked at her communications officer. "I don't like being stuck with a bunch of outpost jockeys checking on damage to my ship in the middle of nowhere. I want to know every damned thing they're doing or somebody's butt is going to be up here in Ops telling me themselves."

Lieutenant Kelta quickly replied, "Yes, ma'am. Right away, ma'am."

The lieutenant keyed her mic.

"Bay Control. This is Ship Ops. Colonel Dobbie wants an immediate update on the damage to the bay door."

"Ops, this is Bay Control. I've got to raise one of the Dagars to locate Colonel Hajeck or Master Chief Achted. I can't see any of the work that's being done. The extraction ship is still blocking the entrance to the bay."

Dobbie snapped, "Inform him that I don't care if he has to go himself. Get me some answers." She turned to her second-in-command, Major Qwan, and asked, "Can you tell me why I agreed to transport the savior extraction ship to this forsaken place? I must have been intoxicated."

"No, ma'am," Qwan answered as she quickly stood while addressing her superior. "The Supreme Commander said he only trusted you to bring the Zaw One here."

"Well, why didn't someone just fly it here?"

Qwan smiled. "The colonel must have forgotten that the technicians were still working on the SOD components during our trip here. We were on an accelerated schedule."

Dobbie put her hands on her hips and looked at the Major.

"You remember every little detail, don't you?"

Qwan shrugged. "It's my job to support you, ma'am."

"Well, this has nothing to do with you personally, but I wish they had chosen someone else to pilot Zaw One back to Terlokya."

"Sorry, ma'am. Wasn't my choice. After we return, I'll be at my post under your command."

"I wouldn't count on that just yet. You're one who's going to go far," Dobbie said over her shoulder as she walked back to her console.

Hajeck pulled on his tether to maneuver himself closer to the two specialists who were working on the bay door. He adjusted the tether so he could maneuver around the edge of the frame.

Without looking at Achted, who was floating next to him, he said, “It seems to me that if they got it in here, they should be able to get it out.”

“One would think that. Who piloted this thing in here?” Achted asked as he looked over the damage himself.

“That would be Major Qwan. She’s in command of Zaw One when we extract the Savior. She’s piloting the ship back to Terlokya.”

“That’ll be a tricky ride back.”

“I know.”

“Wait, who attempted to fly this out of the bay then?”

“I’m not sure but I’ll find out. Bay Control, this is Colonel Hajeck out by bay one’s door. I’m inspecting the work on the damage here with GAIA Base Master Chief Achted and two specialists. Who was piloting Zaw One when the door was hit?”

“Uh, Colonel, this is Bay Control. That was one of our bay pilots who was moving the ship out. Do you need me to find out who it was? I wasn’t on shift then. I can check the logs for you.”

“No, that won’t be necessary.”

“Achted, did you hear all that?”

“Affirmative. What I want to know is why Major Qwan wasn’t at the helm?”

“I’m not sure but when we get back on dock, I plan on finding out.”

A short time later in the Ops of Mover One, Dobbie and Hajeck were nose to nose in a heated discussion.

“Colonel Hajeck, being the Supreme Commander’s Apprentice & Chief of Staff does not allow you to disrespect a ship’s commander.”

“Colonel Dobbie, with all due respect, now is the time for Major Qwan to take command of Zaw One. A Bay Control pilot should never have been at the helm of that ship.”

“Qwan has her second in command duties to perform,” Dobbie declared.

“She has been ordered to command that ship,” Hajeck countered.

Dobbie crossed her arms and glared at Hajeck.

“I know you have issues with your second in command being taken from you,” Hajeck continued. “But she tested out as the best for this mission. She needs to take her command. Lieutenant Kelta is perfectly capable of being your second. If you need me to contact Colonel Braaddy about this, I'm sure you'll find him in total agreement with me."

The crew on the bridge was transfixed at the scene playing out if front of them. There wasn't enough room to slide your hand between their faces.

"Colonel Hajeck, the only thing preventing me from putting you in the …"

"Colonel Dobbie," Qwan barked after having just arrived from Bay Control. "It appears that the damage to the blend cameras and transmitters on Zaw One has been repaired. The bay door frame has also been repaired. There is no other damage. The door is operating normally now."

"Excellent news, Major," Dobbie continued to glare at Hajeck who stared right back.

"With your permission, ma'am, I would like to go ahead and assume my command of Zaw One and take it out of the bay. It seems that the bay pilots can't make the angled squeeze through the bay door."

Not taking her eyes off Hajeck, she replied through pursed lips, "Fine. Please take Colonel Hajeck with you. I'm sure he wants to make certain that nothing happens to his precious ship."

On the way down to bay one, Hajeck asked Qwan, "Did you do that on purpose? You interrupted just in time back there. My Trace was on and Colonel Braaddy was listening to everything."

Qwan smiled. "Yes and I was afraid of that. Colonel Dobbie has a certain way she likes things done. Anything that comes along to disrupt that is met with strong resistance."

"Well, your timing was impeccable. You are aware that I'll be on your ship for the trip back."

"No, I didn't. I think it will be great to have someone with your experience there to help out. Since we can't always travel at Speed of Dark, do you have an estimate on how long it will take us to get back?"

"About two months."

Qwan looked puzzled. "Why so long?"

"Oh, wait. I just gave you an Earth time estimate. A lot of us have been here so long that we are used to communicating dates and time by Earth standards, not Terlokyan. So it'll be about a month in Terlokyan time. You know we have to travel with the fleet. Since there will be a layover when we stop at Kekter for Mover One to pick up a load of Costine, we will stay there and perform the medical procedures on the Savior to youthinize him."

"I see. You will need to go back to our ways since you are going home."

"It's actually pretty easy to convert. Earth revolves around their sun in about half the time it takes Terlokya to revolve around our suns."

"Interesting. Are you looking forward to getting off this rock?"

"Without a doubt. Now let's go get this ship out of here."

During the first week of July, final preparations were underway for the mission. Not only was there to be the extraction, but a mass exodus of about half of Base GAIA's research operations would occur. While the Savior was away from Earth, the base would be in a low-key military only operative state waiting for his return.

Unaffected by the activity around Base GAIA, Major Qwan and her copilot Lieutenant Roial were flying Zaw One on a July 2011 morning. Hajeck and Achted were accompanying them on the third and final test of the EET, the External Extraction Tube.

"We are passing over Tsiolkovskiy right now. In four minutes we should be over the test site at Mendeleev," Lieutenant Roial announced as she scanned her monitor for landmarks.

"Thank you, Lieutenant." Based upon flight headings on the screen in the control panel, Qwan made a slight bank to the left. "Hajeck, this was much easier to fly these maneuvers with an atmosphere. Even on Donar, the EET operated smoothly."

Hajeck was still marveling on the advanced technology aboard the ship. His seat, located behind the pilot, had its own thermostat. Achted sat next to him but was staring straight out the front. He hadn't said a word since they departed.

"But Terlokya's moon has an atmosphere."

"It's thin but works better than here. It was even easier on Terlokya. I just want you to know that I feel these tests on this moon are not really indicative of the way this EET operates. It will go much smoother on Earth."

"I hope so," Achted finally spoke. "These first two tests would have killed the target if it were an actual extraction."

Hajeck shook his head. "I don't think so. Besides, Colonel Braaddy is the one operating the EET. He's the best."

"Well the Dagar is already on site and Specialist Tuu is ready and waiting," Qwan said.

"Don't kill him, Qwan. He's on the Intervention Team and Jzet claims Tuu is the best specialist he has," Hajeck joked.

"Sir," Roial interrupted, "I just got word that Admiral Kaioc just flashed in on the dark side of the Moon in his Battle Cruiser, the TRAZ. He is accompanied by two War Carriers, the TAAN and the KILD."

"That's some power," Hajeck noted. "This latest Veloptor push really has the Supreme Council on edge. Sounds like they aren't taking any chances for our trip back."

"Let's hurry up and complete this test." Achted sounded tense. "We've still got a lot to do and little time to do it in."

The next morning, Extraction Day, Braaddy, Hajeck, and Major Qwan were walking across the hanger's tarmac toward their waiting Dagar. They had just gotten out of their final briefing with General Jhall who was just arriving at the shuttle.

Hajeck saw the Dagar in the next slot being loaded under Zenta's watchful eye. Everyone saluted the General.

"You must have flashed down here from the briefing, General," Hajeck commented jokingly.

"I've learned to move quickly during critical missions, Colonel." He gave a slight smiling nod to Hajeck, then turned his attention to the group.

"At ease, everyone. We have all devoted years of work and preparation for this moment. I am very proud of each and every one of you. Your accomplishments have been noted and will be recognized. Colonel Braaddy, let's touch on our next step after the extraction."

"Yes, sir," Colonel Braaddy responded. "After we complete the Extraction Phase of the Savior, we move onto the next phase; training. But I prefer not to get ahead of ourselves. We need to pull this extraction off without a hitch. Then, of course, we have a long trip back including all of the medical procedures. And let's hope the Veloptors don't get wind of our plans."

"Agreed," Jhall nodded. "Let's just do our jobs so the Savior can do his. It's departure time. Fly forcefully."

After some goodbyes and the boarding, Hajeck piloted the Dagar out of the base to Zaw One. Zenta's Dagar had already docked and unloaded by the time Hajeck arrived. He saw their Dagar exiting the single bay door.

"It's a shame they only built one bay for a single Dagar, but I guess space is at a premium," Hajeck noted.

"I would say so with all of this medical equipment onboard," Braaddy added. "At least there are external docking capabilities for two more shuttles."

"Are we the last three to board?" Qwan asked.

"That's it. This shuttle stays onboard," Hajeck answered. "We have about eleven hours until the actual extraction time." He maneuvered the Dagar into the bay and docked it. "But we need to have Zaw One above the target area by nine o'clock this evening."

Braaddy gave the final instructions before departing. "We meet at three o'clock in the medical lab for the briefing, but we all have assignments to complete before that. Let's move it."

A few minutes before three, Braaddy caught up with Zenta in the medical lab. The huge Reconditioning Hydro Chamber dominated the lab from its place in the middle of the room. Workstations adorned the walls with various team members manning each one. Colonel Prahash, the Chief Health Officer, was at the assessment table with two assistants. Tish and Xander were next door in the Command Center. Others were filtering in.

Zenta, seated at one of the workstations next to the hydro chamber, felt a tap on her shoulder.

"Oh. Sorry, sir," she said to Braaddy." I was so focused on this that I didn't hear you."

'That's all right, Major. Is the synthetic ready?" Braaddy asked.

"Looks like the real thing. It's been tested and retested; fully knowledgeable. Acts and talks just like him, including the limp."

"You know, we've never made one look and act like an Earthling." Braaddy marveled at the likeness as he looked at the images on Zenta's monitor.

"We've never had to."

"Do you think he'll believe it's real?"

"He'll catch on eventually. But we'll get his subconscious to conscious flow engaging before he figures it out. Then I'll bet he compliments us on doing such a fine job," Zenta said with pride in her voice.

"We'll see," he said as his attention was diverted by the swishing of the lab doors.

Jzet and his Intervention Unit of Dlocto, Tuu, and Bal, entered. Jzet had a certain mischievous look to him. Everyone was arriving for the briefing now. Xander and Tish came in right after them.

Braaddy focused back on the synthetic. "How long before he figures it out?"

"Maybe five minutes. That's all we need. Don't worry, sir. Worst case scenario is that I'll have to go in there."

"Well, I hope it doesn't come to that. You've only been with him in mind meetings."

"Trust me. A lot can happen in mind meetings. It'll work if I have to go. He's so advanced now. He won't panic."

"Trust is not the issue; timing is. But I do trust in your assessment. This is great work you've done here. I'd better start the briefing."

Colonel Braaddy went over to Colonel Prahash's table and raised a hand. The room fell silent.

"Each of you is aware of how important this is. Many years of hard work have gotten us to this point. The test we did a few months ago of the probes at the extraction point was successful. The few Earthlings that heard the sound did so without causing alarm. Tonight we'll have that sound at full volume." He looked around the room to make sure he had everyone's attention.

"I will be operating the EET. For those of you who aren't familiar with this new technology, the External Extraction Tube is a cylinder device made of the translucent material, X4E. It can be extended from a ship for short distances to a surface of a planet or another ship. When capturing an object, it is designed to scoop below the target just enough to secure it. Whatever debris is captured in that process is also extracted."

Colonel Prahash put a hand on Braaddy's shoulder. "I think everyone should know that Colonel Braaddy helped design this device."

"Thank you, Colonel." Braaddy then began ambling around the room as he spoke.

"We will leave for Earth at six o'clock. This ship, Zaw One, has the new, advanced Magnetic Field Realignment, or MFR, so we will arrive in orbit above our destination at half past eight. A half hour descent puts us above target at nine PM. The moment the extraction is complete; we cut the blend and illuminate the bottom of the ship. The specific outline of lights will make the shape of the ship appear round like an old fictional flying saucer. All sound, including the probes, will be silenced at that time. Then we get out of there. Everyone knows their assignments. Questions?"

"Sir?" Jzet asked. "How are we to going to guarantee that our target is in a clear space for us?" He shot a quick glance at Zenta.

"I will let Major Zenta explain that." He gestured toward her. "Major?"

"The Savior will be playing a game. His position is somewhat in the middle of the field of play. On his left hand, he wears a large protective glove to be able to catch a ball that is either thrown or hit at him. These gloves are necessary for the participants that play this game. The glove the Savior uses is one we designed and we were able to have him acquire it. There is a small device inside the glove that when activated, will send a shock through his hand causing him to drop the glove. We are hoping this bit of distraction will keep him there just long enough for the field to clear. He will pick the glove back up."

"How can you be so sure that he will?" Jzet asked with a sardonic smile.

"We know through years of observation and knowing the Savior and his traits," Zenta countered confidently.

"Okay, everyone." Braaddy quickly got the focus on him and away from the brewing conflict between Zenta and Jzet. "We all have our orders. Extraction personnel will reconvene in the Command Center at eight, medical personnel will meet here. If there are no more questions, let's get started."

At 8:27 PM, Qwan started angling Zaw One for the descent through Earth's upper atmosphere.

"It's going to look like a meteor when we've passed through this part," Qwan said. "Lieutenant Roial, when we enter the atmosphere, you will fire off the decoy burner," Hajeck ordered. "I'll watch the monitor and tell you when to deploy it."

"Yes, sir."

Qwan keyed her mic to the ship's communications system. "Attention everyone, secure items. This may get bumpy."

Zaw one passed through without a hitch. The decoy was launched successfully.

"Blend on," Qwan announced.

"Fully active," Roial confirmed.

"All right then." Hajeck rubbed his hands together. "Major Qwan, take us over our target.

Earlier, at a few minutes before eight o'clock, Chris and Cory had been warming up next to the ball field.

"Do you feel stiff after that semifinal game?" Cory asked.

"Nah. I feel great. I'm just glad we beat the Dirtbags." Chris rubbed the ball around in his glove before throwing it back.

"Who do you think is gonna win this game, the Roadies or the Dining Club?" Cory asked nodding his head toward the field.

"I'm hoping it's the Roadies. They're ahead right now. Those guys beat us earlier this season. I'd like to return the favor."

"Me too." Cory fumbled a catch and picked the ball up.

"Wow. What a full Moon," Cory noticed while staring up into the night sky. "It's so bright out here. What a beautiful night."

Chris was also taking it all in.

"Yeah, you're right," Chris said. "Check out those ugly, dark clouds off to the southwest. They sure look like rain clouds."

"Well, hopefully they'll hold off dumping on us till the game is over." He threw the ball to Chris.

"Hope so." Chris caught it and threw it back.

"There sure are a lot of people here tonight," Cory said in between throws.

"You got that right. They all came to see the awesome Boys win a championship." Chris heard cheering from the field. "Hey, it looks like the Roadies won." He pulled his glove off and threw it toward his bag. "Let's get the guys out there and warm up."

"Lowering to three hundred feet," Qwan announced. "One hundred feet … fifty feet …we are on target."

"Blend working perfectly," Roial added. "The video feed from the probe shows twinkling stars."

Hajeck slapped his knees. "This is perfect. I'm going down to the Command Center. Great work you two." He got up and exited Ops.

In the Command Center, the huge screen in the front had an overhead shot of the playing field below. The center was filled with personnel and humming with activity. The room was set up in a similar fashion to the Savior Project Lab on GAIA.

Tish, sitting in the front row section of workstations announced, "The intervention team is aboard the two Intervessels and are ready to deploy if needed."

"Good," Braaddy replied as he entered another command into his system. "The EET is fully energized and ready to go."

"There are two outs so if we are going to extract during this inning of the game, it has to be now," Zenta informed everyone. "We've completed the organized flyovers of probes over the Savior. He is definitely aware that something is amiss."

"Very well," Braaddy responded. "Start the sound sequence."

Zenta keyed in the command for all the X13 Probes in the trees next to the left outfield fence to begin transmitting a different buzzing sound. This was an altered version of the normal buzzing sound which came from the beating of their wings. The probes were now emitting a deep, mid-level tone that had been felt in test subject's chests. Its purpose was to instill fear with no physical harm.

Everyone in the Command Center watched as panic erupted at the softball park.

"I just engaged the shock tab in the glove," Zenta announced as she zoomed her monitor's view and watched Chris throw his glove down.

"Engage the flood lights," Braaddy ordered.

All eyes were glued to their monitors as the field was illuminated brighter than daylight.

"Major Zenta. Run down the probe checklist," Braaddy barked.

"Probes are installed and activated in the receiving room, in the top of the EET, and on the edge of the pitcher's mound," Zenta responded. She looked back at her monitor and saw Chris pick up his glove.

"Lieutenant Tish, has the Earthling who is to receive the ship's video feed been located and is his communication device identified?" Braaddy asked.

"That's affirmative," Tish answered. "The Earthling operating the video camera will receive the feed to his phone device on a two minute delay."

"Good. I'm launching the EET," Braaddy announced.

Zenta watched as an intense beam of light bathed Chris in whiteness. He looked up. Zenta saw no fear, just intensity.

On half of the screen up front, an X13 probe transmission showed the tube extending toward the ground. In a manner of seconds, Chris was encased inside the tube.

"Extracting!" Braaddy yelled.

The bottom of the tube sealed itself. Chris could be seen doing a little hop as the ground shifted beneath him. Then he began to slowly rise as the tube collapsed into the ship's storage ring.

Tish leaned over to Zenta and whispered, "I would hate to be Chris' wife right now."

"I agree," Zenta said as she switched views and had a probe zoom in on Lisa's face.

Lisa was hysterical with fear. Tears were streaming down her face as she watched her husband being taken away. Cory and Diane were holding her, trying to keep her calm. Taylor and Michelle were clinging to her.

Zenta switched the view back to Chris. "I can't imagine having someone like that taken away from me," she lied.

The other half of the front screen showed Chris nearing the receiving room.

"Ten more seconds ... five seconds ... he's onboard," Braaddy announced.

The room erupted in cheers and applause. On the front wall screen, Chris could be seen inside the receiving room still standing on the EET trap door. He was scraping the dirt away from the bottom of the tube trying to look down at the field through the clear bottom door he had just come through.

"Let's stay focused everyone. We're not done yet. Give it a second ... cut the blend."

Zenta entered the command to turn off the Blend Technology Unit that renders the ship invisible, thus allowing everyone at the softball park to see Zaw One.

"Lieutenant Tish, has the video feed been transmitted to the camera man?" Braaddy asked.

"It just completed," Tish responded.

"Major Zenta, engage the blend."

"Done," Zenta replied.

"All right then. Tell Ops to get us out of here."

"Yes, sir." Zenta keyed her Trace. "Major Qwan, mission accomplished. Take us home."

34 – TEARS FROM THE MOON

Pandemonium reigned. The bright lights had suddenly gone out revealing a huge ship covered with a multitude of lights and emitting a blue glow. It began to slowly rise into the night sky trailing a sprinkling of white sparks. Then it vanished leaving all of the onlookers in shock.

The television crew, which had been interviewing Bernie Gold of Parks & Recreation, had filmed the entire event.

"Did you get all of that, Lance? Melissa Howard of Channel 29 News screamed over the chaos surrounding her.

"Is that a trick question?" came the sarcastic reply from her cameraman, Lance Utley. His camera was aimed right at the unfolding spectacle. Lance felt his smart phone vibrate so he pulled it out of his pocket. "Someone is sending me a video."

"Lance, put that thing away and let's move," she ordered.

Melissa scrambled to get to some players and spectators who were still around the softball field. Lance tried to keep up, but fell behind having to lug the camera and equipment. Melissa ran breathlessly toward a group of distressed and clearly frantic people. She glanced up, stumbling over a parking curb, and saw the empty sky.

"Anyone here see what happened?" Melissa said out of breath as she reached the group nearest the dugout. A cloudy haze of dust hung everywhere around the field, settling in your nostrils as you breathed the night air. Everyone in the group fell silent. Some were still staring up into the night sky, watching as if the ship was going to come back.

Cory exclaimed while holding a sobbing Lisa, "Are you for real? You had to of been blind to have missed it!"

Lance zoomed his camera in on Cory and Lisa.

A broken voiced plea came from Lisa, "Get that camera out of here. Why do you news people show up when you aren't wanted?"

Cory spun Lisa around and walked away from the group. As Lance and Melissa started toward them, Alex, Ian, and David stepped in, blocking their path.

"Going somewhere?" snarled Alex as his brown eyes darted back and forth between Melissa and Lance. Sweat was still dripping down his face from playing softball. He was visibly angry.

"I just want to talk to people who saw what happened," Melissa stated defiantly. "Especially you guys who were on the field. This is really important and I want to make sure we get all the details."

Lance slowly lowered his camera.

"I'd put that away right now if I were you. Can't you see these people don't want to talk to you? You were here. You saw what happened," David said staring at Lance.

Melissa put her hand on his shoulder. His jersey was still wet from sweat.

"I know everyone is upset," she said. "But if we are ever going to do anything about this, we've got to let people know what happened."

David looked at her. He noticed Lance raising his camera so he turned his face away.

"I really can't believe any of this," David began. "This is small town USA. We're just some everyday guys playing softball." He shook his head in disbelief and looked out toward the woods. "That buzzing sound was so loud that I couldn't hear anything else. Then came the blinding, bright lights."

"Yeah. When the lights finally went out, everyone could see that ship just floating up there," Ian added. "That thing was huge."

Melissa moved her mic over to Ian while Lance continued filming.

"I watched everyone race off the field in a panic," Ian continued. "But Chris didn't run. He just stood there and looked up at the lights with everyone screaming at him to get off the field." Ian was staring at the pitcher's mound. "Why didn't he run like everyone else?"

Ian stopped talking when Alex grabbed his arm.

"Come on. Let's get outta here."

As Ian took a step away, Melissa blurted out, "You don't remember me do you?"

Ian stopped as Alex and David kept going. His expression confirmed the recognition.

"That was a long time ago and has nothing to do with this," he said.

"But you could at least talk to me," came Melissa's reply. "I want to know all the details about Chris."

Lance looked a bit confused. He had long ago given up trying to figure out these crazy Americans.

Ian saw Lance's puzzled expression. "We used to date, okay? It didn't end well."

"Thanks to you," she added.

"Sorry." Ian avoided eye contact. "Like I said, it was a long time ago."

"Well?" Melissa had her hands out.

Ian finally looked up and said, "There's not a whole lot to this. A spaceship took away my best friend. I just can't believe it happened."

Lance nodded his head and chimed in, "That does sum it up. A big spaceship grabbed this chap and flew off."

"Shut up, Lance," Melissa commanded.

"You can't tell me to … "

"He's right," Ian said while he scrapped his cleat on the pavement. "That's all there was to it. He's gone."

"Can I ask you something about Chris?" Melissa quickly said.

"I guess," Ian said dejectedly as if he was trapped. He wanted to go see what was happening with Lisa and the kids. He caught sight of them from across the parking lot. Watching them depressed him even further.

"Why do you think they took Chris?" Melissa asked. "Does it look like he was the target?"

Melissa's question brought Ian out of his fog.

"Well, it did appear like they specifically chose him," Ian said glaring at Lance who had the camera on his shoulder filming everything.

That made Lance a bit nervous.

"I feel like he was the chosen one too," Lance responded hoping to soften Ian's angry gaze.

"Well, I don't know why he was picked," Ian added. "But it really looked like it targeted him. I don't know how else to break that down. Can you sum it up any differently?"

Suddenly, Melissa jumped off the curb and went running to where police cars had started arriving. "I've got to go check this out," she yelled over her shoulder.

"Witch," Ian muttered.

Lance started after her when Ian grabbed his arm.

"Will you answer a question?" He let go of his arm. "Did you see anything different?"

Lance stopped for a moment and noticed Ian's dirty handprint on his sleeve. It had only been minutes since these guys had just been playing ball. They were just having fun and minding their own business. It seemed like hours ago.

He looked at Ian with all the sirens and people yelling and crying and quietly said, "I saw the same thing you saw. I didn't know Chris Gates, but I've covered him for the news." He paused, then asked, "How close were you guys?"

"Real close. We're still real close," Ian replied. "We grew up together. You didn't see anything else, maybe some markings or something on that ship?"

"No. I guess I was too busy filming. I did hear that awful sound when Melissa was interviewing Bernie. And then the sky just lit up." He noticed Ian's nervous fidgety movements. "Do you think that ship was something man made, like from Earth?"

Ian didn't answer. He was now watching the commotion

surrounding the ambulances and police cars.

Their talk was cut short anyway when Melissa yelled from across the parking lot, “Come here Lance! The emergency people have Lisa Gates in an ambulance and she’s screaming about buzzing noises and aliens.”

Lance turned to Ian and said, “I’ve got something for you if you’ll promise to give it to Chris’ wife or his brother; no one else.”

“What are you talking about?” Ian asked.

“It’s a video you’ll want to see,” Lance said as he put his camera down and pulled out his cell phone.

Ian watched as Lance removed his Micro SD card from his phone.

“I don’t know who sent this video,” Lance said as he handed the card to Ian. “I’ve still got a copy of it on my phone. Someone downloaded it to me shortly after Chris was taken away and that someone was not from around here.”

“Did you watch this?” Ian asked while pulling out his phone.

“Lance, get over here!” Melissa screamed at him.

“I saw bits and pieces. You won’t believe it. Here, take this too,” Lance said while handing Ian his business card. “Call me tomorrow. I want Chris’ wife to also have a copy of the video I shot tonight too. I’ve already put a copy onto that card I gave you. It’s no telling what is going to happen before I get out of here tonight.” Lance looked at Melissa who was waving at him. “I gotta go.” He gave a parting nod and left.

Ian shouted, “Thanks, man! I’ll call you tomorrow!” He stared at the SD card for a few seconds then put it in his phone. He looked up at the ambulance where Lisa was jumping up and down, screaming hysterically. Diane and one of the EMTs were trying to get her back into the ambulance. Ian cringed and turned toward the ball field. The lights were still on. Some guys in suits were now walking around and investigating the pitcher’s mound. Ian watched as they hovered around that area, scooping up dirt, and putting it into bags. A hand on his shoulder made him jump.

“Here, you could use this.” Cory slipped a cup of beer into Ian’s hand. “I think I’m going to need about ten of these before the night is over.”

“Are you seriously drinking beer at a time like this?”

“I needed something to take the edge off considering …” Cory said pleadingly. “Alex handed me one so I took it.”

Ian didn’t drink, but he chugged it down anyway.

“How’s Lisa?” Ian asked. “It doesn’t look good from here.”

“She’s cracking up so the EMTs just gave her a sedative,” Cory answered as he kicked a broken branch across the pavement spilling beer on his hand. “Diane has been trying to calm her down and Jay and Lynn are hanging onto the kids over there.” He pointed to the concession stand.

"I don't know what to do now." He took a drink from his cup and looked at the field.

"Where in the heck did the suits come from so fast?" Cory asked. "These guys look straight out of the 'men in dark' movie or whatever that was."

"They just showed up and have been digging around in the dirt."

Ian threw his cup down.

"What the hell just happened?" he asked as if Cory was going to suddenly have all the answers. "I just can't believe any of this."

Ian considered telling Cory about the phone card but didn't think it was a good time to look at it right there with the looming possibility of having to deal with those suits who were now in the dugout. They were obviously from some specialized service. Ian remembered Lance saying that he didn't know what the rest of the evening would bring.

"I dunno," Cory went on. "I just saw a big ass space ship show up and take my brother away." He turned away from the field. "I mean here we are playing softball, this buzzing sound starts, and then a huge spaceship shows up. Was it from Earth? If it wasn't, well, that's a whole new set of issues."

"I've never seen a ship like that anywhere," Ian added. "Not even a picture of one."

"I'll tell you this," Cory continued. "Right before that tube disappeared into the ship; I could have sworn I saw Chris looking at me. And I got this feeling … that … uh …" Cory stopped.

"What?" Ian asked. "Why did you stop?"

"Eh. You won't believe me anyway," Cory said while staring at his beer.

"Well, I can't believe you unless you tell me."

"It was weird," Cory started again. "Chris and I were always able to, in a way, send feelings to each other."

"Yeah, so?" Ian shrugged his shoulders. "You guys have always been able to do that."

"Well, right at that moment when I thought we made eye contact, I felt like he was trying to tell me something."

"Okay," Ian said getting a bit impatient. "Tell me what it was."

Cory paused and looked down for a couple of seconds. He looked real calm considering everything that had just transpired.

"I felt like he was telling me that he was okay."

"Are you nuts?" Ian asked in disbelief.

"No," Cory said irritably. "I know when my brother is telling me something and I …"

Ian glanced up and saw one of the suits walking toward him. He knocked Cory's beer out of his hand spilling it on the ground, and bolted into the crowd.

"Come on," he said. "We need to talk over here."

The suits were coming off the field and were fanning out in different directions into the crowd. All games had stopped long ago but nobody had left. If anything, with all of the commotion, more people had come to the park.

As Ian and Cory quickly slid into the crowd, Ian heard a voice behind him say, "Hey, hold up. I want to ask you some questions."

Ian and Cory kept moving through the mass of people until they bumped into David.

"Bunch of suits coming our way. Know who they are?" Ian asked David.

"Not sure. They don't look like cops. Maybe they are UFO specialists," David said as he fell in behind the others. "What if they're some kind of special group that investigates stuff like this? We should talk to them, right?"

"I don't know," Ian answered, slightly out of breath from walking so fast. "But I think we should go to the picnic shelters and get our stories straight before we talk to them. They obviously know something about this considering how quickly they showed up. We need to find out who they are."

David, Cory, and Ian kept moving across the parking lot, putting as much distance as they could between themselves and the suits.

"Did you see the size of that ship?" David asked. "It had to have been as big as an aircraft carrier. I swear that thing could have filled the football stadium. I couldn't hear anything in left field with all that buzzing. Then the sky lights up. What the heck did it want with Chris? And why did he just stand there on the mound like that?" They finally got to the side of the shelter.

"I don't know. We've been wondering the same things," Ian said then took a sip of David's beer.

"Hey, I've got an idea." David's face lit up. "I'm going to go question the suits and bring any info to you guys before you talk to them. They must know something. You stay here. I'll be back."

"Cool. Good idea," Cory said. "Don't tell 'em anything, though."

"Got it."

David ran toward the crowd as Ian stomped his foot in frustration.

"What a dumb ass." Cory threw his cup against the picnic shelter's outer brick wall. "Chris just froze. Why didn't he get off the field?"

"I know. He just kept looking up. I really think the ship came for him," Ian added.

Cory spun around and looked at Ian.

"It did look like it came just for Chris. But why?" Cory asked. He sat down in the grass and put his face in his hands.

Ian didn't answer. He watched Cory for a couple of seconds then felt a drop of rain on his arm. He raised his face to the night sky and felt more misty droplets splash on his forehead.

"It's starting to rain," Ian stated quietly.

"Yep." Cory said as he looked up and stuck out his arm. "That's all we need." He stood up and pointed up. "But look. The full Moon is still out."

"That's weird ..." Ian stopped and glanced at the parking lot, his attention diverted by the sound of a child crying. He listened and heard others sobbing. "Geez, listen to all the crying."

"I hear it," Cory said while still looking up letting the rain hit him in the face. "I guess these are tears from the Moon."

Neither one spoke for a minute, both just standing there letting the rain hit them. Ian broke the silence.

"Hey, step under the picnic shelter. I want to show you something," he said as he got his cell phone out.

Cory followed him.

"What is it?"

"Dude, the cameraman gave me this." Ian began fiddling with his phone to get the video on the SD card to play. "The guy's name is Lance and he told me that he had no idea who sent this to him."

The video started.

"Holy crap," Cory said in disbelief as he watched it. His jaw dropped.

"Yeah, holy crap," Ian agreed nodding his head. "They really did come for him. Now the question is … will they bring him back?"

ACKNOWLEDGMENTS

I am so grateful for the support of my family in writing this book. My wonderful wife Jan, stood by me through thick and thin, along with taking the lead in finding time for me to write. She sacrificed so much for this. I will always strive to repay her. To my children: Christopher's unwavering belief in the story, Ryan and her artistic/computer talents, Scott with his attention to detail and his feedback, and Karl who's technical expertise was essential. They helped with everything. To my Step-Father Wes, for his support in helping me finish the editing. And to my brother Brad, for his constant encouragement and timely phone calls. I would never have been able to write about the closeness of brothers if it weren't for him. He's always been there for me.

None of this would have been possible if it weren't for the most awesome Heather Hummel, the award winning author who discovered me in a creative writing class where she was a guest lecturer. Her skill, guidance, and wisdom taught me how to really be a writer in actions, not just words. She edited this entire book. It would be an understatement to say I owe her everything. She's my mentor and truly a best friend.

To my heroes, Diane Bahler, Philip Day, and our missing comrade, Denise Demitris. Our Heroes Writers Group is forever. And kudos to Professor Henry for starting it all.

Many thanks to my reviewers, especially Kristin Franke Mann, my wonderful niece who always knows how to redirect me to a different and better way of seeing things. And to Tom Rowe, a part of my conscious; always has been, hopefully, always will be.

I owe a huge debt to superman Ian McDaniel of Gravitys Edge for his fantastic photography work and book cover enhancements. We started working together back in the mid-90s and it appears there is no end. And to Rob Browning, artist extraordinaire, for his right on character sketches that are on the book series websites. It's like he could see what I saw.

A great big thank you goes out to Pat Sweeney and the gang at my new publisher, Imagination Pro, for coming to the rescue at the last minute.

To the real Bros. You know who you are. Thanks for being you.

I need to thank my fellow writers, Heather, Mike Sullivan, Cari Kamm, Phil James, and Susan Ricci who encouraged me along the way. Through their words, actions, and deeds, I learned so much about what it means to be a writer. And from Heather, I learned HOW to be a writer.

And I'll never forget Ross who kept my head on straight throughout this journey. To Toan – thanks for keeping the coffee going.

To each and every one of you, I couldn't have done this without you being there for me every day and in every way.

THANK YOU SO MUCH.

COMING SOON

TERLOKYA
Book Two from the Savior Project Series
FRITZ FRANKE

FRITZ FRANKE

Fritz Franke is a story teller who recently began putting his stories to paper.

'The Chosen One' is the first of six books in 'The Savior Project' series.

Currently a member of the Heroes Writers Club, Fritz continues to write and has had some recent stories and articles published in local newspapers and magazines.

Fritz's previous writing experiences were as a newspaper columnist in the early 1980s with the University Journal; one of the student newspapers at the University of Virginia. In the early to mid-80s, Fritz was the Marketing Manager and Editor for the advertising firm, Word Merchants. In the late 1980s, Fritz designed, edited, produced, and wrote for the employee newsletter of Blue Cross and Blue Shield of Virginia. Recently, he has written and edited numerous IT technical articles and documents for the University of Virginia and other technical and marketing documentation in both the private and public sectors.

Additionally, Fritz is a graduate of the University of Virginia's McIntire Commerce School in 1983 with a double concentration in Management Information Systems and Human Resource Management and an undeclared minor in Psychology. He currently resides near Palmyra Virginia with his wife of 25 years, Jan, and his three children, Christopher, Ryan, Scott, and his nephew, Karl.

Visit Fritz's website and find out about his other projects - www.FritzFranke.net

Keep up with the Savior Project - www.saviorproject.com

Discover more about Chris Gates and follow what happens to him - www.saviorproject.net

Follow Fritz's blog and his story: 'The Odyssey of This Writer' - www.fritz-franke.tumblr.com

Join Fritz's Author Group on Facebook - https://www.facebook.com/groups/279978775413902/

Be a member of Chris Gates' Facebook Fan Club - https://www.facebook.com/groups/104534649514/

Thank you for reading my book.

CPSIA information can be obtained at www.ICGtesting.com
Printed in the USA
BVOW012135070413

317438BV00008B/15/P